Praise for Ellen Hart and her Sophie Greenway mysteries

THIS LITTLE PIGGY WENT TO MURDER
"Strong characters and a rich Lake Superior setting make this solidly constructed mystery hard to put down. Another winner for Ellen Hart!"
—M. D. LAKE

FOR EVERY EVIL
"A dilly . . . A fair-play plot and contemporary characters that leap off the page . . . Stir in Martha Grimes with P. D. James and add a dash of Christie and Amanda Cross and you begin to get the idea: a cozy with a brain."
—*Alfred Hitchcock Mystery Magazine*

THE OLDEST SIN
"A brisk, lively plot that melds religion and food and realistic characters make Ellen Hart's third Sophie Greenway novel a solid mystery. . . . Hart does a first-rate job with this intelligent mystery."
—*Fort Lauderdale Sun-Sentinel*

Please turn the page for more reviews . . .

Praise for Ellen Hart and her Jane Lawless series

FAINT PRAISE
"Wit, charm, and fine writing."
—*Library Journal*

HALLOWED MURDER
"Hart's crisp, elegant writing and atmosphere [are] reminiscent of the British detective style, but she has a nicer sense of character, confrontation, and sparsely utilized violence. . . . *Hallowed Murder* is as valuable for its mainstream influences as for its sexual politics."

—*Mystery Scene*

VITAL LIES
"This compelling whodunit has the psychological maze of a Barbara Vine mystery and the feel of Agatha Christie. . . . Hart keeps even the most seasoned mystery buff baffled until the end."
—*Publishers Weekly*

By Ellen Hart
Published by Ballantine Books:

The Jane Lawless Mysteries:
HALLOWED MURDER
VITAL LIES
STAGE FRIGHT
A KILLING CURE
A SMALL SACRIFICE
FAINT PRAISE

The Sophie Greenway mysteries:
THIS LITTLE PIGGY WENT TO MURDER
FOR EVERY EVIL
THE OLDEST SIN
MURDER IN THE AIR

MURDER IN THE AIR

Ellen Hart

BALLANTINE BOOKS • NEW YORK

Copyright © 1997 by Ellen Hart

All rights reserved under International and Pan-American Copyright Conventions. Published in the United States by Ballantine Books, a division of Random House, Inc., New York, and distributed in Canada by Random House of Canada Limited, Toronto.

http://www.randomhouse.com

Library of Congress Catalog Card Number: 97-93707

ISBN 0-345-40203-0

Manufactured in the United States of America

First Edition: December 1997

10 9 8 7 6 5 4 3 2 1

For Kathy.
Twenty wonderful years together,
and an infinity to come.
Happy anniversary!

CAST OF CHARACTERS

SOPHIE GREENWAY: Owner of the Maxfield Plaza Hotel in St. Paul; part-time restaurant reviewer for the *Minneapolis Times Register*; Bram's wife; Rudy's mother.

BRAM BALDRIC: Radio talk-show host at WTWN in Minneapolis; Sophie's husband.

HEDA BLOOM: New owner of WTWN Radio in Minneapolis; Alfred and Justin's mother.

BUD MANDERBACH: President and owner of Manderbach's department store.

B. B. MANDERBACH: Bud's sister.

ALFRED (ALF) BLOOM: CEO of Bloom Enterprises; Heda and Cedric Bloom's son; Justin's half brother.

WISH GREVEEN: Radio scriptwriter.

VALENTINE ZOLOTOW: The voice of *Dallas Lane, Private Eye*.

DOROTHY VENEGER: Heda Bloom's personal assistant.

MITZI QUINN: Radio actress.

GEORGE CHAMBERS: Radio sound-effects technician.

JUSTIN BLOOM: Heda Bloom's son.

KAY COLLINS: Justin's girlfriend.

SALLY NASH: Kay's roommate.

JONNIE APFENFORD: Kay's roommate.

Man is the only animal that laughs and weeps;
for he is the only animal that is struck by the
difference between what things are and what
they might have been.

—WILLIAM HAZLITT

December 24, 1958

Mother:

I haven't got much time. By now, you've heard what happened. Don't believe what the police tell you, please! Wait until you hear the story from me. I know I haven't been around much lately, but I've had my reasons. All I ask is that you don't close the door on me. Don't tell Cedric or Alf I've sent you this note. Hear my story out first—that is, if I can get away from this god-awful town without getting caught. If I can, I'll write. If I can't—just know that I love you. You've always believed in me and for that I'm grateful. Pray for me now. It's night here and it's cold, and I'm more scared than I've ever been in my entire life.

Justin

1

the present, late November

"She bought the damned radio station!" announced Bram, dumping himself into a chair on the other side of his wife's desk. It was nearly four-thirty in the afternoon, exactly four weeks before Christmas. After entering her office at the Maxfield Plaza, St. Paul's most famous downtown hotel, he'd tossed his camel wool coat on the sofa, but had forgotten to remove a red wool scarf. It was still wound snugly around his neck.

"I already know," said Sophie, organizing some file folders into a lower drawer. She eyed her husband warily, knowing that the flush climbing his cheeks wasn't because the scarf was cutting off circulation.

"How could you possibly know the station had been bought? I just found out myself a couple of hours ago."

Sophie could read the frustration in his voice. Bram had one of the most expressive radio voices in the country. That, and his freely expressed opinions, were all part of what made him such a great talk-show host. "Well, actually, dear, Heda Bloom checked into the hotel this afternoon—complete with a body-guard, her personal secretary, and four trunks of clothes."

"She's staying *here*?"

"Afraid so. As a matter of fact, I gave her the executive suite directly across from our apartment. For the duration of her visit, we're going to be neighbors."

Bram's expressive voice failed him. "Ugh," was all he could squeeze out.

1

"I tried to call you with the news, but you weren't in your office. I didn't think I should leave a message. It's not *bad* news, is it? I mean, she's such a nice woman."

"A nice woman," he repeated, leaning forward and running his fingers absently through his graying temples. "I'll be sure to remember that when I'm standing in line at the unemployment office."

Sophie assumed he was joking. "You know," she continued, glancing at a newly framed snapshot of her mom and dad standing in front of the Eiffel Tower—they were currently on a round-the-world tour. "My parents knew the Blooms back in the Fifties, when they owned WPXL. That was before Dad bought the Maxfield."

"Do tell." Bram's interest wasn't overwhelming.

"I even met Justin Bloom once."

"Who's Justin Bloom?"

Sophie was aghast. "You've never heard of the infamous Justin Bloom?"

"I grew up in Chicago, Soph. We thought of St. Paul as a suburb—and not a very interesting one at that."

"You may be in a bad mood, dear, but you don't have to insult my hometown." She fussed indignantly with her short, reddish gold hair.

"Just finish the story. If he's related to my new boss, I want to hear it."

"Well," said Sophie, folding her arms over her chest, "if I recall correctly, Justin Bloom killed a woman by the name of Kay Collins back in the late Fifties. It was a real *cause célèbre* in the Twin Cities. He was engaged to someone else at the time, but the reports said the woman he murdered was his lover."

"No kidding." He stopped fidgeting with his tie clasp and gave her his full attention. "What happened to him?"

"Nothing. He fled the country. I was just a kid at the time, but I remember my parents talking about it. The police kept the heat on him all over Europe. Eventually, I suppose, it just got to be old news and we didn't hear about it anymore. But as far as I know, he was never caught."

"Fascinating." Bram scratched his chin. "How was he related to Heda Bloom?"

"He was her son. Seems to me there was another son, too. I don't recall the name. Her husband, Cedric, died about a year after Justin committed the murder. I remember my parents saying he probably died of shame."

"That must have been rough." Unwinding the scarf from around his neck, Bram added, "I wonder if he really did it."

"Oh, he did it, all right. There was an eyewitness. A police officer."

"I guess my new boss has a few skeletons in her closet." His manner grew distracted as he glanced at his watch.

Sophie assumed that when he'd walked into her office, he was home for the night. "Do you have to get back to the station?"

"Afraid so. It's a command performance. Heda is going to meet with us at five and give us all our walking papers."

"You can't be serious."

"Completely."

She hadn't taken his agitation seriously before, but she certainly did now. "Bram, you have a contract."

"Contracts were made to be broken." He rose and walked to the window overlooking the garden area between the two towers, where mounds of snow now covered the ground. As he pressed his hand to the cold glass, Sophie moved up behind him, rested her head against his back, and slipped her arms gently around his waist.

"They've already put up the Christmas lights in the garden," he said, unable to keep the melancholy out of his voice.

"Every year. Right after Thanksgiving. It's tradition at the Maxfield."

He was quiet for several seconds. "They look . . . pretty."

"Everything's going to be all right, sweetheart. She won't fire you. Your ratings are the highest in the Twin Cities."

"You can't argue with a pink slip."

"But you don't know for sure that's what the meeting's about. She never said anything to me about letting you go."

He turned around. "I have to prepare myself for the worst,

Soph. New owners like to bring in new talent. The problem is, I'm not fit to do anything else. And, since you run this hotel now, it's not as if we can move to another city so that I can pursue my career elsewhere."

That stung. In the eight years they'd been married, career conflict had never been an issue before. True, Sophie loved running the Maxfield—every bit as much as Bram loved his job. In September, she'd inherited the hotel from her parents. Henry and Pearl Tahtinen had announced their retirement at a birthday celebration, passed the reins—and the owner-ship—of the hotel on to Sophie the next day, and then imme-diately took off for Finland. Eager to leave a job that no longer held her interest, Sophie tendered her resignation at an arts magazine and, in early November, began her new career in the hospitality business.

"I wonder if I could learn to sell aluminum siding?" said Bram listlessly, his chin sinking to his chest.

Sometimes he was *such* a drama queen, thought Sophie. "Surely Heda Bloom wouldn't buy a station and then institute some hideous shake-up. She's a professional, sweetheart. She owns many other radio stations around the country." Then again, what did Sophie know about the radio biz?

"If I don't get going I'll be late."

"Will you come back as soon as you're done?"

"Sure." He said the word a little too quickly.

The tension surrounding him unsettled her. She couldn't remember when he'd ever been this upset. After helping him on with his coat, she straightened his tie and then took hold of his lapels, drawing him close. "You're not going to be fired, sweetheart. Trust me. I have a sixth sense about these things."

"Right."

"You'll probably come back with a big fat raise."

He kissed the top of her head. "Hold that thought." Squaring his shoulders like a man readying himself for battle, he walked to the door and, with a less-than-enthusiastic wave, left without a backward glance.

2

Bram sat morosely next to the conference-room door, glaring at one of the morning producers who seemed completely unaffected by the tension in the air. Between loud slurps from his can of Coke, the man stuffed a turkey sandwich into his mouth. Bram found the man's appetite both difficult to fathom and obnoxious since his own stomach was doing flip-flops.

At exactly five P.M., a small, white-haired woman entered the room and, with the help of two silver-handled canes, took a seat at the head of the table. Bram wasn't surprised by Heda Bloom's advanced age. One of the assembled crowd had already mentioned that she was well into her eighties. She was still a handsome woman, with high, sculpted cheekbones and bright blue-green eyes. Bram assumed that in her youth she must have been a real knockout.

Placing a briefcase on the table in front of her, she turned her attention to her new employees. "I'm delighted so many of you could come." There was no trace of age in her firm, clear voice. She folded somewhat arthritic-looking hands on the tabletop and looked down at them with an expression Bram could only read as resignation. Unhappy resignation.

Here it comes, he thought. The pink slips have already been signed, sealed, and are about to be delivered. He steeled himself for the worst.

As Heda looked up, a forced smile replaced the sadness. "By now," she said, somewhat haltingly, "you all know that I've recently become the new owner of WTWN. My assistant, Dorothy Veneger, will assume the role of interim general manager until a new general manager can be hired. That, by the way, is the only staff change I plan to make."

The silence lasted for a few seconds as everyone digested the information. Finally, a woman near the back began to clap. The rest of the crowd followed with a burst of relieved cheers and applause.

Heda's smile broadened. She seemed pleased with the response. Her face lost some of its strain as she drew a file folder from the leather briefcase. "I bought this station because it was a good investment. I applaud you all on your consistently top ratings. My philosophy has always been a simple one: If it ain't broke, don't fix it."

Bram eased back in his chair and tugged his French cuffs out from underneath his herringbone jacket. He'd dodged a bullet, that was for damn sure. Even so, he wasn't entirely comfortable with the situation. He'd been in radio for over twenty years and during that time he'd seen many stations change hands. Most often, personnel changes followed soon after, no matter how hard management tried to put everyone's mind at rest.

Sitting quietly, he listened as a barrage of questions was directed toward Heda.

"What about your son Alfred?" asked one of the production assistants. "We'd heard he might be our new boss."

"Alfred is holding down the fort in Palm Beach. That's where our general offices are located."

She seemed so lively and enthusiastic now, Bram couldn't imagine what that initial look of resignation had been about. Had he projected his own anxiety onto her? Sophie often said he didn't translate other people's emotions all that well. Well, blast. Intuitive genius or not, he'd bet an entire pitcher of martinis that she was worried about something—and that something had to do with the station. She'd come here specifically to make everyone feel at ease with the transition, and yet she obviously wasn't.

"There is one new programming addition I'd like to discuss with you," continued Heda. Mustering up another strained smile, she said, "You people are the first to hear this bit of good news and I hope you'll be as excited as I am. The fact is, we're about to make radio history. WTWN is going to bring back the half-hour serial on commercial radio." She waited, allowing the import of her statement to sink in. "I'm fairly confident that there's still life in that dramatic format. I've been looking for just the right venue in which to test my theory, and I feel this market is just about perfect."

"A radio serial?" repeated Bram's producer, Mary Landis. "You mean, like . . . *The Shadow*?"

"I mean specifically," said Heda Bloom, "the program my late husband created for WPXL. *Dallas Lane, Private Eye.*"

"Hey, I remember that," said Dorie Hennessy. Dorie's confident, deep tones had been the voice of WTWN local news for almost thirty years. He was a true radio buff, probably knew everything there was to know about the old-time serials. "I used to listen to that when I was in college. It was never syndicated, was it? Just a local Twin Cities show?"

"That's right," said Heda. "As a matter of fact, I've even convinced three people from the original production to do the first six episodes. Valentine Zolotow, the voice of Dallas Lane, and Mitzi Quinn, the voice of Dallas's girlfriend, Lucy DuFour, are landing at the airport even as we speak. So is George Chambers, the man my husband considered the best live-sound-effects technician in the business."

Bram sat up straight in his chair. "Pardon me, but you're not suggesting this broadcast will be live, are you?"

With a twinkle in her eye, Heda said, "Live radio is always the best. You of all people should know that."

"Well, sure, I agree, but—"

"I want you to be the announcer for the new show, Bram. It will be broadcast from this very studio every Sunday evening from six-thirty to seven P.M."

"But . . . what about my sports talk hour?" demanded Larry Blodnik in his trademark whiny, nasal, heavily supercilious voice. He was an airline executive who moonlighted as a talk-show host. An angry vein throbbed in his thick neck. "May I remind you we're in the midst of football season. The Vikes are six and three."

"As of next Sunday, your show will be cut to one half hour. There's too much emphasis on sports in this country already, Larry, don't you agree? The arts deserve far more attention." She looked innocently around the room for support.

Bram couldn't help but laugh. The lady had balls. Anybody who'd challenge even a small part of America's sports monolith was okay by him. He glanced over at Larry, who looked as if he was about to chew off the end of his tie. Too bad, thought Bram acidly. Perhaps with his time off, old Larry could get some professional voice training so that he wouldn't sound so much like a rusty door hinge every time he opened his mouth. His opinions, on the other hand, weren't so easily fixed. As far as Bram knew, there was no professional remedy for arrogance.

"We begin work on the first episode bright and early tomorrow morning," continued Heda. "Bram, I'd like you to be here at nine A.M sharp. George, Valentine, and Mitzi will also be here. The timing needs to be worked out as soon as possible. We have the half-hour newsbreak to think about, as well as commercials."

Since Bram's talk show had been switched to afternoon, his mornings were usually spent in bed reading the local newspapers, *The New York Times,* and the *Chicago Tribune.* Living in a four-star hotel was a terrific arrangement as far as he was concerned. Not only had he escaped the drudgery of mowing grass and shoveling snow, but he never had any handyman chores waiting to destroy his weekends. Even better, he had room service available to him at any given hour of the day or night. The idea of spending a Saturday morning in Heda's office didn't exactly appeal, though he had to admit he was intrigued by her desire to bring back the radio mystery. "Do you already have the story?" he asked.

"Not to worry," said Heda. "I've got some heavy talent working on that one. We'll have the first half-hour script in front of us by tomorrow morning."

"May I ask who will be producing this new show?" Bram

knew that no one currently employed at the radio station had any experience with radio drama.

"My assistant, Dorothy Veneger, will," said Heda. "You'll all get a chance to meet her tomorrow."

Heda cut off any further questions by pushing abruptly away from the table. Standing with the help of her canes, she said, "Let me just say by way of parting that I look forward to working with all of you. And although I'll miss my home in Florida, I intend to remain in the Twin Cities, living at the Maxfield Plaza, for the next six weeks." Glancing from face to face with a warm, exuberant smile, she added, "It's my fondest hope that our new association will be a profitable one for each and every one of us. And now I bid you all a good evening."

Since Bram was seated right next to the door, he was the only one able to see her face as she walked out of the room. Consequently, he was the only witness to a curious transformation. As soon as the elderly woman's back was turned to the crowd, her cheerful enthusiasm evaporated. In its place, Bram now saw an entirely different Heda Bloom. This one looked tired, drawn, and much to his surprise, even a little frightened.

December 29, 1958

Dear Mother:

Sorry it's taken me so long to write. I've spent the last four days traveling—running as fast and as far as I could on the money I was given. Sometimes I wonder if I'm losing my grip on reality. I feel as if I'm being watched constantly. This morning I was at a train station just outside London. I'm pretty sure two men were following me.

I lost them by ducking into an alley, but then I'm almost positive I saw them again in a café near my hotel. I couldn't go back there, I knew that much. So I'm sitting on a park bench right now, wondering what to do next—until my boat leaves, that is. I'll be in Amsterdam tomorrow night. After that, I'm not sure. I'm not sure of anything. My life has taken on the quality of a dream. Nothing seems real, nothing, that is, except the growing fear that I'll be caught and brought back to stand trial. As traveling companions go, terror is a hell of a mate. But I have my freedom. For now, until I get my bearings, until I figure out what to do next, that has to be enough.

I took a chance sending you that first letter, Mom, but I can't do it anymore. I'm afraid my whereabouts could be traced if your mail is being watched. That's why this letter's been forwarded to you—under a different cover— from a friend in New York. Do you remember him? I brought him home with me for Christmas several times. Once, we got drunk at a bar downtown, and when we got back to the house, he threw up in the clothes hamper. To make up for it, he bought you that beautiful green scarf, the one you always wear with your cashmere coat. I realize that by not giving you his name, I sound completely paranoid. Perhaps my precautions aren't necessary, but for now you'll have to bear with me.

Anyway, this old friend of mine is the only one I can trust. I phoned him the other night, explained everything. I almost cried when he said he believed me and that he'd help me any way he could. He sounded so normal, so—regular. It made me realize how much I've lost. Anyway, from now on, I'm going to mail all my letters to him, and he'll pass them on to you without a return address. At some point, I hope I can remain somewhere long enough so that you can write me back. Right now I feel pretty safe sitting here on this park bench, but I know it's only temporary.

I need to get my mind on something else for a while, Mom, so I thought I'd spend some time today telling you about Kay—what she meant to me, how we got involved.

*In the past few days I've come to see that my feelings for
her were all bound up with my desire to succeed at the
paper. I guess it's fair to say that I wanted to be the best
reporter St. Paul has ever seen, to follow in Dad's footsteps and do some good in the world. And I was on my
way, too. Late last summer I got wind of a story that was
going to knock the socks off of every guy on the city desk.
Kay became part of it—the key, so to speak. It's just—I
never counted on falling in love with her.*

*I'll never forget the night I first laid eyes on her. It was
at the Westgate Country Club out near Lake Minnetonka.
A late-summer evening. I was sitting at the bar having a
quiet drink when she came in on the arm of some guy.
Maybe I'm just being a romantic sap, but there was a kind
of a hush while every head in the place turned to watch.
She was stunning, Mom. Tall. Regal. Dark gold hair. I
asked the fellow sitting next to me what her name was. He
said it was Kay Collins. He said it with a kind of reverence. All I could do was stare.*

*—I'm hurrying now. There's a man sitting across
the park on a far bench reading the paper. He's—I can't
tell, but I think he's watching me. I'm probably halluci-
nating, but I figure the authorities back in the States are
passing my picture around to people over here. Everyone
looks suspicious.*

I love you, Mom.
Don't forget me. And don't judge me, at least not yet.
                                                Justin

3

Sophie switched off her computer monitor, took off her glasses, and rubbed her sore eyes. As the new owner of the Maxfield Plaza, she had much to learn about the running of a large metropolitan hotel. She'd been working late for so many weeks now that spending the evening in her office almost felt normal. Bram was generally being a good sport about it, and yet she could tell that her constant absence was creating a strain in her marriage.

The problem was, Sophie was in way over her head, and everyone on her staff knew it. The only solution was to work extra hours—to sit up nights reading reports, digesting information, to get to work early and stay late. It wouldn't be like this forever, but for now, it was the way it had to be. She had ideas for the Maxfield—new ways of dealing with old problems. She wanted to make her father proud of her. He'd been right when he'd said that the Maxfield Plaza was in her blood. She loved every inch of the old place, but sometimes she felt like a drowning woman desperately treading water. There simply weren't enough hours in the day.

Checking her watch, she saw that it was after seven. She'd been on pins and needles waiting to hear how Bram's meeting had gone at the radio station. She couldn't imagine why he hadn't called. Making a quick decision, she turned off her desk light and headed out the door.

Riding the elevator up to the sixteenth floor, she entered her apartment, glad to be anywhere but her office for a few minutes. She flipped quickly through a stack of mail on the table next to the door. As she did so she noticed that Ethel, the ancient black mutt who spent most of her days guarding a bevy of devious green tennis balls, had fallen into exhausted slumber under the dining-room table. When it came to energy, Ethel had never been a ball of fire, but her age was slowly creeping up on her.

Last week, in an effort to give the poor thing a break from constant tennis-ball surveillance, Sophie had gathered up the balls and put them in a box in the closet. Instead of breathing a sigh of relief, Ethel had slipped into a depressed funk, refusing even to take pleasure in having her ears scratched. She'd emerged from her melancholy only when the tennis balls miraculously reappeared. Sophie had come to the conclusion that everyone needed a reason for living. Remaining vigilant in the face of sneaky tennis balls was Ethel's.

Rounding the corner into the living room, she was surprised to find Bram seated on the couch, feet propped up on a footstool. The light from the Christmas tree in the corner suffused the room with a kind of mellow, peaceful glow. By the look on his face, he was deep in thought. She studied him for a moment, but saw no overt depression, only contemplation.

Placing the manila envelope she was carrying on a table just inside the arch, she cleared her throat. "Are you . . . still among the ranks of the employed?" she asked softly.

He looked up, his face inscrutable. "Would it really be so bad if you had to support me for the rest of my life?"

"What?" He'd caught her off guard. It wasn't the response she'd expected. "Well, I, ah—"

"If I told you I wanted to retire, spend my remaining years painting bleak but poignant seascapes, you wouldn't mind?"

"Where do you plan on finding a seascape in Minnesota?"

"Don't change the subject."

"But . . . retire? You're only forty-eight."

"Isn't that just like you?" He sniffed. "Dismissing my desire to become an artist by shifting the subject to my age."

She caught his drift and smiled. Everything was all right, she could tell. "I don't like seascapes," she said, sitting down on the couch next to him. "How about clowns? Now, there's a subject no one's ever explored before."

"You're mocking me."

"No, dear, I'd be mocking you if I suggested you do Elvis portraits on black velvet."

"Ah." He pulled her close.

"So, give. What happened?"

"Well," he said, kissing the top of her head, "I was wrong. Heda Bloom wasn't planning to fire everyone."

"See! I told you."

"She's happy with the current programs, but informed us that she does intend to add something new." He paused for dramatic effect. "Starting tomorrow morning, we begin work on a new radio mystery theatre."

"You mean like the old radio serials? *Mr. District Attorney*? *The Green Hornet*? *Mr. and Mrs. North*?"

"For someone with such a youthful appearance, you're pretty knowledgeable."

She knocked him on the arm. "I used to listen to radio shows when I was a kid. One was even produced here in the Twin Cities. I was probably seven or eight at the time. Let's see. What was that name?" She tapped the side of her face.

"*Dallas Lane, Private Eye.*"

"Hey, that's it." She raised a suspicious eyebrow. "Say, you're not from around these parts. How come you've heard of it? You're a Chicago boy, as you're always so quick to point out."

"I'd never heard of it. Until this afternoon." He rose and walked over to a glass cart near the dining-room arch. "Something to drink?" he asked, holding up a martini glass.

Since she planned on working late tonight, she probably shouldn't. And yet, now that she'd had a moment to relax, she realized how exhausted she really was. "Sure. Why not?" She watched him open a new bottle of gin. "Are you telling me WTWN is going to bring back that *specific* mystery series?"

"To quote that great Minnesota philosopher, Swen Swenson: *you betcha.* Starting next Sunday evening, we'll be up and running. Live, as they say, from the beautiful downtown studios of WTWN."

"What beautiful studios? It's a dump."

"Okay, live from our crummy, dust-ridden suburban Roseville studios. Do you like that better?"

"Back up a minute. You're doing it *live*?"

"We are."

"What do you mean, *we*?" She narrowed one eye.

He turned and gave her a smirk. "You're looking at the new announcer for the program."

"Bram, that's . . . that's wonderful!"

"Is it?" He kept his back to her as he loaded the martini shaker with ice.

"Of course it is."

After shaking—not stirring—he strained the liquid into two glasses and then returned to the couch and handed her one. "A salute to the radio mystery. May we breathe some life back into its moribund form."

They clinked glasses.

"There's only one problem," he added, lifting his feet back up on the footstool.

"And that is?"

"Well, to be succinct, Heda wants this rushed into production by next weekend. I mean, we don't even have the script yet. I don't get it. Why don't we take our time, promote the hell out of it, and then begin the show right after the new year?"

Sophie could see his point.

"Giving us one week to prepare is like setting us up to fail. And when we do, she's going to have the perfect excuse to fire everyone involved. I'm not out of the woods yet, honey. Mark my words."

"Did Heda say why it was so important to get it on the air by next weekend?"

"Not while I was in the room." He took several sips of his drink. "She may think she has the best idea since Darwin invented corporate downsizing, but if she pushes too hard, the whole thing is going to fall flat on its face. In an anthropomorphic sort of way."

Sophie glanced down at her drink. "You forgot the olive."

"So sue me. The other thing is, she projected this sort of . . . confident well-being, but I saw right through it."

"You're masterful when you're intuitive."

"Thank you. Something's up with that woman, Soph. And I'd like to know what it is before I get mixed up in some new radio fiasco."

"You mean . . . other than your *own* show."

"Exactly." He did a double take. "Hey."

"Well, darling, all I can say is, give it your best shot."

"Gee, dear, I'll have to commission someone to do a needlepoint of that so it can hang on my office wall."

"If you're going to go to all that trouble, I'd prefer it went on a pillow for your couch."

"What couch?" He grinned at her. Finishing his drink, he leaned close and nuzzled the side of her neck. "I love to play with you—verbally, and otherwise."

"I know." She nibbled his ear.

There was a loud rap on the door.

"Now what?" groaned Sophie, annoyed by the interruption.

"Why don't you find out who it is while I make us another drink." He grabbed her empty glass.

"Fine. But this time, don't forget the olive." As she stepped over to the door she whispered, "What would you think of doing some Christmas shopping tonight over at Manderbach's department store?"

"Oh, Soph, let's just stay home. We haven't spent a quiet evening together in ages."

She could hardly argue the point. Swinging open the door, she found an attractive, middle-aged woman standing outside in the hall. "May I help you?" she asked. She'd never seen the woman before.

"I'm sorry to bother you. I'm Dorothy Veneger—Heda Bloom's personal assistant." She brushed back her blonde hair and tugged somewhat nervously on a large, gold earring.

Sophie had never cared for curly bangs on women, especially older women, but on Dorothy, they seemed to fit. "Of course. I'm Sophie Greenway. We just missed each other this morning. Won't you come in?" The words were a reflex, though by the tight way Bram now held his shoulders, she could tell the invitation had been a mistake.

"Thanks," said Dorothy. The horn-rim glasses, tailored navy blazer, and beige slacks made her look a bit like a college professor, albeit a fairly glamorous one. Her manner was businesslike. She also appeared to be in a hurry.

"I believe you have a fax that belongs to me," said Dorothy, standing just inside the door.

"Oh, that's right." Sophie retrieved the manila envelope and handed it over. "I assume that means you got my message. The fax came through a few minutes ago. Since you're just across the hall, I thought I'd bring it up. Unfortunately, when I knocked, no one answered."

"I was out grabbing a bite of dinner, and Heda was asleep. But I wonder where Gerald was."

"Gerald?"

"Heda's bodyguard." She noticed Bram standing next to the refreshment cart and gave him a pleasant if somewhat preoccupied nod.

"I'm sorry," said Sophie. "This is my husband, Bram Baldric."

"I assumed as much. It's nice to meet you. Actually, I'll be seeing you tomorrow morning at the station. We've got a lot of work to do if we're going to make next Sunday's schedule."

"I thought you didn't have the script yet," said Bram, his hands sliding casually into the pockets of his slacks.

"We do now," said Dorothy. She held up the envelope. "This should be the entire first episode. Wish Greveen, the writer we've hired to do the first six episodes, promised he'd have it to me by dinnertime. It looks like he's a man of his word. Actually, I need to make several copies to pass out to the other cast members. They're no doubt in their rooms waiting for their first glimpse of the script."

"You mean *they're* staying here, too?" said Bram. "The three people Heda told us about?"

Dorothy nodded. "I'll drop off your copy within the hour. You might want to look it over before tomorrow morning. Get a feel for the story line. By the way, Sophie, is there a copy center around here somewhere?"

"Just go down to the front desk. They'll make as many copies as you want."

"I need them right away."

"Not a problem."

"Thanks." This time, her smile was a bit more relaxed.

"You're sure you won't stay and have a drink with us?" asked Bram. His voice dripped charm as he held up the martini shaker.

"I'm sorry," said Dorothy. "Perhaps another time."

"We'd both like that," replied Sophie. She bid Dorothy good night, then closed the door and leaned against it, eyeing her husband with amusement. "You like to play dangerous, don't you? What if she'd taken you up on that offer of a drink?"

"She didn't."

"But what if she had?"

He patted the pocket of his shirt. "A powerful sedative, specifically designed for glamorous, middle-aged matrons."

"Oh, please."

"You don't believe me?" he said, moving slowly toward her, a seductive look in his eyes.

"What else have you got in that pocket—and up your sleeve?"

"Gee, Soph, I don't know. I guess you'll just have to take my shirt off to find out."

4

Bud Manderbach sat behind the desk in his office, willing the phone to ring. He might own the most exclusive department store in the Midwest, but when it came to the opposite sex, his success had been something less than stellar. He was waiting for a call from Giselle Tannanger, his newest paramour. Giselle was angry at him for failing to keep their usual Tuesday-night dinner engagement. He was a bastard, no doubt about that, and to make it up to her, he was planning to take her on a shopping trip to New York over Christmas. He liked Giselle. Maybe even more than liked her, but he hated being tied down, always having to toe some imaginary line. The truth was, Bud had forgotten about the dinner date. The reason he'd forgotten was no one's business but his—and the young woman he'd met at a bar down on Wabasha.

After four marriages and countless affairs, Bud Manderbach remained a sucker for a pretty face and a sexy voice—at least that's what he told himself. Women were a necessary evil.

Three of his wives had demanded he get some therapy for his drinking. The last one insisted he was sexually addicted and that if he didn't get help, he'd end up dead of AIDS. But Bud knew how to take care of himself. He was sixty-eight years old and still kicking. He intended to stay the same fun-loving, randy bastard he'd always been until the day he checked out permanently. He'd inherited a department store from his father and turned it into a multimillion-dollar business. No doubt about it, he was a success. Except, well, for one small point: Bud Manderbach couldn't stand to be alone.

From the time he was a child, he'd lived in the family home

on Summit Avenue in St. Paul with his sister, B.B. His mother
had died when he was seven, and his father when Bud was in
his late twenties. B.B. was four years younger. While B.B. provided some companionship, it wasn't the kind he craved. Oh,
he loved his sister, and was as protective of her as any good
brother should be. She'd always been the "strange duck" in the
family, as his first wife lovingly referred to her, and Bud had to
admit, she'd gotten even stranger with the years. She drove
him nuts with all her quirks. Two of his wives had actually
blamed B.B. for breaking up their marriage. They'd refused to
live any longer under the same roof with her. But since he
couldn't exactly throw her out, and he wasn't about to move
out of the family home himself, that was that. What was the old
saying? Women were like buses. Another one would be along
any minute.

Bud buzzed his secretary. "Have there been any calls
for me?"

"No, Mr. Manderbach," came the swift but polite reply.
"But you did just get a fax. Would you like me to bring
it in?"

"A fax, huh." Giselle had never sent him one before, but
there was always a first time. "Who's it from?"

"The name on the form is Wish Greveen. I don't have any
other information. Would you like me to read it to you?"

"No," said Bud gruffly. "Just bring it in."

Damn. Giselle was playing with him, he could tell. She
was going to make him squirm. He thought about it for
another minute and then slammed his fist down on the desk.
Why the hell didn't she call? He'd left several messages on
the answering machine at her home, and a couple with her
secretary at work. Maybe he should try again. He hated it
when women reduced men to the emotional level of a
teenager. He had better things to do with his time than worry
about Giselle's *feelings*. Nobody was worried about his.

A knock on the door announced the entrance of Bud's secretary, Loretta Nallen. She was a fortyish woman with dyed
blonde hair and a schoolmarmish voice. She approached the
desk and handed him the envelope containing the fax. "Were

you expecting an important phone call?" she asked, straightening the papers in front of him.

"Yes. No. Never mind what I'm expecting."

"Of course, Mr. Manderbach."

Flicking his eyes to hers, he added, "I'm sorry if I snapped. This hasn't been a good day."

"Maybe you should go home. Have a nice dinner. Watch a movie."

Home, thought Bud sourly. What was there to go home *to*? No one was there except B.B., and she was probably engrossed in her newest collection of whatever trivia had currently caught her fancy. B.B. *always* collected. The house was stuffed to the rafters with her ridiculous "collections." Bud wasn't sure, but he thought her newest passion was lamps. God, what was he going to do with fifty new lamps? B.B. never stopped at one, or ten, or fifteen of anything. She found seemingly endless joy and contentment in all her labeling and cataloguing and comparing. Without her shopping trips, she'd have nothing to do but watch TV.

Neither Bud nor B.B. was very good at maintaining friendships. Bud didn't have the time. He had a business to run, so his lack of interest was understandable. B.B., on the other hand, well . . . even he knew that it would be much easier if she didn't dress so outlandishly.

When B. B. Manderbach stood still in a department store, people always thought she was a mannequin, part of a store display. Over the years she'd become a curiosity, something grandly decadent and hopelessly outdated. With her heavy, ill-applied makeup and clothes that smelled of mothballs, B.B. looked a bit like Queen Victoria sweeping through the corridors of power. Bud had no idea where his sister found the ridiculous garments she wore, and he didn't want to know. B.B. was B.B., just like Bud was Bud. In a way, he respected her as a true iconoclast. His wives may have thought she was mentally ill, but Bud knew B.B.'s heart. She was a good person who had struggled hard against lifelong bouts of depression. Since money had never been an issue in their family, Bud left his eccentric sister alone to pursue her interests. What was the harm?

"I'll go home later," said Bud dismissively. He glanced at his watch. It was nearly seven. "How come you're still here?" He gave his tie a yank, leaned back in his chair, and watched Loretta adjust her pink cashmere sweater.

"Well, I thought I'd finish up a few projects and then go downstairs and do some Christmas shopping."

Manderbach's corporate offices were located on the eighth floor of the downtown St. Paul store. Bud had moved the offices from the Minneapolis store in 1967. He often worked late himself and then had dinner at the Hunter's Grill, the ninth-floor restaurant. "Well, you better get moving. We're only open until nine."

"Ten," said Loretta, correcting him. "We're open an hour later until Christmas."

"All this Christmas crap is enough to drive a man to drink." He hated all holidays, but Christmas was the worst.

"You sound like Ebenezer Scrooge." Loretta smiled. "Maybe you need a visit from the Ghost of Christmas Past." The smile faded when she saw the startled look on Bud's face. "That was a joke, Mr. Manderbach."

"Get out," he snarled. "Leave me alone."

"Of course." She scurried to the door and closed it softly behind her.

Immediately, Bud opened his bottom desk drawer. He withdrew a fifth of Scotch and a paper cup. After swallowing several gulps, he sat back, waiting for the booze to take effect. He shouldn't let silly comments like that get to him. Christmas was something to survive. Surely he wasn't the only human being on earth who felt that way.

He gave himself another minute and then grabbed the envelope Loretta had given him. Opening the top flap, he withdrew a single sheet of paper. It was a typed note, signed in an unreadable scrawl by someone named Wish Greveen. He wouldn't have been able to read the signature except that the sender's name was typed at the top as part of the transmission record. Bud had an Uncle Wish, so the name wasn't foreign to him, not that he knew how Uncle Wish came by it. His given name was Darby.

The note was simple and to the point.

Dear Mr. Manderbach:

I'm writing to call your attention to a new program airing on WTWN radio next Sunday night. It's an updated version of the old *Dallas Lane, Private Eye* mystery series, the same one that ran on another local radio station from 1954 to 1959. I have reason to believe that this program will be of great personal interest to you, and I strongly encourage you to tune in. As I have been commissioned to write the script for the show, any comments you have would be welcomed. I will be checking into the Maxfield Plaza sometime later in the week.

Sincerely,
Wish Greveen

Bud read it through one more time and then tossed it aside. There were a lot of crackpots in this world. He had the distinct feeling he'd just heard from one of them. Pouring himself another inch of Scotch, he sat back and sipped it slowly.

The fax was obviously a joke. Commercially backed radio drama died years ago. Nobody in their right mind would fool around with it today—not with movies, video games, and the Internet to entertain the masses. Nah, someone was pulling his leg.

Still, maybe he'd ask Loretta to call WTWN next week and see if the information was accurate. Manderbach's regularly advertised on WTWN. Maybe the fax was some kind of veiled pitch to get him to sponsor the show. If it was, he might have to listen—or have Loretta listen—just to see what it was all about. Not that he was interested. On the other hand, if some poor son-of-a-bitch really wanted a piece of helpful criticism from a man who prided himself on his business acumen, who was Bud Manderbach to deny this guy a bit of hard-won wisdom?

Dear Mother:

1959 arrived without so much as a handful of confetti or a glass of champagne. I spent New Year's Eve alone in a crummy hotel room in Eindhoven. I felt more cut off from the world in those few hours than I've ever felt before in my entire life. If I'd picked up a gun and blown my brains out, no one would've cared or, for that matter, even noticed. The streets were full of revelers, but I was afraid to go out.

That was almost two weeks ago. Last weekend I found another hotel, in a safer part of town. I still don't go out much. It's just better that way. I had such hopes for the new year, Mom, and for what it would bring. I never dreamed I'd be in Europe, away from home. Depressed. Alone. I know you're not much for reading the Bible. I'm not either, though I did pick up a used King James version in London before I left and read it on the boat coming over.

Do you remember this? "And the Lord said unto Cain . . . now art thou cursed . . . a fugitive and a vagabond shalt thou be in the earth."

I can't help but wonder if that's my fate. I've done more thinking about my life in the past three weeks than at any other time in my life. It's funny, but before I left Minnesota, I'd convinced myself that all my actions were noble. I see now that I was kidding myself. I thought I could control events, protect the innocent, punish the guilty. I was on a mission, Mom, and in the bargain, my career would zoom into the stratosphere.

In the end, all I accomplished was saving my own hide while the woman I love is dead. I have no one to blame but myself. I'm almost afraid to give you an address for fear of what you might say to me when you write. I know what the newspapers must be reporting. I promise, I'll tell you the entire story, but you have to be patient because it's complex. I need to take my time. It's the puzzle of my life that I want to piece together, Mom, as much for me as for you. In many ways, I suppose I was the victim of my own arrogance—that and the arrogance of another man, someone I'll tell you about in due course.

Let me continue with how I met Kay, how we both got mixed up in something neither of us recognized as dangerous.

Okay, in my last letter I began telling you about the night I first saw Kay. I was at the Westgate Country Club and I was there for a very specific reason.

If you recall, in late August of last year, Olga Landauer, the younger sister of Kurt Landauer, owner of Landauer Construction, was killed in a hit-and-run accident outside her home on Fairmount Avenue in St. Paul. I covered the story for the paper. The police had some good leads early on, but none of them panned out.

Kurt Landauer happens to be a good friend of Martin Donovan, the publisher of the St. Paul Daily News & Examiner. Through him, Landauer was able to keep the heat on the police by making sure the paper continued to report the story. With Olga Landauer's name appearing on the front page several times a week, the public couldn't exactly forget what happened. People were demanding answers. Yet by late summer, all the leads were cold. I was eventually pulled off the story and assigned to something else.

On the morning of September 15, I received an anonymous note. There was no return address on the envelope, and the message inside was typed. It said something like, "If you want to know who killed Olga Landauer, talk to

Sally Nash. She lives in an apartment on Bryant Avenue in south Minneapolis." It was signed, simply, *"A Friend."*

I decided to check on it myself before I informed anyone at the paper. You remember that old newspaper maxim Dad used to quote? *"If your mother tells you she loves you, check it out."* I figured that if it was a prank, as I suspected it was, the note would go in the trash with everything else I'd written that day.

I found Sally Nash's number in the telephone directory and phoned, but no one was home. I decided to take a short drive. I stopped at Porky's Drive-in first to wolf down a couple of hamburgers, and then arrived at the Bryant Avenue apartment around two. I buzzed number 213, but just like before, no one answered. By the looks of the names above the mail slot, Sally lived with two other girls. At the time I didn't take much note of the other names.

Later that afternoon, back at the paper, I tried calling again. This time I reached a woman named Jonnie Apfenford, one of her roommates. She informed me that Sally wasn't in and probably wouldn't be around much for the next couple of days. She asked if there was a message. I gave her a fake name and said that it was urgent. I wanted to make it sound important so that she wouldn't forget to give Sally the message. She inquired what it was about. I told her it was personal. She tried to worm it out of me, but I just kept asking when and where I could reach Sally. So finally she said something like, "Well, if you're really that interested, Sally usually spends her weekend evenings over at the Westgate Country Club. That's the only place I can guarantee you'll find her because I know she's got a date this Friday night."

I thanked her and said goodbye. That was Wednesday. Two nights later I drove to the country club. The place was a little rich and formal for my tastes, but I managed to find the bar and order a beer. I waited there a good hour before I saw Kay come in—as I said, on the arm of a guy I didn't know. I thought she was lovely. More than *lovely. I had to meet her, but knew my other business had to come first.*

I studied her from a distance for a few minutes and then caught the bartender's eye and ordered another beer. While he was pouring I asked if he knew a woman named Sally Nash. Sure, he said. She was sitting right over there. He pointed to the table Kay was at. Sally and her date had apparently arrived while my back was turned.

Sally Nash was pretty, but nothing like Kay. She had platinum-blonde hair—kind of a poodle cut—a loud laugh, and from the looks of her, a little too much to drink. Since her date seemed to be hanging on her every word, I wasn't sure how I should make my approach. A frontal attack seemed out of the question.

For the next forty-five minutes I watched Sally drink Manhattans. Her boyfriend tried to get her to stop, but she just kept ordering them. Finally, the music started. People began to gather on the dance floor. I waited and watched as Sally finished her drink and then got up. Mr. Muscles might have been great on the football field, but he wasn't exactly light on his feet. He obviously felt uncomfortable and after the first number pulled her back toward the table. Sally resisted. She wanted to keep dancing. I saw my chance and moved in.

As Muscles sulked off I asked Sally to dance. She was a real flirt and also very drunk. When the next slow song came on, I asked her a couple of innocent general questions just to get the ball rolling. She cuddled up, and I let her.

Somewhere along the line I let it slip that I'd heard she had the real dope on the Landauer murder. She stiffened and drew away. She knew something all right, but she wasn't about to tell me. As she stumbled off she turned and for one brief moment stared me straight in the eye. "I don't know who you are, but stay away from me." She spoke precisely, the way people do when they're afraid they might slur their words, but I still couldn't miss the fear. I should have taken the warning to heart, but I was much too intrigued.

I knew I wasn't going to get any more out of her that night, so I paid my bar tab and left. On the way home, I considered my options. Sally and Kay were obviously friends. That fact alone would have compelled me to continue my search for answers from Sally Nash, even if I wasn't already fascinated by the entire situation. In retrospect, I see that I approached this almost as a game. And that was the biggest mistake of my life.

It's nearly eleven, Mom. I need to breathe some fresh air. I like to go out after dark. The countryside isn't far, and I can lean against a tree and look up at the stars. I have to put my life in some kind of perspective before I can go on. I've got plenty of money, so don't worry about that. I haven't seen anyone following me since I left Amsterdam. I'll pick up some bread and cheese, maybe some wine on the way back to the hotel.

Just remember—if, for some reason, you don't hear from me again, know that you're in my thoughts. Always.
Justin

5

George Chambers nursed a brandy and watched the after-theatre crowd filter into the Maxfield's bar. It was late Friday evening. After the long plane ride from Arizona, he was tired, but not tired enough to go to bed. As he watched the bartender mix one drink after another, his thoughts turned to the radio show he would be working on starting tomorrow morning.

George remembered fondly the good old days of radio. Before he'd entered the army and been shipped off to Korea, he recalled one particular show where he'd spent hours working in frenzied conditions, always pushing a deadline. Rehearsals often took place in absolute chaos, and yet it was gloriously energizing. Back then, he'd spent days trying to replicate certain sounds. The lonely wind on the moor, a dog's plaintive howl, creaking carriage wheels as horses charged into the night. The sounds of terror and the screeches of simple city traffic. The microphone had its own distinctive ear. It wasn't an easy taskmaster, but the truth was, he'd loved every minute of it. He'd helped to project larger-than-life images onto the listeners' mental screens, plundering the audience's own memories to tell the tale. An extraordinary body of work had been created for the radio, and yet most of it was lost as the new medium of television trampled everything in its path.

George freely admitted to himself that he still missed the excitement of his radio days. And yet he wasn't a fool. He knew that not everything about the good old days had been good.

Looking up from his drink, he noticed an old acquaintance amble into the bar. "Hey, Zolotow," he called, waving the man over. He stood and then stuck out his hand. "I thought I might run into you if I waited in the bar long enough."

Valentine Zolotow walked up, but gazed at George uncertainly. "Have we met?"

"Don't you remember me? George Chambers?"

"Hey, sure." He cocked his head. "God, but you've changed."

"Have I?"

He stared at the long white ponytail and full white beard. "You trying for a Santa Claus gig somewhere?"

George laughed. "Not really, although every year I do play Santa for one of the local department stores in Phoenix. I'll miss it this year since I won't be around."

Valentine scratched his chin. "Well, hell, what am I talking about? We've both changed. Look at me." He stroked his balding crown, then snorted. "This is *some* hotel, huh, George? Did you ever think an old junk heap like the

Maxfield Plaza would look like this? I mean—" He straightened his garish plaid sport coat and eyed two young women at the next table. "This must be a four-star joint now. It could even be a 1930s movie set. I worked in Hollywood for a while, in case you didn't hear, so I know about these things." He lowered his voice to a more confidential tone. "I don't suppose you caught me in that movie with Clint Eastwood? Most of my scenes ended up on the cutting-room floor. Schmucks. I coulda won an Oscar for best supporting actor if they'd listened to me instead of the assistant director. But, yeah, I feel expansive in a place like this. It's got glamour. Old-fashioned class. Hey, isn't that Joan Crawford up at the bar?" He elbowed George in the ribs and let out a belly laugh that was half laugh, half deep, wheezing cough.

As they sat down George saw that Valentine had a thick envelope tucked into his sport-coat pocket. If he wasn't mistaken, he knew what it was.

"Look at you, Georgie. You must be what—seventy?"

"Sixty-seven."

"Gee, I thought you were older than me. Well, at least you've got some hair. Other than the beard, you look fabulous. I suppose you're still a lady-killer."

George bristled. "I was never a lady-killer, Valentine."

"Sure, George, sure. So, how've you been? I heard via the grapevine that you were coming." He motioned to the waitress to come take his drink order. "My plane was delayed because of bad weather. I should've been in around six. Actually, I've been upstairs for the last hour unpacking and reading this goddamned script." He yanked it out of his pocket and dropped it on the table. "It was shoved under my door when I arrived. You gotta have eyes like a ten-year-old to read such small print. And tell me something else. Who the hell is Wish Greveen?"

George shrugged. "I've never heard of him."

"Yeah, but . . . the name kind of rings a bell, doesn't it? I think maybe he and I might've worked together on a project some buddies of mine were putting together for Disney a few years back. Bad writer. No talent at all."

Same old Zolotow, thought George. Loud clothes and tall tales. Except that now the clothes looked old and frayed, and the tales sounded like what they were—bluster and braggadocio. The years had obviously manhandled him. He was as thin as a reed, and his skin color betrayed a man whose health was failing. "Where are you living these days?" asked George, sipping his brandy.

Valentine ordered a whiskey sour and then sat back and lit a cigarette. "Here and there." He flipped the top of his lighter closed.

George remembered now that Zolotow never could hang on to a job—or a dime. "So," he continued, "did you read the script?"

"Well, I read some of it." His eyes shifted to the bar entrance and then back to the tip of his cigarette. "But not much. I'll read it later. I got lotsa time before tomorrow morning."

"I read it. The whole thing." He couldn't help but notice that the topic seemed to cause Zolotow some discomfort.

Picking a piece of tobacco out of his teeth, Valentine leaned into the table. "Say, George, I'm curious about something. How did you get involved in this revival?"

"Heda Bloom's assistant called me with the invitation. I believe her name was Dorothy."

"Right. Me, too." He stroked his receding chin with a hand liberally peppered with age spots. "She offer to pay you?"

George nodded.

"A lot?"

"Enough."

"I told her I wasn't interested." He tapped his forehead. "Always thinking, pal, always thinking. I know how to play these games. We talked for a while and finally I told her I wouldn't do it for less than three thousand dollars an episode."

"Really?" That surprised George. "You got more than me."

"Damn straight I did," snapped Valentine, giving the waitress a seductive wink as she set his drink down in front of him.

"I *am* the voice of Dallas Lane after all. They couldn't exactly do it without me. I figured I had them over a barrel."

"I suppose you did."

"Even got a written contract. Did you?"

George nodded.

"Well, good. But I'll bet they don't have to pay you if you get sick. I insisted on that clause. The old ticker isn't what it used to be." He tapped his heart. "Not that I'll *get* sick. Valentine Zolotow never disappoints his audience."

"I remember that." What George actually remembered was a young man with immense talent, but terrible work habits. Valentine rarely ever made it to appointments on time. When he did show up, he often railed at the text and cursed the writers. Yet to be fair, much of the show's success depended on Zolotow's perfectionism. If the camera is said to love certain actors, the microphone positively adored Valentine Zolotow. He was a master of pitch, accent, rhythm, and character. Radio suited him down to the ground. Yet like so many other radio stars, Zolotow's leading-man voice was packed into an unattractive, Ichabod Crane body.

"Don't tell any of the others what I'm being paid," said Valentine, smoking now in quick jabs. "I don't want to create any bad feeling."

"The secret of your good fortune is safe with me."

"Because I really need the money," he added, taking one last puff and then stubbing out the cigarette. "You understand."

"Sure."

"Times have been tough."

"You still gambling?"

He shrugged, picking up his drink and then setting it back down without taking a sip. "Now and then."

"You married?"

"Nah." The grin returned. "I'm too smart for that. I'm not the family-man type. Say, did this Dorothy mention anything to you about the next six episodes?"

"There won't be another six episodes."

"Why?" He studied George for a moment and then took out another smoke, tapping it against the pack. "Oh, I get it.

You don't think people listen to radio anymore. Well, I happen to agree with Heda. Radio drama is just itching to make a comeback. It might as well be us. Don't get all negative on me, Georgie. We're going to make a big splash. Everyone in the Twin Cities will be listening to our show."

"Of that I have little doubt."

Valentine did a double take at George's certainty. "Glad to hear you think that, pal. Anyway, the way I figure it, we'll be asked back for six more episodes. Then another six. Before you know it, we'll be rich men. We've finally hit pay dirt, George."

"I don't need any more money."

"Well, I do," snapped Valentine. "What the hell do you think I'm here for?"

"Oh, I don't know. Maybe to renew old acquaintances."

Valentine smiled as he lit up again, blowing smoke out of the side of his mouth. "Good one, George. Very good. Say, speaking of old acquaintances, I wonder if Mitzi's checked in yet?"

"I don't know," said George wearily.

"Now, there was a real looker. I could never understand why that Justin Bloom dumped her for another woman. I mean, to look at the guy, he seemed so normal."

George finished his drink. "I suppose we never really know what's in another man's mind."

"True. I see you're still the philosopher. After all these years we don't change much."

"I guess not." It struck George that he was bored with the conversation. Or maybe he was just tired. Either way, he wanted to pay his bill and leave.

"I think maybe I'll go give Mitzi's room a call. It's not late. You game, Georgie? We could have another drink. Reminisce about the good old days. Those were some wild old times, weren't they?"

"Not tonight."

"Yeah, I suppose you're right. We've all gotta be up at the crack of dawn."

"You want me to give you a wake-up call?"

"Thanks, pal, but I haven't needed a mother since I was five years old."

"Fine," said George, rising and tossing some cash on the table. "See you in the morning."

6

Mitzi Quinn had a bad case of cold feet. Coming to Minnesota as she had, accepting the invitation so quickly, before she'd really had the time to think it through, had been a terrible mistake, one she had to remedy right away. She'd taken a taxi in from the airport yesterday afternoon, been shown to a lovely room on the fifth floor of the Maxfield Plaza's north wing, yet as soon as she'd set foot in downtown St. Paul, she knew she was in big trouble.

She couldn't imagine what she'd been thinking when Dorothy Veneger had called to offer her the chance to reprise her role in *Dallas Lane, Private Eye*. It was some youthful fantasy, no doubt. Perhaps she'd been seduced by the notion that the stardom that had eluded her in her younger years was finally within her grasp. Except that real life didn't work that way. Dreams didn't always come true. If anyone should know that, Mitzi should.

All night the memories had come flooding back, haunting her thoughts so relentlessly that she couldn't sleep. The years spent trying to land a job with a radio station—any radio station. Then, success with WPXL. And finally, the icing on the cake: meeting Justin Bloom, falling in love with him, and planning a life together. Yet here again, Mitzi knew she'd used a bit too much magic in her thinking. She assumed that because she loved Justin more than life itself, that he would love her back the same way. That small delusion had gotten her into big trouble—trouble that had almost ruined her life.

No, the only way out of this current dilemma was to talk to Heda Bloom face-to-face and get her to see that this reunion of old radio talent—as Dorothy had put it to her—was out of the question. It was never smart to reopen old wounds, and that's what staying in the Twin Cities would accomplish. If it created bad feelings between them, well, so be it.

Mitzi actually remembered Heda quite fondly. For several years of her young life, Mitzi had thought of Heda Bloom as her future mother-in-law. Heda had been unusually kind and generous to her back then, taking her under her wing, helping her shop for clothes, learn about politics and culture, all the things she knew Justin valued. Neither she nor Heda had come from money—or politically sophisticated backgrounds—but the younger woman was willing to learn just as the older woman was willing to teach. For a short time Mitzi even counted Heda as a close friend. Of course, after Justin murdered his paramour and then went into hiding, they'd lost track of each other. It was a situation that might have brought them closer, but, for whatever reason, it hadn't. Yet Mitzi felt confident that their old friendship would make it easier for her to back out of this business deal.

After a quick breakfast, Mitzi left her room and took the elevator upstairs to Heda Bloom's suite. Before she completely lost her courage, she lifted a shaky hand and knocked on the door. It took almost a minute before anyone answered.

"May I help you?" asked a muscular young man dressed in a business suit.

Mitzi had no idea who he was, but forged on. "I'd like to speak with Heda Bloom if I may." She grew ill at ease under the man's scrutinizing stare. Not many manners, she thought to herself silently. Straightening the collar of her dress, she continued, "I know it's early, but this is important."

"What's your business with Ms. Bloom?"

"Well, I, ah, that is to say . . . my name's Mitzi Quinn and—"

A voice from behind him called, "It's all right, Gerald. Let her in."

As she entered the suite Mitzi saw an older woman emerge from a side hallway. She was carrying a stack of file folders.

"Ms. Quinn," said the woman, placing the folders on the end of the marble bar. "What a pleasant surprise. I'm Dorothy Veneger. We spoke on the phone." She moved toward Mitzi, her arm extended.

"Oh, yes. Nice to finally meet you." They shook hands.

"I see you've already met Gerald. Actually, I didn't expect to see you until our meeting later this morning over at the station."

"No, well, I—"

"Mitzi!" called a surprised voice from the other end of the room.

Mitzi turned around.

Heda Bloom stood framed in her bedroom doorway, her face lit by a warm smile. "What an unexpected treat. I'm delighted to see you." Leaning heavily on her canes, she crossed to where Mitzi was standing.

They hugged briefly. Mitzi thought the embrace was a little stiff.

Holding Mitzi at arm's length, Heda gave her a long, measuring look. "How could the years have left you untouched while they've beaten me to a bloody pulp?"

Mitzi couldn't help but laugh. She remembered now that Heda had grown up with a prizefighter father and a vaudeville-star mother. Polite conversation, while an acquired skill, had never been her normal mode of expression. Mitzi was pleased with the compliment. She'd always tried to keep herself up. She selected clothes to highlight her still-slim figure, and with an occasional nip and tuck to keep her face tight and firm, she continued to feel reasonably young and attractive. She'd dithered for almost a year about whether to let her hair go gray, but finally decided her old shade of brown was much more youthful. Mitzi was pleased with her image. She didn't look a day over forty-five; at least, that's what her daughter always said.

Heda looked wonderful as well. Energetic as ever. Older, yes, but still kicking, as they say. Still very definitely alive and kicking.

"What brings you here this morning?" asked Heda, sitting down with some difficulty in an armchair next to the window. She pulled her skirt down over her knees, and then gave Mitzi a pleasant if somewhat curious smile.

"Well, actually, I was hoping to talk to you alone." She took her cue from Heda and sat down on the sofa.

Dorothy moved to a chair halfway across the room. "If this has something to do with the new radio show, I'd like to stay." Glancing over at the bodyguard, she said, "I'm sure Gerald wouldn't mind busying himself somewhere else for a few minutes. Would you, Gerald?" She nodded her head, silently telling him to get lost.

"Of course, Ms. Veneger." He quickly opened the door and stepped outside.

Mitzi could have sworn she saw the butt of a gun under his suit coat as he left the room. It gave her a funny feeling. She couldn't imagine why Heda would need that kind of protection.

"So," said Heda, folding her hands in her lap, "shoot. What can I do for you?"

"Well, actually," said Mitzi, feeling as if she were standing center stage with a spotlight shining on her, "I've changed my mind about starring in your new radio project. I no longer want to be a part of it."

No one spoke for several seconds.

Finally, Dorothy said, "I'm afraid that's not possible, Mitzi. For one thing, we have a signed contract. For another—"

Heda held up her hand for silence. "No, I want to hear this. Why don't you want to remain with us, Mitzi? Are you . . . unhappy with the script?"

Mitzi shook her head. "I haven't read it yet."

"Then what?"

She bit down hard on her lower lip. She wasn't prepared to tell Heda the truth. Consequently, she had to come up with something plausible to extricate herself from this tight spot. "I . . . you see, it's just that this town holds so many bad memories for me. You of all people should understand."

"I do," said Heda gently. "But surely you considered that before you agreed to our proposal."

Her eyes drifted to the window. "Well, somewhat."

"Is it your husband? Is he putting pressure on you to come home?"

"I've been divorced for many years."

"Oh," said Heda. "I didn't know."

"Well, actually . . . now that you bring it up, you *have* hit on the crux of the matter. It's a family problem. I was hoping my daughter could come up from Texas to spend the holidays with me here in St. Paul, but I found out yesterday that she can't. I've never been away from her at Christmastime before. We're very close. It's simply too much to ask. So . . . you see, I have to decline your offer. It's nothing personal. I simply have to withdraw."

"I didn't know you had a family," said Dorothy. "You didn't mention it on the phone."

"Didn't I? Well, anyway, she doesn't have the money to fly up from Houston. And being away from her during the holidays is just too big a sacrifice."

"Well, that's no problem," said Dorothy, smiling calmly. She lifted a pad from her blazer pocket and began jotting down some notes. "We'll send her a plane ticket. We'll even put her up at the Maxfield free of charge. How's that?"

"Good idea," agreed Heda. "Now, Mitzi, you have to admit, that takes care of your crisis quite adequately. And this way, I get to meet her. We'll all get to meet her."

This wasn't working, thought Mitzi. She was making her usual mess of things. "No, but it's more than that. It's . . . it's the memories, too."

"I can't do anything about those," said Heda. "And I understand that this is hard on you. It's hard on me, too. The last time I was in the Twin Cities, I lost my eldest son and my husband."

"And I only lost Justin, is that what you're saying?" She shot to her feet. "Your loss is greater than mine? Because if it is, for your information, I lost a lot more than that." She knew she had to calm down. She was on the verge of saying too much. "I'm sorry," she said, turning her back on Heda and pressing her fingers to her temple. "I'm more emotional about this than I thought. Don't you see? That's why I mustn't stay."

As Mitzi turned back to them, looking from face to face, she could tell what the verdict was before either of them spoke.

"I'm sorry, too," said Dorothy. "But a contract is a contract. We've already begun to advertise the show, complete with old-time cast members. We have big plans for promotion, for radio and TV spots. If you back out on us now, you leave us no alternative." She paused. "We'd have to sue, Mitzi." Staring at her intently, Dorothy lowered her voice to a deeper, more serious register and added, "And we will sue, have no doubt about that."

Mitzi felt flattened. She hadn't expected that Heda would put up such a fight. After all, if anyone could understand why she might rue her decision to stay in Minnesota, even for six weeks, Heda should. Still, the idea of spending the next year of her life dealing with lawyers and judges, schlepping in and out of courtrooms, was too much. "All right," she said with a shrug of resignation. "I guess you win."

"I don't want to win, Mitzi." Heda's expression had grown sad. "I just need for you to stand behind your commitment."

Mitzi looked Heda square in the eyes. She could feel the old anger rising in her chest. "You know, if your son had done that, we all would have had much happier lives." Her voice was icy with a rage that surprised even her.

Heda looked stricken. "I don't know what to say to you. I can't go back and change what my son did. You have to believe me. I'm so sorry, far sorrier than you'll ever know."

Mitzi desperately wanted to tell Heda the truth—how she was sorry herself for *her* actions. But almost forty years after the fact? What was the point? Some secrets were best left in the past, buried under layers of time. At least there, they couldn't hurt the living.

January 24, 1959

Dear Mother:

I've moved again. I thought I'd managed to give my pursuers the slip, but I saw them outside my hotel, five nights ago. One guy—the tall, skinny one—was standing in a doorway. If he hadn't been smoking a cigarette, I never would have seen him. The other guy was sitting in a parked car half a block away. I'm not sure why they haven't arrested me yet. As far as I can tell, they've had plenty of opportunities. I managed to escape through a basement door that led to a parking garage. I had to leave most of the stuff I've accumulated since I left Minnesota in my room, though I did manage to take my backpack and a small suitcase with me. In the past few weeks I've learned to travel light. Material possessions don't matter as long as I've got my freedom.

I spent one night sleeping in a train station, the next in a barn. For the last few days I've been staying just outside Koblenz, but it's not safe here. I know now that I'm not safe anywhere as long as I remain in Europe. The problem is, I'm sure the train stations and airports are being watched. I've thought long and hard about this, Mom, and I finally came up with a plan. I've already dyed my hair black, and I'm in the process of growing a beard, which I'll also dye black. Today I was thinking it might be better—and faster— if I bought a fake beard somewhere. I can't tell you the rest of my plan just yet, but I'm going to be traveling for the next few weeks—possibly longer, so don't get upset if you don't *hear from me for a while. When you do, I'll be in a much better position to write more regularly, and, hopefully, to finally hear back from you.*

Since I've got about an hour to kill before I have to leave the hotel to meet a man in town, I thought this might be as good a time as any to resume my story. I feel pretty safe here for now, but I know it won't last. This time, I intend to get a jump on my pursuers before they can locate me. It's the only way I can give them the permanent slip.

Okay, to continue:

After that first night at the Westgate Country Club, I felt confident that the anonymous note I'd received was on the level. Sally Nash did know something about Olga Landauer's death, I was sure of it. But how was I going to get her to talk?

Since I wasn't exactly sure how to proceed, I decided to tail her to see what I could learn. On Monday morning, I sat in my car outside her apartment and waited. I figured she'd come out sooner or later and I could follow her to work. Once I discovered where that was, I thought maybe I could get one of her coworkers to give me a lead—tell me what kind of girl she was, who she associated with, how she spent her time and money.

The only problem was, she never came out. By ten, I'd drunk an entire thermos of coffee, smoked my remaining five cigarettes, and eaten three jelly doughnuts. I figured it must be her day off. Since I had a meeting at eleven over at the paper, I'd have to resume my surveillance later in the afternoon.

I was about to pull away from the curb when I saw Kay come out of the building. She checked her watch and then proceeded quickly toward the bus stop. The funny thing was, in my mind I'd pegged her as the kind of person who probably lived in a Kenwood mansion. She was dressed so elegantly on Friday night and looked so regal, I assumed she was rich. As I sat in my car and watched her, I thought back to the names above Sally Nash's mail slot. I wished now that I'd taken better notice of them. Kay might very well be one of her roommates. But any way you sliced it, Kay was a link to Sally. I decided to take a chance and follow her. My meeting could wait.

Fifteen minutes later she got off the bus on Eighth and Hennepin and walked several blocks to Marquette Avenue, where she entered Manderbach's downtown Minneapolis store. I parked across the street, fed some nickels into the meter, and headed inside myself. I quickly spotted her stepping onto one of the elevators. I ran to catch up, but the doors closed in my face. Feeling incredibly frustrated, I got on the next available car and then got off on the third floor— women's clothing. I figured that was a good bet. I hurried through the various departments, but again struck out. After dashing around madly for the next half hour, I gave up and took the elevator back downstairs. I had nothing to show for the morning except an acid stomach and a bad case of caffeine jitters.

As I charged through the cosmetics department I stopped dead in my tracks. There she was, standing behind the counter, showing a fancy bottle of perfume to an elderly woman. I mean, I was floored. Kay Collins was a salesgirl? Again, this didn't fit my image of her. Right then and there I settled myself down. Romantic notions or no romantic notions, Kay was obviously nothing like the way I'd envisioned her. She lived in a modest apartment and she worked in a department store.

I waited until she was done with her sale and then walked up and pointed to a couple of the bottles. Actually, I'd been meaning to get Mitzi something for her birthday— which, of course, reminded me that I had no business being attracted to another woman. As you may or may not know, Mitzi and I, though not officially engaged, had talked about getting married. I assumed she'd filled you in on the big news because it seemed to me that at her birthday party in late September, you were just bursting with joy that your oldest son was about to tie the knot. I never confirmed or denied it, because by then I wasn't sure it was what I wanted. Unfortunately, I didn't tell Mitzi about Kay.

And, much to my later embarrassment, I didn't tell Kay about Mitzi.

That morning, standing in front of the perfume counter, I convinced myself that talking to Kay was simply part of the research I needed to do on a potentially hot story.

Kay was polite and helpful. She found me just the right scent in a price I could afford. When she asked who it was for, I said it was for my mother. She smiled and told me I was a thoughtful son, though I'm not sure she entirely believed me. I tried as hard as I could to engage her in a conversation. I can be pretty charming when I want to be, and whatever I said, it must have worked. She agreed to have dinner with me the following evening.

When I came to pick her up, I found that she did indeed share an apartment with two other women. Both Sally and Jonnie were sitting on the couch when I arrived, but thank God, neither of them recognized me. I'd spoken to Jonnie on the phone, but it had been brief and I hadn't given her my real name. Sally, on the other hand, had seen me face-to-face at the Westgate, but since she'd been pretty smashed, she didn't connect the dots.

As you might imagine, I breathed a sigh of relief when Kay and I finally left. I wanted to get to know her better, pump her for information, but subtly. I figured that if Kay thought I was using her to get the lowdown on Sally, she'd not only be angry, but she'd dump me without so much as a backward glance. Taking Kay out, showing her a good time, easing slowly into a friendship was simply good investigative journalism. I was protecting myself, and my story.

Three weeks later, after our tenth date, I knew better than to think our time together had anything to do with research. I was falling in love with her. Maybe I'm flattering myself, but I think she was falling in love with me, too.

She was incredible, Mom. Beautiful. Funny. Smart. She'd attended the university for a couple of years, but couldn't afford the tuition, so she'd taken a job at Manderbach's until she could save up enough money to go back. Her family was from a small town in Michigan, but Kay wanted to be independent. She was starved for adventure in the big city. I guess, in a way, you could say we had a lot in common. She and Sally and Jonnie had all moved to Minneapolis together in the spring of '55. Sally and Kay were now twenty-three. Jonnie was twenty-six, exactly one month younger than me, and in graduate school over at the U. She wanted to be a psychologist. Sally was nowhere near as serious about life as Jonnie and Kay. Attending the U was just her excuse for getting away from home. She'd been the first one to quit her studies and apply for a job at Manderbach's. Kay followed a year later.

As the weeks progressed I began to get a clearer picture of the kind of girl Sally was. She'd grown up poor and had to fight her brothers and sisters for everything she ever got. Basically, I guess you could say she liked men and liked money. In that order. Kay confided to me that it was Sally's dream to one day marry a rich man. Kay felt Sally could be disgustingly shallow at times. When I asked her if Sally had been dating anyone in particular recently, she explained that she'd dated a guy pretty steadily back in July and August, but had stopped seeing him during the first week in September. Interestingly enough, Kay said that a day or two after the breakup, Sally had quit her job at Manderbach's and signed up for driving lessons. One week later she passed her driving test and drove home in a new car. She started taking day trips all over southern Minnesota. Sally called it "seeing the countryside."

Kay admitted she had no idea where Sally had gotten the money for the car or her new—far more affluent—way of life, but she seemed to have plenty of ready cash whenever she needed it. I smelled a rat. When I pressed Kay to tell me the identity of the man Sally'd been dating, she clammed up. My instincts told me I'd hit pay dirt. If I found out who this boyfriend was, I might also find the identity of the man who'd killed Olga Landauer.

Of course, my first thought regarding Landauer's death was that it might actually have been Sally herself driving the car the night of the hit-and-run. Yet if she didn't know *how to drive until the middle of September, that seemed to rule her out.*

Funny, as I think about it now, it never occurred to me that either Kay or Jonnie might've had something to do with the Landauer hit-and-run. No, it was the boyfriend that sounded my journalistic alarm. The way I had it figured, Sally was being bought off, paid for her silence. I wanted to know who was behind it; I already had a good idea why.

More later, Mom.

My love always,
Justin

7

Shortly after eleven on Thursday morning, Bram was standing next to the second-floor reception desk at WTWN sifting through his mail when the elevator doors opened and out walked a massive, bearlike creature, undoubtedly human, but endowed with so much hair—or was it fur?—that Bram could barely make out a face. The man's wiry beard was dark brown. No mouth was visible. And although the hair on his head was reasonably short, it was so thick and unruly, it looked like a wig. Bram tried not to stare, but it was a struggle.

When the man opened his mouth and spoke to the receptionist, Bram did a startled double take. Whoever this guy was, he had a voice as deep and loud as Duluth's famous foghorn. Actually, he kind of reminded Bram of the cartoon likeness of Paul Bunyan, Minnesota's answer to Rip Van Winkle—or was it Arnold Schwarzenegger?

"Where is Heda Bloom's office?" demanded the bear, mashing a paw down on the desk.

"May I ask your name?" said the receptionist, attempting to be as polite as possible. Bram could see she was every bit as astonished as he was.

"Alfred Bloom," boomed the voice. "Your new boss."

"But—"

"But what?"

"Well, Ms. Bloom and Ms. Veneger said you wouldn't be coming to Minnesota."

"I like surprises."

Bram cleared his throat to draw Bloom's attention. "Mr. Bloom. I'm delighted to meet you." He extended his hand. "My name's Bram Baldric. I do the afternoon show. And I'm also announcing WTWN's new radio mystery."

Alfred Bloom looked like a man who'd just been severely annoyed by a buzzing gnat. Turning his dark brown eyes on Bram, he snapped, "What radio mystery? They went out with spats and zoot suits. I've seen the program roster. It's not on it."

Bram lowered his hand to his side. So much for social niceties. "You haven't been told about the program change on Sunday night?"

"No. Where's my mother? We need to talk."

"She's not in here, Mr. Bloom," said the receptionist. "But Ms. Veneger is. Would you like me to buzz her and announce you?"

"No. I'll announce myself," said Alfred curtly. "Just tell me where to go." He returned his attention to Bram. "I've seen your ratings. They're good."

"Thanks."

"But you surprise me. You're the suave, sophisticated type. Nice, expensive threads." He brushed a hairy paw across Bram's lapel. "Not what I expected."

"I prefer the term 'gritty' myself."

"I usually don't get along with suave types. Anybody ever tell you you look like Cary Grant?"

"Just my mother."

The whiskers around Alfred's mouth moved. Bram couldn't tell if it was a smile or a snarl.

Alfred returned his glare to the receptionist. "So which office is it?"

"Right down the hall, Mr. Bloom. Third door on your left."

"Call me Alfred. And find me a bottle of Evian water. I'm thirsty."

"Of course, Mr. Bloo—I mean, Alfred."

Fascinating, thought Bram. He looked more like the type of bear that foraged for his food-and-beverage needs in garbage cans.

As Alfred Bloom lumbered off down the hallway Bram turned to the receptionist, raised an eyebrow, and whispered, "Remember. Only you can prevent forest fires."

By four-thirty, Bram had finished his program and was preparing to leave. As he stuffed a copy of the *Christian Science Monitor* into his briefcase, he heard a knock on the door. "Come in," he called, quickly brushing the cookie crumbs off his desk. If Alfred Bloom was about to enter, he didn't want to damage his sophisticated image. Grabbing a pen, he pretended to be deep in thought as he pored over some important papers.

The door opened.

Bram lifted his head with great solemnity. "Oh hell, it's just you." He tossed his pen down.

"Not a very nice welcome," said a police officer ambling into the room. "Cops usually command a little more respect." The man lowered himself into a chair on the other side of the desk.

"Sorry," said Bram. "I was expecting someone else."

Al Lundquist was a sergeant with the St. Paul police. He and Bram had gone to high school together in Chicago, and had stayed friends ever since. Every now and then, Bram would pass him some tickets to a local sporting event in return for a bit of inside police information.

Glancing contemptuously around the messy office, Al cracked his knuckles and said, "This place is a firetrap. You got more books and magazines in here than most libraries."

"How long has it been since you were in a library?"

"None of your damn business."

"Want a cookie?" Al was easily placated by food.

"Don't mind if I do."

Bram lifted a sack from his top drawer and pushed it across.

"Thanks. Hey, these look great. You always get the gourmet kind. I should swing by here more often. By the way, I got that stuff you asked for."

"Tell me the truth, Al," said Bram, leaning back in his chair. "Do you think I'm suave?"

"I think you're a smart-ass."

"That's what I figured. What've you got?"

"This." He dumped a manila envelope on the desk. "It's a copy of the entire police file on the Kay Collins murder. It took me quite a while to dig it up."

"You have my undying devotion."

"Just keep your promise abut the Vikings tickets and we'll call it even. Oh, and if you've got any questions on the file, direct them to me."

"Will do." Bram slipped the material out and paged through the top few documents.

As Al munched on a cookie he continued, "The file included some of the newspaper clippings from the *St. Paul Daily News & Examiner* back in fifty-nine. They covered the story pretty straight. Well, as straight as any two-bit newspaper can ever do. I thought you might find it interesting."

"I do," said Bram. His attention was completely captured by the information in front of him. This was just what he'd been looking for.

"Hey, buddy, you gotta answer me a couple of questions before I go." Al twisted his head around and cracked his neck.

"Sure." Bram flipped to another page.

"No, asshole. Look at me when I'm talkin' to you."

He glanced up. "You have such a delicate verbal touch, Al. Has anyone ever told you that?"

"Save the charm for your radio audience. First, I want to know what caused this interest in Justin Bloom."

And wasn't that the question of the hour? How could Bram have failed to miss the significance of the story line in the newest *Dallas Lane* mystery? The names might've been changed to protect the innocent—if there were any—but the fictionalized account was a dead ringer for the real one.

The story concerned a young newspaper reporter wrongly accused of the murder of his girlfriend. While the kid rotted in jail, Dallas Lane was hired to prove his innocence. Not only could Bram see the similarity to the Justin Bloom case, but as soon as it aired on Sunday night, so would most of the listening audience, at least those who were old enough to remember.

Bram assumed that Heda was setting up the story to retell the events surrounding the murder, but from a different point of view. This would be Justin's account. Bram didn't know what specific knowledge Heda had, but figured that she'd been in contact with her son after he'd left the country. Since he was now dead, clearing his name fell to her. The case had never gone to trial, so technically it was still an unsolved murder.

"So give," said Al, stuffing the last cookie into his mouth. He chewed for a few seconds and then said, "You got any coffee?"

Bram pointed to a coffeemaker on a table in the corner. "I turned it off a few minutes ago, but it's still warm."

"Great." He got up and poured himself a cup. "So, answer the question."

"Well," said Bram, leaning back in his chair and clasping his hands behind his neck, "Heda Bloom, the mother of Justin Bloom, just bought the radio station."

"No kidding." Al sipped his Colombian Supremo as he stood next to the window overlooking the parking lot. "So what?"

"So, you should listen to our new radio mystery. It debuts this Sunday night at six-thirty."

"Is this a joke?"

"No, I'm serious. I may be wrong, but I think it's going to be a new take on the Kay Collins murder."

Al screwed up his face in thought. "You mean, that's how you're advertising it?"

"Of course not, lunkhead."

Al cracked another couple of knuckles. "Well, maybe I'll give it a listen. If I'm not too busy."

"You do that."

"You part of this program?"

"I'm the announcer."

"You mean like Ed McMahon?"

"No," he said, deeply annoyed by the comparison. "Like Orson Welles."

Al pushed his hat back on his head with one finger. "This isn't going to be another *War of the Worlds* fiasco, is it? We don't want any of our good citizens frightened for their lives."

"You've got a twisted mind, pal."

"Since *you're* involved, I had to ask."

Bram couldn't imagine how it could escalate into something quite so morbid. "I have every confidence that Heda Bloom knows what she's doing. In a way, it's her son's last hurrah, posthumously speaking. And I, for one, am curious how it's going to play out."

"*Curious,* huh?"

"Aren't you the least bit interested in what really happened to Kay Collins?"

"I know what happened to her. It's right there in that police report." He nodded to the manila envelope.

Bram sighed. "You have no drama in your soul, Al. No drama at all."

8

"More coffee?" asked the waiter, the pot poised next to Sophie's cup.

She glanced up at him with a weary smile. "Sure." This was round number three.

"We could switch to decaf."

"No, we couldn't."

"Would you like to order now?"

She could feel her stomach growl. "I better wait until my husband gets here."

For the past half hour Sophie had been sitting at a table in Manderbach's ninth-floor restaurant, studying some menu notes she'd made earlier in the week for a party she was throwing for her son.

Rudy and his companion, John Jacoby, had planned a commitment ceremony the week before Christmas. Sophie had suggested that once the service was over at the church, everyone come back to the Maxfield for a champagne buffet. Rudy and John had been so touched by her enthusiasm that they'd accepted immediately.

Sophie was truly happy for the two of them, and she eagerly looked forward to the event. And yet, with everything already on her plate, the added responsibility of organizing a large party had turned out to be far more stressful than she'd imagined. At this time of year the Maxfield's banquet facilities were booked solid. The kitchen was always in a state of frenzied chaos and staff hours were pushed to the maximum. But Sophie knew what an important step it was for Rudy and John, and to show her love and support, everything had to be perfect. Disappointing her son was out of the question.

Rudy would finish his degree in theatre arts at the University of Minnesota next winter. John was an artist whose drawings had appeared in several local galleries. To support himself, he worked a day job at a brewery in St. Paul. They'd met shortly after Rudy had come to Minnesota. As Sophie recalled it now, it had been a hard time for everyone.

Sophie's ex-husband, Norman Greenway, had raised Rudy since he was a boy. Much to her great pain and regret, Sophie hadn't been allowed to see him much while he was growing up. For the past twenty-four years Norm had been a minister in a cultlike fundamentalist Christian church in Montana. He'd sued for custody as part of the divorce proceedings. With the unlimited funds of the church behind him, the ensuing custody battle had been a *fait accompli* from the outset.

Sophie had left the church as a result of a conflict over the doctrine of healing. As a young child, Rudy had become ill—so ill, in fact, that Sophie had feared for his life. Defying her husband's wishes and the church's moral teachings, she'd taken him to a doctor. She'd never had any doubt about her actions. She knew Rudy wouldn't be alive today if he hadn't received medical treatment. Yet she also knew that as soon as she set foot inside the hospital door, her marriage was over. Even if Norm had been willing to take her back, she was finished—with him *and* the church.

After the divorce, Norm, in his infinite wisdom, had cut Rudy off from his mother's influence. And yet once Rudy was old enough, he'd left Montana. Sophie wished she could say he'd turned up on her doorstep because he missed his mother and wanted to mend an important relationship in his life, but the truth was, he was running—from his father and the church.

Rudy was gay. He knew that as long as he stayed with the Church of the Firstborn, he would have to hide that part of himself. In the end, it was too much. Sophie was glad that he'd come to stay with her, even if his reasons had been simple expediency. He was a confused young man, in most ways a stranger to her, in need of a safe place to stay while he figured out what to do next. It had been a hard road back to each other, but they'd finally made it.

Checking her watch with growing impatience, she saw that it was almost six. Bram had called around five to say he'd come across some important information he needed to discuss with her right away. He'd suggested that they meet at Manderbach's for a quick dinner. Sophie had tried to beg off, explaining that she had a ton of work to do before she could call it a night, but Bram had insisted, and reluctantly, she'd agreed. Since he was now half an hour late, she was beginning to regret her decision.

Sophie did have to admit that she was curious about what this important information might be. Bram wouldn't discuss it on the phone. He relished life's little dramas, wherever he could find—or create—them. It could be just about anything. His afternoon radio show had become a kind of gossip central for all the hot dish in the Twin Cities. Callers phoned in from all over the state with tidbits of this and that new rumor. As a matter of fact, *The Bram Baldric Show* had been instrumental in breaking the Prostitution-gate scandal at the state legislature last year. All in all, Bram liked his status as the guru of Minnesota gossip. It certainly kept his radio show at the top of the ratings.

By six-thirty, Sophie was completely out of patience. As she was about to call for the check, she saw Bram breeze through the front entrance and snake his way through the dark, oak-paneled room toward her. He approached the table with a harried look on his face, tossed his coat on an empty chair, and sat down with a sigh.

"Sorry I'm late. The driving's getting nasty out there. I'll bet we got three inches of snow this afternoon. The roads are a mess."

"Five, according to the weather report."

"Really. Well, it's coming down again. And the wind's picked up." He smoothed back his hair. "But I still look pretty as a picture, right?"

Her smile was thin. "Right."

He eyed her a moment, then glanced down at the menu. "I meant that, Soph—about being sorry."

"I know. It's just . . . I'm really under the gun right now, Bram. This was kind of a bad night for me to go out to dinner."

"It's been a bad night for the past two months."

His frustration instantly put her on the defensive. "Look, you're the one who was an hour late. Why are you trying to make *me* feel guilty?"

"Because I hardly see you anymore, Sophie. And I don't like it."

She lowered her head, knowing this was a no-win situation. If she didn't work extra hours at the hotel, she would end up making mistakes—maybe even big mistakes. But if she didn't back off from all her overtime, her marriage would suffer.

Bram had made her a deal early in their relationship. His first marriage had ended because of all the hours he'd spent building his career in radio. He had no time for anything but work. Taking the job at WTWN had been a compromise, a wedding gift to Sophie. He wanted to put their relationship first. Sophie was thrilled—it was what she wanted, too. Bram worked now for less money, but it was also less of a time commitment. He didn't want to make the same mistake twice.

Sophie never dreamed that she would be the one swept up by a career move, and yet she couldn't exactly turn her back on the hotel, or give it over to some flunky to manage. She knew, given enough time and experience, that she was the best person for the job. Running the Maxfield Plaza was the most absorbing work she'd ever done. Bram would simply have to understand. He surely didn't doubt her love. And besides, all these extra hours wouldn't last forever. "Things will change, honey, I promise—just as soon as I get my feet on the ground. The more I learn about the hotel business, the more I realize how much I don't know. And you know me. I can't do anything halfway."

The waiter arrived with a basket of bread. Once they'd placed their orders, Sophie leaned forward, rested her chin on her hands, and said, "So, what important information did you want to talk over?" She hoped the change in subject would ease the tension between them.

"Did we finish our fight?"

"I think so. At least for now."

Gazing at her for several long seconds, Bram nodded. "All right. For now." Pulling some notes out of his coat pocket, he smoothed them out on the tabletop. "Believe it or not, this is everything you'd ever want to know about the Kay Collins murder case."

Bram had talked of little else all week. "Where did you get the report?" she asked.

"From Al Lundquist."

"Ah, yes. Mr. Knuckle Cracker. You can hardly hear his voice over the din his joints make."

"Cute."

"So what'd he have to say?"

Bram buttered a cardamom roll. "He gave me the official police report along with a bunch of newspaper clippings."

"And?"

"In a nutshell? I don't see how this Justin Bloom could possibly be innocent."

Sophie was intrigued. She was also glad to be concentrating on something other than hotel business for a few minutes. "Start at the beginning, honey. I don't want to miss a thing."

"God, I love it when you're as pruriently morbid as I am." He took a bite of the roll and chewed while he searched for a particular page. "Okay, here's the scoop. Kay Collins was murdered on December twenty-fourth, 1958. Christmas eve. It was late afternoon, sometime around four. An off-duty police officer named Arn O'Dell was walking near Bryant and Minnehaha Creek when he heard what he thought was a gunshot. He rushed down the embankment toward the water and saw a man shouting at a woman. They were clearly fighting about something, though O'Dell couldn't make out the words."

"It was Collins and Bloom?"

"Exactly. Now, even though it was getting dark, the cop still got a good look at both of them. He later picked Justin Bloom's photo out of a file. At the time all he knew was that the two people were young, and that the man was very, very angry. About twenty yards away, O'Dell slipped on a piece of ice and landed in a snow pile. When he looked up, he saw the man level a gun at the woman's head and shoot. Since O'Dell didn't have a gun himself, he shouted for the man to stop, but Bloom took off up an embankment. Thinking that the woman might still be alive, he raced to where she'd fallen and checked her vital signs. It was too late. She'd been horribly disfigured by the gunshot. The medical examiner said she died instantly. There was a citywide search that lasted for days. The police even found the clothes Bloom had been wearing that night. They were hidden in his bedroom closet, and they were covered with blood, Sophie—Kay's blood. The upshot was, Bloom got away. The story made the headlines for weeks afterward. It was a brutal, bloody murder, and no one had a clue where Justin Bloom had gone."

Sophie shook her head. She, too, was amazed by the brutality.

"And it doesn't stop there," continued Bram. "From what

others pieced together after the murder, Justin and Kay had apparently been dating. They told friends they were in love. Bloom even broke an engagement with another woman to be with Kay. Guess who that other woman was?"

"Who?"

"Mitzi Quinn."

Sophie was surprised. "I met her the other night when she checked into the hotel. She's very attractive. Didn't look a day over fifty. But"—she did the math in her mind—"she must be in her sixties."

"Fascinating, huh? And there's more. As I understand it, Kay had two roommates. They were all close friends, all from the same small town. They'd come to Minneapolis together to attend the university. But get this. Neither of the two roommates could be found for questioning after Kay's death. They'd disappeared. Vanished into thin air. As a matter of fact, they never even came back to the apartment to get their clothes or any of their belongings."

"Creepy."

"I agree. All I can say is, there was something pretty intense going on in that group of friends. Beyond that, it's hard to speculate."

"What about the gun? Seems to me I remember something important about it."

The waiter arrived with their drinks and two dinner salads.

"That's another interesting point," said Bram, picking a crouton off the top of his salad and popping it in his mouth. "The gun was left at the scene. The only fingerprints on it were Bloom's."

"Pretty incriminating."

"The police shared the same opinion. The gun was registered to Cedric Bloom."

"Justin's father?"

"His *step*father. And interestingly, Cedric Bloom had reported the gun missing just the day before. He usually kept it in his desk at the radio station. He sometimes worked late at night. As I understand it, he'd been mugged once, so he said it made him feel safer to have one available."

"You think Justin took it?"

"That's what the police think. Who had easier access?"

"Well, lots of people, I suppose," said Sophie. "What about all the station employees?"

"Cedric maintained that only a few people knew about it. Since he didn't want any problems, he kept the drawer locked, and the key taped inside a filing cabinet."

"So who knew about both the gun and the key?"

Bram ticked the names off on his fingers. "Besides Cedric and Heda Bloom, there were five people he mentioned specifically in his statement. Justin. Alfred Bloom, Justin's half brother. Valentine Zolotow. Mitzi Quinn. And George Chambers. Cedric said the last three people often worked late with him if they got behind on a *Dallas Lane* episode. They'd all seen him take it out of the drawer at one time or another."

"Fascinating," said Sophie under her breath. "And now they're all back in town for *Dallas Lane*'s last hurrah."

"*Dallas Lane*'s last hurrah, or is it Justin Bloom's?"

They both sipped their drinks for several moments in silence. This was a lot of information to digest. Sophie wanted to read the report herself. "So what about the rumors that Justin spent the remainder of his life in Europe? That he died in a car crash sometime in the early Eighties."

Bram shrugged. "It's just that. Rumor. Although I did read something in the police report that suggested the FBI had watched Heda off and on for years after Bloom skipped the country. Sometime in the early Sixties she began taking a yearly holiday to Europe. They were never able to connect it to any kind of encounter between the two of them, so if they did meet, it was very discreet. I think the FBI probably gave up on the whole matter by the mid-Sixties. They had way too many civil-rights workers and antiwar demonstrators to harass to bother with small fry like Justin Bloom. Not that they still wouldn't like to get their hands on him, if he's still alive."

"Do you think he is?"

"Well, it seems Heda attended a private funeral in Stressa,

Italy, sometime in the early Eighties. It was autumn. She was
alone and came by rental car. It was mentioned in an
addendum to the police report Al gave me."

"You think it was her son?"

"The authorities weren't sure. She was apparently very
closemouthed about the entire matter, but it was definitely a
middle-aged man who died. No one knew much about him.
And there's a picture taken of her coming out of the church.
She had on a dark veil, but you could see she'd been crying."

Sophie had no trouble picturing it. Heda, leaving the
church. Walking alone back to the car. Standing for a
moment and gazing at the damp Italian countryside. Was she
mourning the son she'd lost so many years before? A mother
who was denied her son's company in life, but refused to be
parted from him in death? "Except, if it wasn't Justin, and he
did come back to the U.S., he'd still be a wanted man, right?
And if he was discovered, he'd still have to stand trial."

"What's your point?"

"Just that the state might have a hard time proving its case
against him. I mean, it's been so many years."

"True. It has been a long time. But the facts seem fairly
incontrovertible."

"Is the cop still alive? The one who was the eyewitness?"

"He died years ago. But he left behind a sworn statement
naming Bloom as the shooter."

Sophie agreed. It did seem pretty cut-and-dried. "But—"

"But what?" Bram was almost done with his salad. Sophie
had barely touched hers.

"There's something that doesn't fit. Why would a man
who'd professed his love for a woman shoot her in the head?
The stomach, maybe. The chest, the leg, the heart, but not
the head. That's so disfiguring. So brutal."

"Maybe that's the kind of guy he was."

"Maybe," said Sophie. "Except, I remember that he had a
reputation as an honest reporter and a decent man."

"Even decent men can go wrong."

She could hardly argue the point. "So what do you make
of it?"

"That Justin Bloom probably killed Kay Collins. *Why,* we may never know."

"But doesn't that lack of motive bother you?"

"Sure. It's a huge hole, but not one we're likely to fill up at this late date."

"Maybe. Maybe not." She had a feeling the newest edition of *Dallas Lane, Private Eye* might do just that. "So, is that it? That's all you found out?"

"For now, yes. Actually, I accomplished exactly what I set out to do."

"Which was—"

"I wanted to prepare myself to handle the calls that will undoubtedly deluge my show. This is going to be a hot topic for a while, Soph. At least now I've got some background." He took a sip of his drink, his eyes straying to the front entrance. "Say, isn't that B. B. Manderbach over there?"

Sophie looked around and saw a short, rotund woman dressed all in blacks and browns being shown to a table near the fire. She looked typically ridiculous in an old-fashioned hat with a veil that swept dramatically over her forehead and down over one eye.

B. B. Manderbach was one of those characters common to every city and small town. Her claim to fame, other than her place in one of the oldest, richest, most successful business families in the Twin Cities, was her status as fashion nightmare. People pointed, whispered, even snickered, but most everyone left her alone. Normally, her clothing was eclectic, tending toward the Victorian. Tonight, however, she was dressed as a matronly 1940s woman-about-town. Instead of eyebrow pencil, her eyebrows looked as if they'd been painted on with black tempera. Her heavy makeup—especially the poorly applied red lipstick—made her look hard, and at the same time silly and rather sad.

"Boy, she's a case," said Bram, leaning back as he was served his stew.

"You could say that," said Sophie, delighted to see the food arrive. "You know, you should have her on your radio show."

"My producer tried. She doesn't give interviews."

Sophie watched her a moment longer and saw that underneath her coat, she was hiding a small table lamp. As she placed it on the opposite chair and then draped her coat over it, her eyes darted suspiciously around the room. "Strange," said Sophie under her breath.

"What's strange?" Bram's dinner now commanded his full attention.

"B.B.'s got a lamp under her coat."

"Really. Well . . . maybe she's been out looking for an honest man."

Sophie stared at him over the rim of her wineglass. "At least I'm having dinner with a classically educated man."

"You are."

"Eat up, dear. I hate to be a broken record, but I have to get back to the hotel."

Bram's head popped up. "Does that mean we don't have time for dessert?"

"You sound like you're four years old."

"I know." He grabbed another roll. "That's what makes me such a hit on talk radio."

February?

Dear Mother:

I'm sorry if you're having trouble reading this. My hand is pretty shaky because of the drugs I've been given for the pain, and to help bring my fever down. I tried to get one of the other men in the ward to write this for me, but while several of them speak English, no one knows how to write it.

I'm not sure of the date. I know it's been a long time since my last letter. Right now I'm in a hospital in Tel Aviv. I've been ill. I'm stronger today. I even walked for a few minutes in the yard. I don't want you to worry, Mom. I'll explain everything in my next letter. The problem is, most of my money is gone, stolen on the boat.

I talked to my friend in New York last night. I was surprised to hear you'd phoned him several times. I'm glad you didn't call from the house. Anyway, even though my friend's a great guy, he doesn't have much money right now. I assume he told you he was in medical school. The hospital won't release me unless I can pay my bill. Can you send him some money and then he can wire it here? I'm in a bad spot, Mom. Really bad. I don't mean to sound desperate, but I'm not sure what I'll do if you can't help me. I need about three hundred dollars for the bill, and another three hundred for living expenses when I get out. He'll wire the first three hundred directly to the hospital authorities. I don't want the money sent to me personally because in my present condition, I'm afraid it might be stolen as soon as it came into my possession.

I need you to do this right away. Don't fail me, Mom. Please.

Justin

9

On Sunday afternoon, several hours before the first radio mystery broadcast, Sophie sat at her desk poring over the Maxfield's new environmental policy, the one she planned to institute come the new year. As she made some notes about the new soap-and-shampoo dispenser she wanted to use, the phone interrupted her concentration.

"Sophie Greenway," she said, grabbing it on the second ring.

"Sophie, hi. It's John."

"Hey, kiddo. What's up?"

"Do you have a minute to talk?"

"For you, I've got more than a minute. Say, I bet I know why you're calling. You're curious about the plans for the champagne buffet. Would you like to know what's on the menu—so far?"

"Well, sure—"

"Okay. You can pass this on to Rudy." She pulled a notebook from the top drawer of her desk. "We're going to do a beautiful spread, John, starting with crab-stuffed avocados, prosciutto and fresh figs in a citrus sauce, a lovely Roquefort mousse, and a duck terrine."

"Stop, you're making me hungry!"

She could hear the delight in his voice. "Then, for the main course, I'm thinking salmon—perhaps the whole fish covered in a light whipped cream. What would you think of a hint of horseradish?"

He laughed. "I'd say I'm going to have to make myself a sandwich or I'll never survive until dinner."

She smiled. "When I have everything firmed up, I'll give you two the entire menu. I'm trying to include some of Rudy's favorite desserts, as well as yours."

"This is so great of you, Sophie. I really don't know how to thank you."

"Just make my son happy, John. That's all I ask."

"That won't be hard. I care about him a lot. Actually, that's why I called."

She could hear a certain strain in his voice now. "What's wrong?"

"It's Rudy. I'm worried about him. See, he hasn't been feeling well for the past few weeks, but he won't go see a doctor. He's pushing hard to get through school early. I keep telling him to slow down, but he ignores me. He's, well, kind of stubborn, Sophie, if you don't mind my saying so."

It wasn't something she hadn't already observed herself. As a matter of fact, if Rudy had inherited his stubbornness from anyone, it was from her. "You say he's not feeling well. Can you be more specific?"

"Sure. Last week he said he thought he had the flu. He slept most of one day, but then the following day he went on just like normal. He seemed real tired, but that was about it. Then, last night, we went for a walk. When we got back, he had to rest before he could make it up the stairs to our apartment. He was really winded. Later, after we'd gone to bed, he woke me up to ask what some clunking noise was. I had no idea what he was talking about. I mean, I didn't hear any noise, but he was adamant. He said it sounded like a tennis shoe in a dryer. To be honest, Sophie, I'm worried. I'm pretty sure it's got nothing to do with his back problem."

"What back problem?"

"Didn't he tell you? He tripped and fell off the stage over at Rarig Center."

"That's awful!" It was the first she'd heard of it and she felt instantly guilty. Had she been *that* out of touch? Sure, she'd been working long hours, and maybe it had been a while since she and Rudy had talked— "When did it happen?"

"Three weeks ago. It was during a rehearsal for the play he's working on for his senior drama class. Anyway, it messed his back up pretty bad. But the painkiller he was prescribed seemed to do the trick."

Sophie was shocked and more than embarrassed that something like this could happen and she knew nothing about it. "I think you're right, John. He needs to see a doctor."

"I was hoping you'd agree. Will you talk to him? He'll listen to you."

She was afraid that John was overestimating her influence on her son, but knew something had to be done. "Where is he this afternoon?"

"Over at Walter Library. I don't expect him back until close to six. I know he wants to listen to that new radio show

Bram is announcing. We sort of made a date to listen and then have dinner together."

"Okay, here's the plan." She had to think fast. "I'll call your apartment right after the show's over. That way I know Rudy will be there and I'll have an excuse. I can say I wanted to know what you two thought of the first episode. And then I'll ease into the part about seeing a doctor."

"Great. Except . . . maybe it's best that you don't tell him I called. I wouldn't want him to think we were ganging up on him."

"No problem. I'll think of a way to say it without including you." She hesitated. "Listen, John, he's not in any real danger here, is he? I mean, he's not *that* sick."

"No, I didn't mean to upset you. And I don't want to make this sound worse than it is. I just think he needs a vitamin shot or something. And he needs to slow down and take life a little easier, even if everything doesn't get done perfectly."

She smiled. He was a chip off the old block. She was grateful that Rudy had someone like John in his life. "All right, I promise. I'll speak with him tonight."

"You're a lifesaver, Sophie. Talk to you later."

After they hung up, Sophie sat for a few minutes going over in her mind just how she would broach the subject of a doctor. She decided that the best way to proceed was to suggest that he get a flu shot. If she had to drag him into the office herself, Rudy was *going* to see a doctor.

After spending the next hour working on a new program for frequent business travelers, Sophie felt the need to stretch. Rising from her chair, she headed out to the main desk. She nodded a quick greeting to Celia Walker, one of two women working registration this afternoon. Joan Zimmer, the other woman, was nowhere in sight.

"Where's Joany?" asked Sophie, straightening some papers next to one of the computer terminals.

"She was only here until three," said Celia. "She left about half an hour ago."

Since there was a line of people waiting to be checked in,

Sophie nodded to the next person, tapped her code number into the computer, and began the registration process.

As the late afternoon wore on she could feel herself growing more and more nervous for her husband. Talk radio was one thing, but this new venture of his was more on the order of live theatre. Bram had even been given a small part in the production in addition to his role as announcer, and needless to say, he was loving every minute of it. He was already over at the station, and knowing him, he was probably as cool as the proverbial cucumber. Sophie, on the other hand, was dissolving slowly into a mist of opening-night jitters.

"Excuse me," said a voice from behind the roped-off waiting area.

Quickly returning her attention to the business at hand, Sophie smiled a greeting. "Welcome to the Maxfield."

The man moved toward her. In his right hand he was carrying a small, bulging suitcase. Setting it down on the floor, he removed his gloves. "I, ah, have a reservation. The name's Greveen. I'm part of the Heda Bloom party."

Sophie recognized the name at once. "It's very nice to meet you, Mr. Greveen. I'm Sophie Greenway, the owner of the hotel. My husband, Bram Baldric, is the announcer for the new show. As I understand it, you're the writer."

He adjusted his wire-rim glasses to get a better look at her. "That's right."

"Do you have your confirmation number?"

"Yes, it's . . . right here." He searched in his pockets for the information.

Sophie found the man's wavy white hair quite attractive. Actually, everything about him was impeccably turned out. The final touch was an expensive camel wool coat draped over his shoulders.

After handing her the slip of paper, he leaned on the counter while she found the reservation.

"Have you been to Minnesota before?" she asked, continuing to make small talk.

"Yes. A long time ago. But I prefer warmer climates."

His voice was low and pleasant, yet it was so soft that she

could barely hear him. Pushing a signature card across the counter, she waited while he signed his name. "Have you been writing long?"

"Most of my life." He glanced over his shoulder.

"Are you expecting someone?"

"No. Actually, I'm rather tired, so if I could just get my key?" He stuffed his gloves into the pocket of his coat and then placed both hands on the counter.

Sophie couldn't help but notice a square-cut tiger eye on the ring finger of his left hand. She'd never seen one like it before. "That's a beautiful ring you've got there."

He removed his hands.

Not the friendliest fellow she'd ever met. "All right. You're all checked in. Room 743, south wing. The elevators are right around the corner. Here's the door key, as well as a key to the mini-bar. If there's anything we can do to make your stay with us more enjoyable, please don't hesitate to contact the front desk."

"Thanks."

"If you're interested in fine dining, Fitzgerald's restaurant is located in the south wing on the fifteenth floor. Reservations required. The Fountain Grill is located on the mezzanine level, right up the lobby stairs. It's more informal. No reservations needed. And Scottie's Bar is located near the front entrance on the lobby level. You can get a sandwich in there until midnight."

"I'll remember that." He reached down for his bag. As he straightened up he said, "Actually, I do have one question. I haven't been feeling well all day. I wonder if you could point me to the nearest clinic or hospital."

"Is it an emergency?"

"No, no. Nothing like that. I'm sure any clinic you recommend would do just fine. I'm just a little under the weather. It's probably the flu."

Sophie took out one of her cards and wrote the name of a clinic on the back. "Here you go, Mr. Greveen. This is right up the street. I know Dr. Fredericks personally. He's a GP, and one of the best in town."

"Thanks." He slipped it into his pocket.

"I hope you feel better soon."

"Me, too. I have a lot of work to do while I'm here." He turned to go.

"Writing the scripts, you mean?"

Again, he turned to face her. "Why, yes."

"Have you completed the next *Dallas Lane* episode?"

"No, but I'll finish it tonight. For some reason, I find it easier to work in a hotel. When I'm home, there are too many distractions."

"Where are you from?"

"Florida."

"Same as Heda Bloom."

"Yes, I believe she lives there, too."

"I'm just curious." She could read his impatience, but forged on. "How does someone come up with a story like the one you've just written? Did you borrow the idea from real life?"

Containing his impatience behind a forced smile, he said, "I assure you, Ms. Greenway, my story is purely the result of a fruitful imagination. The central truth of all fiction is, it isn't fact."

"I see."

He stared at her. "You disagree?"

"In theory, no."

"Have you ever written any fiction, Ms. Greenway?"

"No."

"Then trust me. I know what I'm talking about." His voice had taken on a professorial tone.

"Right . . . well. I have to say, I admire your talent. After tonight's broadcast, lots of people are going to be banging on your door, wanting to speak with you. If you don't mind a prediction, I'd say you're about to become the talk of the town."

All vestiges of good humor were now gone. "Then I shall expect the Maxfield to provide me with the privacy I not only crave, but demand. Good afternoon, Ms. Greenway." He turned abruptly and walked away.

10

On Monday morning, Bud Manderbach crept into his office without so much as a simple hello to his secretary. His hangover was so gigantic, he couldn't bear any extraneous sounds. Even the creaking of his leather chair as he sat down behind his desk caused him a moment of pure pain. But it was happy pain—at least he thought it was. He and Giselle had made up last night. He'd wined her and dined her until the wee hours.

Later, back at her place, she'd even admitted that she loved him. Over the years many women had professed their love for Bud. As far as he was concerned, it was a pointless exercise, yet for some odd reason, one he still coveted. Where were all these loving women now? What the hell did it mean if nobody stuck around? Women were as faithless as the day was long.

Bud had always gotten a certain pleasure out of making women fall in love with him. With his money and dark good looks, it wasn't hard. Sure, he might be getting older and his hair might be receding, but it was also as brown as the day he turned thirty, and so was his mustache, which he kept trimmed and narrow. At heart, however, Bud was a realist. Women, whether they declared their undying devotion for you or not, always left, sooner or later. And then, once more, you were alone. That's why he always had another woman waiting in the wings ready to take over for whoever was on their way out the door. To his way of thinking, it was simple logic.

The problem was, Bud didn't have anyone but Giselle right now. Oh, he had an occasional sexual dalliance, but there was no one else who cared about him. Without his usual safety net, he was like a man trapped in a burning building. For the moment the fire against his back felt warm and pleasant, but when the flames got too intense and he was forced to jump, no one would be there to catch him. You never knew what a woman was going to do, and Bud wasn't going to be alone for Christmas, that was for damn sure. Maybe it was time to go on a little shopping trip downstairs. He'd been shopping at Manderbach's for years—and not just for his suits and ties.

As he eased his head back against his leather chair, there was a knock on the door. "Come in," he said, cringing at the sound of his own voice.

His secretary, Loretta Nallen, breezed into the office. She was wearing her usual Monday-morning navy-blue suit. Setting a yellow file folder down in front of him, she began to straighten his papers.

Her energy was making his headache worse. "Do that later," he grunted, slumping forward and resting his head on his hand.

"Still feeling like old Mr. Scrooge, are we?"

Loretta might be the best secretary he'd ever had, but she talked like a grade-school teacher. It drove him nuts. "What if *we* are?"

She tsk-tsked.

"Look, Ms. Nallen, if you're waiting for the Ghost of Christmas Past to provide me with a Yuletide epiphany, it's not going to happen. Let's just can the Christmas crap for the duration, okay?"

"Whatever you say, Mr. Manderbach."

He knew he was being humored. "What's this?" He flipped open the folder and found some typed pages.

"Don't you remember? You asked me to call WTWN to see if that program Mr. Greveen told you about in his fax was on the level. When you found out it was, you ordered me to listen to it last night and then make a full report. That's the report."

With his personal life in such upheaval, he'd completely forgotten.

"I had dinner over at a friend's house," continued Loretta. "Carol Richards? She works in housewares down on four.

Anyway, when we were done, we listened together. I hope you don't mind that I added some of my opinions to the report." She picked up a crystal paperweight and began polishing it with a clean tissue. "I could be wrong, Mr. Manderbach, but I think that show's going to be very popular. It has the nostalgia factor working for it. And the first episode really grabbed me."

"Do tell."

She tapped the pages. "It's all right there."

"Dandy. Thanks."

"Anything else you'd like before I go?" She placed the paperweight back on the desk.

"No. Yes. Bring me two aspirin. And a glass of water."

"Of course."

"And hold all my phone calls."

"Certainly."

"Oh, and send a dozen roses to Giselle Tannanger. You've got her address."

"Long-stemmed?"

"Whatever."

"Any particular color?"

"Pink. No, red." His last girlfriend had liked pink. Giselle's favorites were red. Or—was it yellow?

"Is that all?"

"For now."

After Loretta was gone, Bud grabbed the report, slipped on his reading glasses, and skimmed the first page. He might as well get his mind off his headache.

Loretta had been her usual thorough self. She'd covered everything from the opening music to the end credits. The *Dallas Lane* theme song was "I've Got My Love to Keep Me Warm," an old Irving Berlin piece done by Les Brown's great swing orchestra. She'd even included the names of the actors. Much to his surprise, Bud recognized them. "My God," he whispered, massaging his brow, "they've hired back the old cast and crew." Everyone was there, from Heda Bloom right on down to the sound-effects technician.

His interest now piqued, he read on:

* * *

I found the opening episode quite gripping. Dallas Lane, a tough, tall-dark-and-handsome ex-GI from "nowhere in particular," runs his PI business out of a sleazy downtown bar called DuFour's. It's on Sixth Street, just south of city hall, in a fictitious Midwestern town called Mill City. When he's not out on a case, he's sitting at the bar having a sandwich and a beer, or using the bar phone to make phone calls, or talking to his girlfriend, who works as a waitress in the late afternoons and evenings. Her name is Lucy DuFour.

Lucy is the daughter of the bar owner, and of course she's blonde and gorgeous. While Dallas hasn't exactly proposed marriage, we all know they're sweet on each other. He bounces his theories off Lucy. That's partly how we get to know what he's thinking, and partly how we learn that he and Lucy are in love.

Dallas meets with all his prospective clients at DuFour's. The bar is dark and the drinks are cheap, a perfect business office as far as he's concerned.

Dallas is irreverent, wisecracking, and street-smart. A typical PI. He's concerned about people, wants to help the underdog—the little guy. Perhaps the actor's voice adds to his appeal. Whatever the case, we learn all of this information through the opening dialogue. It's a cold winter night. Lucy is just about to close down the bar and make Dallas take her home.

Enter a woman. We can tell by her voice that she's older. Since we can hear Dallas's thoughts, he describes her as "in her mid-forties, rich-looking and scared." She's says she's come to DuFour's looking for Dallas Lane. The bartender checks her out briefly and then points her to the end of the bar where Dallas and Lucy are talking.

The woman introduces herself as Irene Hewitt. She explains that her son is in trouble and she's come to ask Dallas for help. Dallas takes her over to a booth, where the woman opens up with a terrible tale of woe.

It seems her son, Judson Hewitt, has been accused of

the murder of his girlfriend. It happened at Wallace Pond, a lake right on the outskirts of the city. It's a wooded area, and since the murder took place on a cold January night, the only witness was a priest, an older man who was headed home from a wake.

The story the priest later tells the police is this: He was walking along a section of the lake when he heard some shouting. A second later there was a loud bang, like a gunshot. He took off running toward the sound and came upon two young people. A man was standing with a gun in his hand, staring quietly at a woman lying on the ground at his feet. She wasn't moving.

Fearing the worst, the priest shouted for him to stop. The man seemed startled by the sound of the priest's voice. He dropped the gun and rushed up an embankment to his car. The priest watched him drive away. When the priest finally reached the woman, she was dead. Shot in the head.

Dallas asked where the young man was now. The woman answered that he'd tried to get away, but the police had found him in a hotel room in Seattle. He'd been brought back to stand trial. All she had to prove her son's innocence was a letter, one he'd written to her just before he left.

Dallas asked to see it. It said something like, "Mom, by now you've heard what happened. Don't believe what the priest says, please! Wait until you hear the entire story from me. Your son, Judson."

Bud looked up. He didn't have to read any more. He already knew the end of the story.

Without wasting a minute, he buzzed his secretary. "Get me Wish Greveen on the line. He's staying at the Maxfield Plaza. I want to talk to him right away. No excuses, Loretta. If he's not there, find him."

Bud felt a sinking feeling inside his stomach. This *was* the Ghost of Christmas Past come to torment him, to take his revenge. The funny thing was, he wasn't surprised. He'd been expecting the ghost for years.

Dear Mother:

Several days ago I left the hospital in Tel Aviv, thanks to you and the money you sent me. However, I was too weak to travel. I spent some time resting at a friend's home, someone I met while I was in the hospital, a man I've grown to trust. He's a businessman, a Polish Jew who went to school in England. I'm almost certain now that I've eluded my trackers, but he knew I didn't feel entirely comfortable in Tel Aviv, so he convinced me that I should move one last time. On his recommendation, I traveled by bus to a smaller town.

I'm now renting an apartment. My friend's brother-in-law owns the building and has given me a remarkably cheap rate. Here, finally, I believe I can recuperate.

Today, I thought I would try to fill you in on what happened to me after I left the Continent. I'll be brief, since sitting up for prolonged periods still leaves me exhausted.

The day after I wrote you from Eindhoven, I bought a motorcycle from a man in town, and then hit the road the same night. I hardly stopped to rest for the next two weeks. During the entire time I never saw a single person following me. I ended up in Athens, where I booked passage on a boat to Palestine. It was on that boat that I was mugged and lost most of my money. Thank God I was able to retain my passport. Even though it's a fake, it's served me well.

When I arrived in Haifa, I knew I was ill, but I thought it was a result of the beating I took. The man who attacked

73

me kicked me in the stomach. The pain in my lower abdomen grew so intense that when I got to Tel Aviv, I fainted in the doorway of a restaurant. I woke up in a hospital, where I was told my appendix had to be removed immediately, before it ruptured.

The first few days at the hospital are a complete blur to me now. I believe I was operated on late on a Wednesday afternoon. By the weekend I'd recovered sufficiently to call my friend in New York and ask him to wire me some money so that I could pay my bill. He, of course, had none to offer, and that's when I wrote to you. Your speedy reply saved my life, in more ways than one. It also told me you still care about your wayward son. I hold on to that thought, Mom, and hope that soon you can write to me here.

But back to my most recent odyssey. I'd no sooner been given the okay to leave the hospital than I developed peritonitis. From what I was later told, I was in a coma for almost a week. I'm not sure I was expected to live.

But I did live, though I've lost a lot of weight and I'm very, very weak. The worst part for me now are the night sweats. I wake up soaking wet, disoriented, and jittery. Unfortunately, I've used up just about every dime you sent me, and I'm afraid I have no other choice but to ask you for more help. I hope someday to be able to pay you back. Right now could you see your way to wiring my New York friend another several hundred dollars? Whatever you can spare would be a lifeline for me until I can resume a more normal existence.

Although I feel much safer here, I'm still concerned that you're being watched, and that your mail may be opened and read. That's why this letter has come to you in a different manner. My friend in New York is sending it to a friend of his in Minnesota, who will pass it on to you as discreetly as possible. I hope this doesn't present you with any problems. When I've recovered a bit more, and continue to remain certain of my invisibility here, I'll give you my address and we can begin a real correspondence. Be sure that you destroy my letters. If they fell into the wrong hands, both our lives would again be in great danger. I don't have the strength to run any longer, Mom. At least, not until my health improves.

Next time I write, I hope to resume my story. I find myself dissecting the events of last fall almost continuously now. But thankfully, my more comforting thoughts of you, and of home, are never far from me.

With much love,
Justin

11

As soon as Bram arrived at the station on Monday morning, he was informed that Dorothy Veneger had summoned the cast and crew of *Dallas Lane, Private Eye* to discuss last night's premiere. Hurrying down the hall, he couldn't wait to hear the initial reports. Was it a hit? A miss?

Heda Bloom hadn't shown up for any of the rehearsals and probably wouldn't make it to the meeting either. Everything had been left to Dorothy to arrange, and in Bram's humble opinion, she'd done a highly professional job. He liked Dorothy. She was smart and sensible, two qualities often lacking in management and creative types, as far as he was concerned. Yet nobody felt particularly at ease in Dorothy's presence. Not only was she always in a hurry, but she never engaged in small talk. Still, the success of the first episode had depended almost entirely on her unflagging energy. Dorothy brought a tremendous infusion of confidence to the proceedings, something everyone needed.

As Bram entered the room he saw that most of the chairs

around the long conference table were already taken. Some people were laughing and talking as they sipped their morning coffee, while others nibbled a doughnut or a sweet roll, compliments of WTWN and its consistently blind eye toward nutrition.

Bram took an empty chair near the door.

A few moments later Valentine Zolotow ambled into the room, sliding his lanky frame into the seat next to Bram. He reeked of tobacco smoke. "God, I'd forgotten how cold it gets in Minnesota. I nearly froze to death walking from the cab into the building." He chewed his gum with annoyance. "I don't know why on earth we have to get here this early. I just hope Dorothy makes it short today. I need a smoke."

Since the building was smoke-free, most people chewed gum as a way of assuaging their oral needs, a habit Valentine had obviously adopted.

"I got better stuff to do with my time," he muttered.

It seemed inconceivable to Bram that such a weaselly-looking old guy could project the voice of the young and handsome, sexy and tough PI. Yet Valentine did it with ease. "Grab a doughnut and relax," said Bram. He helped himself to some coffee.

Valentine snapped his gum. "Our fearless leader's probably checking her makeup in the ladies' room. Vanity, thy name is woman. Jeez, I wish she'd get a move on."

"You could be trampled to death for a comment like that. Want some coffee?"

"Nah." Again, he checked his watch.

By now, everyone had become well aware of what Valentine Zolotow's "better stuff" was. Put simply, he gambled. So far he'd been late for two rehearsals because he "couldn't tear himself away from a previous engagement." Everyone knew that the engagement was a casino. Last Thursday, in front of everyone, Dorothy had informed him that if he was late one more time, contract or no contract, he'd find himself out of a job. Whether he'd lost most of his ready cash at the tables or Dorothy had really put the fear of God into him, he hadn't been late since.

"When do we start work on the next episode?" asked Bram, waving the smell of Juicy Fruit away from his face.

"Whenever we get the next damn script," replied Valentine.

Bram blew on his coffee. This guy was a real character. Yet in spite of his flaws, Bram admired him. Valentine Zolotow had seen and done just about everything in radio.

"You know," continued Valentine with a sour look on his face, "I was hoping to talk to this Wish Greveen, but so far, I haven't caught up with him. Dorothy said he'd checked into the hotel, but he hasn't answered my phone messages, and when I knocked on his door earlier this morning, there was no answer." He turned and looked Bram square in the eye. "I don't suppose you'd know where I could find him?"

Bram shrugged. "Sorry."

"Well, I'll just have to take my chances."

"With what?"

Valentine smiled. "Not with what, pal. With *who*."

"Meaning?"

"Skip it." He unwrapped another stick of gum and jammed it into his mouth. After a few seconds he seemed to reconsider. Leaning close to Bram, he whispered, "That first script. Did it remind you of anything?"

"You mean the Kay Collins murder?"

Valentine seemed startled. "Hey, kid, you're smarter than you look." He grinned, revealing a set of badly nicotine-stained teeth.

"Gee, thanks."

"Nah, I mean it." He flicked the gum wrapper into the trash. "We've all been beating around the bush this past week, but I'll bet everyone feels the same way I do."

"And how's that?"

"That, you know, this rebirth of the radio mystery is just a vehicle to vindicate Justin Bloom."

Bingo. This was the first time Bram had heard anyone in the cast touch on his own suspicions. "And you think Wish Greveen is behind it?"

"Of course not, asshole. Use your brain." He lowered his voice even further. "Heda's orchestrated the whole damn thing, but nobody, including yours truly, is going to get a straight answer out of her. I thought maybe Wish and I could have a drink. You know, for old times' sake."

"You know him?"

"Hell, yes." Looking off into space, he added, "That is to say, I'm pretty sure we met back when I was in Hollywood. In any case, I know I could get the story out of him—man-to-man."

"Man-to-man?" repeated Bram, raising an amused eyebrow.

Valentine gave a serious nod.

"But, how come you care? I mean, so what if the stories are similar?"

Valentine's smile grew sly. "You never know, kid. There may be someone out there who'd care. The way I figure it, if this story continues on the way I think it will, they might care a lot."

"You sound like you know who that someone is."

He glanced slowly around the room. "Maybe I do. Maybe I don't."

"Not much of an answer."

Valentine's smile was as thin as a razor, but he added nothing more. "Hey, this is bullshit. Look at the time."

Boy, this guy really is hot to trot, thought Bram. It had only been five minutes since the last time he'd mentioned it.

Folding one thin leg over the other, Valentine continued in the same confidential tone, "You know, I thought when Alfred Bloom arrived, he'd take over the reins of the station. Mark my words, if he was in charge, this meeting would already be over and I'd be outta here. Funny thing is, I haven't seen him around."

Come to think of it, Bram hadn't either. After his grand entrance on Wednesday afternoon, he'd seen him briefly at the hotel, but that was it. "Maybe he only stayed the weekend."

"Maybe. But if I remember Alfred, he has to have his hand in everything. He's what they call a control freak."

"Say, I suppose you knew him back in the Fifties when you worked at WPXL."

"Everybody knew Alf Bloom. He was that kind of guy. Just itching to take over the business from his father."

Bram was intrigued. "What'd you think of him? Personally, I mean."

"Alf? Eh, you know. He was a hustler. Young and on the make. Then again, so was I, but I didn't have a rich daddy lookin' out for me. Just between us, I don't think it broke brother Alf's heart when his half brother took off for points unknown. There was no love lost between those two."

This was news to Bram. "Why was that?"

"Well, this is just my opinion, you understand, but it always seemed to me that there was a rivalry between them. Justin was the oldest, but he had a different father. I think Alf was jealous that he had to share Cedric—and his potential inheritance—with anyone. Especially with Justin. They were so different."

"In what way?"

"Every way. Alf was a climber—a real material guy, if you know what I mean. He wanted money, power. Justin was a do-gooder. A journalistic crusader. As far as I could see, he wanted no part of the radio empire Cedric Bloom was creating. Oh, he worked for a while on a couple of shows before he went into the army, but it didn't stick. He had his own career plans in mind. What he really wanted was to follow in his own father's footsteps. His dad was a newspaper reporter, you know."

"I'd heard that."

"Physically, they couldn't have been more different. Alfred was a giant. Dark hair, dark eyes. Looked a lot like Cedric. Justin, on the other hand, was thin, not terribly tall, and fair. No one would ever have taken them for brothers."

"Have you talked to Alfred since he's been here?"

Valentine uncrossed his legs and sat forward in his chair. "Nah. I've been busy with other stuff." Glancing at Bram out of the corner of his eye, he added, "But we'll talk. I have no doubt about that."

Dorothy Veneger chose that moment to enter the room. She didn't seem merely happy, she looked positively triumphant.

Bram wanted to continue his conversation with Valentine, but it would have to wait.

Dorothy set a stack of papers down on the table. "Well, everyone," she said, standing behind her chair, "the verdict is in. *Dallas Lane, Private Eye* is a winner!" Her smile lit up the room.

Everyone cheered and clapped.

"You all deserve this moment. Well done, everyone. Now, I have interviews scheduled for Valentine this afternoon with the feature editors of both local papers, and tomorrow, George and Mitzi, you've been invited to talk about your work on *Morning with Donna King*. It's the hottest locally produced TV show in town. Then, on Thursday, the two entertainment weeklies are going to be at the station for a photo shoot. They want some candid shots of the rehearsal, so everybody, make it good. Camp it up. I'm talking to a woman this afternoon who owns a vintage clothing store in downtown Minneapolis. You'll all be fitted with vintage Fifties suits and dresses for the occasion. I want this to look fabulous. Whatever it takes to grab the audience, we're going to do it."

She continued by holding up a fistful of pink notes. "For your information, these are phone calls I haven't returned yet, all people wanting to talk to me about the new show. The *Star Tribune* is running a review in tomorrow morning's paper. In part it will say—" She adjusted her oversized, horn-rim glasses. " 'This is an idea whose time has come! *Dallas Lane, Private Eye* has all the wit and charm of the old radio serials, and a story that will intrigue even the most jaded TV viewer. Mark Sunday night down on your calendar as a time to turn *off* your TV and turn *on* your imagination!' "

Dorothy looked up, making sure she had everyone's attention. "Now, as you may have guessed, we've got our work cut out for us. We can't let the momentum drop. Before Christmas, I want every radio in this state tuned to WTWN on Sunday nights."

It was curious, but as Bram listened he felt less and less like he was in a business meeting, and more like he'd become part of a crusade. He raised his hand. "When do we get the next script?"

"Good question," said Dorothy. She tapped the stack of papers in front of her. "They're right here. Everybody take one on your way out. Read it through several times today, and then tomorrow, I want you all back here bright and early. Eight A.M. sharp. We'll run through the initial reading to get our timing down. Any questions you have, bring them with you tomorrow. Valentine, be back to the Maxfield Plaza by three. Your first interview is with the *Star Tribune* reporter. He'll meet you in the lobby."

Valentine lifted his finger. "I've got a question."

"Yes?"

"What's the best way to get in touch with the scriptwriter?"

Dorothy's hands slid into the pockets of her blazer. "Mr. Greveen is staying at the hotel."

"I know that, but he hasn't been around, at least not when I tried to contact him. Will he be at tomorrow morning's rehearsal?"

"I don't know. Is there something you'd like me to pass on to him?"

"You mean, I'm never going to get a chance to meet the guy face-to-face?"

"I didn't say that. But it's up to him whether or not he comes to the rehearsals."

Valentine seemed annoyed by her answer. "Just forget it. I'll handle it myself."

She pulled on one of her large gold earrings and then went on. "Now, if that's it, I believe we've all got work to do. See you tomorrow."

Bram waited until she'd left the room and then grabbed his copy of the script. The only one who beat him to the stack was Valentine.

"Hey, let's have a cup of coffee after rehearsals tomorrow morning," he called to Valentine's retreating back. He wanted to finish their conversation.

"I'll check my social calendar." He waved over his shoulder

but kept right on walking. Catching the elevator just as the doors opened, he stepped on, pushed a button, and then gave Bram one last wave as the doors closed in front of him.

12

"Amazing," whispered Valentine, flipping to the next page. He was sitting in a coffeehouse on St. Peter Avenue, sipping a latte and reading the script for the second episode of *Dallas Lane, Private Eye*. If this didn't convince those in the know that the story was genuinely about Justin Bloom and his ill-fated love affair with Kay Collins, nothing would. Not that Valentine was personally familiar with all the details, but he knew enough.

The episode started with Dallas doing some snooping at the apartment building where the fictitious Kay, called Darla in the radio script, had been living before her death. While exploring the basement, he ran into one of Darla's second-floor neighbors, an old woman who admitted that there had been plenty of shouting recently inside the girls' apartment. It had gotten so bad, the woman had considered moving. She said she was sorry about Darla's death, but was glad that the fighting had stopped and the apartment had returned to peace and quiet.

As Dallas was about to go the elderly woman put a hand on his arm and stopped him. There was something that had been bothering her, something she'd witnessed and couldn't make any sense of. Maybe Dallas would have an opinion.

Dallas said sure. If it had to do with the young woman who'd been murdered, he was all ears. He listened as the old woman told him a story.

Last summer, Peggy, Darla's roommate, had been dating

a man for several months. The neighbor insisted that she wasn't a snoop, but how could she miss what was happening right outside when her front windows looked directly down on the street? She'd never actually seen Peggy's new boyfriend because he always waited for her inside his large, very expensive Cadillac. Yet the neighbor always knew when he was outside the building. How? Because he honked. Three times. No more. No less.

One night, the woman heard a commotion outside. It was close to two A.M. She often suffered from insomnia and that night was a particularly bad one for her. Glad for an excuse to get up, she slipped into her robe and went to see what was going on. The Cadillac had pulled into a parking spot and then backed up onto the curb, knocking over several metal trash cans in the process. Trash littered the street behind the car.

The woman could make out two pinpricks of light in the front seat. She assumed Peggy and her date were smoking as they sat and talked. For whatever reason, nobody made a move to right the cans and pick up the mess. A minute or so later a man erupted out of the driver's door. He was tall, wearing a dark raincoat and narrow-brimmed felt hat. As he rushed around to the front of the car, she noticed that he wasn't very steady on his feet. She assumed he'd been drinking.

After flipping on a flashlight, the man spent the next few minutes critically examining every inch of the left front fender. The headlight was out, but that was all the old woman could see that might be wrong. The whole situation seemed sort of odd because it was the left *rear* fender that had hit the garbage cans.

On his way back to the driver's-side door, the man stopped and leaned against the hood. She wasn't sure, but through the open windows, she thought she heard him crying. After a few moments he returned to the front seat and slammed the door shut.

Since the old woman was wide-awake now, she kept her vigil at the window. She got herself a glass of milk and waited to see what would happen next. The car sat there for a good half hour before the passenger door opened and

Peggy got out. She just stood for a long time looking at the man inside the car. The engine was running, but he made no move to drive away. The young woman didn't wave, or smile, or say a word. Nothing cheerful. Nothing romantic. She just stood there. Finally, she stepped back and pushed the door shut. The car immediately lurched forward and skidded into the street. In a second it disappeared around the corner. The old woman said that after that night, she never saw the Cadillac again.

Dallas agreed that it was an interesting story, but he had no idea what to make of it. He thanked the old woman, and said that if he figured out what it was all about, he'd let her know.

During the next segment Dallas drove over to visit the priest who'd witnessed the murder. He found him in front of the church, shoveling snow. The man seemed credible and sincere—yet a little too sincere for Dallas's liking. He had a hunch the guy wasn't telling the truth. The problem was, how was he—or some high-paid defense attorney—supposed to impugn the testimony of a priest on the witness stand? The man was adamant about what he saw, and there were no inconsistencies in his story.

On his way back to DuFour's Bar, Dallas stopped for a sandwich at a popular downtown restaurant. As he was about to pay the bill and leave, he felt a hand grab his shoulder. It was an old friend, a well-connected criminal type named Walt Rollins. Rollins had his finger on just about everything that happened in Mill City. Taking Dallas aside, he warned him off the case. He said Dallas didn't know what he was getting himself into. The Big Guys were involved with this one. That meant only one thing to Dallas: Organized Crime.

"You saying the murder was a hit?" asked Dallas.

"I'm not sayin' nothing," replied Rollins. "Just keep your nose clean and back the hell off. It's the only way you're gonna live to see forty."

As Dallas left the restaurant he was immediately jumped by two men who dragged him into an alley. Even though he fought valiantly, he was beaten up and left bleeding and unconscious. As the episode ends no one is even sure Dallas is still alive.

Bravo, thought Valentine, tossing the script down on the table next to his cup. Greveen had used many of the standard old techniques, just as he had in the first episode. A rapid succession of short scenes. Complete freedom of location. And lots of narration. As far as Valentine was concerned, the genius of radio was that it got inside your head the way no other medium could. The narrator, in this case, Dallas, had your ear. It was a fabulous part and it was all his. And even better, this episode was an old-fashioned goddamned cliffhanger. Greveen knew what he was doing. But organized crime? Where the hell was he getting his facts? As far as Valentine knew, Collins's murder was a simple crime of passion.

Not that it mattered. Valentine knew a gold mine when he was sitting on top of one. He'd always been a believer in free enterprise, and damn if he didn't have something to sell.

Rising from the table, he walked over to a wall phone right outside the men's rest room and quickly placed a call.

He waited until he heard a familiar voice and then, using his best highbrow English accent, said, "I daresay, I'm delighted to find you in. I do so hope you have a moment. I rang your flat earlier, but no one was home."

"Who is this?" came an impatient voice.

Valentine moved into a sturdy, metal-voiced Cockney. "Aye, gov. It's me. Don't you recognize me voice?"

"Who the—"

Next came a Southern accent. A soft, womanish voice this time. "Ma daddy used to tell me to be polite, but I declare, you're makin' this as hard as a Georgia peach—or is that an Alabama walnut?"

"Look, you've got one second—"

This time, Valentine used his own voice. "It's me. Valentine Zolotow. I assume you got my message, so this call shouldn't come as a surprise."

Silence. Then: "What the hell do you want?"

"I'll get right to the point. Twenty-five thousand dollars. In small bills, just like last time."

"That was forty years ago!"

"Listen, friend. You and I both know you got a problem. I could create a real mess for you—if I wanted. But hey, look at it this way. A few thousand dollars every forty years isn't such a bad investment."

More silence. "Once a thief, always a thief."

"Let's not get nasty."

"You're as mixed up in this as I am."

Valentine chuckled. "There are levels of guilt. I got you the gun. The way you used it was up to you."

"I wasn't even there when Kay Collins was killed!"

"Okay, fine. Whatever you say. But you paid me to lift it from Cedric's office. I've had years to work it all out in my head. Here's my theory. You wanted to teach Justin a lesson, but things got out of hand. Collins got shot. Who cares who pulled the trigger, friend. All our hands are dirty."

"Stop calling me *friend*!"

"Sure, friend, sure. Except, you have to admit that your hands are worth more than mine. Your involvement would be a national headline. Mine would be a minor story on the back page. So let's get back to the matter at hand, shall we? We've got twenty-five thousand dollars on the table. The fact is, *you've* got a hell of a lot more to lose than I do if this all comes out."

"We'd both go to prison."

"Hell, no. Not me. I was just a pawn in your game. Just doing a friend a favor."

"Right. For money."

"Damn straight, for money. Come to think of it, twenty-five thousand dollars is a pittance to keep your good name out of the tabloids. I want thirty."

For several seconds all Valentine could hear on the other end was heavy breathing.

Finally: "All right. How do you want me to get it to you?"

Valentine's lips thinned into a self-satisfied smile. "I'm being interviewed this afternoon in the lobby of the Maxfield

Plaza. A reporter from the *Star Tribune* should be there around three. I want the bills placed in an unmarked manila envelope and delivered to me before the interview. Got that? *Before.* If I don't have the money in my hands by three, that reporter is going to get an earful. Do we understand each other?"

More silence. "We do. But one word of caution. After today, the bank is closed. I don't want to hear from you again—ever. You'll get your money, and that will be the end of it."

"Of course," said Valentine sweetly. "Hey, you can trust Valentine Zolotow. If you couldn't, you'd be in jail right now."

March 9, 1959

Dear Mother:

For the last two months, fear has been my constant companion. It went to bed with me at night, dominated my dreams, and then woke me in the morning. All day it sat on my shoulder and taunted me.

But here in this apartment, I've finally found a refuge. When I go out, I'm not looking over my shoulder every minute wondering who's following me. Yet though the fear has retreated somewhat, in its place I feel something even more powerful. In a word, anger. It's like no other emotion I've ever experienced before. Since I can't do much now except rest, I've watched myself sink into a kind of furious bitterness. I spend whole days obsessing about how my life's been stolen from me. Sometimes I actually feel like two different people. While one is slipping into fury, the other is aloof, watching the disintegration, waiting with a kind of detached patience. But waiting for what? I have no answer to that question, and yet I know there is one.

Sometimes the depth of my anger terrifies the observer in me. At what do I direct my anger, you ask? At an arrogant man, one who is wholly unscrupulous and evil. How am I ever supposed to come to terms with what's happened to me, especially while that bastard is still enjoying a life of affluence and freedom?

What's even worse is that a friend, someone I trusted, betrayed me, and I don't even know who it is. I try to think it all through. I devise scenarios and solutions, but then that's just theory, isn't it? Worthless, impotent conjecture. Not knowing eats away at me. All I know for sure is that it's one of the people you work with at the station. George, Valentine, even Mitzi.

My worst fear, one I've resisted until now, is that my Judas is Alfred. What if my own brother sold me down the river? We were never close, and there's always been that stupid rivalry between us, but surely he wouldn't condemn me to a life of wandering, of fear and emptiness? Do you know what the mark of Cain is, Mom? It's something I've been thinking about for months. I think it's cynicism. I was always such an idealist, such an optimist. Now I understand the world better. I bear the mark of Cain in my soul.

It's hard to keep any perspective when all you have are your own thoughts—and an active imagination—pounding away at you, day after day, night after night. Yet perspective is what I crave. That's why I want to continue with my story today. I have nothing but time on my hands now, Mom, so I hope you'll understand that I want to take it slow. I'm writing the story of what happened last fall and early winter through the eyes of the observer I have become. This account is as much for me as it is for you.

If you recall, I wanted to find out the truth behind the Landauer hit-and-run so badly I could taste it. I was never assigned anything really big at the paper, I was too young and inexperienced. But this case had the potential to make my career—if I could solve it and then break the story. The problem was, even though I'd begun dating Kay— and had quickly made friends of both Sally and Jonnie—I knew approaching Sally directly was out of the question. I'd already tried that once and failed. I had to come up with another plan.

For most of October into early November, Kay and I, and Sally and whoever was currently tickling her fancy, double-dated at least once a week. Jonnie usually stayed home, her nose in a book. She didn't go out much other than to work and to school. During those dates, I talked privately to Sally's steady stream of new boyfriends, usually over a drink at the bar while the girls were in the ladies' room. Unfortunately, none of them seemed to know anything about Sally's former beaux.

I was starting to become frustrated. There had to be some way I could find the information I wanted. Sometime in mid-November I suggested we throw a party at their apartment. I figured it might provide me with the perfect opportunity to meet more of Sally's friends. I needed to find a confidant, someone who wasn't so ignorant or reticent about Sally's past love life.

Kay and I started planning the party right away. She loved the idea, said it would be a great chance to "show me off." I suppose I was flattered. By then, I was sure that I loved Kay. Anything she wanted was okay by me.

I know what you're thinking, Mom. What about Mitzi? That was my number-one problem. With each passing week she was acting more and more like my fiancée. I know she wanted a ring for Christmas. "Wanted" isn't the right word. She "expected" it. I was in a jam. I had to tell her the truth, but she was so happy. You were so happy. Everybody, it seemed, was happy-happy-happy. Everyone, that is, except me. Alfred asked me a couple of times if we'd set a date. He really liked Mitzi. Said that he envied me. I was getting a great gal. Cedric kept suggesting

"romantic spots" for a honeymoon. I never felt so trapped
in my life. Mitzi wanted to spend every night with me, cook
my dinner, watch TV together snuggled on the couch. I
used my job at the paper as an excuse to beg off, but in
reality, I spent every free minute with Kay.

For most of November, I was miserable. I felt like
a fraud. I'd never thought of myself as cowardly before,
but when it came to facing Mitzi, telling her the truth, I
lost my nerve. I'd looked at rings and found a simple, elegant diamond, but it was for Kay, not for Mitzi. My plan
was to give it to Kay on Christmas eve. I was a man
leading two lives. I was excited one minute, depressed and
ashamed of myself the next.

I'd determined that on the night of the party, I was
going to tell Kay I loved her. If she said she felt the same
way, then I'd talk to Mitzi the next day, after Thanksgiving
dinner. I guess I needed Kay's strength to go through with
it. I would never have married Mitzi, even if there had
never been a Kay, it just would have taken me longer to
tell her. What made it so hard for me to face was that
everyone seemed to be lined up behind Mitzi. If I broke it
off, I was not only the bad guy in her estimation, but in the
estimation of my entire family. Except, isn't it better to tell
the truth? Even if it hurts someone you love? I did love
Mitzi, Mom. Just not enough.

When the night of the party finally arrived, I was in a
terrible mood. I felt apprehensive about talking to Kay,
and even more conflicted about talking to Mitzi the
next day.

Sally was in her usual high spirits, oiled by several
glasses of the cheap wine we'd bought for the occasion, as
well as some Elvis Presley 45s she'd put on the phono-
graph. Kay and Jonnie had been preparing canapes for
hours in the kitchen. I could tell Kay was exhausted. To
make a little extra money for Christmas, she'd worked
both the morning and afternoon shift at Manderbach's
that day. While Jonnie was tired, too, she also seemed
unusually impatient, mostly with me, though I couldn't

imagine why. I hadn't done anything to upset her, I was pretty sure of that. I'd dutifully cleaned the bathroom and vacuumed the living-room rug, uncorked some of the wine bottles, and set up a couple of card tables for the food. I even helped hang some of the red-and-blue streamers Sally had bought at the neighborhood five-and-dime. She'd placed Hula Hoops all over the apartment. We were going to have a contest later in the evening.

About fifteen minutes before people began arriving, Jonnie cornered me in one of the bedrooms, made sure we were alone, and then insisted that she had nothing but disgust for men who "used" women. I didn't have a clue what she was talking about, but she was on a roll. Didn't I know Kay was in love with me? How could I hurt her that way? I was so stunned, I didn't utter a word in my defense. I asked her to explain what this was all about. She just turned on her heel and left. She obviously wasn't interested in a conversation. She just wanted to take her shot.

Well, fine, I thought to myself. My personal life is none of her damn business. I was so agitated when I came out of the bedroom that I asked Kay if she'd like to take a walk with me. She lived close to the creek, and earlier in the fall, we'd often taken long walks along the banks. We had some of our best talks sitting by the water. Kay had even begun calling the place where I'd first kissed her "our spot." Her sweetness never ceased to amaze me.

Anyway, in late November, as you well know, night comes early. But again, luck was on my side. There was a full moon that night to guide us down to the water. Kay cuddled close to me as we walked. There wasn't much snow, so the path was pretty clean. I just needed some fresh air to clear my head. Jonnie's comments had cut deep, not that she was right about my relationship with Kay, but she was dead-on when it came to Mitzi.

After a few minutes we stopped. I pushed Kay playfully up against a tree and then bent close and kissed her. It was just the moment I'd been waiting for. I'd never told anyone I loved them before. Mitzi made assumptions, but I never said the words. But with Kay, it all flowed so easily. If I'd ever had any doubts that she returned my feelings, she put them to rest that night. My heart was so full that on our way back to her apartment, I think my chest almost burst. We danced for a while in front of the building. We were so silly, giggling at anything and everything. There were no stairs leading to the second floor that November night, only air under our feet. We were both glowing when we entered the apartment. The universe was a fabulous place and we were the center of it. And then the bomb I'd participated in creating blew that universe to smithereens.

Mitzi was sitting in the living room making small talk with one of Sally's girlfriends. She didn't see me right away. If I'd backed out of the door right then, I could have gotten away. If I'd feigned illness, or said I'd remembered something at the paper that I needed to get, Kay would have understood. But I couldn't move. My legs felt like lead. And an instant later Mitzi looked up—and I was a dead man.

She cocked her head and gave me a surprised smile. As I helped Kay off with her coat she came over. "I didn't know you were going to be here tonight, Justy," she said. I can still hear her words. "I thought you were working late." She took my arm, gave me a kiss on the cheek, and then walked me into the dining room. I looked over my shoulder at Kay. She was just staring at us, a confused look on her face. God, I couldn't believe this was happening.

As we were standing at one of the food tables, Kay appeared next to my shoulder and introduced herself to Mitzi. Mitzi smiled and said it was a great apartment, and a terrific party. She was glad Jonnie had invited her. Snuggling close to me, she added something like, "I see you've already met my fiancé."

I could have killed her. Kay's face went completely blank. Mitzi instantly sensed that something was up and moved away from me, giving herself a few moments to let the situation sink in. Finally Kay said, "How nice for you, Mitzi. I'm sure you and Justin will be very happy together."

I tried to stop her, but she was out the kitchen door before I could catch my breath. Mitzi, on the other hand, stayed put. She just kept glaring at me. She wasn't stupid. She got the point, saw that Kay and I were much more than friends. Finally, in a cold voice she said, "You bastard. You goddamned bastard!" Backing away from me, she shouted, "I trusted you, you miserable lowlife. How could you do this to me!"

We were creating quite a scene, one Sally and Jonnie watched with great interest. I was glad now that Kay had left. She didn't need to see this. I'd hurt her enough for one evening. I grabbed Mitzi's arm and whispered, "We need to talk."

"I'm not going anywhere with you, you two-timing piece of shit." She yanked her arm away. I got her coat from the bedroom, found mine, and pulled her out the door. She was spouting a stream of venom the entire time. To be honest, I had no idea she even knew some of those words.

When we got outside, I offered to take her to a bar so we could talk. She refused. Did I love that girl? she demanded. I told her I did. How long had the affair been going on? I objected to her choice of words, but said I'd known Kay for a few months. So what does that mean for us? she asked. Was the engagement off? I told her that I was sorry things had worked out this way, but the truth was, there never had been an engagement except in her mind. Again, I told her I was sorry. I said I knew I was a rat for not nixing her marriage fantasy before she got everyone in the family all worked up about it. I pleaded for her forgiveness. Took all the blame on me. She asked if I intended to continue to date Kay. I said that I wanted to, though after tonight, I wasn't sure what Kay wanted. She walked away from me. I ran after her, but she told me to leave her alone. I waited until I saw her get into her car. As she drove off I decided it was best to let her go. I would no doubt be hearing from her soon. I figured there were a few choice swear words she'd forgotten to call me.

The most important thing now was to find Kay, tell her the truth, get her to understand. I had an idea where she might be. I set off at a dead run for the creek. As I scrambled down the steep embankment I saw a small form huddled near the water. Even in the weak moonlight I could tell it was Kay. She was sitting on a rock, her head in her hands. As I approached I could see her wipe a hand across her eyes. She'd been crying.

Since she made no move to leave, I sat down next to her. I waited for a few seconds, hoping beyond hope that I could come up with the right words to explain what had just happened. I started talking. She listened. I talked on. Told her how Mitzi and I had met at the radio station right after she'd started working there. How much you and Cedric had liked her, had encouraged our relationship. I told her the good and the bad. I explained that I'd been a coward. That I should have broken it off with Mitzi long ago, but hadn't. I never anticipated meeting anyone like Kay. I didn't know the feelings I had for her even existed before we met. It was like dreaming in black-and-white, and suddenly I saw everything in Technicolor. I loved her. I'd broken it off with Mitzi. I had no plans to ever see her again. I pleaded with Kay to give me a second chance. I touched her hand, and miracle of miracles, she didn't pull away.

That night, she made me promise I'd never lie to her again. I took that promise seriously. I still had one secret left to tell, and I told it. I said I'd show her the note I'd received at the paper, the one telling me that if I wanted to find out who murdered Olga Landauer, I should talk to Sally Nash. I explained why I'd followed Kay to Manderbach's that first day. How attracted I was to her, and yet, at the same time, how I hoped she could give me some information about Sally. I knew I was taking a big chance, but I couldn't allow any more secrets to exist between us. She asked me a lot of questions. I tried to answer them as best I could. I wanted her to know that I thought Sally was being paid for her silence. Her ex-boyfriend, the one she'd dated in July and August, seemed the most likely candidate.

Kay took it all in. Finally, she said she didn't know the identity of the man Sally had been dating. I believed her. Apparently Sally had been unusually closemouthed about the guy, which suggested to Kay that he was probably married. Kay felt uncomfortable even talking about it. I suggested that Jonnie might know more than she did, but Kay doubted it. On the other hand, she thought my theory was not only plausible, but likely. Amazingly enough, she offered to help. I was so relieved I let out a whoop and then kissed her. We held each other for a long time that night. It's strange, but I think it brought us even closer.

So, I guess you could say I'd dodged a bullet. What I didn't know was that Mitzi's little scene in the apartment would soon help me find the information I needed. I'll tell you more about it next time, Mom.

Until then, all my love.

Justin

13

Heda was having a late breakfast in her suite when she heard a knock on the door. "Now what?" she muttered, turning and looking around the living room for Gerald. He'd been sitting by the bar reading a magazine just a few minutes before. He'd probably gone back to the kitchenette to get himself a cup of coffee. "Gerald, will you answer that?" she called, taking a bite of toast.

Dorothy wouldn't return to the Maxfield until close to noon. Heda hoped the meeting with the *Dallas Lane* cast and crew had gone well this morning. It felt strange not to attend the meeting herself. She hated being trapped in a hotel suite day after day, but for the duration it was the only safe way to proceed. Outside of these rooms, Gerald would have a harder time protecting her. She would be a sitting duck.

Gerald lumbered out of the hallway, stuffing the last bite of a Pop-Tart into his mouth. "Sure thing, Ms. Bloom." He adjusted the holster under his suit coat.

As he drew back the door Heda was surprised to see Santa Claus standing outside. She smiled, motioning him into the room. "Where on earth did you get that costume?"

George Chambers set his heavy sack down and removed his red cap. "Didn't I tell you? I often play Santa for the kids in Phoenix. Since I've got so much free time on my hands here, I offered my services to a local hospital. I'm going to spend the afternoon visiting the children's ward."

"How wonderful." She beamed at him with great fondness. "It will also be good PR for the radio show. Be sure to mention it tomorrow morning when you're interviewed on TV."

"Will do. How are you feeling?" he asked, making himself comfortable on the couch.

"All right. At my age, it's a long road back from hip surgery." As she picked up her coffee cup she studied him a moment. "You know, it's just so funny to see you looking like Santa Claus. I can't get used to it."

"I can't get used to many things," said George, looking wistfully down at his cap. "Returning to the Twin Cities has really brought back the memories. I suppose I knew it would. I took a cab over to Minneapolis yesterday. Walked around the downtown like an archaeologist searching through the ruins. The Foshay Tower is still there, but so much is gone. Some of it truly breaks my heart. I guess I thought places like Charlie's Café and the Curtis Hotel would always be there. I mean, they were landmarks. But they've been erased, just like so much of my past. One minute you're young and the next you're old, and yet the connecting years have all vanished in the mist. Where did the time go? Where did my life go?"

Heda had no answers, and knew he expected none.

"Mitzi looks great," continued George, crossing his legs and revealing white socks under his red pants. "But Valentine has really aged. And Alf. God, what happened to him? On the positive side, there's you and Dorothy Veneger. By the way, Dorothy is quite the dynamo. Where'd you find her?"

"She's been my personal assistant for about six years. She loves radio almost as much as I do."

"You can tell. She's done a bang-up job on the new show. We've got a real hit on our hands with that one. I never doubted it for a minute."

A knock on the door interrupted their conversation.

"I'll get it," said Gerald, rushing out from the hallway. This time he was holding a can of Coke. Opening the door, he was nearly knocked down by Alfred Bloom as he steamed into the room.

"What are you doing here?" asked Heda, unable to hide the surprise in her voice.

"Keeping an eye on you," he said, swirling around and glaring at Gerald. "My mother and I would like some privacy."

"Of course, Mr. Bloom. I'll go sit in the hall."

"That goes for you, too, Chambers," snarled Alfred, jerking his head toward the door.

"Alf!" said Heda. "Where are your manners?"

George held up his hand. "It's fine, Heda. I've got a script to study and I should probably get to it." As he stood he turned to face the younger man. "You look pretty hot under the collar, son."

"If I am, it's none of your damn business."

He shrugged. "Maybe you're right, but Heda is an old

friend of mine. And old friends are often protective of each other."

"I hardly think she needs protection from me."

"Take my word on this, Alf. Family can hurt you worse than anyone." Picking up his sack, he walked over to the door. "Maybe we could have dinner tonight, Heda. What do you say? We've got a lot to catch up on."

"I'd love it."

"Good. I'll call you later. Nice to see you, Alfred. I'm sure we'll run into each other again."

Alfred waited until the door closed. When they were finally alone, he crossed his arms menacingly over his chest and returned his attention to his mother. "What are you up to?"

"What do you mean? George and I are old friends."

"I'm not talking about George."

She tapped a napkin to her lips. "I thought we agreed that you would fly back home yesterday afternoon."

"That was your idea. Never mine."

"But . . . your meeting. Didn't you say you had something important scheduled for today?"

"The meeting was canceled. I canceled it."

She touched the pearls at her neck. "Oh."

"Is that all you've got to say? Oh!"

"Well—" She placed the napkin next to her plate and attempted a smile. "A few more days of rest will be good for you. I'm . . . glad you're still here."

"No, you're not."

"Alfred, why would you say something like that?"

"Do you need a list?" He ticked the points off on the fingers of his right hand. "First, you push the WTWN acquisition through behind my back. Did I get the chance to voice any opposition? No. Second, you arranged the financing through Tri State Bank. We haven't used Tri State in years. Sam Nielson isn't the kind of man I do business with."

"He's an old friend and he's as honest as the day is long. I trust him implicitly."

Alfred ignored her. "Third, I didn't even know you'd left

Palm Beach until one of the junior vice presidents mentioned it to me. You've kept me completely in the dark on this, Mom. Now I know why."

She gripped her canes and got up. "I've done nothing your father wouldn't have done. The station came on the market. I was informed about it, and I made the decision."

"Without informing me?"

"I don't answer to you, Alfred. I'm still the head of Bloom Enterprises."

"Right. I'm just the CEO. Trivial baggage in your estimation."

"If we hadn't acted quickly, we would have lost out. You were busy with the new station in Tucson, so I didn't bother you with it."

"Oh, please," he said indignantly.

"Look, I've wanted to buy a station up here for years."

"I don't doubt that," he snorted. "Not after what I heard last night."

She moved over to the windows, where Dorothy had set up an easel. Turning her back to her son, she opened the blinds, allowing the morning sunlight to flood into the room. After a nasty hip-replacement surgery last year, she'd taken up oil painting as a way of staying active. She was currently working on the downtown St. Paul skyline. "I don't appreciate all this negativity," she said, sitting down on the stool.

"Oh, cut the act, Mom." He sank down on a brown mohair club chair next to the couch. "What's going on? I think I deserve some sort of explanation."

"I assure you, Alfred, the station is as solid as a rock."

"I've got meetings all week to make sure that's the case. And I'm having one of our analysts go over the numbers, so forgive me if I say it remains to be seen. But that's not what I'm talking about."

She looked down at her box of paints. "No, I suppose not."

"Tell me about the broadcast, Mom. *Dallas Lane, Private Eye*."

"Does that mean you listened last night?"

He bristled. "Of course I listened. It's my job to listen."

It was clear that she was fighting a losing battle. Since he'd already figured some of it out, she might as well come clean and tell him the truth. "What do you want to know?"

"Is the story about Justin?"

"Yes, dear, it is."

"But why?"

"It's very simple. I want to set the record straight."

Heda was thoroughly disgusted by this turn of events. Alfred wasn't supposed to find out about the radio broadcast until after the fact. In six weeks everything would be said and done. The show would vindicate Justin, at least in the eyes of some, and she could go home again, if not a happy woman, then at least content that she'd done what she could to restore her son's good name.

Alfred put his head in his hands. "You don't know what you're doing, Mother. This is a hornet's nest. Controversy is the last thing we need."

"On the contrary. I welcome it."

"You always did think you had some special corner on the truth. But you don't. Your oldest son was an evil man. Now that he's dead and buried, why can't you leave it alone?"

"Because I'm his mother! And what was printed about him in the papers wasn't true."

Alfred shot to his feet. "But we have an eyewitness, a police officer, who swears he saw Justin murder Kay."

She watched him pace off his frustration. "I have Justin's word, Alfred. That's proof enough for me."

He whirled around. "You what?" Marching back to the easel, he stared down at her. "What do you mean you have Justin's *word*?"

"I've never told anyone this before, but Justin wrote me from Europe for many years. Before he died, he told me the entire story."

"What entire story?"

"Of how Kay really died."

Alfred eyed her with deepening suspicion. "You say . . . you have letters?"

"I do."

"Where are they?"

She smoothed her white hair into place. "That's not important."

"Of course it is. I want to read them."

"What *is* important, dear, is that, by the end of *Dallas Lane*'s premiere run, the truth will be told."

Alfred crouched down next to her. "You're going to name names? Mother, you could be sued! We could all be sued."

"Don't worry." She patted his hand. "No names. At least, not on our part. If there's conjecture by the media, what can we do about that?"

"But . . . the scriptwriter? He's putting his neck on the block, too."

"You're such a catastrophist sometimes, Alfred. Everything's going to be fine. Actually, finding Wish Greveen was an incredible stroke of luck. He's really good, don't you think? Apparently, he wrote for a number of shows in the late Forties and early Fifties. Dorothy found him through an ad she placed in the newspaper. I explained to her that I needed someone who could write me a radio drama, and she did the rest."

"You fed him all the pertinent details?"

"I did. Dorothy said he was so thrilled by the prospect of returning to radio, he never even batted an eye about having to collaborate with an old bag like me."

"Mother!"

"Oh, Alfred, don't be so prissy."

"But . . . does Greveen know about Justin? That he's telling a real story?"

"Of course not."

Alfred seemed to consider it for a moment and then shook his head. He kept shaking it as he moved over to the window. "I don't like it."

"Well, like it or not, it's the way it's going to be."

"You're . . . getting bad advice."

"From whom?"

"Dorothy, for one."

"Dorothy's completely in the dark about my motives, Alfred. If she's heard about Justin, it wasn't from me." Heda knew that convincing Alfred would be a struggle. That's why she'd kept her intentions a secret. "Listen, son. I've explained everything to you—what I'm doing and why I'm doing it. Now, you *must* back off. The topic is no longer open for discussion."

"But, Mother!"

"Presenting Justin's case by using a radio mystery is simply good marketing. It's a perfect way to entertain and at the same time introduce our side of the story. Think about it, son. Radio is the only forum open to me. It's all I know and it's all I need."

As he stood looking down on the street below, he muttered, "Anybody ever tell you you're a tough old broad?"

"Just your father. Nobody else would dare."

"Well, he was right."

She smiled, though at this moment, with her stomach doing nervous flip-flops, she was feeling far from tough. The truth was, not everything was as cut-and-dried as she made it sound. Something was at work here, something she didn't entirely understand.

Alfred sat down on the couch and spread his arms across the back cushions. "Well, I'm here for the next week at least, like it or not."

She couldn't force him to go, and yet she didn't want him to stay. Not only was she concerned for his safety, but she wasn't interested in having someone watch her every move. She wanted to pursue her mission in peace. When all was said and done, she would pack her tent and quietly steal away, leaving the pieces to fall where they may. Dorothy would object to his continued presence, too, but what could she do? The bottom line was, Heda loved both her sons. It pained her deeply to think they would never be friends. "All right, dear. Stay as long as you want. But on one condition."

"What's that?"

Never being one to beat around the bush, she said, "What happens on *Dallas Lane, Private Eye* is my call. Stay out of my way, Alfred. And keep your mouth shut. That's an order."

14

"The number is 555-4905, and I'm not making this up, my friends. Some people in this country *would* rather die than live with horrible pain. As far as I'm concerned, it's their right. You wanna fight about it, give me a call. This is *The Bram Baldric Show*, and don't touch that dial. We'll be right back."

As they went to a commercial break Bram leaned back, pulled off his headphones, and stretched. He'd been broadcasting his show from Studio B for several years now, and yet today the room struck him as unusually claustrophobic. Remembering the maxim *It can't be the hour, it must be the company,* he smiled. That old saying should be laminated and tacked up all over the gray, acoustic foam walls. Someday it might even be his epitaph.

Every weekday afternoon, Bram sat at an ancient scuffed table and talked to the public. In front of the table was a glass booth where his producer and a technician sat amid a tangle of technology. Radio stations were notorious for their lack of ambience. What the public couldn't see didn't matter. Only what they *heard* had any significance.

Bram glanced briefly at today's guest. The man was a doctor and looked like he needed a stiff drink—or a couple of Valium. "You doing okay?"

"Jeez, do these people eat raw meat for dinner or what?"

"We've got about ten minutes left in this segment. After that, you can take off."

"Good."

Bram felt sorry for the guy. He usually did a one-on-one interview for the first hour, and then opened up the next two hours for listeners to call in and ask questions or make comments. Maybe it was a full moon or an explosion of sunspots, but whatever the case, most of today's callers had gone into attack mode right from their opening statement. Bram figured it was only fair to let this poor schmuck off the hook, even though he had an hour left to fill.

Through the glass, he could see the producer hold up her hand, counting down the seconds until they would be back on air. He put his earphones back on. "Five, four, three, two—" She pointed at him.

"This is Bram Baldric and you're listening to WTWN, 1630 on your radio dial. Again, we have with us today one of the country's foremost medical ethicists, Dr. Lloyd Bergstein, professor of medical ethics at the University of Minnesota. The topic? Assisted suicide. Back to the phones. Gary, you're on." Bram heard nothing in his earphones. He waited a second more and then said, "I guess Gary was disappointed Jack Kevorkian couldn't be with us. Let's move on to line two." He checked the computer screen in front of him for the name. "Betty, you're on with Dr. Bergstein."

"Me?" came a weak voice. "Am I on?"

"Talk now or forever hold your opinions."

"Bram?"

"Yes, Betty?" He tried to be patient. Sometimes it was a struggle.

"My husband and I listened to the new radio mystery theatre show last night. It was the second episode."

"We're off topic now, Betty. Did you have a question for—"

"The story reminded me of that Kay Collins murder case back in the Fifties. Do you remember it? My husband says I'm crazy, but I'm sure I'm right."

It had started as a slow trickle on last Friday's program. One caller noted that Heda Bloom had recently bought the station. The next fellow, a self-professed geezer from Lake Elmo, brought up the subject of her son Justin Bloom. From there, the floodgates had opened. Smelling potential public interest, several local TV stations had picked up the story for their weekend ten o'clock reports. Interest in the topic was beginning to snowball.

Bram tried to head Betty off at the pass. "In our next hour I'll open the lines up to anything and everything my listeners want to talk about. However, right now, Doctor—"

"I think you make a great announcer, Bram. Did anyone ever tell you you have some of the same qualities in your voice as Orson Welles?"

He couldn't cut her off now. She was making too many salient points. "Why . . . thank you, Betty."

"My husband thinks you're a pathetic liberal fruitcake, but I don't agree. Hey, tell me. On the mystery broadcast, didn't you also play the bartender? I loved every minute of it!"

"Yes, that was me. But back to the pathetic-liberal-fruitcake comment."

"And tell me another thing. Is Valentine Zolotow, the actor who plays Dallas Lane, really as handsome as he sounds?"

"Oh, Betty. Valentine is . . . something to behold. On a scale of one to ten—" He couldn't help but smirk. "He's off the scale."

"I knew it. I just knew it. Thanks. Bye."

Bram glanced at the time. Five minutes to the top of the hour and the phone banks were full. "I've got room for a couple more calls. Raymond from St. Paul, you're on."

"Bram? Thought I'd rescue your guest for a moment. I've got a few comments I'd like to make on the Kay Collins murder case, on the off chance you're interested in a lawyer's point of view."

"Ray, this is great. For those of you who don't know who I'm talking to, this is Raymond Lawless, St. Paul's most famous defense attorney. The F. Lee Bailey of the North."

"If you're trying to flatter me, it's not working."

Bram laughed. "Thanks for the call." He could both feel and see Dr. Bergstein's relief as the subject of assisted suicide was temporarily put on hold. "Actually, Ray, I've wondered how a defense attorney would view Justin Bloom's innocence or guilt. I mean, if he'd gone to trial, was he a doomed man?"

"Absolutely not," said Ray. His voice projected quiet authority. "We have an eyewitness account of the murder, but we have no motive. That would have been a huge hole in the county's argument, a critical gap that a good defense lawyer could have used to Bloom's advantage. Why would a man, Justin Bloom in this case, murder a woman he supposedly loved? As far as I know, no one has ever come up with an answer to that."

"Interesting point."

"Secondly, in the Fifties, a police officer's word was inviolate. Today, however, we know that police officers do lie. People are people. Some are honest, some aren't. The point is, if they lie now, they lied back then, even though in the age of Eisenhower, society wasn't willing to admit it. Recently, we've heard a lot of talk about 'dirty cops.' Well, maybe the cop who witnessed the Collins murder was dirty. Maybe he was paid to give a false statement. Who knows? He's dead now, so he can't be cross-examined, but just because a man gives his word about something doesn't make it true."

"These are all fascinating points," said Bram, pulling the mike closer. This was the meatiest conversation he'd had so far about the murder case. He assumed his listeners were eating it up. "But what about the gun? It was registered to Justin Bloom's stepfather. Justin had easy access to it. And, if I recall correctly, only his fingerprints were on it. No one else's. Isn't that pretty damning?"

"Well, let's talk about that for a moment. First, why would Justin murder his girlfriend and then leave the gun at the scene of the crime? Seems kind of silly to me. Of course you're right. It's a damning piece of evidence. But assuming Justin Bloom wasn't a stupid man, why would he leave the murder weapon for the police to find? You could argue that the police officer startled him. He dropped the gun as a reflex. But if he'd stolen a weapon to kill his girlfriend, this was a premeditated act. He'd thought about what he was going to do, planned the time and place. That requires a cold, calculating mind, Bram, not the kind of mind that would panic easily and leave incriminating evidence at the scene."

"When a defense attorney gets his hands on a case, nothing is cut-and-dried, is it?"

"No, and it shouldn't be. The last point I want to make is this: You mentioned that only Justin Bloom's fingerprints were found on the gun. Now, if the gun belonged to his stepfather, then why weren't the stepfather's fingerprints found on it as well? Obviously, it was wiped clean. But why? Why would Justin wipe the gun clean of prints, and then drop it at the crime scene with only his prints on it? It makes no sense. And furthermore, it was no doubt cold that day. Christmas eve, if I'm not mistaken. Why didn't he have on a pair of gloves? If you ask me, all of this begins to sound more and more like a setup. At least, as his attorney, that's what I'd argue."

Again, Bram checked the time. "You got any more thoughts on this subject?"

"Many," said Raymond. "But right now I'm due in court."

"Thanks, buddy. If you don't mind, I'll have my producer contact you off air. Maybe we can get you on the program sometime soon."

"It would be my pleasure."

"All right," said Bram. There was only one minute left. "Let's get back to our topic. Dave from Blaine, welcome to *The Bram Baldric Show*."

"Hey, man. My mother-in-law worked with the infamous Kay Collins at Manderbach's department store back in the late Fifties. She said Collins was a slut. Deserved everything she got."

Bram cut him off. "On that inspiring note, we better head to a break. Next hour it's going to be open mike. All you good folks out there get to entertain *me*, and boy do I need it. I expect our usual Monday-afternoon free-for-all. 555-4905. And, as always, this is the pathetic liberal fruitcake, Bram 'Rosebud' Baldric, speaking to you from Xanadu. Be right back."

The "On Air" light went out.

"You know," said Dr. Bergstein as he yanked off his headset

and scrambled to his feet, "they couldn't pay me enough money to do your job."

Bram's smile lacked its usual luster. "Some days I feel the same way. Thanks for coming."

"Don't mention it. And don't call again. Try one of my associates next time." He bolted for the door.

An hour later Bram limped back to his office. It was only Monday and here he was, already sick to death of discussing Justin Bloom and company. Unfortunately, the subject wasn't about to disappear, not as long as the intrepid Dallas Lane, Private Eye was on the case. Bram would have welcomed another topic, even subjects he loathed such as the English royals or the dreaded gun-control rant—anything but more speculation on a question that was, by its very nature, unanswerable.

Easing down onto his tired but soft leather chair, Bram grabbed a package of chocolate-chip cookies from his top desk drawer. A little R & R was in order. He hadn't eaten any lunch and knew he'd never make it to dinner on the bagel, cream cheese, and coffee he'd had for breakfast. So what if this wasn't one of his better nutrition days? He'd make up for it tonight by eating . . . a celery stick. In his Bloody Mary. That would take care of two of the four vegetable servings he should be eating each day. Sophie would be proud.

The phone next to him gave a jarring ring.

"Ugh," he grumped, gazing forlornly at the uneaten cookie in his hand. The last thing he wanted was another phone conversation. "Speak," he said, hoping his lack of manners would make the call a short one.

"Is this Bram Baldric?"

It was a female voice. Pleasant. Not young. "Last I heard."

"I, ah, was hoping to talk to you privately."

"What about?"

"The Kay Collins—"

"Lady, look, I don't mean to be rude, but why don't you call me on air tomorrow afternoon. I'm pretty busy right now, and to be honest, I'm kind of sick of the whole subject. By tomorrow, I should have my second wind."

"What I've got to say will interest you."

"Fine. Call me tomorrow and—"

"Like I said, we gotta talk about this privately. I've listened to your program for years and I know you're a good guy. I need someone I can trust."

"That's very kind of you. And of course, true. But right now, I'm a starving man. I'm sitting here, staring at a cookie—"

"I have a letter, one you might want to look at. It was written by Arn O'Dell, the police officer who saw Justin Bloom murder Kay Collins."

He was instantly intrigued. As he was about to respond a button on his phone lit up. "Listen, I have another call, but I'll be right back. I promise. Don't go away, okay?"

"I'll wait."

He switched to line two. "Bram Baldric. Make it fast."

"Bram, you have to come right away!"

It was his Sophie. She sounded upset. "What's wrong?"

"It's Rudy. He collapsed. John came home from work and found him facedown on the bathroom floor. He was—" Her voice broke. "Unconscious. John just called. I'm at the Maxfield right now, but he said the paramedics were taking Rudy to St. Jude's emergency room. Can you meet me over there? I'm leaving right now."

"I'll be there in twenty minutes. Sophie?"

"What?"

"Are you all right?"

"No! I'm terrified. I should have pushed him harder to see that doctor. This is all my fault. Just come soon, okay. I need you."

"Don't worry, sweetheart. Twenty minutes."

He returned to the first caller. "I'm sorry, but I'm afraid I've got a family emergency."

Silence.

"Hello? Ms.—I don't know your name." He waited. After several seconds of dead air it was apparent she'd hung up. Hell, there was nothing he could do about it now. Grabbing his coat and scarf, he rushed out the door.

March 21, 1959

My dearest Justin,

I've thought long and hard about what I would write to you if and when I got the chance. So much is in my heart, and on my mind. I remembered, finally, what my father always used to say to me. Heda, he'd say, don't ever pull your punches. I'm going to follow his advice.

First, let me tell you that I love you. I will always love you, Justin, no matter what you've done. I miss you and I want you to come home. It's been terribly hard for me these past few months, not knowing where you are or if you're safe.

Alf and Cedric don't know that you've written to me. It's taken every ounce of discretion I possess not to let them know. I'm aware that you and your stepfather haven't always seen eye to eye, but Cedric has been beside himself with worry ever since you left. He wants you to come back and stand trial. For the first few weeks he talked about nothing else. If you're innocent, then you have to prove it, and I agree. Money isn't an object. You know we're not poor. He'd find you the best lawyer in the state. Truth always wins out, son. If I didn't believe that, I couldn't get up in the morning. Think about it. I see no other way for you to clear your name.

You're right about the newspapers. They've tried and convicted you. While I know that in your own way and in your own time, you're trying to give me the details leading up to Kay's death, I have to be honest with you. It's very difficult for me to understand why a well-respected police

110

officer would lie about what he saw. Cedric and I even went to the station and spoke with him personally. He seemed like a decent, honest man, and he's adamant that you were the one who pulled the trigger that night, the one who ended Kay's life. He's been on the force for over twenty-five years. Don't be upset with us, Justin, but it's a hard matter for me to resolve, especially when I don't have all the facts.

I want desperately to believe in your innocence, son. And yet I must say that it fills me with horror to hear you suggest that your brother or one of our friends at the station had something to do with Kay's murder. You've got to explain that to me. I simply don't understand.

Since you left, Alf has said very little. He's in pain, I can tell. I know you think Cedric has always favored Alf because he's his natural son while you had a different father, but if you could see the two of them now, you'd know they love you, and that they want to help prove your innocence to the entire world. I'm sorry, but I cannot believe Alf would ever hurt you in any way.

As for Mitzi. I thought you should know that she's left town. She was so devastated by her breakup with you that for a time I wasn't sure she'd survive it. She's a high-strung, emotional young woman, and whether you believe this or not, she loved you deeply. Since I was never able to meet Kay, I have no way of knowing what kind of woman she was. From your account of her, she sounds like a good person. I can only say that I wish matters had been handled differently. I had no idea why the breakup happened until I read your letter. You were your usual tight-lipped self about it before Christmas, and all Mitzi would say was that it was over. Like any woman, she has her pride, and I didn't want to force the information out of her. I thought that eventually one of you would come to me and I'd be told the truth of the matter. But that won't happen now.

Mitzi's contract wasn't renewed at the station because, as of February 1, Dallas Lane, Private Eye is no longer part of our radio schedule. It was simply becoming too costly, and our advertising base for this kind of program is drying up. Television's challenge to the radio industry can't be overestimated, and I'm afraid Mitzi got caught in the cross fire. I was, however, terribly upset that she left without saying goodbye. She hasn't been herself since you left, Justin. Perhaps, someday, her wounds will heal. I pray for that every night.

Several weeks after you left, your landlord called us. He said you'd paid your rent early, so your belongings could stay put until the end of the month. But he wanted everything out by the thirty-first of January. So I went over and boxed everything up and then we hired some men to move it to a storage locker down on Lake Street. That's where it is now. And your car is in our garage. Oh, I should tell you that I took all your personal papers and put them downstairs in a wooden storage box just outside the rec room. I promise, I'll keep everything safe for you until you return.

I've taken every precaution to make sure this letter travels by trustworthy hands. I believe your friend in New York and I have worked out a reliable system for funneling your letters to me. You're right about the house being watched. Several times in the last few months I've noticed men sitting across the street in a car. They pretend they're reading a map, but I know better. Actually, I even saw one of them following me once when I went into the downtown library to check out a book. I assume they're FBI agents, although they look like thugs. Cedric mentioned that he'd seen some men, too, outside the radio station.

Don't worry, we're keeping our distance. I wish I could say the same for our postman. A month or so after you left, I saw one of the agents talking to him. You remember Hank, don't you? He's delivered mail to the house for years. Anyway, I always thought he was a friendly old guy, which was why it didn't surprise me to see him exchanging a few words with the man. After talking for a couple of minutes, the agent pointed to our house and then pulled some cash out of his wallet. It all happened so fast, I could hardly believe my eyes. Hank took the money, stuffed it into his shirt pocket, and then the two of them walked off just as nonchalantly as you please. If you ask me, it was pretty low behavior for an FBI agent and a man entrusted with the U.S. mail. I've kept my distance from Hank since then. I can't prove he's done anything illegal, mind you, but I'll never trust him again.

I find it hard to end this letter, Justin, but if I don't, it will never reach you. I'm going to make sure you receive a regular monthly income until you're on your feet. I can't imagine where you got the money to take you this far. But whatever the case, I'm just glad you're safe and feeling better. Rest now, son, but when you're stronger, I hope you'll come back home. We can see this through together. If some core part of my being didn't believe you were innocent, I'd never suggest that. I believe in you, son.

I miss you, and I send all my love.

Mom

15

Sophie dashed into the emergency waiting room and immediately spotted John sitting at a table in the rear. Since his back was to the door, he didn't see her come in. "John!" she called, rushing up to him. "Is Rudy here yet?"

Solemnly, John stood. "Yes, but I don't know anything about his condition. They won't tell me."

"Why not?"

"Because . . . I'm not family."

She was stunned. His outrage was so palpable, she could feel it hit her like a blow. "Oh, John. I'm so sorry." She took him in her arms. Even through his heavy coat, she could feel him trembling.

"Sometimes I think the world is changing," he said, stepping back. "But then I get dumped on by a good dose of reality."

"It is changing, John."

"Not fast enough. Rudy and I were going to talk to a lawyer, give each other power of attorney just in case something like this ever happened, but we've both been so busy, we haven't gotten around to it yet."

Sophie looked up into his eyes. "Did you tell the doctor that the two of you were partners?"

"I told the nurse. That's when she turned into the ice princess."

Feeling her own anger rise in her chest, she marched straight out of the room and up to the nursing desk near the front entrance. "Who's in charge here?" she demanded. There were times she wished she were big and tall, not barely five-three in high heels.

An older woman looked up from a stack of file folders. "May I help you?"

"My son was just brought in. The name's Greenway. Rudy Greenway."

"Right," she said, glancing down at a chart. "Dr. Sibley is in with him right now. If you'd like to take a seat—"

"I want to see my son."

"Of course. As soon as the doctor's done, I'll take you back."

"Are you the one who refused to give information to his partner, John Jacoby?"

The woman took off her glasses, giving Sophie a hard, appraising look. "I'm afraid I can only give out medical information to family members."

"He *is* a family member."

"Not legally. The hospital has rules. We could be sued if we gave out information to anyone who asked."

"Sued by whom?"

"The family, for one."

"He *is* the family. A life partner isn't just anyone!"

"Please, if you'll just calm down." She watched with

impatience as John walked up and stood next to Sophie. After eyeing him with undisguised distaste, she continued, "You have to understand, Mrs. Greenway, some families don't feel the way you do."

"Listen, Ms."—she read her name off the plastic name tag—"Hansrude. You're going to be sued if you *don't* give information to Mr. Jacoby. I don't mean just the hospital, but *you*. Personally. How someone could be a nurse and lack simple human kindness is beyond me. Give me a reason to make your life as miserable as you made John's a few minutes ago, and believe me, Ms. Hansrude, I will. Now," she said, unbuttoning her coat, "do we understand each other?"

They stared at each other across the deepest, darkest, and widest abyss of all: ideology.

After several silent seconds Nurse Hansrude said, "I'll make a note on his chart that this, as his mother, is your wish."

Sophie knew it was the best she was going to get. She locked arms with John. "John and I expect to be informed as soon as the doctor's done with Rudy."

"Of course." Her politeness was pure acid. Sophie knew she'd won the battle on a technicality and it made her sick. John was right. The world wasn't changing fast enough.

Once they were back in the waiting room, John gave Sophie a hug. "I can't thank you enough."

She touched the side of his perfectly groomed beard, motioned for him to bend down, and then gave him a kiss on the cheek. "I wish it hadn't been necessary."

"Me, too. But . . . I want you to know how good it feels to have you on our side. So many of my friends don't have any support from their family. To be hated simply for being who you are is . . . well, it's intolerable." He took a deep breath. "Okay, enough said. Except, well, one other thing."

"Yes?" She removed her coat and placed it on an empty chair.

"Don't tell Rudy this happened. It would only upset him. He doesn't need any more upset right now."

Her smile was tender. "He won't hear it from me."

They each took a seat near the door.

In the next few minutes both Sophie and John turned into balls of nervous energy.

"Have you had any dinner?" she asked, examining a magazine without really looking at it.

"No."

"Look, if you want to go get a bite to eat—"

"I'm not hungry. Thanks. You?"

She shook her head. "Did Rudy ever regain consciousness while the paramedics were working on him?"

"Yeah. He was kind of embarrassed when he woke up. Two guys were bent over him, taking his blood pressure and his pulse. He tried to stand, but he was too weak—or dizzy, I couldn't tell which. They put him on a gurney and took him away almost immediately. I locked up the apartment and then followed in my car."

"Did the paramedics give you any indication what might be wrong?"

He shook his head. "Nothing. I wish I could tell you more."

What had been left unspoken was her concern about AIDS. She knew that both Rudy and John had been tested twice, but the last test had been a good year ago. She felt ill at ease discussing their sexual relationship, so she'd never pressed him to get another. She assumed that he was monogamous, though she didn't know it for a fact. If either of them *were* sleeping with other men, then AIDS couldn't be ruled out, and that made her feel as if she were sitting on top of a ticking time bomb.

Hearing footsteps in the hall, she shot to her feet as Bram entered the room. "Oh, honey, I'm so glad you're here."

Bram wrapped his arms around her and held her tight. "It's going to be all right."

"God, I hope so."

"Where is he?"

"The doctor's looking at him right now."

"When can we see him?"

"As soon as he's done."

Bram nodded to John. "Are you okay?"

"Yeah. Fine."

"So," said Bram, sitting down next to Sophie, "what do we know so far?"

"Nothing," she replied. "Just that he was weak and collapsed." She gazed wearily around the cheerless waiting room. Chairs. A few lamps. No other people. Nothing to take her mind off the grim reality that her son was sick, possibly even gravely ill. She tried not to let her imagination get away from her, but it was a struggle.

Half an hour later a woman in a white coat entered the room.

"Are you the Greenway family?" she asked, glancing from face to face.

"Yes," said Bram, getting up.

"Then you must be Ms. Greenway."

Sophie nodded. Turning to John, she said, "And this is John Jacoby, Rudy's partner."

The doctor shook John's hand. "I'm Dr. Sibley." Returning her attention to Sophie, she said, "I caught some of what you said to the head nurse. I just want you to know, you have my complete support. My sister's gay. I'd hate to think she'd be treated like that if her partner became ill. The nurse was right about the policy, but most of the time nobody pays any attention to it." Glancing from face to face, she added, "If you feel the urge to file a complaint, I'd do it. The sooner the better."

John seemed visibly relieved by her comments. "Thanks."

"No problem. Now," she said, looking down at the chart in her hand, "Rudy is stable, but very weak. We're running some tests, but after talking to him, I think it's fair to say that he's been bleeding internally for quite some time. As soon as I get the results of his blood test, we'll need to transfuse him. The sooner the better since his hemoglobin is undoubtedly very low. Any effort on his part causes him extreme fatigue and, it appears, some trouble breathing."

Sophie cleared her throat. "Doctor? Has my son had an AIDS test recently?"

She shook her head. "But we did one tonight. We should have the results very soon."

"You think this is AIDS-related?" asked John, his voice trembling.

Sophie looked up and saw that he'd gone white as a sheet.

"We don't know yet. He says he's only had one partner since last year. That would be you, Mr. Jacoby."

"That's right. And it's been the same for me."

"Well, if that's the case, then I think we can rule it out. But let's wait until we get the results of his blood work back. In the meantime we're going to run some further tests. The next step is to put a small tube down his throat and take a look at his stomach. If we don't find anything, we'll do a colonoscopy. I'd like to do both tonight. I'm not going to minimize this. Rudy is in serious condition right now. But I'll have more to say on that in a few hours."

Sophie felt her stomach go hollow. "Can we see him?" she asked.

"Of course. But he's going to be moved to another room very shortly. Actually—" She glanced at her watch. "Why don't you meet him upstairs." Again checking her notes, she said, "He's going to be taken to 823. West wing. It's a private room."

"That's fine," said Sophie.

"You can take the elevators right outside the door all the way up to the eighth floor. As soon as I know more, I'll let you know. Oh, one other thing. I think it's great to let Rudy know you're here for him. If he wants you all to stay in the room, I suppose that's fine. But remember. He's very weak. You might want to visit him in shifts, one at a time. And if he wants to sleep, I'd encourage it. I don't want to give him any medications until I know what we're dealing with."

"I understand," said Sophie. She felt Bram's arm ease around her shoulder. She was so grateful for his strength and concern. "We'll wait to hear from you."

The doctor nodded, and then left.

Two hours later Sophie and Bram sat in Rudy's hospital room, staring at an empty bed. Rudy had been taken down for tests and wasn't expected to return for at least another hour. In hospital speak, that probably meant three hours. Feeling the need to do something—anything—John had gone to scout out some coffee.

During their brief time together, Sophie had been trying to give Rudy every positive vibe she could muster, but he was so pale it almost took her breath away. "Bram?"

"Um?"

"Did Rudy seem, I don't know—confused to you?"

He folded his hands over his chest and looked up at the TV set hanging on the wall. "Yeah," he said somewhat hesitantly. "A bit."

"I wonder why."

He shook his head, but said nothing.

"How do you think John's taking all this?"

"I don't know. He's been pretty quiet."

"That's not like him."

"He's worried, Sophie. We all are."

"But . . . do you believe him?"

Bram caught her eye and then looked away. "You mean about not having sex with anyone other than Rudy for the past year?" He shrugged. "I guess so. I have to believe both of them."

Her frown deepened. "If we just had more information."

"We will," said Bram. "But it's going to take some time."

Absently, she began playing with her diamond ring. "Say, what time is it?"

Bram checked his watch. "Five after ten."

"Do you want to watch the news?"

"Sure. It might help pass the time until Rudy gets back."

Sophie switched on the TV set and found their favorite local station. As she was about to turn up the volume, a woman backed into the room pulling a cleaning cart with her. She nearly bumped into Sophie as she turned around. "Oh, sorry. Didn't know anyone was in here."

Sophie moved her legs so that the woman could push the cart around her.

"Do you mind if I clean the bathroom?"

Bram shrugged. "Whatever. It's empty."

"Hey, don't I recognize the voice?" Her hands rose to her hips. "Say something else."

"Something else."

"No, I mean talk for a minute."

"Look, I'm kind of tired." When she kept staring at him, he added, "I'm all talked out for the evening."

"You're that radio guy, right? Bram Baldric?"

"That's me." His tone was something less than friendly.

"I listen to your show all the time."

"Really. That's . . . nice to hear."

"Caught your show today. Kind of depressing. Assisted suicide isn't my bag."

"That's probably fortuitous, madam, since you work in a hospital."

Sophie watched the woman empty the wastebasket next to the bed. She was middle-aged and a good fifty pounds over-weight. Her curly red hair, tinged with gray, had been pulled back into a tight bun, revealing a broad forehead and intelligent blue eyes. Watching her replace a box of Kleenex, Sophie decided she must have once been pretty, though now her face was coarsened by age and, if the high color in her cheeks was any indicator, too much alcohol.

The woman kept stealing peeks at Bram as she bustled around the room, never quite making it into the bathroom. Sophie knew that women often found her husband attractive. She couldn't blame them. She shared the same opinion.

"Hey, Molly." A man pushed his head into the room. Seeing Sophie and Bram, he said, "Oh, sorry. Say, Molly, you're not on this floor tonight. Didn't you read the schedule on the bulletin board?"

"I'm not?" she said, giving him a disgusted look.

"You better get down to sixth pronto."

"Oh . . . hell." She pulled the cart toward the door. "Nice meeting you, Mr. Baldric." She gave him a flirtatious smile.

"Likewise," said Bram.

"We'll meet again."

Sophie found the entire interaction thoroughly obnoxious.

After the woman had banged her way out the door, Bram shot Sophie a pained look. "It's hard being the object of so much adoration."

"It's your cross, dear."

"It doesn't get on your nerves that women find me utterly irresistible?"

"Should it?"

He took her hand and drew it to his lips. "No."

They both looked up as John entered the room carrying three cups of coffee.

"I had to go all the way down to the basement," he said, handing the cups around. "There's supposed to be a coffee machine on this floor, but it's out of order." Sitting down, he looked at the empty bed and said, "I don't suppose you heard anything while I was gone."

Bram shook his head. "I think we better prepare ourselves for a long night."

Sophie's eyes rose to the ten P.M. report. She wished she were home in bed and this was all a dream. Just yesterday she'd put the finishing touches on her plans for Rudy and John's commitment party. Everything was all set. The menu. The flowers. The champagne had been ordered. The room had been reserved. She was so happy for them she could have burst. Now Rudy was fighting for his life. She felt tears well up in her eyes as she realized how desperately she wanted yesterday back.

16

The mechanical whir of slot machines droned heavily inside Valentine's alcohol-soaked consciousness. It was Monday evening. Since he never wore a watch, and there wasn't a window or a clock in sight, he wasn't sure of the time. The cab had dropped him off at the casino around four, the frigid Minnesota winds dissolving into luxurious warmth as he pushed through the front entrance. It was like walking through an air lock into instant sensory overload. On the ride down from St. Paul, he'd been lulled by the calm of the winter-white landscape, yet once inside the casino, a brilliant mixture of light and sound assaulted his senses. The contrast staggered him. For almost a full minute all he could do was stand and blink his incomprehension at the crowds milling around the slot machines.

In Minnesota, as his cabdriver had pointed out, the best gambling establishments were owned by Native Americans. The River Bend Casino was set smack in the midst of a frozen tundra. From many miles away, the casino and the twelve-story hotel that sat directly next to it loomed large and luminous in the growing dusk.

As Valentine was counting out the cash to pay for the cab ride, the driver asked him where he was from. "Southern California," he responded.

"Well then"—the cabby grinned—"welcome to Siberia."

"That about covers it."

"Good luck in there." The cabby nodded to the casino doors. "The wife made me promise to swear off slot machines, otherwise I'd join you."

"Maybe you should swear off the wife."

They both had a good laugh as Valentine disappeared inside.

For the next several hours alcohol and adrenaline kept him warm as he sat perched on a stool in front of a blackjack table. Whatever he did, his moves were golden. The chips piled up in front of him so relentlessly that the stacks looked like mini-skyscrapers, the makings of a small metropolis.

This, of course, was all part of his master plan. The thirty thousand he'd received was going to be his seed money. He would parlay it into a small fortune—or at least a hefty retirement income. Once he was all set up in a nice little condo in the Hollywood Hills, he might start playing the stock market. Or maybe he'd take a Caribbean cruise. He'd always wanted to do that.

Valentine knew his jobs had never been the kind that would provide him with a comfortable old age. People in the arts were often paid shit all their lives, and then, when they got old, were dumped into the ranks of the poor by a society that only valued the assholes who managed—deservedly or undeservedly—to become stars. That was exactly what Valentine had to look forward to until he'd stumbled over a goddamned gold mine.

"It's up to you, sir," said the dealer, his hand poised next to the deck.

Raising a cigarette to his lips, Valentine lifted the bottom card and stared at it. He knew the card hadn't changed since the last time he'd looked at it, but he was uncertain. He was struggling to maintain an air of confidence, but it was becoming more and more difficult. In the past half hour his luck had begun to change. In response, his frustration was making him reckless. Tapping the green felt, he said, "Hit me."

As soon as he saw the card, he let out an audible groan. "Shit." It was a ten of spades. He'd lost again.

The next few hours proved even more disastrous. He'd always known that his worst failing as a gambler was that he didn't know when to quit. Maybe that was a problem in life, too, but this was no time to get philosophical, not when the stakes were this high. He had only four thousand dollars left. If he lost much more, he'd never make it back.

Thinking that it was perhaps time to take a short break, Valentine pocketed his remaining chips and went to the men's room, where he splashed water on his face. He stood for a few minutes, hands on the sink, staring at his reflection in the mirror, trying to figure out what had gone wrong. What sort of character flaw made a man a loser—in blackjack or in life? He had as much natural talent as the next guy. Maybe he wasn't great-looking, but then at sixty-nine, who was?

Entering the bar a few minutes later, he made himself comfortable on a red leather stool and ordered a vodka martini. He had to figure out his next move. He'd always loved to think his problems through in bars, especially in the quiet of the early evening, before the crowd arrived. There was something about the emptiness that appealed to him. This joint was a little too busy for his tastes, but it would do.

After he'd been served his drink and had taken a couple of sips, he grabbed the pretzel bowl, but found that it was empty. He couldn't be expected to enjoy his drink without something salty to go with it, so he waved at the bartender. That's when he noticed a woman across the room making eyes at him. She wasn't young, but she wasn't old either. Platinum-blonde hair. Heavy makeup. Tight red dress. Probably a hooker, not that he had any particular problem with prostitutes. He gave her a seductive wink, motioning her over. He might as well see what she wanted.

"Hi," she said, easing onto the stool next to him.

Seeing her up close, Valentine decided she wasn't a hooker—probably just a lonely woman looking for a little adventure. In his experience, even with his limited looks, American women couldn't resist a foreigner. "Good evening, my dear," he said, using his best British accent. It rarely fooled a genuine Brit, but American women were easy. "May I offer you a drink?"

She gazed up into his eyes. "Are you English?"

"I'm afraid you've found me out."

She smiled. "I was in London once. Where's your hometown?"

Since he'd never been to England, he gave his standard lie. "Bricketwood. You've probably never heard of it."

"Actually, no. I haven't."

His smile broadened.

"Are you in town on business?" she asked.

"Yes, I'm staying at the Maxfield Plaza in St. Paul. I just came down to the casino tonight because I had a few free hours on my hands."

"The Maxfield," she said, almost reverently. "That's an expensive place."

"It's quite lovely, my dear. Perhaps we could share a glass of wine . . . some evening soon?"

"Well . . . sure. I'd love that."

"What's your name?"

"Mandy. Like the song." She giggled, then put her hand over her mouth.

They talked amiably for the next few minutes while Mandy downed a double Scotch and soda, on top of the several she'd already had. If Valentine couldn't get lucky at the tables, he might as well get lucky somewhere else. There was a hotel right next door. Judging by the weather and the relatively thin crowd, it probably wasn't full.

"You know what?" he said, slipping his arm around the back of her chair. He finished his vodka martini in one gulp. "I feel lucky."

"You do?"

"Yes, my dear, I do. And do you want to know why?"

"Well . . . sure. I suppose."

"Because of you."

"Me?"

"Indeed. I want to try my luck one last time at the black-jack tables. If you would accompany me, be my good-luck charm, I'm certain I'll win." The fact was, he *was* feeling better. His confidence had returned.

She looked at him uncertainly. "Are you sure?"

"One hundred percent."

Her face brightened into a smile. "You're on."

Valentine selected the highest-stakes table in the casino. In very short order, his instincts proved correct. He quickly doubled his money. "We're on a roll now," he said, squeezing the woman's waist and giving her a kiss. He didn't know how she would react to the intimacy, but when she moved closer and rested her hand on his thigh, he knew the night was his.

After a few more rounds he whispered in her ear. "I need to ring a friend."

"Oh. Ah, sure."

"I'll cash in my chips first. When I'm done with my conversation, I'll meet you back at the bar."

She looked crestfallen. "No, you won't, Val. You're going to take off. I'll never see you again."

He took her hands in his and looked deep into her eyes. "Why, my dear, you're my good luck tonight. I need you. Perhaps I'll always need you, who can say? You make me feel as if I can walk on water. Reach for the stars. But, you see, now that my luck has changed, I need more money. We're going to make a fortune tonight, my darling." He was getting a little too Ronald Colman for his tastes, but what the hell. She was mesmerized. "But first, I'm going to ring up that friend. Believe me when I tell you, it won't take long. As soon as I'm done, I'll rejoin you in the bar."

"You mean this . . . friend is going to bring you some more money? All the way out here?"

"Oh, it won't be a problem. My friend is very old, and very dear."

"Well—" She rolled her eyes as she thought it over. "Why can't I come with you while you make the call?"

Good question. She was beginning to annoy him. Still, she was bringing him luck, he could feel it. "All right, Mandy my dear. Come with me, then." He pocketed his chips, took her by the hand, and dragged her through the crowd over to a bank of phones near the men's room. "Remain here on this bench," he commanded, waiting as she sat down.

He found the number in his wallet, approached the phone,

and quickly punched it in. "Please God, be home," he said, praying silently.

After the fourth ring, a groggy voice answered, "Hello?"

"I'll make it quick. It's Zolotow."

"Who? Christ, do you know what time it is?"

"No, I don't. Now listen. I need more money—twenty thousand will do."

"Are you nuts? Have you been drinking?"

"I need it now." Valentine could hear rustling on the other end.

"Go to bed. And don't call again."

"Maybe you didn't hear me. I need it *now*." His tone carried a distinct threat.

"Look, even if I had twenty thousand just lying around, I wouldn't give it to you. We have a deal."

"All bets are off."

"Wait a minute—"

"You might be interested to know that I've got a letter in my pocket, unsigned, of course. It details your involvement in the Kay Collins murder." It was a lie, of course, but it was all he could think of on such short notice. "If you don't bring me the money now, it goes in the mail—tonight. Straight to the police."

A long pause. "Where are you?"

"At the River Bend Casino south of the Twin Cities. You know the place?"

More silence. "I don't have twenty thousand here."

"How much do you have?"

"Well, I could get you half of it."

"*Tonight.* I've got to have it tonight."

"All right."

"You can get me the rest tomorrow. How long will it take you to drive out here?"

"Give me an hour. And I don't want to hand you the money in the casino. Too many interested eyes."

"That makes sense. I'll be at the front door in one hour. We can pass the package outside."

"Fine. And listen, Valentine. Don't make me wait. I don't like driving around in the middle of the night."

"I won't be late. You can count on that."

At the appointed time, Valentine stood alone near the front doors, eyeing the frozen drive in front of the casino. After another couple of drinks and a whole lot of sweet talk, he'd managed to convince Mandy that he wasn't going to take off on her. He'd ensconced her at a roulette table, given her a couple of hundred to play with, and told her he'd be back shortly.

Towering bright lights illuminated the parking lot. It looked a lot emptier now than it had when he'd arrived. He figured it must be the wee hours of Tuesday morning, which was just fine with him. He always felt more alive at night than he did during the day. As soon as he got the dough in his hands, maybe he and his new lady would find a place and grab a bite to eat. A meal would steady him. He'd need all his wits about him to win the kind of money he intended to win.

A dark sedan came rolling down the off-ramp from the highway a few minutes later. The car parked twenty or so yards from the front door, switched off its lights, and waited.

Valentine took it as his cue. He plunged through the doors into the frigid night air. Since he didn't plan on staying outside, he hadn't brought his coat. He trudged quickly out to the car and stood rubbing his hands, waiting for the door to be unlocked. Instead, the electric window came down.

"All right. So, where is it?" he demanded.

"Get in."

"Just give me the money."

"Not here. We'll drive a short ways—away from the lights. There's a convenience store about a mile down the road. I'll give it to you while we're driving and then drop you there. You can get a cab to bring you back."

Valentine looked around the lot. There wasn't a soul in sight. "Damn it, just give it to me!"

The window went up.

Valentine banged on the hood as the car backed away. "Stop, for chrissake. Wait."

The car stopped.

Valentine flipped the lapels of his thin jacket up around his neck. The night wasn't fit for man or beast. His hands and ears were already going numb.

The window eased back down. "Are you coming?"

Valentine knew he had only seconds to decide. "You say there's a convenience store around here?"

"A 7-Eleven. Just up the service road."

He couldn't see any lights. The hills were probably blocking his view.

"Do you want this money or not?"

Valentine's eyes darted back to the casino entrance. Two people were coming out, running, not walking, to their car. He had to think fast. "Oh, shit," he said, throwing open the passenger-side door and jumping in. "Let's make it fast."

April 17, 1959

Dear Mother:

I can't tell you what it meant to me to receive your letter. So much is in my heart. I promise, I will respond to everything you've written, but first, I have to get this note off to you right away.

You must listen to what I'm about to tell you. Even if you don't believe me, it's imperative that you do as I say. I had no idea he would go this far. When you mentioned that the house was being watched and that you were being followed—even to the library!—my blood turned cold.

*You've got to promise me, Mom. You mustn't go out
alone. Stay away from those men across the street at all
costs. They're not with the FBI. I can't prove it, but I know
it, more profoundly than I've ever known anything before
in my entire life.*

*I thought that if I left the country, promised to stay away
and never return, he would leave you alone. I can see now
that I was wrong. It drives me crazy that I can't be there to
protect you. I thought my silence would keep you safe. We
simply have to wait this out, Mom. I don't know what else
to do. In my more rational moments I don't think he'd dare
touch you. And yet, he's a ruthless man. I plan to write him
and tell him that if a hair on your head is harmed, he can
forget his own life. I'll end it—one way or another. If that
sounds cruel, all I can say in my defense is that this is a
cruel game, and not one of my own making.*

Be careful, Mom. Please!

Justin

17

Bram was startled awake by the sound of a ringing phone.
Disengaging himself from the blankets, he glanced over at
the other side of the bed and saw that Sophie was gone. She
must have gotten up sometime during the night.

Wondering who had called, he fumbled for his bathrobe
and headed out of the room. He could smell the results of
Sophie's sleepless night long before he saw it.

Bram found his wife in the kitchen, standing amid piles of
freshly baked Christmas cookies. She usually baked them in
huge batches before the holidays and then gave them away

s gifts. With all the overtime she was putting in at the hotel
his year, he didn't think she'd have time for this long-
standing tradition. He never counted on Rudy getting sick.
Whenever Sophie was worried, needed some quiet time to
hink, or simply couldn't sleep, she always baked.

"It's John," she whispered, holding her hand over the phone.

Sleepily, Bram shifted his gaze to the clock on the stove.
t was just after seven A.M. Last night's crisis had barely left
is consciousness. He and Sophie had stayed at the hospital
until after two. Rudy was back in his room by then, resting
comfortably. The doctor seemed fairly confident that he was
out of immediate danger. More tests had been ordered for
his morning.

"I'm so glad you called," said Sophie, leaning against the
ink. "How is he?"

Ethel dragged herself into the kitchen and nudged Bram's
eg, gazing up at him with undisguised gloom. She wasn't a
morning dog.

"Yes," said Sophie, making notes on a pad. "I understand.
Did you just get there?" She paused. "John, you must be
exhausted!" She put her hand over the receiver and whis-
ered, "He never went home."

Bram wasn't surprised.

"Sure, that's no problem. I'll get dressed right away. I can be
here in less than an hour. Is Rudy awake?" She listened, wrap-
ing the phone cord around her finger. "I see. And when did
ne doctor think she'd be in to talk to us? Okay, that's fine. Yes,
'll see you soon." After she'd hung up, she turned and leaned
er head against Bram's shoulder as he took her in his arms.
They're about to do another test. It seems the current theory is
nat he may have a bleeding ulcer."

"Then it's not HIV?"

She held him tight. "I won't feel confident of that until we
et the results of the blood test."

He could read the worry in her face. "You look tired. Did
ou get any sleep?"

"I'm fine." She pulled away and wiped her hands on her

apron. "Just think, if I didn't need to sleep, look how much I could get done." She swept her hand to the mounds of cookies. "Don't eat them all while I'm gone."

"Sophie, I'm worried about you."

"Why? I said I was fine." She busied herself turning off the oven and switching off the lights.

"You were already exhausted before this happened. You're going to get sick if you keep pushing so hard."

She turned her back to him. Resting her hands on the sides of the sink, she said, "I can't have this conversation right now. I've got to get dressed."

"You're going to crash and burn, sweetheart. You're not superhuman. Rudy needs you whole and healthy. So do I. Promise me that you'll come back here this afternoon and get some sleep."

"Sure," she said, turning around. Her smile was full of fake lightness. "I promise."

He didn't believe her, but knew it would only add to her stress if he pressed the point. "I'll hold you to it, Sophie."

"Good. You do that."

Following her into the bedroom, he asked, "What else did John say? I mean, it seems pretty strange that someone Rudy's age would get an ulcer."

She stood in front of the closet and lifted her jeans off a hook. "According to the doctor, some ulcers are caused by a virus. She'll be in to talk to us as soon as the procedure is over. It only takes an hour."

Bram had already pulled on his jeans. As he buttoned up a fresh shirt Sophie said, "Don't you have a *Dallas Lane* rehearsal this morning?"

"Sure, but this is an emergency. Dorothy will understand."

"No. We're not at emergency status yet. I'll be fine driving over by myself. And I won't be alone. John will be there."

"But—"

"I'll call you with any new developments."

"All right," he said hesitantly. "If that's what you want." He knew it was useless to argue. Sitting down on the bed, he watched her dress. "Sophie? Is something wrong? You seem . . . I don't know . . . kind of distant this morning."

"My son is in the hospital and I'm terrified he's got a disease that will kill him. I'm sorry if you think I'm being distant."

"Sophie . . . I love him, too."

"I'm aware of that."

"Then don't shut me out."

"I'm not."

"It feels like you are."

She turned around, her eyes narrowing in anger. "It's all my fault, right? I'm not paying enough attention to you. I'm not home enough. I'm a failure as a wife *and* a mother."

"I never said that."

"You didn't need to." She pressed her lips together. Turning her head away, she put her hands up to her face and started to cry.

In an instant Bram was by her side. "I know this is hard on you, sweetheart." He held her, stroking her hair.

"God, it's all my fault. I'm his mother, Bram. I didn't even know he'd hurt his back until John told me. I've been so busy, I haven't seen him in weeks."

"He's been busy, too, sweetheart. It's not a one-way street."

She bit her trembling lip. "That's no excuse. I'm the parent. I should have talked to him about having another AIDS test."

"It's not your fault that he's sick."

"Then why do I feel like it is!"

All he could do was hold her in his arms until she stopped crying. He had to fight back his own tears. Rudy was such a great kid, with so much to look forward to. Thrashing around for some words of comfort, he noticed Ethel drag herself into the room, a leather leash clasped between her teeth.

Sophie heard the movement, too, and looked around. "I guess she wants to go out." She sniffed.

"We're kind of busy, Ethel. Go find a tennis ball and guard it."

Pulling away, Sophie said, "You better take her out."

"I'd rather stay here and hug you. Besides, it's ten below zero out there."

She gave him a crumpled smile. "I guess she doesn't watch the weather report as faithfully as you do."

"Well, she should."

Wiping her nose on a tissue, Sophie tried another smile. "I love you."

"You better."

She brushed his graying brown hair away from his forehead. "Be patient with me, honey. This has been a rough couple of months."

"I know. We'll work it through."

Ethel dropped the leash at his feet.

"You better get going," said Sophie, moving over to their bureau and lifting a sweater from the top drawer.

"You *will* call if you need me, right? Someone can come get me out of the rehearsal room." He drew her close one last time and kissed the top of her head.

"Don't worry. I mean it."

"All right." He sighed, grabbing Ethel's leash. "Come on, Ethel old girl. Let's go take a brief walk by the mighty Mississippi."

"Put a sweater on her first," said Sophie. She disappeared into the bathroom.

"Which one?"

She stuck her head out of the door. "I think her 'Thank God I'm Swedish' sweatshirt is clean. It's by the front door."

Ethel was the only dog in the known universe who needed to make a fashion statement before breakfast. Hooking the leash to her collar, he dragged her out of the room.

Bram arrived at the station half an hour late. Since he'd only had four hours of sleep, it was the best he could do under the circumstances. As he headed down the hall to the conference room where the rehearsals were held—now referred to by one and all as the greenroom—he saw everyone milling around outside the door. Surely Dorothy hadn't postponed the entire rehearsal just because he was half an hour late.

"What's up?" he asked, approaching Mitzi Quinn. She

was sitting next to the water cooler, paging through a fashion magazine.

"Oh, morning," she said with a vague smile. She adjusted the collar of her red dress and gave a resigned shrug. "What else? We're waiting for Valentine to get here."

"Where is he?"

"We don't know," said Mitzi. "Dorothy called over to the hotel, but he wasn't there. I guess she figures he's on his way, so we're just waiting until he arrives."

An hour later they were still waiting.

At exactly ten-thirty, Dorothy's office door opened and she hurried out. "Everyone, we've got to get started," she ordered.

Bram was a bit startled by her abrupt appearance. He was also irritated that his leisure was about to end. For the past half hour he'd been sitting on a bench talking quietly to George Chambers about some of the sound effects he planned to use for the third episode. Everyone in the old cast agreed. George had changed more than any of them. The guy was a character, all right. Not many men his age would wear a ponytail and a thick white beard. Bram was fascinated by his stories, especially the one about his search for the perfect way to represent leaves rustling in the wind.

Dorothy clapped her hands. "Everybody, take a seat. I assume you all brought your scripts."

"But . . . what about Valentine?" said Mitzi, walking into the room behind George. "He still isn't here." She touched a hand lightly to the side of her dyed brown hair. It was a casual enough gesture, and yet Bram could read a certain nervousness in it.

"I'm well aware of that," said Dorothy, sitting down in the head chair. "But we can't put this off any longer. We have to do our first read-through today—and start working out the timing." She waited while everyone took a seat. "Now," she said, folding her hands on the table, "since we don't have understudies, I'm going to appoint one for Valentine. Until he shows up, Bram, I'd like you to take the part of Dallas Lane."

"Excuse me?" Bram nearly choked on his coffee. "But . . . I'm already the announcer."

"Historically, the announcer often took part in the show, often as the main character."

"But . . . I'm not an actor."

"Of course you are. You've done one role already and, I might add, you did it extremely well."

"But it was just a bit part."

"Look," said Dorothy, leaning forward in her chair, "this is just temporary, so don't get opening-night jitters on me. Valentine will show up sooner or later. Although," she added somewhat curtly, "I've just about reached my limit with that man."

Alfred Bloom entered the room, a cigar stuck in his mouth. It wasn't lit, but it still conveyed an attitude of defiance. As he sat down in an empty chair he gripped the stogie in his teeth and said, "Don't mind me. I'm just here to observe."

By the look on Dorothy's face, Bram could tell that Bloom's presence was not only unexpected but unwanted. It was the first time he'd shown up for a rehearsal, or, for that matter, the first time Bram had seen him at the station since last week.

Dorothy eyed him with thinly veiled annoyance as she continued, "So, Bram, I'd like you to pick up the narrative on page two. It's only Tuesday, so we've got plenty of time to polish the dialogue before we go on air."

Once again, her words startled him. "You sound like I'm definitely going on in place of Valentine next Sunday night."

"I won't lie to you. I'm mere inches from firing that man. He's tried my patience far too many times."

"But—"

"You're a natural actor, Bram. Hasn't anyone ever told you that? And your voice is perfect for the part. I'm not just making it up either. I've thought that all along. Remember, you don't have to memorize the lines, you merely have to read them." She paused, then continued. "I'm afraid that Valentine's absence this morning may have forced me into making a decision before I was entirely ready, but decide I will. Nothing comes before this program."

There it was again, thought Bram. The crusade.

Her eyes traveled from face to face until they came to rest on Bloom. "After this morning's run-through I'll have a better idea of how to proceed. So, let's just take it one step at a time, shall we?" She glanced down at the script in front of her. "Now, Dallas, you're talking to your girlfriend, Lucy." Her eyes shot to Mitzi. "Are you ready?"

"Yes," said Mitzi, though she didn't sound all that certain.

"Cue the music," said Dorothy, nodding to George.

Two hours later Bram returned to his office, feeling like a limp dishrag. His head was still spinning from the rehearsal. It was funny, but Dorothy had been right. He *did* have a certain flare for radio acting. Reduced to a voice, relieved of the tedium of having to memorize the script, get into makeup and a costume, and move around on a stage, he was free to concentrate on the words, to create a mood, a character. He felt an instant intimacy with the microphone, as if he'd been acting in front of it for years—which, in many ways, he had. Talk radio was nothing if not theatre.

But back to the matter at hand. He searched his desk for phone messages. He found two, but neither was from Sophie. He also found a sack of pretzels—not exactly what he had in mind for lunch.

Buzzing the secretary at the main desk, he said, "Judy, did I get any other calls while I was in rehearsal?"

"Hi there, Mr. Private Eye. What's this I hear about you becoming the station's newest leading man?"

"The stories of my death are greatly exaggerated."

She laughed. "That's not what I hear. We took an official office poll and decided that you'd make a much better poster boy than Valentine Zolotow."

"So would Pee-Wee Herman."

"Now, now. Don't sell yourself so short. With that handsome, wolfish smile of yours—"

"I do *not* have a wolfish smile."

"Ever looked in a mirror?"

"Are you flirting with me, Judy?"

"Would it do any good?"

He cleared his throat. "What about my messages?"

"Actually, I just got off the phone with your wife. She has nothing new to report about Rudy, but he's feeling better and you're not to worry. She'll call you later."

"Good." At least it wasn't bad news.

"Oh, and someone else called. A woman. I left the two messages on your desk. She called again just a few minutes ago. She wouldn't leave her name."

He wondered if it was the same woman who'd called yesterday, the one who said she had a letter from Arn O'Dell. "Was there a message?"

"No, nothing other than she'd try you later."

"All right," he said, glancing at the bag of pretzels. "I'm going over to Salisbury's for a quick lunch. If anyone's looking for me, I'll be back in twenty."

After taking the elevator down to the first floor, Bram dashed across the street to a small, one-story café sandwiched in between a mystery bookstore and a one-day photo shop. Most everyone at the station ate lunch at Salisbury's a few times a week. It was the closest restaurant around, and the food was cheap and pretty good.

Standing just inside the front door, Bram waited to be seated. There were several open spaces at the counter, but he wanted more room to spread out his reading material. He'd brought two newspapers with him, thinking he'd spend some time catching up on the day's headlines before his show started at one.

"Hey, Mr. B," said Jerry Dimitch, the restaurant's owner. He waved at him from behind the cash register. "Good to see you."

"The weather sure isn't hurting your business," said Bram, rubbing his hands together.

"Nah, we're lucky. We got lotsa regulars." He grabbed a menu and walked out from the back. "As a matter of strict fact, there was a lady in here a few minutes ago looking for you. She took a seat right over—" His eyes moved to the end of the counter. "Huh. She must have left. I been so busy, I never noticed."

"Who was she?" asked Bram.

"No idea. She didn't give a name. She just asked if you ever ate lunch here, and when I said you did, almost every day, she ordered a cup of coffee and acted like she was going to wait."

The *every day* part was an exaggeration, but Bram let it pass. "Did she say why she wanted to talk to me?"

"Like I said, she just asked if you ever came in. I got the impression she knew you worked across the street. But she was kinda jumpy. She kept looking around behind her, watching the door. And she had a purse with her that she clutched, you know, with both hands, right in front of her, like it had diamonds or gold in it and she wasn't going to let anyone take it away from her."

Bram was intrigued. Maybe it was the same woman who'd been trying to reach him all morning. "What did she look like?"

"Jeez, I'm terrible with faces, Mr. B. Middle-aged, I guess. Kinda hefty. Sorry, I don't remember anything else. Do you want a booth?"

"That would be great."

"You betcha, Mr. B. Our best booth, coming right up."

Bram followed him to a window table.

"You want to order now, or are you waiting for someone?"

"Give me a hot turkey sandwich and a cup of coffee. Black. And can you make it quick, Jerry? I'm in a hurry."

"Coming right up."

"Oh, and if you ever see that woman again, call me, okay? You've got the number of the station, right?"

"Sure thing." Jerry scurried off into the kitchen to place the order.

Bram waited until he was served his coffee and then he took out the Minneapolis paper and began looking over the front page. Nothing was particularly new. A national athletic franchise was strong-arming the state once again, insisting that another new stadium be built with local tax dollars, the fourth in recent memory. An animal-rights activist had attacked a truck carrying fur coats to a local department store, seriously injuring four people, including the activist himself. And the weather was cold and getting colder, just like the world was crazy and getting crazier.

Finishing his coffee, Bram decided to peruse the *Chicago Trib*. As he opened it to the opinion page his attention strayed to the street outside. There, standing next to him on the other side of the glass, was a woman, a hood pulled up around her head and a scarf covering her mouth. A purse was clutched nervously in both hands. The only part of her face not covered were the eyes, and they looked wary, like a scared animal's. She was undoubtedly the same woman who'd been asking about him earlier. He smiled pleasantly and nodded to the front door, hoping she'd take it as an invitation to come inside and talk.

She didn't move.

Bram began to feel uneasy. He didn't understand her reticence. After all, if she'd come here to find him—indeed, if she'd been trying to reach him by phone all morning—what was stopping her now? "Come inside," he mouthed, waving her inside.

Looking frightened, she backed away from the window and took off running.

"Damn," he muttered, feeling completely thwarted. Bursting out of the booth, he sidestepped a waitress and rushed to the door. As soon as he hit the street, he saw that it was too late.

Halfway down the block, a bus was pulling away from the corner. As it roared past, inside, near the back, he could make out a hooded profile. For one brief moment the woman turned and their eyes met. In that millisecond Bram could tell that her fear was gone. She was safe now, removed from danger—whatever she perceived that danger to be. He flailed his arms, urging her to stop, to come back. If she wanted to show him Arn O'Dell's letter, he was eager to see it. But she'd lost her nerve, and in turn, Bram had lost his one potential link to Justin Bloom's past.

18

By the time Bud Manderbach dragged himself into the office on Tuesday, it was nearly four in the afternoon. He nodded to his secretary on his way past the reception area, asking her to bring him a cup of coffee. It would be his first of the day.

Once seated behind his desk, he flipped through the stack of papers ready for him to sign, wondering how long it would take to finish it all. He had no taste for business today, yet he never put his name on anything without a thorough examination of the material—especially personal letters, ones he'd dictated. Bud didn't have a hangover, but he did have a splitting headache. Concentration wouldn't come easily.

When Loretta entered the room a few minutes later, he scowled as she set the coffee down in front of him. "Is this fresh?"

"Yes, sir. I just made it."

"Good." He took a sip, savoring the bitterness. He loved a strong cup of coffee. "Say, have you reached Wish Greveen yet?"

"No, I've left several messages for him at the Maxfield, but so far, he hasn't returned the calls."

"Well, damn it, that's not good enough. It's essential that I talk to him."

"I realize that, sir, but I don't know what else I can do."

"He's the writer of that radio program, for chrissake. A public man with public responsibilities."

"How would you suggest I proceed, Mr. Manderbach?" Her reasoned tones grated on his already raw nerves.

"Call him again. Leave another message. Threaten him with legal action if he doesn't return the calls. Next, call the radio station. Rattle some goddamn cages, Ms. Nallen. You've got to be aggressive. Determined."

"Yes, sir."

He narrowed one eye. "Loretta?"

"Yes?"

"This is all going in one ear and out the other, isn't it?"

"Why, no, sir. I'd be happy to"—she frowned in distaste—"rattle some goddamned cages, if that's what the job requires."

At first he thought she was being funny. The more he studied her perfectly composed face, the more he realized she was merely humoring him. He hated being humored. "Just leave me alone."

"Of course, Mr. Manderbach. If you have questions on any of that correspondence, just let me know."

Ten minutes later a knock on his door interrupted his reading. Looking up from the stack of papers, he said, "Come in."

Loretta popped her head inside the door. "I'm sorry to disturb you, but we've got a situation developing on the sixth floor. I think you should take care of it personally."

"Why?"

"It's your sister, B.B. I'm afraid . . . she's about to be arrested for shoplifting."

"What!" He shot out of his chair. "Call store security and tell them to meet me there right away."

"Of course."

Was that a smirk he saw on her face? "You think this is funny, Ms. Nallen?"

"No, of course not."

He gave her a nasty look as he bumped past her.

When the elevator doors finally opened, Bud followed the commotion to the furniture department, where he found B.B. standing in between two beefy policemen, looking fearful and contrite. He knew for a fact that neither emotion came naturally to her. Heavy red lipstick was smeared across one puffy, powdered cheek, while her eye makeup, applied with all the delicacy of a cement trowel, seemed to be dripping from the edges of her eyes. If she wasn't so overweight, she would have looked like a sad mime, all pathos and silence, dressed all in black—wool coat, tam, dress, and suede boots. As it was, she just looked dreadful.

"What's going on here?" demanded Bud, pushing past the knot of people gathered to watch his sister's public humiliation.

"Mr. Manderbach," said the floor manager, stepping forward out of the crowd. He appeared red-faced and nervous. "I just got here myself. It seems . . . actually, you see, Ms. Fillmore here"—he nodded to a young woman standing behind the cash register—"who is one of the new clerks we just hired for the Christmas rush—well, it appears she witnessed your sister take . . . I mean, ah, *remove* one of the smaller Swiss clocks from the store display and then hide it under her cloak. She thought, well, I mean, what *could* she think?" He tittered. When he saw that Bud wasn't smiling, his face lost all color. "It's just . . . somehow we must have failed to inform Ms. Fillmore about Ms. Manderbach's"—he cleared his throat, bent close to Bud, and whispered—"proclivities."

Bud glared.

"So, you see, Officers," continued the floor manager. He was beginning to sweat. "There's no problem. This was all a silly mistake." When neither of the men made a move to go, he added, "We apologize for any inconvenience this may have caused you, but you can leave now. Please. We can handle it from here."

The officers exchanged glances.

"Come on now, everyone. The show's over." The floor manager's attempt at lightness died in his throat. Returning his attention to the policemen, he said, "I mean, how can Ms. Manderbach steal from this department store when she owns it? Anything Ms. Manderbach takes from the floor is automatically covered by Mr. Manderbach's personal account. So you see, nothing is amiss. We can all go about our business."

"Shut up," snarled Bud. He'd had enough. This guy was a sniveling mass of incompetence.

Part of the basic instruction for every new Manderbach employee was a warning. On peril of losing their jobs, employees were instructed to look the other way when B.B. took something from the showroom floor—as she had, several times a week, for the last thirty years. B.B. was, very simply, a thief. Shoplifting was part illness, part hobby.

After Bud had bailed her out of jail for the third time back in 1961, he insisted that from then on, she do her shoplifting only at Manderbach's. That way, she wouldn't end up in prison. Thankfully, B.B.'s addled brain was able to grasp the value in the arrangement. This was the first problem they'd had in years. As he watched her now, standing alone, wrapped in her black garb and her sullen pout, he couldn't help but feel sorry for her. She was his sister and his best friend, but she was damaged. He usually managed to protect her from the outside world. His responsibility to her, indeed his love *for* her, mandated that sort of brotherly protection. And now, thanks to this jerk of a floor manager, he'd failed her. Heads would roll, that was for *damn* sure.

"You're positive everything's all right?" asked one of the officers, resting his hand over his gun.

"We're fine," said Bud. "We appreciate your time. If you'll pardon me now, I'm going to take my sister home."

B.B. looked up at him with grateful eyes.

"Sure thing, Mr. Manderbach," said the other policeman. "Say, just for your trouble, go get yourselves a cup of java and a slice of cake at the coffee bar downstairs. It's on the house."

The officers tipped their caps and left.

As Bud took hold of his sister's arm, ready to lead her to the elevators, he whispered to the floor manager, "Sack Fillmore. Immediately."

He swallowed hard. "Of course, Mr. Manderbach. Whatever you say."

"By the way, what's your name?"

"Me? I'm Ted. Ted Anderson."

"Well, Mr. Anderson, for the record, as soon as Ms. Fillmore is out of here and you've found a suitable replacement, you can leave. Take the rest of the day off."

"Really?"

"Sure. You've earned it."

"Why . . . thanks, Mr. Manderbach. That's really kind of you."

"No problem. Oh, and Ted, don't bother coming in tomorrow. Your services are no longer required."

The man's mouth dropped open.

Bud left him standing in the aisle, stunned and shaken. Under the circumstances, it was the least he could do.

Bud drove B.B.'s Cadillac home. He left his own car parked in the department-store ramp, thinking that he'd come back downtown later in the evening to get it. It was a short drive to the house on Summit Avenue. B.B. sat silently in the front seat, solemnly contemplating the growing dusk. Bud could tell she was upset. He wished that she'd talk about her feelings now instead of waiting until the middle of the night when her depressions were the worst. His sister often crept into his room to talk out her troubles. None of his four wives had welcomed these nocturnal visitations, though Bud could hardly turn her away.

"Maybe we should break out the Christmas ornaments and buy a tree." He hoped the idea would cheer her up. As he glanced at her, trying to gauge her response, he saw that amid the smear of her lipstick, the corners of her mouth had turned down. A single tear had escaped her left eye, rolling slowly over the rouge and the white powder. Up this close, B.B. looked like an embittered clown. A caricature. They were both caricatures, really. The clown and the aging pretty boy. Without the family largesse, they would have been a sorry pair. It was only the patina of wealth that kept the wolves at bay.

"Could we find a Norway pine?" mumbled B.B., sniffling into an Irish linen handkerchief.

"What?" The sound of her voice pulled him back from his reverie.

"You said we should get a tree. You know I only like Norway pines."

"Oh, sure. Whatever you want."

"Could we get it now?"

God, why had he suggested it? The thought of trimming a Christmas tree gave him a pain in the you-know-what. "I suppose."

"You don't sound very eager."

"It's been a bad day."

"In other words, I humiliated you."

"No, B.B., that's not what I meant."

She removed her tam and placed it in her lap. Keeping her eyes fixed straight ahead, she continued, "Why didn't you tell me you were going out last night?"

He waited a moment before answering. "How do you know I went out?"

"I came to your room. It was the middle of the night. You weren't there. You weren't anywhere. I even went out to look for you in the cook's cottage."

"You know you're not supposed to go out there." He was angry now. The cook's cottage, a small servants' residence behind the main house, was the only private spot he had in the world, the only place where he would brook no visitors, no interruptions to his solitude. A few years back he'd even removed the phone. Oh, every once in a while he'd take one of his girlfriends out there for a romantic evening, but whoever came inside did so by invitation only. B.B. wasn't allowed. Nor were the cats. The cook's cottage had been his retreat and his sanctuary ever since the last full-time servant had been let go, sometime during his first marriage. Bud still employed a cook and a housekeeper, but they didn't live in.

"You didn't answer my question," said B.B., twisting the tam around in her hand.

"I got a call from Giselle. I spent the night at her place."

"But why didn't you let me know?"

"What do I always tell you, B.B.? We're both adults. My comings and goings are no one's business but my own."

"But . . . I worry. Why don't you ever bring your girl-friends back to the house anymore?"

"Because you spy on us through the keyhole."

"I do not."

He put on his right-turn signal and turned the corner onto Summit Avenue, then looked over at his sister with an amused smile. "You haven't changed since you were ten years old."

"What a terrible thing to say."

He laughed out loud. As he was about to flip on the radio, he saw her take a small clock out from under her cloak and begin to examine it. "We've switched to clocks now, have we?"

"Don't be patronizing."

"What happens to your lamp collection now that your interests are elsewhere?"

"I've moved it all to the basement."

He groaned.

"Don't worry. It's perfectly organized."

"Of that I have little doubt."

"I ordered a subscription to *Antique Clock Digest* a while back. Timepieces are so fascinating, Buddy. I'll read some of my articles to you when we get home."

Oh, goody, he thought to himself. Thankfully, he had the presence of mind not to say the words out loud.

"Turn left up there." She pointed to the next stoplight.

"Why?"

"There's a Christmas-tree lot near Grand and Selby. I'm sure we can find something nice. Now, let's see. I wonder where I packed all the ornaments. Won't Mom and Dad be surprised when they walk in tonight and see a tree."

Sometimes B.B. got mixed up. Most of the time Bud just let it go. After all, at her age, what would be the point in sending her to a lot of doctors and therapists. She wasn't hurting anyone. And if she did occasionally forget what year it was, or who was alive and who was dead, what was the harm? Her consciousness, like her collecting instinct, was eclectic.

Bud felt B.B. lay her hand gently over his.

"I love you, Buddy. You're a dear brother. I'd do just about anything for you."

"I love you, too," he said, touched by her sweetness. "Very much. You're all the family I've got left." He felt tears well up behind his eyes.

"Merry Christmas." She smiled, holding the clock up to the fading light. "I think I'll put this under the tree when we get home."

April 18, 1959

Dear Mother:

Hope you got yesterday's letter. I didn't mean to frighten you, but you've got to be careful. Stay away from strangers. And let me know right away if you see that goon again.

Your letter of last week gave me a lot to think about. I was sorry to hear that Mitzi left town. I know she was hoping to make it big in radio. Dallas Lane, Private Eye was going to be her big break. I hope this cancellation hasn't wrecked her chances. In a way, I guess it's better that she left. The Twin Cities probably hold too many bad memories for her now. She's young. She should make a fresh start somewhere else.

I'm also glad to know that you've stored my belongings—that they weren't tossed out on the street. It just feels good to know that part of what was once my life still exists somewhere. I don't know when or if I'll ever return to the States, but it's just good to know my things are safe. I don't really think there's anything in my papers that would require special treatment, but since you have them at the house, they might as well stay there.

I've thought about my response to your letter and the only way I believe I can answer your questions is to go on with my story. That's exactly what I intend to do today.

After the night when I came clean and told Kay everything, we spent the next few days brainstorming, trying to come up with the best plan of action. As I said, Kay wanted to help me in my efforts to find out who was behind the Landauer hit-and-run, and offered to talk to Sally. You have to understand, Mom. Kay is—was—a very honest person. She thought the truth would be the most effective. She wanted to appeal to Sally's better self, tell her about the note I'd received, everything.

Of course, Sally already knew I worked as a reporter on the St. Paul paper, but since she never read newspapers, she didn't know I'd covered the Landauer case. The problem was, I felt that if Kay talked to her openly, bluntly, that Sally would get spooked and clam up. She was being paid well for her silence. She might even fear that her silence made her an accomplice in the whole mess. And frankly, in the light of what I already knew about Sally, I wasn't sure there was a "better self" to be appealed to. Still, Sally's cooperation was crucial. This boyfriend of hers wasn't going to incriminate himself. While somewhere down the line there might be some independent evidence that might establish his guilt, an eyewitness was the best means to put him behind bars. And, if I wasn't badly mistaken, Sally was that witness.

Kay and I dithered about it for days. Finally, I hit on an idea that I thought would work. I told her to make Sally swear to keep a secret, and then confide in her, woman-to-woman, that she, Kay, was attracted to a married man, someone she'd met recently. Sally knew that Kay and I were serious about each other, but she had a roving eye herself. She could easily understand an illicit sexual attraction. I thought that maybe the confession would get Sally to open up about the guy she'd been dating in July and August. Kay's theory, if you recall, was that this man *was married, and even if he wasn't, that kind of admission on Kay's part might lead to greater trust, and eventually, greater confidences. At least I felt it was worth a try.*

Kay waited until the following night when Jonnie was away at class. She poured some of the leftover wine from the party, and then popped some popcorn. She was trying to make it as relaxed an evening as possible. After Sally's third glass, Kay broached the subject. She said she'd met this guy. She told her about his sensual mouth, his sexy eyes, or whatever the hell women talk about when they gossip about men. To Kay's surprise, Sally demanded to know where she'd met the man. What was his name?

Well, Kay hemmed and hawed and then made something up, but Sally seemed to sense the lie. Except, the lie she sensed wasn't the underlying charade. She thought Kay was keeping this guy's identity from her for a reason and she was furious about it. Later, when Kay was recounting the story to me, she said it was almost as if Sally was jealous—like this man was someone she knew, but wouldn't name. Kay was nonplussed. The conversation ended by Sally stomping out of the room and taking the bowl of popcorn with her.

So much for my idea. Yet the more I thought about it, the more I realized we were on the right track. That's when I got another idea. I decided to talk to Sally myself, follow up on Kay's admission of a mystery man with deep depression on my part. I drove over to the apartment two nights later and knocked on the door. I'd already pre-arranged with Kay for her to be gone. I knew Jonnie was at class again that night, and hoped that Sally would be home. Luck was with me. I explained that I'd come to take Kay out to dinner, and acted angry, like I'd been stood up when she wasn't there. In a huff, I asked Sally if she'd like to join me for a drink at the nearest bar.

Well, Sally was never one to turn down either male company or the offer of a drink. She grabbed her coat and ten minutes later we were sitting at a dark table in Turner's Tap on Hennepin. I decided to go with Kay's instincts. I let

Sally get well oiled on several whiskey sours and then con-
fided that I was worried about Kay. I said I thought she
might be losing interest in me. I explained that I'd seen her
with another guy a few nights ago. They were in his car.

Sally jumped on the comment. What did the man look
like? What kind of car? I said that I couldn't see his face
very well and I didn't remember the make of the vehicle,
but they were parked right in front of the apartment
building. I was so stunned when I saw her kiss him that
everything just went out of my head, everything, that is,
except the desire to beat the crap out of him.

Sally grunted. "Was it a big Chrysler New Yorker?"
Her voice was eager. "Dark green? Plush seats?"

I took her lead and said, yeah, that sounded right.

She mumbled a few words. The only one I caught was
"bastard," but that was enough. I felt sure I'd struck a
nerve. Time would tell if it was the right one. I said to her,
"You seem like you know the guy."

"He's bad news," she said. Then she explained that if it
was the same guy she was thinking about—one they both
could have met at Manderbach's department store—that
Kay was in way over her head. This man preyed on
women. Used them. Hurt them. I said that I couldn't
believe Kay would get involved with a married man. "Oh,
he's really smooth. He's very unhappy in his marriage,
you know. Misunderstood. If he ever found a woman who
truly loved him, he'd divorce his wife in a minute." Her
laugh was so bitter, I cringed. Men really could be bas-
tards. As I thought of Mitzi I knew I was one myself. I also
knew then that Sally had really cared about this man, and
that she'd been dumped.

"What's his name?" I asked.

"Mr. Bigshot Shithead." By then, she was on her fourth
whiskey sour. Her words were kind of slurred, but the
venom was crystal clear.

"How come you know him?" I asked.

"I dated him late last summer. It was a complete
disaster. I just want to forget about it now."

But, I told her, she couldn't let Kay get hurt, especially since there was something she could do to prevent it. She had to tell me who he was. If I knew, I'd go right over there—wherever there was—and wipe up the floor with him. I'd make him pay. Maybe I'd even tell his wife. Get him in big trouble. She smiled at that, saying it would almost be worth it to give me his name. But not quite, I guess, because she left it at that.

I worked on her for another half hour, but her silence on the matter never budged. She did urge me to marry Kay, get her out of the situation before it was too late.

Finally, I said I was going to follow Kay until I found out who he was. She said great. She just couldn't pass the name on to me because of a "sort of business arrangement he and I have. I'm not supposed to tell anyone I know him."

I asked her why.

She leaned close and whispered, "It's a secret." She giggled, hiccuped, and then she winked.

I asked her what she meant by that, but she brushed the question aside. She said men were all beasts. By then, I think she'd forgotten she was talking to a man. I bought her another drink, waited until she was almost done with it, and then tried one last time. I knew that pushing this hard was a risk, but I went ahead anyway. I'll never forget what she said. This is as close as I can come to the actual words.

"This guy you dated, Sally, he was really bad news, right?"

"The worst."

"Did you ever see him hurt anyone?"

"He hurt me."

"Other than you?"

"Yeah. Once."

"Who?"

"I didn't know her."

"How'd he hurt her?"

"With something very very big." She said the words teasingly, leaning over and brushing my cheek with her lips.

"*Big like a car?*"

She was too plastered to be surprised by my lucky guess. "*Maybe.*"

"*Did you see it happen?*"

"*Maybe I did, maybe I didn't.*" She dropped her head on my shoulder and batted her eyelashes at me. "*But we can't talk about it because that would get Mr. Bigshot Shithead into trouble, and we couldn't have that. Mr. Bigshot Senior wouldn't like it.*"

"*Who's that? His dad?*"

"*Do you know any other Mr. Bigshot Seniors?*" She gave me another wink.

At this point, even in her drunken state, she saw where I was headed and demanded to know why I was asking so many questions. I told her I loved Kay, that I was simply trying to protect my woman. I needed her help. I needed a name. She lifted her head, thought it over, and then dropped it back on my shoulder. "*You poor sap,*" was all she said. I'm not sure, but as I looked down at her a few seconds later, I think she'd fallen asleep.

I didn't get a name out of her that night, but I was positive now that I was on the right track. I told Kay all about it the next day at lunch. She agreed that Sally held the key, but she didn't know what else to do. I mean, we couldn't exactly beat it out of her.

A couple of nights later Jonnie cornered Kay in one of the apartment bedrooms and said she knew Kay was cheating on me. That meant Sally and Jonnie must have talked. As I reflect on it now I realize that as a young psychology student, Jonnie saw herself as Bryant Avenue's answer to Dear Abby. There was right and there was wrong, and it was her job to point out error, especially when it came to relationships. When Kay asked her how she knew, Jonnie lied, she said she'd seen Kay and this man sitting in a parked car outside the building, necking. Since it never actually happened, the only way she could know about it was through Sally. Jonnie nodded to the ring I'd given to Kay and said, "*Doesn't that mean anything to you?*"

Kay said, sure it meant something. But it wasn't an engagement ring. Which was true. The night of the party, when we were sitting by the creek and I came clean about why I'd been following her that first day, I felt I needed to give her something to show her how much she meant to me. It was the ring you gave me when I got out of the army, the one I wore all the time. I planned to give her an engagement ring later. Anyway, Kay promised Jonnie that she wouldn't see the man again. That seemed to placate her and she left Kay alone for the rest of the evening.

The more I thought about it, the more curious Jonnie's whole approach seemed. I should have seen the writing on the wall, but I missed it completely. The thing is, Mom, if I'd left it there, stopped my search and simply enjoyed my new life with Kay, everything would have been all right. I did think about it. Some days I even forgot about Olga Landauer and Sally's mystery boyfriend. It's just, something inside me couldn't leave it alone. I had no idea then that my pursuit of a good story would put everyone's life in danger—including yours. If I had it it to do over again . . . but then, I don't. And hindsight is a useless exercise, as they say, the refuge of fools.

I did eventually find out the man's name, Mom. And that's what started the chain of events that led to Kay's death. I'll tell you more about it tomorrow. I have to take some medicine now and this particular pill usually makes me pretty sleepy, so I'll stop and resume again in the morning. I am feeling better, although my progress is slow. I go for long walks and struggle to put Kay's face out of my mind. I can't bear to think of her, of what our lives could have been. I simply have to empty myself. Is that what a wanderer's mind becomes? A void? Vacant and inexpressive because to think, to remember, creates too much pain? When I'm done with my storytelling, Mom, will I retreat into cowardice and spend the rest of my life hiding, even from myself?

Until tomorrow,

All my love,
Justin

19

On Friday evening, Sophie pushed through the swinging door into Rudy's hospital room carrying a Scrabble game under her arm. "I'm going to beat the pants off you tonight," she said, setting it down on the bedside table. "I feel lucky." Behind her cheerful smile, she examined her son for a sign, any sign, that would assure her he was getting better.

The AIDS test had finally come back, and much to everyone's great relief, it was negative. And yet, after Rudy's initial euphoria over the death sentence that had just been lifted, he'd sunk into a new depression over his continued illness.

For days now he'd been listless and pale, thwarted by his inability to meet his personal and professional responsibilities. After much agonizing, a decision had been made to postpone the commitment ceremony. It was hard for Sophie to keep encouraging him, especially in the face of such a deep personal disappointment, but she had to try. Rudy had a bleeding ulcer, and he still wasn't out of the woods. The doctor wasn't sure the bleeding had stopped.

Sophie tried as best she could to stay centered, not to give in to her fears. While she didn't want to be a Pollyanna, she knew Rudy needed people around him who were positive. He'd been sleeping a lot the last few days. Yet tonight, he seemed much more alert. She could even see a hint of color in his cheeks.

Switching off the TV set, Rudy stared at the game in front of him. "The problem is, Mom, you can't spell."

"Oh really?" This was the first time he'd joked with her in days and it felt good. She sat down, crossed her legs, and folded her hands calmly in her lap. Nodding to the plants, she said, "This place is starting to look like a greenhouse."

"Yeah." He sighed. He transferred his gaze to the window ledge. "I guess you could call it poinsettia central. A couple of school friends came by this afternoon. They brought the new one with the pink leaves."

"It's pretty. Puny, but pretty. All right," she said, breaking out the board. "Let's get down to business."

"Don't you want to hear what the doctor said? She was in to see me just a little while ago."

Sophie was surprised and more than a little frustrated. Last she'd heard, the doctor planned to come by after dinner. She'd made it a point to arrive *before* dinner so that she could get the latest report firsthand. "Sure," she said, wondering if he could read the anxiety in her face. "What'd she say?"

Rudy clasped his hands behind his neck and gave her a triumphant smile. "I'm being released tomorrow."

"Rudy! That's great news." She released the breath she hadn't even realized she was holding. "What else did she say? Is the ulcer under control? No more bleeding?"

"That's what she thinks. They've been watching me carefully all week. My hemoglobin count is coming back up, so I don't feel so tired."

Sophie relaxed back into her chair. "Good."

"They may give me one more transfusion tonight. I guess that funny noise I was hearing inside my head was actually my heart. I didn't have much oxygen in my blood, so my heart had to work really hard."

"And why did you get an ulcer in the first place?"

"They aren't one hundred percent sure. It could have been stress, or it could have been the pain medication I was taking for my back. If you mix Naprosyn with other aspirin-based painkillers, which I was, you can get in real trouble. Since my back is better, they've taken me off the painkiller."

"What about food? Can you eat normally when you get home?"

"That's the dreary part. I'm being put on a bland diet for a while. Spices don't cause ulcers, I guess, but they can irritate the stomach. Lucky me. Just in time for the holidays." He made a sour face.

But it wasn't the end of the world, thought Sophie. Bland didn't have to mean boring. What bothered her most was that he was so thin. Rudy had always been slender, but now, after not eating for nearly a week, he was skin and bones. She'd need to check with the doctor first about all the particulars, but she had to do something to fatten him up.

"What?" he said, giving her a suspicious look. "What's cookin' inside that devious mind of yours?"

"Perfect metaphor. How does homemade bread pudding with caramel sauce sound?"

He thought it over. "Is it bland?"

"Absolutely. And delicious."

"What are my other options?"

"Custard. You always liked custard when you were a kid. Have you ever had homemade custard pie?"

He shook his head.

"And your grandma's famous chicken stew with dumplings."

"Stop, you're making me hungry."

"Good. Then I'm doing my job." It was going to be so great to have him out of the hospital and on the mend. "When do you leave here tomorrow?"

"I'm being released before lunch. John doesn't work on Saturdays, so he'll come get me."

"All right. But leave dinner to me."

"You're going to bring something over?"

"Rudy," she said, giving him her most pregnant-with-meaning smile, "I'm going to stuff you with marvelous, rapturous, scrupulously bland food until it's coming out your ears."

Her words elicited a wide grin. "That's the kind of pain I can stand. You're the greatest, Mom." He reached for her hand. "I'm a very lucky guy, and I know it."

The sound of the door being opened interrupted them. The same cleaning woman Sophie had seen on the first night poked her head inside the room.

"Hey, Molly." Rudy smiled. "I wondered if you weren't on tonight. How's it going?"

She opened the door farther. "Same old same old," she said, tossing back her long frizz of red-gray hair. "I thought maybe you were alone and might like some company."

"Come in and meet my mother."

"We've already met," said Molly with a mischievous grin. "Sort of. Hey, I hear you're gettin' sprung tomorrow."

"That's what they tell me."

"Congratulations. Say, not to change the subject, but your father isn't around, is he? I thought maybe I'd get his autograph for my girlfriend."

Rudy looked confused. "My father?" He cocked his head. "Oh, you must mean Bram."

"Baldric isn't your dad?"

"Sorry. He's my mom's second husband." He glanced at Sophie. "Is he coming by this evening?"

She shook her head. "He's got a rehearsal."

"Say," said the woman, leaning casually against the doorway. "I hear he's taken over for Valentine Zolotow."

"That's right. You must follow the radio program."

"Now and then."

Sophie knew her demeanor had grown unusually formal, but there was something about this woman she didn't like—or more specifically, something she didn't trust.

"Well," said Molly, lifting a pack of cigarettes out of her pocket, "I guess I'll go take my break somewhere else. Catch you later, Red." She gave him a wink and then backed away from the door, letting it swing shut.

"Red?" repeated Sophie.

He shrugged, pointing to his hair. "Hey, you didn't tell me Bram was going on Sunday night for sure."

"How well do you know that woman?"

"You mean Molly? Not well. She usually comes in to say hi if she's on duty. She cleaned my room the second day I was here. We kinda struck up a conversation. I like her, Mom. She's funny."

"Who is she?"

"Why the third degree?"

"Just answer the question."

He gave another shrug. "She likes boxcar racing and owns a Harley. Other than that, I know nothing about her. Jeez, lighten up, will you? You'd think she was trying to poison my food."

"Has she ever been near your food?"

He shot her a disgusted look.

"It's a reasonable question."

"No, it's not. Besides, until this afternoon, I haven't eaten any food, remember? I've been on IVs."

She knew that. She'd just forgotten.

"Do you realize how silly you sound?"

"All right, all right." She got up to check the plants. They were probably dry as dust. To be honest, she did feel a little embarrassed that she'd reacted so excessively. With her back to Rudy, she decided to introduce a new subject. "The police now consider Valentine Zolotow officially missing."

He whistled. "No kidding. I wonder what happened to the old guy? Do you think he took off, ran away for some reason?"

"I wish I knew. The police came to the hotel this afternoon with a warrant. They searched his room."

"And?" He sat up eagerly.

"It looks like everything was still there. If a guy was going to skip town, you'd think he'd at least pack a suitcase."

"So, do the police think something bad happened to him?"

"One of the officers told me that they interviewed a cab-driver who waits outside the Maxfield for fares. He told the police that he dropped a man fitting Valentine's description off at the River Bend Casino late Monday afternoon. It sounds plausible because Valentine spent most of his free time gambling. At least, it's their best lead so far."

"And what about Bram? Is he prepared to go on the air in Valentine's place?"

Sophie carried two plants over to the sink. As she watered them she said, "He's nervous, and he's milking everyone's sympathy for all it's worth."

"Yeah." Rudy grinned. "That sounds like him."

"But honestly, I think he's in seventh heaven with all the new attention he's receiving. You know how Bram loves the spotlight." She turned around and held up the plants. "These should now survive the night."

"Thanks."

After placing them back on the window ledge, she opened the Scrabble board and set it on the table. "So, let's quit stalling and get down to business."

"You want a chance to redeem yourself after last night's ignominious defeat."

"Pride goeth before a fall, son."

"We'll see."

Around midnight, Rudy woke suddenly from a deep sleep. The lights were off in the room and the door was closed, but a tiny covered bulb next to the bed gave off enough light for him to see. As he raised his head to look around he was startled to find a woman sitting in the chair next to him. It was Molly. "What are you doing here?" he asked, his voice still thick with sleep.

"Thinking," she replied softly.

He rubbed his eyes awake and then pressed a button, raising the back of the bed. Looking at her now, he could tell she was upset. "Is something wrong?"

She watched him, then looked away.

"You . . . want to talk about it?"

"I don't know."

"Sometimes it helps."

"Sometimes it doesn't."

She'd changed out of her uniform into street clothes. A hooded winter coat rested on her lap. On top was a purse.

"How come you came in here?"

She shrugged. "It was quiet. You were sleeping. I figured I couldn't disturb you."

"I see."

"You sound disappointed."

"No, it's just . . . I thought we were getting to be friends."

Her eyes flicked to him and then away. "Is that what you thought?"

"Yeah." He waited, sensing that she might tell him more if he didn't push.

Looking down at her hands, she said, "I've got a hard decision to make. One that involves a relative of mine. See, I . . . have some information that would shed some light on a crime. A bad crime."

"Then you should tell what you know."

"It's not that simple," she said sharply. "If I do tell, I'm putting my life in danger."

That stopped him. "Danger, like in—"

"I could get killed. I'm not joking."

"I didn't think you were."

A frown carved a deep furrow between her eyes. "My conscience tells me to do one thing, my fear, another."

"Is there any way you could provide this information anonymously?"

"I'm not sure. I have a letter, one that no one's ever seen before, but it would need to be verified. At least, I think it would. I'm the best person to do it, maybe the only person who could."

"Why?"

She didn't answer immediately, but seemed to be weighing something in her mind. Finally, she said, "It was written to me. By my grandfather. He's been dead a long time."

"You couldn't, like, verify it over the phone."

His comment caused her to smile. "Rudy, if the letter surfaces, I'm a dead woman."

"I guess you do have a problem."

They sat in silence for several minutes.

Finally, Rudy said, "Maybe you should just forget about it. Put the letter away and get on with your life."

"I tried that. It didn't work. See, I've had the letter since I was twenty-three. My grandfather told me to burn it when I was done reading it. If I'd followed his advice, I wouldn't have this dilemma."

"But you kept it."

"I had to."

Very softly, he replied, "Maybe that's your answer."

She looked up at him, but didn't respond.

"Listen, Molly, I'm probably not the one you should be talking to. I'm sure there's someone else out there who could give you much better advice than me."

She thought about it for a moment, then said, "You better get some sleep, kid."

"Will you be all right?"

She got up, moving her bulky frame closer to the bed. "We redheads gotta stick together."

"I wish you'd let me know how this all comes out."

She said nothing. Instead, she picked up her coat and purse and crossed to the door. Before she left, she turned to take one last look at him. "You'll probably read about it in the obituaries. So long, kid. Take my advice. Stay out of hospitals. They're bad for your health."

20

"A toast to our leading man, Bram Baldric!" Heda's voice rose over the din of laughter and conversations. "Here's to many more successful episodes."

For the past few minutes Sophie had been standing next to the bar in Heda and Dorothy's suite, talking to Mitzi Quinn. When she heard her husband's name being called, she quickly joined everyone by the fireplace for a round of enthusiastic applause. Bram and Heda stood in front of the mantelpiece, both looking flushed by champagne and a third successful broadcast.

After thanking Heda for the opportunity to try his hand at

radio drama, Bram took a rather silly bow and then blew Sophie a kiss. God, but she loved him. At times like this, he was irresistible.

Since Sophie hadn't eaten any dinner, all this toasting and celebration was beginning to make her feel light-headed. This was Heda's sixth toast, all preceded by waiters moving about the crowd, refilling everyone's champagne flutes. It was a lovely party. In lieu of a tree, Heda had decorated the mantelpiece with pine bows, red and gold ribbons, and delicate glass ornaments. Candles burned in every corner of the living room. And the food table looked fabulous. Except, ever since she and Bram had arrived, she'd been so busy talking she hadn't managed to make her way over to it.

Sophie had spent the afternoon at Rudy's apartment preparing him a pot of homemade chicken soup and fresh-baked Swedish *limpa*, his favorite bread. John was working the afternoon and early-evening shift over at the brewery and wouldn't be home until ten. Rudy had been out of the hospital now for one full week. He was still tired and depressed, especially since he'd had to take incompletes in most of his classes. Sophie tried as often as she could to spend time with him. She'd cut back on her hours at the hotel, and yet with the added responsibility of a sick son, she wasn't finding many hours to sleep. She applied more makeup to hide the dark circles under her eyes, but she wasn't fooling anyone, especially her husband.

While Rudy ate his dinner they'd switched on the radio and listened to the third episode of *Dallas Lane, Private Eye*. It was Bram's second time in the lead role, and even though Sophie knew her husband had lots of vocal and dramatic talent, she was amazed at how easily he'd moved into the part, making it his own.

The episode began with Dallas limping into DuFour's Bar, where Lucy, his girlfriend, patched up his cuts and bruises. He'd been beaten badly by several thugs in the previous episode, but not enough to scare him off the case. After a couple of belts of bourbon, he called Irene Hewitt, the woman who'd hired him, demanding that she contact her son right away. Dallas wanted to meet with the infamous Judson Hewitt and ask him a couple of leading questions. He knew Judson had refused to talk to the police or his lawyer about the murder of his girlfriend, Darla, but at this point, Dallas was sick of getting the runaround. If Mrs. Hewitt couldn't convince her son to talk, Dallas was off the case. He thought it would get a rise out of the old gal, and it did.

Several hours later Dallas was shown into Judson Hewitt's jail cell. After some verbal sparring, Judson broke down and admitted that he was scared. He knew it looked bad for him. Little by little, Dallas pulled the story out of him.

It seemed that in his job as a reporter, Judson had been covering a hot story for the local newspaper. It concerned the hit-and-run death of the sister of a prominent manufacturing magnate in Mill City. Officially, no one knew the identity of the person who'd run the woman down, but Judson said he'd discovered the truth after receiving a note from a friend of Darla's. It was this hit-and-run driver who'd set Judson up, who'd made him look like a murderer. At all costs Judson had to be discredited before he could tell what he knew. The hit-and-run driver's name was Rob Singleton. He was heir to the Singleton's department-store fortune. The problem was, Judson had no proof. He hoped Dallas could find some hard evidence before it was too late.

As Rudy ate his dinner Sophie sat next to the bed and listened to the episode unfold. She couldn't help but wonder if this new twist in the story had anything to do with the real-life Justin Bloom and his alleged murder of Kay Collins. Tomorrow, of course, there would be the usual avalanche of speculation about the implications. Bram's afternoon radio show had become the major forum for discussion of the old murder case, especially as it paralleled the new radio drama. Officially, the radio station was still denying any similarity between the two stories. However, in recent days, the denials were becoming not only soft, but less frequent.

After the episode ended—with its usual melodramatic cliffhanger—Sophie hurried to clean up the kitchen in Rudy and John's apartment. Just as she was about to put on her coat to go, Rudy sauntered into the room and sat down at the table, curious for more information about Valentine Zolotow. She quickly explained that the current theory floating around the station was that Valentine had made a huge killing at the gambling tables and he'd simply taken off. The sad part was, no one particularly mourned his loss, or even found it all that surprising. Sophie figured that unless the police found his body, they might never really know what had happened for sure.

Sophie left Rudy's apartment shortly after seven, hoping she wouldn't be late for the Christmas party, which was to begin at eight. It was the first time Heda had invited any of the radio-station employees and their spouses up for drinks, and though Sophie had a mound of work waiting for her in her office, she knew it would disappoint Bram terribly if she didn't attend.

By the time she got back to the Maxfield, all she had time for was a quick shower. As she sat down on the bed to dry off, she closed her eyes and nearly fell asleep. Ethel watched from the doorway as she slipped into her slinky red sequined party dress. After a few extra minutes at the makeup table, she heard Bram come in the front door. She met him in the living room with a big smile and a congratulatory kiss.

Sophie was standing now in front of the fireplace in Heda's suite, her exhaustion held at bay by the champagne and all the praise being heaped on her husband.

Heda looked wonderful this evening in an Italian silk evening gown. Her manner was not only gracious, but posi-tively ebullient. Dorothy was working the crowd herself, talking nonstop about the splash tonight's show had undoubt-edly made. Sophie had come to the conclusion that Dorothy's only interest in the show was a professional one. She seemed entirely disconnected from the larger ramifications of the story line, sloughing off as idle speculation any comments made to her about the Kay Collins murder. She was, however, an astute businesswoman who understood intuitively how to promote. Privately, Bram had wondered aloud if the reason the station continued to deny any correlation between the two stories was that Dorothy realized those denials were a far more powerful tool than admitting the obvious.

Heda, on the other hand, seemed to grow impatient when even the merest hint of the old murder case came up. Sophie had seen her change the subject several times tonight already. As the crowd grew more oiled and tactless it didn't take an Einstein to predict a possible disaster in the making.

Feeling an arm slip around her waist, Sophie looked up and saw Bram smiling down at her. "Having fun?" he asked, kissing the top of her head. Since he was nearly a foot taller, head kissing was one of his preferred methods of affection.

She fluffed her short strawberry-blonde hair, making sure he hadn't mussed it beyond repair. "So far I've resisted that chocolate torte, but it's about to win the battle."

"You'll love it," he said, wiping his mouth with a napkin. "I just had my second piece." Noticing her disapproving stare, he added, "Come on, Soph. Don't be a Grinch. It's a Christmas party. If you don't go home stuffed, you simply haven't celebrated with the right spirit."

"Is that right?"

"Yes," he said, bending down to give her a real kiss. "It is."

"You're in a pretty good mood, buster."

"Wouldn't you be? I'm the toast of the town. Well, part of the town. This living room, to be exact. We'll see how the other part feels about it in the morning. Hey," he said, popping a stuffed cherry tomato into his mouth, "did you see Larry Blodnik go after that new intern? God, he's like a heat-seeking missile."

She held on to his hand as she inched toward the dessert table. "Where's Alfred Bloom tonight? I thought he'd be here."

"Beats me." He reached for a slice of pecan pie, but Sophie slapped his hand. "Let's keep it under one hundred thousand calories for the evening, okay? Otherwise you won't fit into your Christmas present."

"What is it?"

"A tent."

He gave her a pained smile.

Motioning for him to bend down, she whispered in his ear, "Who's that goon standing next to the front door?"

His eyes flicked to the man, then away. "From what I understand, Heda has a bodyguard."

"Why?"

"Good question. One that undoubtedly has an answer, I just don't know what it is." As he straightened up, his gaze traveled around the room. "Have you talked to Mitzi yet tonight?"

"Briefly. We got separated during one of the toasts."

He nodded discreetly to a chair in the corner where Mitzi sat alone. "She's been drinking a lot. Not talking very much. George sat with her for a while, but he's off somewhere else now doing his Santa Claus routine. I wonder what's up."

"Well, she did mention that her daughter is flying into town this week. They've always spent Christmas together, ever since Mitzi and her husband got a divorce. Maybe Mitzi's afraid her daughter won't like it up here."

Bram reflected for a moment, then said, "What's not to like about thirty-foot snowdrifts and four-hundred-below-zero temperatures?"

"Yeah, can't be the weather."

"So, if it's not the arrival of her daughter, what's got her so depressed? You're the one with all the people skills, Soph. Go talk to her again. See what you can find out."

"Where are you going?"

"I want to stick close to Heda, try to head off any unpleasant comments about Justin Bloom and the old murder case. That woman's got a real temper. I haven't seen it firsthand, but believe me, it's legendary. Some poor sap's going to say the wrong thing and she's going to explode all over him."

"Good man."

He gave her a half-lidded smile. "Fasten your seat belt. It's gonna be a bumpy night."

"I'll remember that, Bette."

With one final, amused glance, he was off again, wading into the knot of people surrounding Heda Bloom.

After taking another glass of champagne from a tray of flutes sitting on the bar, Sophie edged her way slowly through the crowd toward Mitzi. On a whim she walked first into the rear pantry area to see if the Maxfield's kitchen had catered the affair. The food didn't look familiar, though Heda may have designed the menu herself. As she passed in front of a rear door, she heard two soft knocks. She stopped and looked around, but no one seemed to be interested in answering it. Moving closer to the door, she waited. After a couple of seconds she heard them again. It almost felt like a signal. As if the person on the other side of the door were waiting for some prearranged person on the inside to respond.

She checked the time. Exactly ten o'clock. She wondered . . . would it be a terrible breach of Heda's security to answer it? Her hand touched the dead bolt, but once again she waited. Almost a full minute later the knock came a third time. Overwhelmed by her own curiosity, she flipped back the bolt and opened the door. At the same moment a woman in a chef's uniform rushed up to her, thrusting out her hand to prevent the door from opening farther. "This door is to remain closed, lady. No one opens it. We've got strict orders."

But it was too late. Outside, Sophie could see a man she recognized. "Mr. Greveen," she said, smiling pleasantly. She turned her back to the caterer, ignoring her angry protests. "I was hoping I'd see you here tonight."

For a moment he seemed confused. "I'm sorry, if we've met—"

"Sophie Greenway," she said quickly, yanking the door all the way open. "I'm the owner of the hotel. I checked you in the afternoon you arrived." She glanced meaningfully at the woman in the chef's uniform until the protestations ceased. "Won't you come in?"

He seemed hesitant. His eyes searched the hallway behind her for signs of life.

"If you're looking for the party, it's in the living room. I'm afraid this isn't the front door."

Fixing the woman behind Sophie with a questioning look, he asked, "I wonder if you'd go find Dorothy Veneger for me. Just ask anyone, they'll know who she is. Tell her there's someone here who would like to speak to her for a minute."

When the woman didn't move, Sophie turned and glared. "Do you mind?"

"Oh, all right," said the woman grudgingly. "But I'm not taking any heat for this door being opened." She turned on her heel and marched off down the hall.

"Thanks," called Greveen to her retreating back.

Sophie noticed now that he was cradling a magnum of French champagne in one arm. "You're sure you won't come in? I know there are lots of people here who'd love to meet you."

A faint smile touched his lips, then faded. "I don't like crowds."

That was an understatement. As far as she knew, with the exception of Dorothy, no one at the station had seen or heard from him since his arrival three weeks ago. He didn't return phone calls and he didn't go out; at least, not that anyone saw.

"You know, Ms. Greenway, I should thank you."

"For what?"

"That doctor you recommended to me. When I arrived at the hotel, I think I had the flu, but just to be on the safe side, I scheduled a full physical. I believe I go in tomorrow morning. It's always best to have a physician recommendation when in a new city, don't you agree? You can't trust just anyone with your health."

As he touched a hand to his tie Sophie once again noticed the unique ring on his left hand. "I'm glad you liked him. He's been our family physician for years."

Dorothy came rushing down the hallway and interrupted their conversation before Sophie could get past the current topic to the questions foremost in her mind.

"Mr. Greveen, what a surprise," said Dorothy, a bit out of breath. "I didn't expect to see you tonight." She seemed at an uncharacteristic loss for words.

"No," he said softly. "But I wanted you to have this." He handed her the bottle. "It only seemed right that I bring something to the party, since I couldn't come myself. I have that previous engagement, if you recall."

"Of course," she said, glancing at Sophie.

Beneath Dorothy's studied calm, Sophie now noticed a certain agitation.

"I'll make sure Heda knows you brought it by." She seemed impatient to return to the living room. "Is there anything else you'd like me to tell her?"

Before he could answer, Sophie heard heavy footsteps at the other end of the hall. She glanced to her right and saw Alfred Bloom's lumbering frame making straight for them. She'd never actually met the man, but Bram had pointed him out to her in the lobby last week. Once seen, Alfred Bloom wasn't easily forgotten.

"Are you hiding back here?" his voice boomed as he got closer. It was a subdued boom, but the sound was so deep it seemed to resonate off the walls.

Dorothy's lips thinned in distaste. As she turned to face him she backed up, closing the door on Wish Greveen. "Alfred, how . . . good of you to stop by."

"You can drop the bullshit, Dorothy. Consider it my Christmas present."

Their annoyance with each other seemed of the long-standing variety. Dorothy gave Sophie a pained smile, as if to say she was sorry for Alfred's rudeness, but couldn't do anything about it.

"We've gotta talk," he snarled.

"I don't have time for one of your tantrums right now," she replied calmly.

"You're an employee. Don't forget it."

She bared her teeth in imitation of a smile. "It may gall you that I'm also your mother's friend, but it's a fact. If you didn't fight me all the time, you might see that we're on the same side. I have only her best interests at heart."

He stood very close to her, obviously enjoying the sense of power his added height gave him. Sophie loathed men who tried to intimidate women with their size.

Thankfully, Dorothy wasn't buying. "What's so important that you need my immediate attention?"

His eyes flicked to Sophie.

As Dorothy noticed his reticence, her expression grew even more distant. "Alfred, you know Sophie Greenway, don't you? She's Bram Baldric's wife. She also owns the hotel, so mind your p's and q's or she may toss you out."

He glared, clearly unimpressed by either piece of information.

Sophie wanted to add that she could also tie her shoelaces and count to ten, but decided that in his current mood, nothing would impress him.

"Make an appointment with my secretary tomorrow," said Dorothy, folding her arms over her chest. "I'm sure I can fit you in sometime in the afternoon."

Alfred grabbed her shoulders. "Listen, you little idiot, the police want to see us right away. They're waiting down in the lobby."

"Get your hands off me."

"Did you hear what I said?"

She straightened the neck of her dress. "Yes. Why didn't you say that right away?"

"They found Valentine Zolotow."

"What?" His news stopped her. She turned to face him. "Where?"

"About half a mile from the River Bend Casino. He's dead."

She searched his face for an explanation. "How . . . why?"

"I don't know. But we're about to find out. Come on. They're waiting for us."

She continued to scrutinize his face. "Have you told your mother?"

He nodded. "And several people who were standing next to her when I gave her the news. It's not a secret, Dorothy. She wants us both to go downstairs and talk to the cops right away. She doesn't feel up to it herself."

Dorothy turned to Sophie. "Will you do me a favor? Tell everyone that as soon as we're done speaking with the police, we'll be back up to explain what we've learned."

"Sure," said Sophie.

Dorothy smiled gratefully. The smile evaporated as she followed Alfred down the hall and out the front door.

For the next half hour Sophie drifted from conversation to conversation. The news of Zolotow's death had spread through the crowd like fire in a tinder-dry forest. Everyone had a different opinion about what had happened.

Around eleven, feeling the need for a respite from the endless speculation, Sophie sat down in a quiet corner next to Mitzi Quinn. Mitzi seemed to be the only one present not interested in talking nonstop about Valentine's untimely demise. Instead, she sat silently near the window, sipping her champagne and gazing down at the St. Paul skyline.

"What an evening," said Sophie, discreetly kicking off one of her red satin shoes. It had been pinching her toes all evening.

Mitzi nodded somewhat formally, but offered no comment of her own.

"I wonder how long Dorothy and Alfred will be talking to the police?"

She gave an indifferent shrug. "It doesn't matter. We all know how he died."

"We do?"

Mitzi nodded to the front door. Alfred had just entered the room, looking suitably grim. "Here comes the announcement."

Holding his hands up for silence, Alfred moved through the crowd to where his mother was sitting. "I'm afraid I have some bad news," he began, waiting until everyone had quieted down before continuing. "It seems Valentine Zolotow has been dead since sometime last week. His body was found earlier today in the woods near the River Bend Casino. He had a bruise on the back of his head, but death was due to exposure. An autopsy will be performed tomorrow. Right now the best guess is, he was hit over the head and left to die in the freezing cold."

"It was murder?" came an incredulous voice from the crowd.

Alfred put his hand on his mother's shoulder and nodded gravely.

"He's here," whispered Mitzi. She let her glass slide to the floor and then lurched uncertainly to her feet.

"Pardon me?" said Sophie, standing to help steady her. She was afraid she might fall over.

"I said *he's here*." Her words were slurred, but she said them more boldly this time. Several people turned to stare.

"Who's here?" asked Sophie. She had no idea what the woman was talking about.

"*He* is," she insisted. Weaving into the crowd, she said, "Are you all blind? Am I the only one around here who can see what's happening?"

"Please," called Heda Bloom. "Someone help her into my bedroom. She's . . . upset. She needs to lie down."

"I'm fine," said Mitzi indignantly. She pushed her way toward the door. "This is a nightmare," she mumbled. "*My* nightmare."

"Help her," said Heda, a frightened look on her face. She motioned to the bodyguard. "See that she gets to her room safely."

"Leave me alone," said Mitzi, shaking off the man's hands. "I can take care of myself." With that, she stumbled out the door, leaving everyone inside, including Sophie, to wonder what she'd been talking about.

April 21, 1959

My dearest Justin:

I'm afraid I have some disturbing news to pass on to you today about Kay's roommate Sally Nash. Last week, Sally's body was found at the edge of a cornfield about forty miles north of the city. The man who owned the land was out looking at his fields when he discovered the body under a pile of wet leaves. Since it's been a late spring, the snows are just now starting to recede. I didn't notify you right away because

I wanted to see what the medical examiner would say about the death. This morning, the story was in both papers. It appears that she died from a gunshot to her head. Her body was dumped in the field sometime last winter. The article said she'd been dead close to four months, so that would put the date near the first of the year, right around the time Kay died. I don't believe in coincidences, son. In my mind, and in many others, there has to be a connection between the two.

As I expected, Kay's and Sally's deaths were linked in the newspaper stories, though the articles stopped short of saying you'd murdered them both. I guess I should be grateful for small favors. The police are investigating the matter. There's still no word about Jonnie Apfenford. If I were her mother, I'm afraid I'd fear the worst.

Justin, do you know anything about this? You must tell me the truth! You say these past few months have seemed like a bad dream to you, but you must understand, they seem that way to me, too—a dream that never seems to end. When I wake in the morning, I wonder what new horror awaits me. I know Cedric feels the same way, though he refuses to talk about your disappearance any longer. He read the papers today and then left for the station without saying so much as a word, not even goodbye. He wants to believe in you, but every day it gets harder and harder. His health is deteriorating because of the strain. This town has convicted you of one murder, and now with the discovery of Sally's body, your name will be smeared all over again. My son has been taken from me and my husband is withdrawing into silence and sickness. And what's perhaps worst of all is that here I am, going on and on about me and mine when two innocent young women have been murdered! Their lives have ended, Justin. What am I to think?

For months I've been desperate to have you come home, to see your face again, hold you in my arms. Now I realize that's impossible. All I can hope for is clarity. Write to me soon, son. Finish your story.

Love,
Mom

21

"Damn it, you can't ignore me forever! Open this door!" When Bud got no response, he pounded harder. "I've had it, Greveen. You don't return calls, you won't even answer your goddamned phone. Who the hell do you think you are?" He knew he was losing control, but didn't care. He'd come to the end of his rope. With one mighty shove, he tried to smash the door down, but it stood solid.

"Hey, knock it off," said a voice from the other end of the hall.

Bud looked over his shoulder and saw a middle-aged man in his drooping pajamas standing in one of the far doorways.

"It's after midnight, asshole. If you want to get tight and have a fight with your wife, do it somewhere else."

"Shut up," snarled Bud. He resumed his pounding.

Across from him, another door cracked open. "We're going to call hotel security if you don't stop." It was an elderly woman's voice this time.

"You can call the National Guard for all I care." He gave the door a loud whack with his foot. "Come on, Greveen. You can't pump slander like that over the airwaves and not expect me to react. I'll sue your ass for every dime it's worth. You picked the wrong guy to mess with."

Both doors shut with a bang.

Earlier tonight, Bud had switched the radio broadcast on before getting into the tub to relax with a glass of Scotch. By the time the program was over, he was fully dressed and speeding toward the Maxfield in his Mercedes. He didn't

even see the jerk who slammed into the side of his car.
Recalling it now, it was a blur. He wasn't hurt, but the police
had arrived on the scene and asked a lot of inane questions.
When he was done with them, he had to call a towing service
to get his car out of the intersection, and then he'd spent the
next two hours on the phone with his agent, trying to get all
the particulars of his insurance straightened out. Finally,
he'd taken a cab to a rental-car company and driven away—
after another hour of haggling—in some crappy piece of tin
that passed these days for a luxury sedan.

His hand was beginning to throb from all the pounding.
Standing back, he looked both ways down the long hallway.
He'd been on automatic since the broadcast earlier in the
evening. Everything he'd done had one purpose: to get himself to the Maxfield and confront Wish Greveen. Now that
his efforts had been thwarted, he wasn't sure what to do.
Obviously, the weasel behind the door wasn't about to show
his cowardly face. Bud would have to smoke him out, but
that would take a plan, and right now he didn't have one.

"I'll be back, Greveen," he called, giving the door one last
whack. As he stepped resolutely over to the elevators it
occurred to him that he didn't have a clue what the hell he
felt so damn resolute about. He needed to do some serious
thinking. And for that, he needed a drink.

Once downstairs, he headed straight for the bar. He'd
always liked Scottie's. It was suitably dark and smoky, and
with all the signed photos of long-dead actors and actresses
who'd visited the place scattered here and there on the walls,
it was even a little glamorous, a place where a guy could get
his head together in comfort.

Easing onto one of the chrome bar stools, Bud caught the
bartender's eye and ordered a double Manhattan on the rocks.
As he waited for it to be mixed he glanced down the length of
the glass-block counter and noticed a woman sitting alone near
the other end. Maybe it was just his mood, but from this far
away, she kind of reminded him of Barbara Stanwyck. It was
probably the slightly curly bangs and the dark red lipstick. He'd
always been partial to Barbara Stanwyck, even in her later

years. Right then and there he decided to put off his contemplation of Wish Greveen's fate, and instead spend a few minutes trying to drum up a little old-fashioned human attraction.

After he was served, he picked up his glass and sauntered to the other end of the room, where he sat down next to her. Since it was late, the bar was pretty empty. He knew some women found the direct approach too predatory. He had other options, of course. For instance, he could have used the bartender to pass along a message. *The man down at the other end would like to buy you a drink.* But Bud was a good judge of character—especially a woman's character. And he had a gut feeling this one would respond more positively if he simply sat down, flashed her a friendly smile, and introduced a subject.

The opening remark was crucial. "I've been coming to this bar since I was in my early twenties."

The woman looked up from her drink and regarded him somewhat coolly. After several long seconds spent appraising every inch of his face, she said, "You must live in town, then. I'm just visiting."

Bud was elated. His foot was in the door. "Really? Where are you from?"

She took a drag from her cigarette. "Florida."

"You in town with your husband?"

"I'm a widow. And I'm here on business."

He thrust out his hand. "The name's Manderbach. Bud Manderbach."

"Dorothy Veneger."

"Nice to meet you."

She gave him another appraising look, this time checking out his clothes. Picking up her glass, she said, "Seems to me I bought something at a department store with that name."

His smile broadened. "I'm the owner. Four stores locally, and two in Chicago."

"Really." She didn't sound overwhelmed. Tapping some ash onto a cheap glass ashtray, she returned her gaze to the ice in her glass.

"Pardon my saying something so personal, but you look like you've had a rough evening."

"I have."

"Care to talk about it? I'm a good listener." The dress she was wearing revealed a slender body, with some nice curves. She wasn't exactly young, but then neither was he. He'd been wrong before, but somehow he had the distinct impression that this particular lady could be much more to him than a one-night stand. He decided to play his cards very carefully. After all, Giselle wasn't as interesting these days as she used to be. He had to think of his future.

Dorothy emptied her drink. "I just spent the last hour at the morgue."

That shocked him. "Why?"

"A man who works for me was found dead. I had to identify his body."

"I'm really sorry, Dorothy. How did it happen?"

She stared off into space. "I don't know. A Native American kid found him about thirty yards in from a main road out near the River Bend Casino. It looks like he froze to death. The police think it may be alcohol-related. Maybe he walked away from the casino and didn't really understand how cold it was that night. He might have fallen, hit his head, and before he could wake up, he—" The sentence was left unfinished. Instead, she held up her glass, signaling the bartender for another.

"What was the man's name?" asked Bud, holding himself very still.

"Valentine Zolotow."

"And . . . you say this man worked for you?"

She nodded. "You don't have another cigarette, do you?"

"Sorry."

When the bartender arrived with her second round, she bought a pack from him.

"So, tell me," Bud continued, attempting to keep his tone light, "what do you do for a living?"

"I'm the executive assistant to Heda Bloom, owner of Bloom Enterprises." She rested her head on her hand and added, "Although that doesn't tell you anything about my current responsibilities. Bloom Enterprises just bought WTWN radio here in St. Paul. I'm currently the interim general manager. I'm also producing a radio drama for the station."

"Dallas Lane, Private Eye."

"You've heard of it?"

He nodded, and kept nodding as he took her in for the first time. Since she didn't seem to know who he was, he figured he may have just gotten lucky.

"Valentine Zolotow was our star," she continued, gazing morosely at her reflection in a mirror that ran the length of the bar. "We really had to scramble the last two weeks to replace him."

"So, Dorothy," he said, lighting her cigarette before she could use the matches the bartender had given her. "I'm fascinated. Tell me . . . how does a radio drama like that get written? Did you do it yourself?" He decided to play dumb.

"No, we pay a professional writer to do the weekly scripts." She took a drag, then lifted her head and blew smoke high into the air. "Just look at me. I gave up smoking five years ago, and after two lousy cigarettes, I'm right back to where I started."

He smiled. "I know what you mean. It's a hard habit to break. But getting back to this scriptwriter. Where would you find a fella like that? I mean, from my limited understanding of the broadcast, it's nothing but geezers on parade, right? Nobody's done an original radio serial in years."

Dorothy shook her head and laughed. "Yeah, you have a point. But we got lucky. I put an ad in the Palm Beach paper explaining exactly what we needed, and two days later this man walks into my office with references that would have impressed John Houseman and the Mercury Theatre."

"What's the man's name? Maybe I've heard of him."

"Wish Greveen."

"No," he said slowly. "Doesn't ring any bells. And you say he made up this tale of sin and corruption all by himself?"

"Not entirely. Heda Bloom gave him a written synopsis of the story she wanted to present. It was up to him to dramatize it."

"I see. They must be pretty close."

"Greveen and Heda? Actually, they've never met. Our writer is kind of a recluse. He insisted on dealing with only one person, and that ended up being me."

Something didn't add up. If it was Heda Bloom's story, why had Greveen sent Bud a fax before the show began attempting to make it personal between them? "You say this Wish Greveen is a pretty private man?"

She nodded.

"What's he look like?"

She shrugged, flicking some ash into the ashtray. "He's in his sixties. Handsome, in my opinion. Wavy white hair. Slim build. He's a little—" She thought for a moment. "How do I put it? His style is somewhat European. Do you know what I mean?"

"How tall?"

Another shrug. "Maybe five-nine. Why all the interest?"

It could be him, thought Bud. If it was, he was pulling a con on everyone, including his mother.

"Bud?"

"Um?"

"You're kind of lost in thought all of a sudden. Do you know Mr. Greveen?"

He sat forward on the stool and rested both elbows on the counter. "Yeah, I think we might've met once." He looked at Dorothy and smiled. "But let's not talk about that anymore. Let's talk about something more interesting."

She returned his smile. "And what would that be?"

"You."

"Me?" She seemed surprised.

"You're an attractive woman. Must be a lonely existence for someone like you here in a new city, especially around Christmastime."

She pulled on her gold earring. "Well, yes. I suppose it is. But I've been so busy, I haven't thought about it much."

"You got a boyfriend back in Florida?"

She shook her head.

"But you do . . . *date*, don't you?" He made sure there was just the right hint of playfulness in his smile.

She lowered her eyes. "I haven't since Elm died."

He slipped his hand over hers. "I understand, Dorothy, truly I do. But there comes a time when a little male companionship is just what the doctor ordered. Here's what I propose. Lunch tomorrow at my restaurant."

"Oh, I don't know if I can get away from the station."

He touched a finger to her lips. "Lunch tomorrow. And then, on Christmas eve, you'll join me at my house for a late-night supper."

"That's next weekend, isn't it?" Her eyes seemed to glow in the darkness as she laughed. "You know, I hardly know you. I'm not usually this impetuous."

"You know what they say, Dorothy. Unexpected invitations are often dancing lessons from God."

She held his eyes. "I haven't danced in years."

"Maybe it's time you begin again."

She smiled, but still seemed hesitant. "We've got to take this very slow, Bud. I'm afraid my dating skills are pretty rusty."

"We'll take it just as slow as you want." He clinked his glass with hers, pleased with his incredible stroke of luck. Not only had he met an attractive woman tonight, but he'd stumbled upon a door that, once fully opened, would lead him straight to Wish Greveen.

22

"We have with us today, defense attorney Stan Tario." Bram smiled at the heavyset bald man sitting next to him, then pulled the mike closer to his mouth. "Welcome, Perry Mason of the North."

Stan grinned. "I always know when I come on your show, I'll get an inspiring introduction."

"Ever the diplomat. The number here is 555-4905 and I'm Bram Baldric. Be back in a flash."

It was Wednesday afternoon. Prior to going on the air today, Bram had attempted to contact Dorothy Veneger. She wasn't at the *Dallas Lane* rehearsal earlier in the morning. In her place, her assistant, John Cofeia, had been assigned the task of putting the actors through their paces. After the rehearsal, Bram once again tried to catch her, but with no luck. He wanted to run today's topic by her, just to make sure she knew what he was doing and didn't object. Unfortunately, Dorothy had left the station shortly before noon. She was having lunch with some new love interest, a man she'd met at Scottie's Bar. While Bram was delighted for her good fortune, he wished she would keep her staff a little better informed about her comings and goings.

Glancing down at his notes, Bram continued. "We're back. This is WTWN, and I'm that man of mystery himself, Bram Baldric. Our topic today: *Dallas Lane, Private Eye.* Is the radio drama some kind of revisionist history? A new slant on the Kay Collins murder? We were hoping to have Raymond Lawless with us this afternoon, but unfortunately, Mr. Lawless is under the weather. Mr. Tario has graciously agreed to take his place."

"Always willing to do a favor for a fellow defender of justice," said Stan.

Bram tried to hide his grimace. Stan Tario was no Raymond Lawless. His reputation had been built on sleazy legal maneuverings and tasteless promotion. Still, Stan had a good legal mind, and that's what Bram needed today. "We'll take your phone calls in a few minutes. But first, again, Stan, thanks for coming on such short notice."

"My pleasure."

"My producer tells me you've been digging into the Kay Collins murder case and you've come up with some startling new information."

"Absolutely correct," said Stan, glancing at his notes.

"You know, I was more than intrigued by the last episode of *Dallas Lane*, the one that suggested Justin Bloom was working on a big story for his newspaper, one involving a hit-and-run death of a prominent Twin Cities woman. If the show's theory is correct, then the person responsible for the hit-and-run death was also the one responsible for Kay Collins's murder. This is a shocking revelation. Nothing like it has come out before. I might also add that if it turns out to have any validity at all, it sheds important new light on Justin Bloom's potential innocence."

"But, forty years after the fact?" Bram's voice was full of doubt. "It would be hard to prove."

"Maybe. But just to see what we could come up with, I had my assistant do some research into the local newspaper archives. He found several articles in the fall of 1958, all with Justin Bloom's byline, and all of them concerning the hit-and-run death of Olga Landauer, the sister of Kurt Landauer, president of Landauer Construction. It seems that in late August of 1958, Olga Landauer was run down on the street in front of her house. It was around midnight. She'd gone outside with her dog before she turned in, which was apparently her habit. And perhaps most importantly, no one was ever charged with the hit-and-run."

Bram was fascinated. "That's amazingly like the story on our radio broadcast."

"It is. But let's take it one step further. In your broadcast, the young man who is in jail for his girlfriend's murder says he knows who was driving the car that killed the Landauer-like woman—but he can't prove it."

"If I recall correctly," observed Bram, "the driver was the son of a department-store magnate."

"Right," said Stan. "Now, by inference, I suppose that could mean the son of any number of business moguls in the Twin Cities. Or"—he paused, prolonging the drama—"it could be very specific information, pointing us to one man in particular. In Minnesota, we have three large, family-owned department stores. All of them were flourishing in 1958."

Bram counted them on the fingers of his right hand. "Fredrickson's, Manderbach's, and R. L. Donovan's."

"Did any of these families have a son in, say, his twenties or early thirties in 1958?"

"I assume you have the answer," said Bram.

"I do. The only family with a son of any kind was Manderbach's. Specifically, William Manderbach, Junior, known more commonly as Bud. He's presently the president and CEO of Manderbach's, and a well-respected figure in our regional business community."

Bram was getting furious messages in his earphones from his producer. "We should point out that this is all speculation. Neither WTWN's radio drama nor this talk show is pointing the finger at anyone."

"It's important to be clear about that," agreed Stan. "Unless your station wants a lawsuit on their hands. I'm merely suggesting some possibilities."

"And don't we all just *love* to speculate." Bram sat back in his chair and gazed at Stan with amazement. The guy had guts. "Speaking of idle speculation, it's twenty past the hour, and time for the weather." He was aware that the worried look on his producer's face hadn't diminished. "For that, let's go to Randy Ellis. Randy, I hear it's going to be the usual three hundred below zero out there tonight."

Randy's laughing voice took over. "Not quite, Bram, but it *is* going to be cold."

Bram pulled off his headset. Now that the "On Air" light was off, he and Stan could talk normally for a few seconds. "That should set some wheels turning—or some teeth grinding. Next time you decide to drop a bomb, let me know ahead of time so I can crawl under something heavy."

Stan smiled. "Sorry, but this is an incredible set of circumstances."

"You mean the radio show paralleling an old murder mystery."

"Yes, that and the fact that we've now been presented with an alternate story. It's exactly what I would have been looking for if I'd been Justin Bloom's defense attorney back in the late Fifties. A different set of circumstances, equally plausible, and yet one that would provide a jury with enough reasonable doubt to get my client off the hook."

Bram's producer pointed at him, then held up five fingers.

"You won't need to put on your headphones until the next segment," said Bram, taking a sip of his coffee.

As the producer pointed at him Bram sat up and spoke directly into the microphone again. "We're back with Stan Tario, Minnesota's answer to Clarence Darrow."

"That's better than Perry Mason," interjected Stan, his voice amused.

"Off air you mentioned that WTWN's radio mystery has provided the public with a new slant on an old story. An 'alternative story,' I believe you called it, one that would allow you, as a defense attorney, a chance to plant some reasonable doubt in a jury's mind. That is, if this murder mystery ever went to trial."

"Quite true. But before we move on to another topic, I'd just like to say that I think what we've been talking about this afternoon is very serious. If the story your radio drama is telling turns out to be accurate, we have a double murderer out there who's never been caught. Possibly even a triple murderer."

"Kay Collins and Olga Landauer. But who's the third potential murder victim?" asked Bram.

"Sally Nash," said Stan. "One of Kay Collins's roommates. Sally's body was found in a cornfield by a farmer several months after Kay was murdered."

"Something else I didn't know."

"It made all the papers back in April of 1959, but people often forget about it today when they speak of the Collins murder case. Why? Because no one could directly tie Sally Nash's death to that of Kay Collins. Yet her death was ruled a homicide."

"How did she die?"

"Another gunshot to the head."

"So, possibly three related murders."

"Also," continued Stan, "I can't help but wonder if, more recently, Valentine Zolotow's death isn't somehow related."

Bram and Sophie had been discussing this privately for days. "In what way?"

"Well, I've been giving it a lot of thought. If Justin Bloom was indeed set up, as your radio mystery maintains he was, then I propose that Zolotow somehow stumbled onto the truth behind the murder. What if he tried to use that information to blackmail the real murderer?"

"And in the process got himself killed?"

"It's certainly a possibility. My second theory revolves around the gun used to murder Kay Collins. If you recall, it was stolen from Justin's father's office. Cedric Bloom, Justin's stepfather, owned WPXL back in 1958. It was the same station on which the original version of *Dallas Lane, Private Eye* was aired. Let's say a radio-station employee was paid to take the gun. Who knows? Maybe it was Valentine Zolotow. Again, he may have had information that was dangerous to someone."

"But again, we have no proof."

"No," said Stan, "but that's partly because none of this has ever been investigated. Look, if Bloom is innocent, if he was set up, we have a man out there walking the streets of our fair city who's killed more than once and gotten away with it. At the very least, it's a matter that deserves much more attention. In fact, I believe the case should be reopened."

"Wouldn't it be interesting," mused Bram, "if Justin Bloom were alive? I wonder what he'd think of the resurgence of interest in his guilt or innocence. On that rather ghostly note"—he checked the time—"we better move on to the news. More thrilling revelations from famous defense attorney Stan Tario after our break. This is Bram Baldric for WTWN 1630. Don't touch that dial!"

Again, the "On Air" light went out. Bram leaned back and took a deep breath, gazing skeptically at Stan. "There *will* be more thrilling revelations, right?"

Stan shrugged. "You sure know how to run with the balls you're passed."

The producer tapped on the glass separating the technical booth from the studio. She pointed at Bram's earphones, motioning for him to put them on.

"What's up?" said Bram, thinking he had a good five minutes to relax before the next segment. He held one side up to his ear.

"You've got a phone call," said the producer's voice. "The woman doesn't want to talk to you on air, but she says it's urgent. She's been holding for almost ten minutes."

"All right." He sighed, pressing the blinking light on his console. "Baldric here."

"Mr. Baldric? I called you the other day and told you about the letter I have from Arn O'Dell. Remember?"

Bram was delighted by this stroke of good luck. "Was that you the other day at Salisbury's Café?"

"Yeah. Sorry I skipped out so fast. When I saw you through the window, I got a bad case of cold feet."

"No problem. So . . . do you still have the letter?"

"Yes. Like I said, it was written by my grandfather."

"Arn O'Dell was your grandfather?" This was new information. He did some quick math. She must have been pretty young at the time of the murder.

"Right. See, I've been thinking about this for weeks, ever since that new radio mystery started. The letter I have tells a different story from the one my grandfather told officially."

Bram was stunned. He glanced over and saw that Stan Tario had picked up on the importance of the conversation. He was listening intently. "What do you want from me?"

"I want you to read it. I've been listening to you for years. I feel like we're friends—in a strange sort of way. Does that make sense?"

"Perfect sense."

"I thought after you read it, you could advise me what to do next."

"Well, sure, I'd be happy to look at it. When can we meet?"

"I was thinking, maybe you could drive up to my grandfather's old hunting lodge out on Pine Lake. I kept it after he died. It's just a shack, really, but there's an oil heater I can light. We'd be warm enough. You know where Pine Lake is?"

"I think so. It's up near Minton. I used to have a buddy who had a hunting cabin up there."

"Just take 94 to Highway 10. When you get to Minton, you'll see a grain elevator on your left. Turn in front of it and take the road toward the lake. Mine is the first cabin on the east side. You'll see a mailbox on your right. Take that turnoff. It's a dirt road, but I have it plowed out. It dead-ends about thirty feet from the front door. I'll put a light on in the window."

Bram wrote quickly on the edge of his notepad. "Okay. But when do we meet?"

"Tonight. It's gotta be tonight."

He looked up and saw his producer counting down the final seconds until they would be back on air.

"All right, tonight."

"And one other thing. You can't tell a soul you talked to me. I'm dead meat if the wrong person finds out about the letter."

"Sure, I understand." He had to get off. "I'll see you around seven."

"Fine." The line clicked.

Bram had just enough time to grab a gulp of coffee before they were once again live. "This is Bram Baldric and my guest today is Stan Tario. Stan, let's get right back to the topic. We're talking about the Kay Collins murder case. Now, before the break, you were doing some mighty interesting speculating."

"What I had to say is nothing compared to your off-air phone call from Arn O'Dell's granddaughter."

Bram's eyes opened wide.

"For those of you who don't remember, Arn O'Dell was the police officer who maintained he saw Justin Bloom shoot Kay Collins. He was the only eyewitness, and on his say-so, Justin Bloom was convicted, if not in court, then in all the local papers."

Bram drew a finger across his throat, trying to get Stan to back off the subject.

"Maybe you'd like to tell us what she had to say?" continued Stan. "I, for one, am dying to hear about this letter she purports to have from her grandfather."

Bram laughed into the mike. "Stan, you're such a joker." Asshole was more like it. "Yeah, it would be fascinating if Arn O'Dell did have a granddaughter and she called old Bram Baldric with some earthshaking new information—"

Stan seemed indignant that his word was being challenged. "But, you're meeting her tonight somewhere up near Minton. A hunting cabin, maybe?"

Bram motioned to his producer to cut him off. He quickly scribbled a note and shoved it across to him. It said, very succinctly, *Shut up about the phone call!!!!*

Stan shook his head. "You can't withhold information like this. It's too important."

"For all of you radio listeners out there, I should point out that Stan Tario has a very unusual sense of humor. Yes, if there is a granddaughter out there somewhere, we'd love to talk to you. In the meantime let's take a call from Marge in Fridley. Marge, you're on." God, where was Raymond Lawless when you needed him? Bram's heart was in his throat as he pressed line one.

"Bram, is that you?" The voice suggested someone who was quite elderly.

"Yes, Marge."

"Did you say a few minutes ago that Valentine Zolotow was shot at Manderbach's department store?"

"No, Marge. I didn't say that."

It was going to be a long afternoon.

May 3, 1959

Dear Mother:

Hearing about Sally Nash really knocked the wind out of me. I wanted to write to you right away, but found that the depression which has dogged me ever since I left home came back with a vengeance. I thought I was getting better, learning to live with my fears and my failures, but I guess not. Running away from Minnesota was far easier than running away from myself.

I knew something had happened to Sally, and while I feared the worst, I hoped she'd gotten away from the Cities, perhaps back to her parents' place. Everything happened so fast that last week, I didn't have time to find her, to make sure she was all right. I knew she'd disappeared, Mom, but I didn't know what to do about it, except to pursue the man I felt was responsible for the death of Olga Landauer. It turns out he was far more treacherous than I ever imagined. My failing was to underestimate him. If I ever get the chance, I won't do that again.

Have you heard anything about Jonnie Apfenford? I tried to contact her on my way out of town, but she didn't answer the phone. She was supposed to be back at the apartment waiting for us, but something must have gone wrong. God, I hope she took off and never looked back. She was in terrible danger, and more than anyone else in this whole mess, I think she knew it. Let me know if you hear anything. It's so hard being completely cut off from news of home.

Today, I plan to tell you how I found out the name of the man who killed Olga Landauer. You'll be shocked when you find out his name, Mom, because you know him. Cedric and Alf know him, too, and so do tons of other people in the Twin Cities. He's from a wealthy family, and he has—or had—everything going for him in life. Money. A beautiful wife. A great job. A terrific future. The world was his oyster, as they say, except for one small flaw. The guy has the Midas touch in reverse. Everything he touches withers and turns to dust. In the army, we would have called him Mr. Misunderstood. Mr. Grand Exception. There's always a few assholes like him in every company, but it's only in business that creeps like him could stay on top.

Okay, so back to my story. In my last letter I explained how Kay and I had hit a dead end when we tried to get the name of Sally's summer boyfriend out of her. She was either too scared or too bought off to talk. Looking back on it now, I think it was a little of both.

I returned to my office at the paper the next day, determined to figure out who had sent me the note, the one that started the whole chain of events in the first place. I mean, whoever wrote to me must not only know who Sally was dating, but that the man had been involved in the Landauer hit-and-run. The question was, how did this person find out? It either had to be a friend of Sally's, or a friend of the man in question, or perhaps an eyewitness to the hit-and-run. Since it was dark, I didn't think it could be an eyewitness, unless someone else was in the car with them that night. Sally didn't have a lot of close friends, people she confided in. In fact, her closest friends were Kay and Jonnie. Kay hadn't written the note, I was sure of that, so that left Jonnie's name with a big question mark attached to it. And frankly, I was beginning to get a gut feeling that Jonnie was the one. The more I got to know her, the more I saw that she was the kind of person who listened at doorways, who knew what was happening in the personal lives of everyone in her small circle of friends. Yet I also knew that demanding that Jonnie talk to me would get me *nowhere fast. Whoever had written the note wanted to remain anonymous. There had to be some other way for me to find out the name of Sally's ex-boyfriend.*

A couple of nights later Kay was working late at Manderbach's department store. It was just four weeks before Christmas, so I knew she couldn't get out of it. Since I had some free time on my hands, I decided to take a drive out to the Westgate Country Club. I hadn't been there since the night I first saw Kay. I knew it was one of Sally's favorite hangouts, so I guess, in the back of my mind, I figured maybe I'd run across something or someone who could point me in the right direction.

After parking my car in the lot, I took a seat at the bar and ordered a whiskey and soda. The place was really jumping. Everywhere I looked I saw holiday decorations. Red and green lights. Pine boughs. The guy leading the band even had a Santa Claus outfit on. Pretty silly, if you ask me. But then, no one was asking. I sat for a while just watching the sights. Finally, about nine-thirty, it was either order my third drink or shove off. I was about ready to leave when a young guy—about my age—sat down next to me. He said, "You're Justin Bloom, aren't you?"

I said, yeah, I was Justin.

"You're the only face I recognize in this entire joint. Let me buy you a drink."

I thought, What the hell? I didn't have anything else to do, so I let him buy it. "Where'd we meet?" I asked him.

"At a party. Remember the one at Sally Nash's apartment, the one she and her two roommates gave right before Thanksgiving?"

I said, sure, I remembered it.

He laughed. "I'll bet you do. Isn't that the one where your girlfriend called you a two-timing piece of shit? That was pretty funny. You must have been in the doghouse for weeks."

He was talking about Mitzi. I wasn't as amused as he was, though I understood now why he remembered me. It had been quite a scene. I asked his name.

"Dave Cordovan," he said, and shook my hand. "I used to date Sally. After she dumped me, I tried to date Kay, but she wasn't interested. I guess you could say I'm not very lucky in love. But then, who is?" He gave me a knowing wink.

"How come you got invited to the party?" I asked.

"Oh, those girls keep me around like a pet dog. I'm harmless—and amusing. A warm body for any unattached female they decide to invite."

I asked him when he and Sally had dated.

"Last summer."

"Really." I turned to look at him, trying not to stare. This might just be the break I'd been looking for. I waited, hoping he'd go on without my prodding.

"Yeah, she dumped me for another guy."

"Who was he?"

He smiled at the memory. "She tried to keep it a secret, but I saw them together. It was Bud Manderbach. You know him? The guy's married. I couldn't believe Sally would be that dumb. But you know her when it comes to money. She can't resist the stuff. And that Manderbach kid's got lots of it. His dad's pretty old. I think he's being groomed to take over the business."

I did know Bud Manderbach. Not well, but socially. "When did she dump you?"

"On my birthday," he said, taking a hefty sip of Scotch. "July second. I think she was already dating Manderbach by then. But what's the difference? If she's that kind of girl, I say to hell with her."

I could tell by the way he said the words that it still stung.

"And then," he added, smiling again, "Manderbach goes and dumps her. According to Jonnie, Sally was foot-loose and fancy-free by the middle of September, and on the lookout for some new sap to draw into her web. I knew it wouldn't work between them, but hell, she wouldn't have believed me. She was so gaga over the jerk." He *finished his drink. Drawing a bowl of peanuts in front of him, he asked, "So, how you doin' with your girlfriend?"*

He meant Mitzi. "We broke up," I said.

"Yeah. The course of true love's never easy." Then he laughed again and ordered another drink.

I told him I had to get home.

"You datin' Kay now?"

I wasn't sure how he knew, but I told him I was.

"She's a real beauty. And a good girl. Nothing like Sally."

I agreed with him, thanked him for the drink, and left. I'd gotten what I'd come for. More, in fact. I was hoping for a lead and I got the guy's name dropped right in my lap.

So, I thought as I drove away, the man in question was none other than one of St. Paul's best-known golden boys. Bud Manderbach had been the driver of the car that killed Olga Landauer. No wonder he was so hot to cover it up. If his father had found out he'd killed someone and then left the scene of the accident, he could kiss his fabulous future goodbye. That fateful night had ended his affair with Sally Nash. To buy her silence, he'd bought her a car, and no doubt given her money. But since she wasn't buying clothes and fancy knickknacks the way she had earlier in the fall, I figured that the money might be just about dried up. Now that I had specific information, I thought maybe I could use her lack of funds to my advantage.

But I needed a plan. If Bud Manderbach was really the hit-and-run driver, as I knew in my gut he was, I had to find proof. I had no idea then that Kay would turn out to be the key.

I better stop there.

Stay safe, Mom. Don't talk about me to anyone. Don't whisper my name or mourn my loss. If you forget about me, at least in every way that's visible, you'll live through this. All I can give you now is the chance to stay alive.

> Much love,
> Justin

23

"This radio show is really taking a toll on you, Heda," said George Chambers. He was seated on the couch in her suite, his feet propped up on a heavy chrome-and-glass-block coffee table. "Are you still convinced it's worth it?"

Heda stood in front of her easel, putting the finishing touches on a painting she'd started weeks ago. The picture had become progressively more somber, filled with dark shadows and an almost palpable gloom. It was a depiction of her mood, rather than an accurate representation of the St. Paul skyline. "It had to be done."

He nodded, puffing on his pipe.

"I'm just so glad you could be here. I don't know what I would have done without you these past few weeks."

"Where else would I be? Besides, I wouldn't miss this for the world."

Heda set the brush down and then eased back onto the stool with a weary sigh. "Alfred continues to be my biggest problem. He's made life horribly difficult for Dorothy. He insists on checking and rechecking every decision she makes."

"Doesn't he trust her?"

"Of course he does. He knows she's a consummate professional. What he doesn't trust is *me*. He'll be damned if he lets anything slip past him again."

"Can't you do something about it? I mean, he's harassing your assistant."

She shrugged. "I suppose I could demand that he leave her alone, but I already feel like I've alienated him enough, buying the station the way I did—behind his back. And if he doesn't harass Dorothy, he's going to be sitting in my living room, dumping his pent-up anger all over me."

George removed the pipe from his mouth. "Well, all I can say is, plant your feet and take your punch. Isn't that what your father always said to do when faced with a problem?"

She smiled, remembering her dad's bulldog determination. "I guess it is."

"And that's what we're doing. Alfred's just throwing his weight around because he wasn't consulted. He'll calm down."

Heda knew George was right. And yet, if only her problems stopped there. She wished she could tell him about Dorothy—how unhappy she was with some of her recent behavior—and yet she knew it was impossible. It would only create new problems.

At the sound of a door being opened, both Heda and George turned. Alfred barged into the room. "Hello, Mother," he said in his deep, ponderous voice.

Her smile dissolved as her eyes locked on the suitcase resting on the floor next to him. "What's going on?"

"I can't stay in Minnesota any longer. My wife and family want me home for Christmas. Christmas eve is only three days away, in case you haven't checked a calendar."

"I know when Christmas eve is. I'm not senile."

George got up. "I think maybe I should leave. You two need some privacy." Nodding to Heda, he said, "I'll see you later tonight, all right? The memorial service for Valentine starts at eight. We should probably head over to the church by seven-thirty."

"I'll be ready." It would be the first time she'd left the hotel since she'd arrived. Even though she was nervous about it, she knew everyone from the station would be there, and she refused to be the only exception. Valentine deserved better than that.

As George moved past Alfred over to the door, he stopped, turned around, and stuck out his hand. "Good seeing you again, Alf."

"Yeah. Good seeing you, too."

George stared at him a moment longer, then shut the door on his way out.

Once he was gone, Alfred walked over to the windows and looked up at the darkening sky. "You two have sure been spending a lot of time together."

"We're old friends."

"How can you call someone you haven't seen in almost forty years a friend?"

"We may not have seen each other, but we've kept in contact. A letter here, a Christmas card there."

He clearly wasn't satisfied, but let the subject drop. Clasping his hands behind his back, he moved around the easel to look at the painting. After studying it for a few moments, he said, "Come home with me, Mother. Surely this fiasco you've set in motion here can run its course without you."

This was the last conversation she needed right now. "Look, Alfred, I understand why you want to leave. You know my feelings on the matter. You didn't need to come to Minnesota in the first place."

"Forgive me if I had to make sure this investment was a sound one. I realize you wanted to play your little game in peace. I haven't interfered, have I?"

"Well . . . not exactly."

"Not that you planned to let me in on your secret."

"Of course I did. I told you the first week you were here."

"Not *that* secret, Mother. The other one."

She didn't know what he was talking about.

He sat down on the couch. "Two words. Wish Greveen."

"What about him?"

"I'm not a complete idiot. I've always wondered if Justin was still alive. Now I know he is."

"What?" she said, blinking back her surprise.

"Sure, that's why he keeps himself hidden. He'd be too recognizable, especially to his brother."

"You think Wish Greveen is Justin?"

"Don't bother denying it." His smile was more of a sneer.

"But that's ridiculous. Absolute nonsense."

"Is it?" He placed both arms on the back of the couch and stared at her, the sneer turning to a scowl. "Oh, that's right, you maintain you've never met Wish Greveen."

"I haven't."

"Then how do you know he's not your son?"

"Justin is dead, Alfred. Dead and buried. I was there." She looked away, first out the window at the fading twilight, then down at her hands. "He died in Italy."

"Those trips you took to Europe in the late Sixties and early Seventies. You went to visit him, right?"

She squared her shoulders. "I did."

"You lied about that, too. You told me you were visiting friends. You even gave me a bunch of bogus names."

"You're smart enough to understand why I had to lie."

"And you're lying now."

"No!"

"I don't believe you," he said flatly.

Her lips thinned in irritation, but she held her temper in check. "I'm sorry you don't," she said finally, "because it's the truth. I swear that to you on my life, Alfred—Wish Greveen is not my son! He was simply hired to write the scripts. If he's a recluse, if he never wants to meet with me personally, that's his business. He's eminently qualified, as our ratings clearly show."

Dorothy picked that moment to come home from work.

Heda was delighted with the interruption. She hoped it would put an end to Alfred's questions.

Dorothy set her briefcase on the table by the door. "I'm exhausted," she said, taking off her heavy wool coat and hanging it in the front closet. Noticing the grim faces staring back at her, she asked, "Is something wrong?"

Heda felt this was a perfect opportunity to change the subject. She hoped Alfred would take the hint and leave. She had other matters that required her attention. "Where were you during lunch? I called, but your secretary said you were out."

"I was," said Dorothy, stepping over to the bar. She began to mix herself a drink. "I had an engagement."

"With whom?"

Dorothy's eyes flicked to Heda, then back to the bottle of sweet vermouth. "Why, I don't think that's any of your business. Would anyone else like a drink before dinner?"

"Was it Bud Manderbach again?" demanded Heda. If Alfred's little tantrum hadn't caused her blood pressure to rise, Dorothy's behavior certainly would.

Dorothy took a taste of her drink before answering. "If you must know, yes, it was." She reached underneath the bar and found a cocktail napkin, then walked over to a chair in a neutral corner and sat down. "What did I walk in on?" she asked, adjusting her skirt over her knees.

"Nothing," said Heda sharply. She didn't know if she was more disgusted by Alfred's constant questions or Dorothy's refusal to listen to reason. Dorothy *had* to stop seeing that man. The fact that she'd even introduced herself to him was an obscenity.

"Well, we were talking about *something*," said Alfred. "I was wondering if Wish Greveen was really Justin Bloom, my half brother."

Dorothy gazed at him for a moment, then started to laugh. "Who told you that?"

"No one. It's just a theory."

Her attention switched to Heda. "Tell him. Justin's dead, right?"

"Pardon me if I don't believe that bit of family bullshit."

"But it's true." Again, Dorothy looked at Heda, this time with a bit more uncertainty. "Isn't it?"

"Of course it is," said Heda firmly.

"Would you like to see a photo of Mr. Greveen?" asked Dorothy, lifting the glass to her lips. "I think I have one in the résumé he sent me. That might set your mind at rest."

Alfred's eyebrow raised. He seemed skeptical, but said, "Sure. Why not?"

Dorothy rose and walked into her bedroom, returning a few moments later with a file folder. "The picture is clipped inside the front cover."

Alfred flipped it open and gazed at the photo. He stared at

it a long time. "There's some resemblance, I suppose. It's hard to tell. I haven't seen my brother since he was in his mid-twenties."

"I've seen the photo *and* your brother," said Heda. "And that's not Justin."

He seemed to mull it over. "Well, of course there's always plastic surgery. You've certainly had your face tweaked and tucked a few times, Mother."

"That's enough," she snapped. She'd had about all she could take of this conversation—from both of them. Rising from her chair, she said, "Alfred, I hope you have a good flight back to Florida. Give my love to everyone. Now, I'm going to lie down before dinner." She turned to Dorothy. "George Chambers is coming by at seven-thirty. We'll all ride over to the church together."

Dorothy nodded. "Alf, are you going, too?"

"Thank God I have an excuse. I'll be winging my way back to Florida by then. I hate funerals." He pushed out of his chair, gave his mother a peck on the cheek, and then grabbed his suitcase. "By the way, Mother, we'll continue this conversation later."

After he'd bumped his way out the door, Dorothy looked at Heda with a pained but amused smile. "God, but he's an oaf."

Heda glared at her. "That's not funny. None of this is funny!"

"No," said Dorothy, crossing her legs and leaning back in her chair. "I suppose it isn't."

24

On Wednesday evening, Bram and Sophie drove up to Minton. They were both sorry they had to miss the memorial service for Valentine Zolotow, but it couldn't be helped. The meeting with Arn O'Dell's granddaughter took precedence. Since Sophie had already planned to take the evening off, she insisted on coming along. Bram was glad for any excuse to get her away from the hotel. At least on the ride up, they'd have some time to talk.

"So," said Sophie, opening the map as they sped along the highway, "if it looks like the letter is authentic, what are you going to advise this woman to do with it?"

Bram signaled and then took the 694 cutoff. "Give it to the police."

"You think you can convince her to do that? From what you told me, she sounds pretty scared."

"Look at it this way, Soph. If Arn O'Dell lied about what he saw the night Kay Collins was murdered, then maybe the killer is still out there. If that's the case, then the only way anyone involved in this mess is going to stay safe is to put the real murderer behind bars."

"I'd never thought about that, but you have a good point." She gazed out the window at the city lights. "You know, that old murder case has become a local obsession. As I was coming out of Rudy and John's apartment this afternoon, I overheard two people in the stairwell talking about it. Then, later, when I stopped at Lund's to get some groceries, two women in front of me at the checkout counter were arguing about whether or not Justin Bloom had really loved Kay Collins. Can you believe it? And then, when I got back to the hotel, the bellman who parked my car asked me if I knew what the next *Dallas Lane* episode was about, specifically what would it reveal about the real murderer."

The real murderer, thought Bram, staring at the road ahead of them. "God, I wish I felt more confident that we *could* find the truth."

"You're pretty bothered by all this, aren't you, honey?"

"Yeah, I guess I am. I keep thinking back to what O'Dell's granddaughter said earlier today. It wasn't terribly specific, just something about her grandfather telling her a different story from the one he told officially. I mean, maybe I'm jumping to conclusions. Maybe what he said was true, but he only told part of the story. Or maybe the whole thing was a lie. I wish I'd pressed her to tell me more." He glanced over at Sophie and saw that she'd closed her eyes. She was exhausted. She hadn't come to bed last night until after two, and then she'd been up and gone before dawn. He decided to let her rest.

Half an hour later he pulled onto the Highway 10 turnoff. Noticing that Sophie was now awake, he said, "We're getting close." He nodded to a lighted billboard: PINE LAKE MOTOR INN, ONE MILE.

She looked out the window as the headlights hit a sign. " 'Welcome to Minton, population four hundred and twenty-eight.' Quite the thriving metropolis." She continued to watch as they sped past an abandoned gas station.

"And there's the grain elevator," said Bram, slowing the car. He turned left in front of it. "Now, we follow this road until we come to the lake. O'Dell's cabin should be the first one on our right."

As they drove down a hill away from the highway, the road became bumpy and narrow. A plow had come through all right, but Bram was glad they'd taken his four-wheel-drive. It wasn't the kind of terrain he wanted to navigate in Sophie's Lexus. The lake was probably out there somewhere in the darkness, but his attention was consumed by the deep, icy ruts in front of him. As they drove on, the road became shrouded in fog.

"Boy, it's dark out here," said Sophie, yanking the collar of her coat more snugly around her neck. "This feels like a werewolf movie."

"Over there," said Bram, pointing. "Can you tell if that's a road? O'Dell's granddaughter said to turn right."

"Didn't O'Dell's *granddaughter* ever give you her name?" said Sophie. She sounded annoyed.

"No, she didn't. And I didn't ask." Bram made a hard right and then pulled onto another deeply rutted road. This one was more of a driveway. Now that the headlights were pointed toward the cabin, he could see it in the distance. It was just a shack, really. One story. Probably big enough for a makeshift kitchen and one main room. He doubted there was plumbing or electricity. As they came closer he couldn't see a light. "That's funny. She said she'd leave something burning in the front window."

"Maybe she's not here yet," said Sophie.

"Since we're fifteen minutes late, I don't know why she wouldn't be." He turned off the headlights, but left the motor running. "So, now what?"

Sophie unbuckled her seat belt. "We wait, I guess."

He wasn't in a waiting mood. Switching off the motor, he rolled down the window and listened. All around them, the night was still and quiet. Bram was a city boy, used to the reassuring hum of traffic. He didn't much care for this remote peace and tranquillity. "I'm going in." He opened the glove compartment and removed a flashlight.

"What am I supposed to do?"

"Stay here. When I'm sure everything's safe, I'll wave to you." Before Sophie could offer any objections, he climbed out of the driver's seat and headed up the front path. Someone had been here all right. He could see footprints in the snow. As he bent down to take a closer look, he heard the car door slam. He turned and saw Sophie hurrying toward him.

"I'm not staying in that car all by myself," she said, pulling on a knit cap. "What are you looking at?"

"Footprints. If I were Sherlock Holmes, I'm sure I'd learn a lot. As it is, they just look like winter boots. It could be a man or a woman. Or both, for that matter." He glanced up at the cabin.

"It seems pretty quiet," said Sophie. As he stood she snuggled close, slipping her arm through his. "Why don't we go have a cup of coffee somewhere and discuss our next move? My treat."

"They don't serve coffee at abandoned gas stations."

"There's got to be some sort of café around here. Small towns have great cafés. I'll bet we could even find one that serves homemade pie."

"Sophie, I'm an adult. You can't bribe me with food."

She shot him a disgusted look. "Of course I can bribe you with food. I do it all the time."

"Look, you were the one who insisted on coming along."

"Yeah, but I didn't think it would turn into an *X-Files* episode. Dark creepy houses and blazing flashlights."

"I thought we were in a werewolf movie."

"I have a fluid imagination."

With their arms locked together, they approached the front door.

"I don't think anyone's here," said Bram, trying the knob. He was surprised when the door opened easily in his hand.

"I have a bad feeling about this," said Sophie, hanging on to his arm as if it were a life raft. "Why wasn't it locked?"

Bram switched on the flashlight. "Is anyone here?" he called, inching cautiously into the front room.

In one corner he could see an oil heater, but it wasn't on. The air inside was every bit as cold as the outside air. The only difference was that inside, he noticed the faint odor of cooking grease mixed with wood smoke, another indication that the cabin had recently been used. And he'd been wrong about the plumbing. Not only did it appear that there was a working kitchen complete with woodstove and sink, but behind it, he could see a door leading to a small bathroom. Undoubtedly, the water had been shut off for the season.

That and the fact that there was no electricity made the cabin an unappealing place to spend a winter's night.

"All the comforts of home," he muttered, shining the light over every nook and cranny. The main room contained a threadbare couch partially covered by a crocheted afghan, a couple of tattered La-Z-Boys, and a small bookcase, mostly filled with junk. The floor was covered by a stained indoor/outdoor carpet.

"I think we've been stood up," whispered Sophie.

It seemed a reasonable assumption. "God, I could strangle that lawyer with my bare hands." As he stood looking over the empty room he gradually became aware of another odor, something more pungent than the grease. "What's that other smell?"

Sophie sniffed the air. "Kerosene, I think. The scented variety."

On a table next to the kitchen window, Bram now spied an oil lamp. "I'll bet that's the light she said she'd have on for us. And it *was* on, or we couldn't smell it."

"Then who turned it off?" asked Sophie.

Their eyes locked.

Bram's whole body felt suddenly tense, alert, as if he could run a marathon. Breaking free of her grip, he rushed over to the table. Removing the glass cover on the lamp, he touched the wick. "It's cold, damn it. Where *is* she?"

Sophie remained near the door. "I hate to sound like a broken record, but I don't like this, honey. Let's go."

"This is so . . . *infuriating*." There had to be some clue, some indication of where she'd gone. "I thought we'd find some answers tonight. Now all we've got are more questions."

"I'm freezing."

"I wonder if there's a back door."

"No, only this one. Come on, honey."

"Just another minute."

"Bram, you know I'm not easily scared. But something's wrong here. I can feel it."

He hadn't checked the bathroom yet. He couldn't leave

without taking a look. Shining the flashlight on the doorway, he stepped inside. Instantly, his eyes were drawn upward. "Oh, my God."

"What is it?" said Sophie, rushing to his side.

He moved to block her entrance. "You're right, let's go."

"But—"

"We need to get out to the car right away."

"Why?" She struggled to push past him.

He grabbed her by the arms and looked her square in the eye. "We have to call the police. She's dead, Sophie. Believe me, you don't want to see it."

Her eyes searched his for an explanation.

"She's hanging by a cord from one of the ceiling pipes. We were too late. Someone got here first."

Giving herself a moment to let it all sink in, she slowly removed a cell phone from her pocket. "I brought it in with me—just in case."

A breath of icy air shot down his spine. Taking it from her hand, he immediately placed a 911 call. "I want to report a murder," he said into the mouthpiece. "What? No, I don't know the name."

"You're sure it was a murder?" asked Sophie, looking at the open doorway.

Covering the mouthpiece, he said, "What else could it be?"

The sheriff held what remained of the cigarette to his lips and inhaled deeply, a bit of the ash falling onto his boot. He'd driven up a few minutes earlier and parked behind Bram's Explorer. The flashing lights from his squad car shot a colored strobe against the cabin's shingled exterior. "We don't get many deaths like this one around here."

Bram and Sophie had given a brief statement to the first officer on the scene. When they were done, the officer had asked them to wait in their vehicle until the crime scene could be examined.

"How much longer is this going to take?" asked Bram, holding his gloved hands over his ears. He wanted some answers, but he didn't want to stand around freezing any longer.

The sheriff flicked his cigarette butt into the snow. He was an older man. Balding, stocky, with large, meaty hands and a deeply lined face. In the harsh, edgy light, he reminded Bram of a badly done woodcut. His name was Olson. Henry Olson.

"Well," said Olson, "what with the cold, it's gonna be pretty hard to tell how long she's been dead."

"I suppose," said Bram. Making small talk about dead people wasn't one of his strong suits.

"You say this woman was a friend of yours?"

"No, we've never met. If you'll read my statement, I explained that she's the granddaughter of Arn O'Dell. This used to be his cabin. I assume she inherited it when he died."

"Yeah, seems to me I do remember something like that," said the sheriff, taking off his cap and scratching his head. "But he's been dead for years." His expression hardened as a man came out of the cabin. "Hey, Tom," he said, his voice deepening. Perhaps thinking he needed to make introductions, he added, "This is Dr. Tom Kowalski. County coroner."

It sounded like a TV show, thought Bram. The inanity of it turned his stomach.

"It wasn't a suicide," said the coroner, ignoring Sophie and Bram as he pulled the plastic gloves off his hands.

"What was it then?" asked the sheriff, lighting up another smoke.

"She was strangled."

"Of course she was strangled, Tom. She was hanging from a cord."

"No, I mean she was strangled first. That's how she was killed. From the looks of her, I'd say someone came up behind her, wrapped that cord around her neck, and . . . you get the picture. He strung her up to that pipe later."

"Why on earth would he do that?"

"Beats the hell outta me."

"Have you ID'd the body yet?"

"Yeah," said the coroner, taking some thermal gloves from his pocket and yanking them on. He looked Bram up and down, then said, "Her name's Betty Johanson. I know her. She plays bridge with the wife."

Bram was confused. "I thought she lived in the Cities."

"Not unless she's leading a double life," said the coroner.

"You're not talking about the Johanson that lives just up the road?" asked the sheriff.

He nodded. "She's a widow. Lives alone. I called her nephew to ask him to come over to the lab. I'll have to do an autopsy, so we might as well get it over with tonight. The nephew said he was in her kitchen a few hours ago when she got a call from some friend in the Cities. A woman. He didn't catch the name. The woman asked Betty to run over to her cabin, stoke up the oil burner, and put a light in the window. Betty said, sure, she'd do it. Apparently she had a key, or knew where to find one. I figure when she got here, someone was waiting for her, surprised her, and, well, that was that."

Bram's confusion finally lifted. "Then it's not O'Dell's granddaughter."

"No, sir. No relation," said the coroner.

Questions raced through his mind. Why had the grand-daughter called this woman in the first place? Was it simply that she was going to be late and wanted a light on in the window just in case he got to the cabin first? If so, had this neighbor woman been mistaken for the granddaughter? Who really *was* the intended victim?

"Well, I guess you two can go home now," said the sheriff, the cigarette dangling precariously from his lips. "Sorry you folks had such a rough night. I'll be in touch. You'll probably be called to testify in a court trial somewhere down the line, after we catch the guy who did it."

"You think you'll catch him?" said Sophie.

The sheriff hooked a thumb through his belt. "Oh, we'll catch him all right. My sergeant tells me we got some great tire tracks in the snow about thirty yards back of the cabin. Footprints leading right to the door. Then more prints back to the car. Tire tracks are like fingerprints, in case you didn't know. In my experience, criminals are stupid, they usually make mistakes." He took a short puff, then continued. "And me, well, I'm too old for snowmobiling. Don't much care for ice fishing. In the winter, I got lots of time on my hands. We'll catch him, all right. What the courts decide to do with him—that's another matter."

May 7, 1959

Dear Mother:

It's nearly midnight. I'm sitting here at my makeshift desk, writing to you by candlelight. The electricity is off, and has been off since I got back this afternoon. I have no idea why, nor have I been able to find out. Most of the other tenants don't speak English, and the two who do are every bit as much in the dark as I am, both literally and figuratively. This is the second time we've lost power in the last two weeks, so I assume it's something I'll have to put up with. I just hope my food doesn't spoil in the refrigerator.

Around eight I went out to sit on the small balcony attached to my apartment. I have a comfortable chair out there where I often spend the evenings watching people come and go down on the street. Did I tell you? I'm on the second floor, though the view is hopeless, nothing lovely or panoramic. Around nine, I closed my eyes and didn't wake until a few minutes ago. The night air is so much cooler than it was earlier in the day. The breeze coming in through the window as I sit here to write is sweet and fresh, yet so different from the smells I was used to at home. How can I put it, other than to say that this town, indeed this entire country, is a strange mixture of the ancient and the pragmatic, utilitarian, almost militaristic modern. Some of it is new, clean, and intensely ugly, while much of it is old, decaying, filthy, and fascinating. The clash of cultures never ceases to amaze me.

Today I rode a ramshackle bus out to the Mediterranean. It isn't far. The cost was next to nothing, yet the reward was immense. This was the first time I'd left town since I arrived, the first time I had a chance to sit alone on the sand and gaze at the water. What they say is true, Mom. The sea is very blue, although to my eyes, it was more of an intense blue-green. I sat for hours just watching the waves splash over the white rocks. Emptying myself. Enjoying the moment. The sun felt good on my body. Better than good. I felt alive again. Sometimes, like this afternoon, I think I'm beginning to heal, both physically and mentally. When I got home, I found myself whistling as I prepared dinner. But then the sun goes down and darkness comes, and once again, I'm alone with my thoughts, my virulent visions, and my rage.

And that's where I am again right now. I want to move on with my story.

I'd finally found the name of the man Sally Nash had been dating late last summer, but I still had no proof of his involvement in the Landauer hit-and-run. Since Sally wasn't about to give me the details, at least for the present, I had to figure out another way to get inside his life—and more specifically his house—to see what evidence might still be there. I knew it was a long shot, but I had to try. I could almost taste the triumph when I broke the story. I felt my career would take off like a rocket if only I could get the information I needed.

Two nights after I met Dave Cordovan at the Westgate and he filled me in on the particulars of Sally's love life, I took Kay out to dinner. It was a celebration. Our favorite spot was Charlie's in downtown Minneapolis, but I wanted to take her someplace new. I made reservations at Sheik's for seven o'clock, picked her up at her apartment, and whisked her downtown. We ordered drinks and *steaks, and sat for a while talking about our future. She didn't know I'd planned to propose to her—officially—on Christmas eve, but it was already a foregone conclusion that we'd marry sometime in the new year. We were both so happy. I could tell by the way people looked at us that our faces were shining.*

And yet I had something else on my mind that night, too, something much darker. As the evening progressed I explained what I'd learned. Kay listened with great interest. I told her I needed to find a way to get into Manderbach's house—and into his life. We talked about it awhile, knocked around a couple of different ideas, and finally Kay hit on one we both felt certain would work. She would become a Trojan horse. In the disguise of a flirtatious, attractive— eligible—young woman, she would enter the walls of the castle. Kay would get to know Bud Manderbach. But first, we had to devise a situation where they would meet. If everything went as planned, he'd then ask her out on a date. Once she had her foot in the door, she could survey the situation, ask a few leading questions, even do some snooping. I was most interested in his car—the one he was driving the night of the accident. Since he was a rich guy, I figured he had access to more than one automobile.

Kay was every bit as interested in finding the truth as I was—at least, I think she was. In many ways, I don't know anymore. By then I was seeing everything through the filter of my own ambition. Yet Kay was willing. I'm sure of that much. She saw the importance of what we were doing. We both knew there might be a certain risk, but neither of us comprehended the overwhelming danger. We were two kids having ourselves a great adventure. In a romantic sort of way, it felt like an old movie to both of us. I was Alan Ladd and she was Veronica Lake. We even laughed about it. The fact that we resembled them wasn't lost on either of us. God, when I think of it now, I could vomit.

For the next week I followed Bud Manderbach around, just to see what his patterns were. Thankfully, he was fairly regular. Always to the store by nine. Parked in the department-store ramp, always in the same spot. Worked most of the day in his office. I learned that his father was apparently too ill to run the store anymore. He was bedridden in the big house on Summit Avenue where the whole family lived. Bud had, for all practical purposes, assumed control of the store. He left anywhere between four and six—never went home. From what I could tell, his marriage must have been a bust. Twice he went to bars and picked up women. Other nights he met friends for dinner. Always, he drank to the point of inebriation. Even with all he had going for him, he wasn't a happy man.

The following Monday morning, we put our plan in motion. Kay didn't own a car, so I let her borrow mine. She parked in the department-store ramp around eight forty-five and waited by the elevators until Manderbach came in. They rode down to the mezzanine level together, where Bud took a different set of elevators up to the corporate offices. My instincts were correct. Manderbach couldn't resist a beautiful young woman, especially when he discovered that she worked at the store. Kay didn't have to flirt with him—Manderbach did enough for both of them. By the third morning, he'd asked her to have dinner with him the following night.

The plan was working. Since we didn't want him to know where she lived, she arranged to meet him at the restaurant and then took her own car—my car—home. He was a married man and she had a reputation to protect. He didn't argue. When she got back to her apartment around ten, I was waiting for her just inside the downstairs door. We sat on the stairs and talked. She said Manderbach was a sad man, but surprisingly fun to be with. She felt it best not to push too much that night. He'd asked her to go skating with him over at Lake of the Isles on Saturday afternoon and she'd accepted. She told him to pick her up outside the drugstore on Franklin and Hennepin. She didn't want her roommates to know she was seeing him. Again, he agreed.

Saturday afternoon came and went. I waited for her at her apartment until six. She was supposed to be back well before that. Thinking that something had gone wrong, I drove straight to the park. I looked everywhere but couldn't find them. I asked some of the people in the warming house if they'd seen a woman with shoulder-length blonde hair, a red coat with black fur around the collar and cuffs. Young. Beautiful. She would have been with a guy in his late twenties. Dark hair. The Fred MacMurray type. I never liked Fred MacMurray and found a secret satisfaction that Manderbach looked like him. One woman said she'd seen a young couple like that. They'd been having a great time. The guy wasn't very steady on his skates at first, but the young woman held on to his arm, encouraging him, helping him up when he fell down. Eventually the guy seemed to get his sea legs. They'd driven off in his car sometime around five.

I thanked the woman and left. The fact that they'd been having such a swell time rankled a bit, but then, that was just her opinion. The most pressing problem was, where had they gone? If they were having a good time, then Kay was all right. But I didn't trust the guy. I hoped Kay had the sense not to trust him either. The only thing left for me to do was to head back to her apartment. Hopefully, she'd be home soon.

I cooled my heels in the entryway until close to nine. I think I must have worn a groove in the rug before she finally arrived home by cab. When she walked through the door, she wrapped her arms around me, kissed me as tenderly as she ever had, and apologized profusely. She had no way of contacting me with the change in plans. Manderbach, or "Bud," as she was now calling him, had asked her out to dinner and she didn't want to refuse.

As we sat on the stairs and talked I could see how excited she was. Her cheeks were flushed not only with the cold air, but with her own sense of mission. She'd finally made some concrete progress. Bud was starting to trust her, confide in her. Over dinner, he'd opened up about his awful marriage, the miserable way his father had treated him ever since he was a child, his neurotic though beloved sister, B.B. Kay said she understood him a little better. He

*was a tortured soul, really. A man who found no joy in
living. His wife was a shrew. She'd only married him
because he was rich. His father belittled him every chance
he got. There was no reason to go home at night. Nobody
except his sister missed him, and she was usually involved
in some TV show. He said his wife was relieved when he
didn't come home until after she'd gone to bed. That way,
there were no arguments. He had his life and she had
hers. The fact that they were strangers didn't seem to
bother her. But it bothered Bud. He was a man adrift,
without moorings or a safe haven.*

As you might expect, about the time she mentioned the
moorings and the safe haven, I was ready to puke. I mean,
I couldn't believe my Kay was this naive. She'd swallowed
his line whole. She was completely blind to how he'd
manipulated her. I gently tried to point that out, but she
got defensive. Said I didn't understand. I hadn't been
there, hadn't witnessed his pain firsthand. Well, I mean, I
still felt nauseous, but then she changed the subject. Said
she was sure she was on the verge of discovering something important. Over dessert, he'd touched on the subject
of some great tragedy that had befallen him recently.
Something he'd never told a living soul about before. But
then, before he could elaborate, Kay's cab arrived. She
was certain that he would tell her eventually. She even
went so far as to say that he might be falling in love with
her—just a little bit.

I asked her if they had another date planned. She said
yes, she was going to a movie and a late dinner with him
the following night.

It all seemed a little too cozy for my liking, but then, this
was what I wanted, wasn't it? Kay was making progress.
Soon we'd know the truth about the Landauer hit-and-
run. When I walked her upstairs and kissed her good
night, she remained in my arms for a long time. "I'm
scared, Justin," she finally said, looking up into my eyes.

I stroked her hair and told her I understood. It wouldn't

*be long now. Once we knew the truth, she'd never have to
see him again.*

*I actually thought I did understand. I figured that even
though Manderbach had sucked her in, she was beginning
to see through his lies. On a gut level, she understood his
essential evil and he frightened her. In retrospect, I'm not
sure we were talking about the same thing at all.*

*The worst part is, now that Kay's gone, I'll never know
what she meant that night. I'll go to my grave wondering
what it was I overlooked. It's like walking in quicksand,
Mom. There's nothing solid under my feet. I'm not sure of
anything anymore, except that I'm alive. And Bud Manderbach is alive. But Kay is dead. It shouldn't have ended that
way, with her bloody body lying in the snow at my feet.*

I'll try to write again soon.

All my love,
Justin

25

"We'd like a table by the windows," said Mitzi Quinn,
smiling pleasantly at the hostess. Making sure her daughter
was safely in tow, she followed the woman through the
room, pointing her daughter's attention to some of the more
prominent features of the sleek, silvery, Art Deco interior.

The Fountain Grill, the Maxfield's famous second-floor
café, was nearly empty tonight. Mitzi assumed that on
Christmas eve most people probably had someplace to be,
somewhere to go. As she sat down at the table and was handed
a menu, she felt herself finally relax, knowing she'd made the
right decision in not canceling her Christmas plans. Just last

night, she'd been on the verge of calling her daughter, but decided that spending the holidays alone was simply too horrible. It was a selfish decision, one she wasn't entirely proud of, but Mitzi was confident her daughter would understand. Once Christmas was over, she would have to leave, of course—instead of staying until New Year's as originally planned. But that was a small price to pay.

"This hotel is *gorgeous*," said Cathy Quinn in her deep Texas drawl. "Far more beautiful than you told me on the phone. Why, a woman could really relax in a place like this. And all the time I thought you were *suffering*." She squeezed her mother's hand and gave her an amused smile.

Mitzi beamed at her proudly. She hadn't seen her in four weeks, though it felt much longer. Catherine Lindsay Quinn, called Cathy by most everyone, was in her late thirties, a good-looking woman with a deep tan and dyed red hair. She was divorced, childless, and currently the director of an exclusive health spa in a ritzy section of Houston. Mitzi was proud of her daughter's good looks and impeccable taste, and especially of her success in the business world. In a way, Cathy was everything Mitzi had always wanted to be. Independent. Confident. Well educated. Well liked. Sought after by an endless stream of handsome, eligible men. And best of all, Cathy was a good girl. She respected her mother's wishes.

"Good evening, ladies," said George Chambers, walking up to the table with a playful smile on his face.

Mitzi looked up. She didn't really want any company tonight, but it seemed awkward not to ask him to sit down. He was such a friendly, good-natured old guy. Everyone had grown terribly fond of him. "Evening, George. Have you eaten dinner yet?"

He patted his stomach. "Just finished. I'm on my way up to Heda's suite for a little Christmas cheer. Would you two lovely ladies like to join us later?"

"I should introduce you to my daughter," said Mitzi, hugging the menu to her chest. "Cathy, this is George Chambers. He's the sound-effects technician for our radio serial."

Cathy smiled. "Nice to meet you, Mr. Chambers."

George cocked his head. "You know, you look awfully familiar to me."

"Do I?"

"Yes . . . come to think of it, you look a lot like—"

"I'm sure the two of you have never met," said Mitzi, heading off any further conversation on the subject. "George, I hope you understand. I haven't seen my daughter in weeks. We've got some catching up to do, so I'm afraid we'll have to pass on your invitation."

"Oh, sure," he said, his eyes still fixed on Cathy. "Well, Merry Christmas to you both. See you at the station on Sunday night, Mitzi."

"You will." She waved as he walked away. Opening the menu, she adjusted her glasses to read the fine print at the bottom. "Are you hungry, honey?"

"Starved," said Cathy, looking around for the waitress. "That guy was sure in a cheerful mood. If you ask me, he needs a good barber. I wonder what he'd look like without the beard and all the hair."

"Probably just another old man," said Mitzi absently.

Cathy had taken a taxi in from the airport. She'd arrived several hours earlier amid a veritable jungle of luggage and packages. Mitzi was waiting for her in the lobby with a bouquet of holly berries and a box of delicate ribbon candy. She always gave these to her daughter on Christmas eve. She couldn't even remember how the tradition got started. Probably a leftover from Cathy's childhood. In her ex-husband's family, it was traditional never to open presents until Christmas morning, so Mitzi was always looking for ways to make Christmas eve special for her only child.

"Let's order some wine," said Mitzi as the waitress arrived. "How about a bottle of the Fetzer Chardonnay." The waitress wrote it down and then left, returning a few minutes later with the wine steward. As he poured she took the orders.

Once the waitress had left, Cathy proposed a toast. "To our Christmas together in Minnesota. May it be everything we hope for."

They touched glasses and then each took a sip. "What are you hoping for?" asked Mitzi.

"Well, I'd like to catch up on what you've been doing here. And then have a good time, I suppose. Oh, and I want to do some shopping at the Mall of America, of course."

"Of course." Cathy loved to shop. She was the original clotheshorse.

"And, oh, I don't know. Maybe see a play at the Guthrie or the Allen Grimby. I read about both while I was on the plane. I hear there's a lot of good theatre in the Twin Cities."

"Actually, your stay is something I wanted to talk to you about."

"Sure. I'm open to suggestions—as long as they don't interfere with my hearing your radio show on Sunday night."

Mitzi had told her daughter nothing of what was really going on. To be honest, *she* didn't know what was going on. Like everyone else at the station, she had theories, but no facts. Yet unlike George Chambers and some of the rest of the cast, Mitzi felt constantly apprehensive and on edge. She'd even had a premonition a few days ago. She'd been standing at a railing overlooking an ice rink, watching a pair of ice-skaters dance and twirl on the ice. In one vivid flash, she saw it all. Something terrible was about to happen. Something hideous, dark, and bloody.

Feeling suddenly overwhelmed, she took another sip of wine to fortify herself. Then another, this one more of a gulp.

"Hey, slow down, Mom. You're drinking that like it's grape juice."

With an unsteady hand, Mitzi set the glass back on the table, noticing she'd spilled some on the tablecloth. "Cathy, I need to talk to you. You're not going to like this, but you *must* do as I say. I want you to leave on Sunday morning. I've already called the airline. There's a direct flight from here to Oklahoma City leaving at ten forty-five. And I've spoken to your father. He said he'd be thrilled to have you come visit him next week. He can show you around the hobby farm he just bought. He's got several new horses. We both know how much you love to ride. And he thought the two of you could drive out and see

Aunt Sal and Uncle Bill while you're in town. You haven't spent any time with them in years."

Cathy held up her hand. "Wait just a doggone minute here, Mom. I just got here and you're already trying to get rid of me? What's going on?"

"Nothing, it's just—"

"Don't tell me nothing. I don't believe you. We haven't been apart at this time of year since I was born."

Lifting the wineglass to her lips, Mitzi gave her daughter a defiant glance and then emptied the glass. She needed it. After pouring herself a second, she began again. "Look, Cathy, I never lied to you. You know Jim Quinn isn't your real father. And you know who is. I've tried to answer all your questions about Justin. I haven't kept anything back."

"I know that. Where's all this coming from?"

Mitzi lowered her eyes. It was all so complex. "When I was offered the job to reprise my role in the old *Dallas Lane* radio series, I didn't tell you that Heda Bloom, Justin's mother, was the one behind it. She's staying here right now. She plans to remain in town for the six weeks the show is on the air."

Cathy leaned into the table, folding her hands over her napkin. "Are you telling me that my grandmother is staying at the Maxfield?"

Mitzi tried to read her daughter's reaction, but it wasn't easy. Ever since she was a child, Cathy could absorb information, even upsetting information, without giving any of her feelings away. Mitzi found it infuriating, but there it was. "Yes, that's what I'm saying. Now, honey, you have to promise me that you'll stay away from her."

Cathy seemed surprised, even a little indignant. "Of course I'll stay away from her, Mom. I've got nothing to say to that woman."

"Good."

"But that doesn't explain why I have to leave."

Mitzi took several more sips of wine. She was beginning to feel the effects of the alcohol, and the mellow sensation was a welcome one. "I don't know how to say this."

"Just spit it out. We've never kept secrets. Tell me what's got you so tied up in knots."

What indeed? thought Mitzi. "Look, Cathy, something funny is going on here. Something to do with your real father."

"Justin Bloom isn't my real father," said Cathy indignantly. "Jim Quinn is my dad. Justin Bloom was just my biodad. He contributed a few sperm and a bunch of genes. That about covers it."

Mitzi felt herself blush.

"Oh, come on, Mom. You were in love. He was a bastard. You'd broken up, but he couldn't leave it alone. He took advantage of you, plain and simple. You've always used the story as an example of how sleeping with a guy, even if it was only once, could mean pregnancy."

Mitzi wasn't sure who'd taken advantage of whom anymore, but let it pass.

"I never gave that man a moment's thought. Certainly not when I had a fine man like Jim Quinn for my dad."

Mitzi began to tear. "Yeah, old Jim wasn't much of a husband, but he always loved you, Cathy. You were the apple of his eye. And I've got to give him credit. Not every man would marry a woman knowing she was pregnant with another man's child. Jim adored you, honey. He still does. Would it be so bad to spend the rest of your Christmas vacation with him?"

"Of course not. But that's not the point. I always spend Thanksgiving with Dad, and Christmas with you. What's so different about *this* Christmas?"

"It's . . . it's just not safe here, honey."

"Safe? Why not?" She looked around the room and shrugged. "This is a luxury hotel. We're in the middle of a big city."

Mitzi grabbed her daughter's arm. "You don't understand. I'm . . . afraid."

"Of what?"

"I'm not sure!"

Cathy's frustration turned to concern. "You're worrying me, Mom."

"Just do what I ask, all right? Promise you'll leave on Sunday morning."

"Well . . . sure, if that's what you really want, but—"

"It is." She finished her second glass of wine. She felt much better now that everything was settled.

"It's just, if it's not safe here for me, it's not safe for you either. Why don't you fly home with me on Sunday morning?"

"I can't," said Mitzi. "I signed a contract. I have to honor it."

"But why? People break contracts all the time."

"No," said Mitzi, pouring herself a third glass of wine. Her hand was steady now. Steady and firm. "I have to see this through to the end."

Cathy shook her head. "You sure are acting strange tonight, Mom. I've never seen you drink so much."

"It's a celebration." Mitzi raised her glass. "My daughter is with me and tomorrow is Christmas. What more can a mother ask?"

"Well," said Cathy, placing her napkin in her lap, "as long as you're happy."

"I am," said Mitzi, gazing at her daughter with great affection. And she would remain happy. Until Sunday morning.

26

"Get away from that door," called Bram. "I mean, really, Sophie. The owner of a hotel, listening at keyholes."

"I'm not listening at keyholes," she said, shushing him. "I'm merely standing in my own living room."

"Right. With the door open, listening to a fight going on across the hall. It's a fine distinction, if you ask me."

Bram busied himself putting the finishing touches on a present he was wrapping for Rudy. Hearing a particularly loud shout, he got up and stood behind his wife, placing a hand on her shoulder. "What are they arguing about?"

"I thought you weren't interested."

"Humor me."

"Well, I'm only catching bits and pieces, but it sounds like Dorothy's got some plans for later this evening. Heda doesn't want her to go out."

"Maybe she doesn't want to be left alone on Christmas eve."

"No, I don't think that's it. She's upset about some man Dorothy's been seeing. She insists that she stop."

"Ah," said Bram, bending down close to Sophie's ear. "The mystery man strikes again."

Sophie screwed her head around and looked at him. "What are you talking about?"

"The gossip around the office says that Dorothy is currently 'involved.' She's had lunch twice this week with the same man." He raised an eyebrow, then gave it a seductive flutter.

"I'd hardly call two lunches 'involved.' Who is he?"

He shrugged. "Nobody's absolutely sure, but I have heard one name being bandied about."

"Bandy it in my direction, darling."

He smirked. "Bud Manderbach."

"No kidding. That guy's been married more times than centipedes have legs. She better watch her step."

"I'm not worried. She can handle herself." Bram walked back to the couch and picked up his empty coffee cup, carrying it into the kitchen. He returned a moment later waving two martini glasses.

"Anybody would be a fool to get mixed up with that guy," said Sophie, sitting down on a wing chair next to the Christmas tree. "Say, isn't he one of the names being discussed as the real murderer of Kay Collins?"

"If there's any truth to it."

"Do you think there is?"

"I think," he said, pouring several inches of gin into a shaker, "that I don't want to talk about Bud Manderbach, Justin Bloom, or Kay Collins tonight."

"Really."

"Yes really. As far as I'm concerned, it's been a bad week for me when it comes to that whole egregious conundrum."

"You mean the murder of that poor woman at O'Dell's cabin."

"Among other things, yes. All I know is, I'll never hear from Arn O'Dell's granddaughter again. The message was clear, Soph. I have every confidence she didn't miss the point. If she surfaces again with that letter, she's a dead woman."

"Who's behind all this?" said Sophie, her voice full of exasperation.

Bram held a finger to his lips.

"Right. The moratorium on the subject begins now."

After adding vermouth to the gin, Bram glanced over his shoulder and saw Ethel's ancient form lurch out of the bedroom. She stood in the darkened hallway for a moment, smacking her lips. Sensing a potential food opportunity in the living room, she dragged herself over to the coffee table, sniffed the air with a certain world-weary curiosity, and then gazed dolefully at a plate of Christmas cookies resting mere inches from her nose.

"Can't I give her one?" asked Bram. "After all, it *is* Christmas eve."

"Well, I did get more of that special meat-flavored toothpaste yesterday, so I guess it would be all right. As long as one of us brushes her teeth before she goes to bed."

"Sure, Soph. No problem."

"Meaning, of course, that I should do it."

"Aren't all women innate caregivers?"

Sophie gave him a half-lidded smile as he handed her the martini glass. "In certain circles, you could be shot for a remark like that. Just to make sure your heart's in the right place, I'll put her toothpaste next to yours tonight. You can do the honors."

"What if I get them mixed up?"

She grinned at him over the rim of her glass. "Plan on sleeping someplace other than our bed."

Bram laughed, then tossed Eithel her cookie. "God, it's so great to have the evening all to ourselves. I love Christmas. Say, what time are Rudy and John getting here tomorrow?"

"Around one. We'll eat at three."

"He's feeling well enough to come?"

Sophie sighed. "He's still not a hundred percent, but he's so much better, and he really wants to come. I've got a big meal planned, so don't feast on too many of those Russian tea cakes."

"Say, didn't you say you'd rented us a movie for tonight?" He snuck Ethel another cookie while Sophie got up to put on a CD. "Panis Angelicus," sung by José Carreras, now wafted softly from the stereo speakers.

"That I did," she said, turning around and eyeing Ethel suspiciously.

"And what did you get us?"

As Sophie sat back down in her chair she merely smiled.

"Oh, God, no. Not *Fargo* again. Since it came out, we've seen it five times. Minnesotans are supposed to hate that movie, Soph."

She continued to smile. "Not me. But rest easy. I've selected an oldie for our viewing enjoyment. Something nice and noir."

"Like what?"

"Double Indemnity."

"Great! Fred MacMurray and Barbara Stanwyck. Perfect. What are we waiting for?"

"Well, I want to take a shower first. Why don't you mix up another batch of martoonies and meet me in the bedroom. I've already got the tape in the VCR."

As Sophie disappeared into the bedroom she called, "Check to make sure the front door's locked before you come in."

"Will do, honey."

After careful consideration, Bram decided to mix the drinks in the bedroom. That way, they would be properly chilled without being watered down. Assembling everything on a tray, he glanced around to make sure no one was watching and then tossed Ethel one last cookie. "Merry Christmas, old girl." He watched her make a mess of it on the Oriental.

As he was about to turn off the tree lights and pack it in for the night, the cordless telephone on the coffee table gave a sudden beep. "I'll get it," he called, realizing as soon as he said the words that Sophie was in the shower.

"Hello," he said, sitting down on the couch.

"Is this Bram Baldric?"

He recognized the voice immediately and his pulse quickened. "Yes, it is."

"Do you know who this is?"

"I do. I didn't think I'd ever hear from you again."

"Believe me, I thought long and hard about making this call."

"Do you still want to meet?"

Silence. Then: "Someone's been watching my house."

"How do you know?"

"I saw them. For the last few nights I've watched the same white van drive back and forth down the street. Every time it comes past my front door, it slows. It's always late, usually around midnight. One time, the driver even got out. I couldn't see his face, but he was short, kind of stocky. I'd never seen him before. He came up to the door. Then walked around the side of the house looking at the windows."

"You're not safe!"

"Do you think I don't know that?"

Bram could tell she was smoking. He could hear her exhale, then take another deep drag.

"Someone made a mistake the other night, Mr. Baldric. I was the one who should have been hanging from that pipe, not Betty Johanson. The guy in the van's just figuring out a way to finish the job."

A shiver ran down his back, as if someone had just run the blade of a knife over his skin. "What are you going to do?"

"I have a gun. For now, it's enough."

"But . . . why did you call this Betty Johanson in the first place?"

"I thought I was going to be late. My supervisor asked me

to put in some overtime that afternoon. I wheedled my way out of it, but by the time I got up there, she was already dead, thanks to you and that lawyer friend of yours. Did you have to announce our plans on the radio?"

He felt his stomach clench. "It was a mistake."

"Sure."

"It was! I tried to get the guy to stop talking, but he wouldn't. He overheard our conversation—I mean, he couldn't help but hear. He was sitting right next to me when you called."

Silence.

"Look, this is awkward. I don't even know what to call you."

"You think I'm going to give you my name? Not on your life. Oh, and it won't help you to look up O'Dell in the phone book either. I was married once for a couple of years. I don't have the same last name anymore."

Bram already knew that. He'd called every O'Dell in the seven-county metro area looking for her, but had struck out. He hadn't even found a relative. Sensing her anger, and fearing that she might hang up, he said the first thing to pop into his head. "Where do you work?" It was meant to be conversational, but it sounded more like interrogation.

"It doesn't matter, Mr. Baldric. I quit my job."

"But—" He struggled for the right words. "After I discovered Betty Johanson's body, I talked to the sheriff, a man named Henry Olson. He said they'd found some tire tracks in the snow about thirty yards back of the cabin. They're confident it will lead them to her murderer."

The woman gave a bitter laugh. "So much for law enforcement. They were *my* tire tracks, Mr. Baldric. It may lead them to my door, but I didn't kill Betty."

"But you know who did, don't you?" It was less a question than a statement of fact.

More silence. After several long, uncomfortable seconds she said, "I still need you to look at that letter. You've gotta help me, Mr. Baldric. I don't know if I'm comin' or goin' anymore, I just know this has got to get resolved."

"Name the place."

"Have you ever heard of the Antler Saloon? It's a bar and hamburger joint on Lyndale and Thirty-fourth."

"No, but I can find it."

"I'll meet you there tomorrow night. Nine sharp. And don't tell anyone this time."

"Of course not. But . . . the bar, will it be open? Lots of places are closed on Christmas day."

"It'll be open." She took another drag on her cigarette. "Oh, and one more thing."

"Yes?"

"Don't bring your wife."

"How did you know—"

The line clicked. She'd hung up.

"Who was that?" asked Sophie, tying the cord on her bathrobe. She'd just come out of the bedroom.

Bram had to think fast. "Old Tony Thompson. He wanted to wish us both a merry Christmas."

Leaning against the door frame, she scrutinized his face. Bram could tell she didn't entirely believe him.

"The curtain goes up in five minutes. I believe I'm on the bill tonight as the 'selected short.' "

An obvious reference to her diminutive height. Bram grinned and replied, "Give me one second to make a phone call and I'll be right in."

"Whatever you say, dear."

"My, but we're in a good mood."

"We're working on it." She disappeared inside the room.

Quickly, Bram tapped in the home number of his friend Al Lundquist. It rang several times before a deep voice answered, "Hello?"

"Al?"

"Yeah?"

"This is Bram."

"Hey, buddy."

"I need a big favor."

"So what else is new?"

"I wouldn't ask if it wasn't important."

Al sighed. "What do you want?"

"I need to know if there's any way you could find out the name of Arn O'Dell's granddaughter."

"O'Dell? You mean the police officer who ID'd Justin Bloom?"

"That's the one."

"You're still beating a dead horse, huh?"

"Yeah, Al. Still flogging the hell out of it."

He was silent for several seconds. "Well, as I think of it, there is one guy I could try. A retired cop. He'd be pretty old now, but I'm fairly certain he knew O'Dell. I think they were even partners for a while."

"Great. Can you call him?"

"You mean tonight? On Christmas eve?"

"Yes, tonight. I've got to find the granddaughter right away."

"Why?" Now he sounded suspicious.

"Look, Al, as soon as I know anything important, I'll tell you."

"Sure. And elephants can fly."

"Will you help me?"

More silence. Then: "Well, I was pretty bored by the TV tonight. When you're a single guy, all this touchy-feely Christmas crap can give you a bad case of indigestion. Sure, I'll give him a buzz. That is, if I can locate him. He could be dead for all I know."

"Thanks, Al. You're a lifesaver."

"What do you mean?" he said gruffly. "Someone's life is in danger?"

"Bad choice of words. Just call me as soon as you know anything. Tonight. Tomorrow. Whenever."

"Have I ever told you you're a putz?"

"Frequently. Oh—wait! I think Santa's about to come down our chimney, Al. I gotta run get his milk and cookies."

"Asshole."

"Night, pal."

May 10, 1959

Dear Mother:

My friend in the States, the man who has been helping
me get my letters to you safely, sent me some recent newspapers from the city where he lives. They arrived in the
mail shortly after lunch. I sat down to read them and
didn't finish until well into the evening. It's funny, but the
advertisements seemed especially strange to me, almost
like I was reading science fiction. None of it has any
meaning to my life now. I guess that's the point, right?
Life goes on. Just because mine ended last Christmas eve
doesn't mean that other lives have stopped.

I did, however, take note of one news story, something I
hadn't heard about before. I don't know if you know Buddy
Holly, Mom, but I read that he died in a plane crash in February. Both Kay and I really liked his songs. I think she even
had one of his albums. It seemed intensely sad to me to think
of a young man being cut down in the prime of his life. His
career was just catching fire. He had everything to live for.
And then it hit me. Buddy Holly and I have much in common.
I'm still walking the earth, while he's perhaps walking some
other plane of existence, but we're both dead men.

You know, reading that story made me feel less alone. It
even picked me up a little, though I should probably
explain what I mean by that. It reminded me of one time
when I was a boy. Remember the piano lessons you insisted I take? I hated them with the kind of passion only a
kid of ten could muster. One afternoon, while I was sitting

*in Mrs. Gruning's living room waiting for her to be done
with the girl who had the lesson before me, I picked up a
copy of* Look *or* The Saturday Evening Post, *or some such
magazine. I started reading an article about a famous
man, an actor I think, who'd been diagnosed with a brain
tumor. Well, I thought to myself with my ten-year-old
brain, I guess there are worse things than having to cool
my heels in Mrs. Gruning's living room. And I used that
poor man's tragedy over and over again, even went back
to it years later when I'd have to take a test I knew I
wasn't prepared for. Just like Buddy Holly's death, it
made me feel less singled out, less alone. The fact that
there was no real comparison between the two never
entered my mind. I immersed myself in that poor actor's
agony and mine seemed less by comparison—although
only slightly less, you understand. I was, after all, a child.
Maybe it's a flaw in my character that I'm still doing it. I
have many flaws, Mom, and won't argue the point.*

All right, back to my story.

*It became increasingly difficult for Kay to always meet
Bud Manderbach at a drugstore or a restaurant when they
went out on a date. I let her borrow my car, but it was still
awkward. The solution turned out to be simple. We'd allow
him to pick Kay up at "her" place, but we gave him my
address, not hers. She'd meet him outside the front door of
my apartment, and then, when they returned, she wouldn't
let him come inside. Anything to thwart that creep and his
lecherous intentions was all right by me. Besides, I could
keep better track of what was happening that way. Kay and
I could talk before and after each "date." I'd get her firsthand reactions. And also, I finally had use of my car to
follow them if I felt even the least bit nervous.*

*As far as I was concerned, Manderbach had taken the
bait hook, line, and sinker. He was pursuing Kay with a
passion. Almost every day he'd stop by the cosmetics
counter where she worked to bring her a flower, or a
small gift. All the while he kept feeding her his lies—lies
about himself, the wife he loathed, the father who belittled*

him, his loneliness, and his desire to meet the woman of his dreams. Of course, he maintained that Kay was that woman, but it was just a line. I could see right through it, though I wasn't always sure Kay could. As time went on I grew more and more concerned that she might believe some of his bullshit. We talked a lot those last few weeks. I tried to straighten out her thinking, and for the most part, I believe I succeeded.

Finally, one night, after dinner at a downtown restaurant, Manderbach invited her back to his house. This was very unusual, and Kay was not only taken by surprise, but she was somewhat frightened. She pointed out to him that he was married. What if his wife saw them together, or his father? It seemed not only risky, but foolhardy. Manderbach explained that his sister had gone Christmas shopping that night, and his wife was attending a concert with one of her many girlfriends. As for his father, he never got out of bed anymore. So, everything was covered. No one would see them.

Well, Kay could hardly say no. I mean, this was just what we'd been waiting for. Our goal all along had been to get her inside the mansion. If Kay was persuasive, she'd be able to convince him to give her a tour of the place. As I said before, I was particularly interested in his automobiles.

That night, Kay hit the jackpot. In thinking about it later, I found it odd that Manderbach would take her into the garage even before they went into the house, but he explained that his father was a great collector of cars, some antique, others he hoped to keep long enough to earn the label. All this collecting was done, of course, before his father had taken to his sickbed. Bud loved cars himself and insisted that Kay see the collection. After all, they were his now—or would be soon enough.

The garage was oversized and unheated. After retrieving an extra key from under a snow-covered flowerpot, Bud unlocked the door. He then took Kay by the arm and waltzed her past a Duesenberg, two Cords, and an old

Packard. These were all in the back of the garage, up on blocks, parked in by five other cars. The first in line was a baby-blue Buick which belonged to his wife. Next was a white Edsel. This was B.B.'s car, though she rarely drove it. She preferred taking cabs. Bud explained that driving made his sister nervous. Next came the empty space where Bud usually parked his car. It was in the driveway at the moment. A dark green Chrysler New Yorker. Third came his father's car, a black Cadillac with gray leather interior. And finally, a silver Rolls-Royce. The last two were hardly ever driven. These were the two newer cars Bud's father wanted to preserve.

Bud maneuvered Kay around the garage like a king showing a queen his kingdom. Even though he rushed her past the Cadillac, Kay spied the damage to the front fender. It was just what I figured. Manderbach had been in no hurry to get it repaired, especially since all the body shops in town were on the lookout for just this kind of damage. Better to wait until the furor over the hit-and-run had died down. Olga Landauer's brother had kept the story alive in the papers, but that couldn't last forever. Soon it would be a dead issue.

After a brief tour of the inside of the mansion— Manderbach skipped the third floor, where his father had his bedroom—he took Kay out to a small, one-story house at the rear of the property. He called it the "cook's cottage." Once inside, he put on some romantic music, dimmed the lights, and then asked her to dance. She said it was a pretty place. A living room with a series of windows facing a garden. They were mullioned windows, the kind with tiny diamond-shaped panes, but that evening they were covered by thick curtains. The interior was comfortable, not at all lavish. Masculine. Lots of browns and golds. An old braided rug covered a polished wood floor. And there was a fireplace. In front of it was a small round table with a cloth over it. On top of that was a bottle of champagne resting in a bucket of ice, two glasses, and some toast points and caviar. Kay had never tasted caviar before. Turns out, she hated it. I guess Manderbach got quite a bang out of that. He said he'd never had anyone refuse his caviar before.

See, Mom, Kay didn't have pretensions. That's what was so great about her. If she liked something, she liked it because it appealed to her, not because other people thought it was good. It was the same way with her looks. I don't think she ever really grasped how lovely she was, how easy it was for men to fall in love with her. She was a straight shooter, and thought other people were, too. That night, Bud told her he loved her. It was the first time he'd ever said anything like that. He explained that he was going to ask his wife for a divorce. While he didn't propose marriage, he did say that when he was a free man, there was something he wanted to ask her.

Well, I mean, it was just more of his bullshit. Manderbach no doubt used that same line on all his girlfriends just to get them in the sack. When I pointed that out to Kay later that evening—after he'd brought her back to my apartment—she grew quiet. Almost distant. At first I was confused by her silence, but after a while I figured it was all part of an important lesson she needed to learn about men like Manderbach, even if it did bruise her ego a little. In an effort to cheer her up, I opened my own bottle of champagne. I mean, she'd found an incredibly important piece of evidence. We needed to celebrate.

The next step was to document it.

Late the following afternoon, Bud came down to the cosmetics counter to tell Kay he couldn't have dinner with her that night. He had an important meeting the next morning and needed to spend the rest of the evening upstairs in his office, going over a report. He was apologetic, even asked for a rain check. He wanted to take her to a new restaurant just down the block, but could they do it tomorrow night instead of tonight? Kay was happy to agree. She called me when she got home to explain the change in plans. Needless to say, this was just the break I'd been waiting for. Emboldened by the assurance that Manderbach wouldn't be around, I told Kay I'd pick her up at her apartment at seven-fifteen. I spent the next hour trying to get hold of a decent camera. I needed a really good one, not the piece of crap I had at home.

After a quick dinner, we drove to the Manderbach mansion in St. Paul and parked about a block away. I don't know if you've ever seen the place, Mom, but it's pretty impressive. It looks like a medieval castle. Under the cover of darkness, we crept silently through the alley to the back of the garage—the side away from the house. I'd already checked out the main house. The only light that was on in the first two floors came from a room at the rear of the second story. Kay said it belonged to B.B. Of course, the third floor, where Manderbach Sr. was now imprisoned, was lit up like a Christmas tree, especially the north turret, but that didn't concern me. The best part was, Manderbach's car was nowhere around. He hadn't been lying to Kay. Actually, it had occurred to me that old Bud might have had other plans for the evening, specifically, another woman. That would have hurt Kay, but it would also have opened her eyes to the kind of man he really was. I half prayed for that to be the case, but if it was, Bud was off somewhere else doing his Mr. Smooth act.

Kay extracted the key from under the pot and opened the door. I'd brought a flashlight and was careful to keep it away from the windows. I quickly located the Cadillac. While Kay stood guard at the door I snapped a bunch of photos. As soon as I got the film developed, I planned to take the evidence to the police. I finally had the proof I'd been looking for.

"All done," I called to Kay. I was still crouching in front of the car.

That's when I saw her strain to see something outside in the darkness. She watched for a moment, then turned and held a finger to her lips.

"What?" I whispered. I switched off the flashlight. Moonlight streamed in through the windows.

"Oh, God," she said, suddenly backing farther into the room. The look on her face was sheer terror.

A moment later I saw him. It was Manderbach. He'd moved into the doorway, blocking her exit. He wasn't wearing a coat, or even a suit coat, but merely his shirt and tie. He slipped his hands casually into the pockets of his slacks and looked around the garage. Even though his demeanor was easy, I could tell Kay was scared to death. So was I. He was like a tiger stalking his prey—cold, calculating, and full of menace.

"What are you doing here?" he asked, removing a cigarette case and lighter from his pocket. After lighting up, he offered one to Kay, but she declined. As he blew smoke out of his nose he studied her. "Well?"

Kay looked around, careful not to give my presence away. "Waiting," she said finally.

He just stared at her, as if they had all the time in the world. "For what, darling?"

She drew her coat more tightly around her. "You."

I'd always known Kay was a clever girl. Right then, that knowledge was the only thing keeping me from jumping out of my skin.

"What do you mean?" he said, flicking some ash onto the floor.

"Do you know what kind of reputation you have in this town?"

"Sure. Not good. I haven't been a faithful husband, but you of all people should know why. Besides, what's that got to do with anything?"

She kept her head down as she continued, "I had to know if you were really working late tonight."

Again, he stared at her with those dark eyes of his. They were like two cold steel balls. "You came all the way over here, stood in this freezing garage for God knows how long, just to find out if I was bringing another woman back here?"

"I called your office around seven. No one answered."

This I knew was a lie. At least I thought it was. Why would she call him after he canceled the date? She was taking some big chances, but I had no other choice than to go along with her instincts. As they continued to talk I eased carefully under the car, taking the camera with me.

"I sent my secretary home at five," he continued. "I never answer my own telephone."

"You weren't with another woman, then?"

"No!" He tossed his cigarette aside, stepped closer, and took her in his arms. She didn't resist when he kissed her. She was a good actress. She made it look like it was what she really wanted. She was so convincing, she almost had me fooled. I knew she loved me, that it was all an act, but watching them, well, it was like someone had strapped electrodes to my brain and then turned up the voltage. I closed my eyes, but I couldn't stand it. I had to watch. I needed every ounce of self-control I possessed not to climb out from under that car and kill him right then and there. But I waited. Fool that I was, I waited.

"Your hands are cold as ice," he said, lifting them to his lips. "Come to the cottage. I'll build a fire and then make us a pot of coffee."

"But . . . your wife?"

He smiled. "I asked her for that divorce today, Kay. She knows the score. She won't give us any trouble."

He led her outside.

I don't know how long I stayed there under that car, but it was a long time. I couldn't move. I was numb, but not from the cold. What I'd just witnessed had left me shaken and confused. I was jealous, unreasonably so, and angry, and yet I couldn't blame Kay. She'd gotten us both out of a jam. But I still couldn't shake my anxiety. Was all of this merely quick thinking on her part? Or was some part of it—any part of it—real?

When I got home that night, I waited for her phone call. I paced the floor, watched some TV, and eventually poured myself a stiff Scotch. As the snow started to come down outside I sat in the dark. It seemed I was doing an awful lot of waiting lately, and I didn't like it.

She never called that night, Mom. I didn't talk to her again until the next day, and when I did, I was dumbfounded *by what she had to say. Manderbach was more slippery than I'd ever imagined. And more dangerous. Even Kay had to admit that she'd been surprised. Believe me when I tell you that what went on inside the cottage that night not only caught me off guard, but started the chain of events that eventually spun all our lives out of control.*

That's all for tonight, Mom.

Till tomorrow,
Justin

27

The lights had been dimmed. A fire was burning in the fireplace. The romantic mood had been choreographed to please long before she arrived. Dorothy entered the small cottage behind the Manderbach mansion and, knowing the fireworks were about to begin, allowed herself a moment to assess the battlefield. The cottage had no doubt been used for the same romantic purposes many times before. Dorothy assumed he had his moves down to a science.

The living room was small. On one end was a short hall leading to a kitchen, on the other were French doors that opened onto a bedroom. The house was comfortably furnished, yet not extravagantly so. That surprised her. She expected extravagance from a multimillionaire. Another unusual omission was the lack of Christmas decorations. Not one ornament, colored light, or pine bough was anywhere in evidence.

Yet the most striking aspect of the room wasn't something she could easily quantify. While none of the 1950s furnishings were the least bit worn or threadbare, everything looked tired and saggy, an unfortunate ambience for a bachelor pad in her estimation. No wonder he had such rotten luck with women. As Bud helped her off with her coat her feeling of discomfort grew. It struck her now that she was standing in a museum—or perhaps more specifically, a shrine to Bud Manderbach's lost youth.

"Have you eaten?" he asked, closing the closet door.

"I had a glass of eggnog with Heda before I drove over. That's about it."

"Good." He smiled. Stepping over to the stereo, he switched on the turntable and then set the needle down carefully at the beginning of a track. "I've got appetizers and champagne for us in the kitchen. Give me a minute and I'll set it up out here."

As Bud busied himself elsewhere Dorothy's attention was drawn to his rather extensive record collection. It ran the length of two bookshelves. She glanced at the first dozen or so titles and saw that most of them were jazz classics and old standards. Since the album he'd chosen to put on tonight was already on the turntable, she wondered if he hadn't been listening to it earlier. The first song was Tony Bennett's version of "I'll Be Seeing You." She knew the recording, and found it heartbreakingly sad. Was it an indication of his mood?

Bud returned to the room a few minutes later carrying a round silver tray. After arranging everything on the coffee table in front of the couch, he poured them each a glass of champagne. "To us," he said, touching his glass to hers.

Dorothy took a sip. "Mmm, this is good."

"I thought you'd like it." He moved in, his eyes rising to the ceiling above their heads.

Dorothy looked up to see what had caught his attention. "Mistletoe," she observed, her voice full of annoyed good humor.

"It's my one sop to the Christmas tradition. Do you . . . object?"

"Of course not."

He set down his drink and then took her in his arms and kissed her. Easing back just a little, he touched her hair, then traced the line of her jaw. "You're a beautiful woman."

She half closed her eyes, like a cat receiving a caress. "And you're a terrible liar."

He kissed her again. "Does that seem like I'm lying?"

"No," she admitted, adjusting the gold necklace around her pink cashmere sweater. "Perhaps I should have said 'a good *actor*.'"

He smiled, then shook his head in exasperation.

She couldn't help but notice that the smile never quite settled on his lips. "Merry Christmas," she said, moving away from him. They needed some distance if they were going to talk.

"Thanks." He took another swallow of champagne.

"You don't have any decorations."

He shrugged. "Christmas eve was never my night."

"No?" She walked over to the front windows. Parting the heavy brown drapes, she looked outside. Deep snow covered a backyard garden. She could also see the rear part of the main house. "Where's your sister tonight?"

"B.B.? Oh, she's probably watching TV."

"She doesn't mind being alone?"

"After all these years she's used to it." He squeezed the back of his neck and laughed. "In case you think I'm a total Scrooge, I let her talk me into getting a huge tree this year. We even decorated it together. And we always have brunch on Christmas day. Well, that is, if I'm in town."

Dorothy turned to look at him. "She must have a lonely life."

"There are lots of ways to be lonely, Dorothy. I was never lonelier than when I was married."

"Maybe you never found the right woman."

He acknowledged this with a slight lift of his eyebrows, then slowly shifted his attention to some indeterminate point in space.

"You seem so . . . distant tonight."

"Do I?" He tried another smile. "I'm sorry. It's just . . . I have a lot on my mind right now. Business problems."

"Believe me, if it's business, I understand." She moved back to the coffee table and withdrew a cigarette from a brass box. "Actually, I've got some news that may cheer you up."

"Really? Let's hear it. I could use some good news." On the end table next to him rested an antique silver dagger complete with jewel-encrusted hilt. He picked it up, flipped open the top jewel, and lit her cigarette. "It's one of B.B.'s," he explained, shutting the top. "She collects cigarette lighters, among other things. I particularly liked this one, so I lifted it from her collection. Trust me. She'll never know it's gone."

"Is it sharp?"

"No." Easing an arm around her waist, he pulled her close again and said, "So tell me. What's your good news?" His gaze shifted to the bedroom and then back to her face.

"I'm not ready for that, Bud. You promised you wouldn't push."

"But why not? We've both been around the block more than once. We like each other. We have fun together. What are we waiting for?"

She disentangled herself from his grip before replying, "When I met you, I didn't know your reputation."

"For what?"

She couldn't help but smile. "Oh, Bud, please."

His scowl slowly turned into a grin. "So what? I appreciate women. Where's the crime in that?"

"I just need . . . more time." She could tell he'd heard that line a thousand times. His reaction almost caused her to laugh out loud, but she restrained herself. Tapping some ash into an ashtray, she said, "Bud, I'm old-fashioned. I need commitment. The possibility of marriage."

"I'm not ruling that out, but . . . I understand. I'll leave it up to you. You tell me when you're ready."

This change in tactics threw her. Tonight, when she'd first walked in the door, his intentions seemed crystal clear. The evening would follow a certain standard course, and eventually they'd end up in the bedroom. He'd push, she'd retreat. He'd push some more. They both knew how to play the game. But now, since he'd given up so easily, she was confused—relieved, of course, that she wouldn't have to fight him off, but still confused.

Placing her cigarette on the ashtray, she spread some pâté on a piece of French bread. "Let's get back to my good news. It's guaranteed to improve your mood." She made herself comfortable on the couch and then patted the space next to her. She waited for him to sit down before continuing. "Now, just so that you understand. This is my Christmas present to you. I hope you like it because it took some real effort to arrange." She paused. "Remember how many times you've pressed me to set up a meeting between you and Wish Greveen?"

"Sure." He shrugged. "Why?"

"Well, I've set one up."

"Dorothy, that's wonderful! Fabulous, as a matter of fact. Just give me the particulars and I'll be there with bells on."

"That's just it. He's coming tonight. He should be here any minute."

Bud seemed truly shaken. "He's coming to the house?"

"Well, not exactly. I told him we'd be in the small cottage behind the main house. He said not to worry. He'd find it. It was his idea, Bud. I didn't think you'd mind."

Resting his fingers against his temples as if to calm a troublesome throbbing, he gazed intently into the fire.

"It's all right, isn't it? I thought this was the perfect opportunity." When he didn't reply immediately, she added, "I mean, you seemed so eager. You talked about setting up a meeting with him every time we've been together."

"No," said Bud, holding up his hand. "It's . . . fine, Dorothy. I just have to think about all this for a minute. Get my bearings."

She retrieved her cigarette, tapping the ash into an ashtray. "Bud . . . what's the problem? You can tell me."

"There's no problem." Again, he smiled at her. "You did just what I wanted you to. I'm very grateful."

The doorbell rang.

Dorothy glanced at her watch. It was nearly ten. "I suppose that must be him."

Bud seemed frozen to his seat, unable to move.

"Do you want me to get it?"

"No." He gave himself a couple more seconds and then pushed off the couch and hurried to the door.

Dorothy leaned back against the couch cushions and watched. At first, the two men just stared at each other. Each seemed to be taking the other man's measure. It was odd seeing them together, both from such different parts of her life.

Finally, Bud said, "Come in."

Greveen stepped hesitantly inside. After taking a brief look around, he removed his coat and hat and set them on a chair. Underneath he was wearing a red wool cardigan over a black turtleneck, and a pair of dark wool trousers. Turning to Dorothy, he said, "Good evening."

"I'm glad you found the place." She stubbed out her cigarette.

"Your directions were letter-perfect."

Bud moved to the fireplace and rested his arm on the mantel. "Welcome to my home, Mr. Greveen."

"Thanks."

"Did you drive over?"

"I took a cab."

Bud seemed transfixed. Finally, he shook his head and looked down. When he looked back up again he was laughing. "You have to admit, this is pretty amazing."

"Life is full of twists and turns," said Greveen. He didn't smile.

Dorothy picked up her champagne glass, holding it delicately between her thumb and forefinger. "You two fellows talk like you know each other."

"We don't," said Greveen coldly.

Bud pointed to the champagne. "Help yourself."

"No thanks."

"I'll have some more," said Dorothy, filling her glass for the second time.

"I trust you've had a . . . profitable stay here in Minnesota," continued Bud.

"I'm not sure I'd use that exact word. Let's just say that I remain confident that matters will turn out the way I planned."

"It's not good to be overconfident, Mr. Greveen."

He dipped a hand into the pocket of his sweater. "I assume you've listened to my radio show."

"*Your* radio show." Again, Bud laughed. "Yes, I guess it is your show, come to think of it. It's been your show all along."

"I beg your pardon," said Dorothy, interrupting them. "We've all got a stake in it. Heda. Me. The actors."

Bud ignored her. Instead, he examined Greveen from head to toe. "Funny how ghosts age."

"Meaning what?"

"I never would have recognized you. That is, if it really is you. I suppose this could all be an act."

"I would have recognized you anywhere." Greveen moved toward the other end of the fireplace.

Dorothy thought they looked like two soldiers facing each other over the field of battle, ready to duel to the death.

As Greveen folded his arms over his chest Bud's eyes were drawn to the ring on his left hand. "Where did you get that?"

"Where do you think I got it? It's mine. My mother gave it to me many years ago."

"But—"

"But what, Mr. Manderbach? Does it remind you of a ring you've seen before?"

"Say, you two *do* know each other," said Dorothy. "I suspected as much. Why don't we all sit down. Enjoy some of this pâté."

Bud stepped quickly away from the mantel. "Listen, Dorothy, Mr. Greveen and I have some important matters to discuss. We need some privacy. Would you mind terribly if I canceled our date tonight? Could you get home by yourself?"

She gave him a disgusted look. "I had no trouble getting here by myself. I'm sure I could get home."

"Fine," he said, retrieving her coat from the front closet.

She could tell he wasn't listening to her anymore. "Will I talk to you tomorrow?" she asked, yanking on her gloves.

"Sure." He gave her a peck on the cheek. "I'll call you."

Something had changed. She didn't need to ask what

it was. Bud had finally achieved his goal—a face-to-face meeting with Wish Greveen. His passionless pursuit of her was over. "No, you won't. It's finished between us, isn't it? Just tell me the truth."

"Don't be silly," he said, pushing her out the door. "We'll have dinner soon. Drive safely, Dorothy." He slammed the door in her face.

At the stroke of midnight, B.B. switched off the TV set in her bedroom, threw on her black cape and her snowmobile boots, and snuck out the back door of the main house. Glancing over her shoulder to make sure no one was watching, she crept soundlessly down the shoveled walk toward the cottage. Chimneys pumped steam, dark and menacing, into the frigid night air as she hurried along the cobblestones. The sky above was a canvas of cold, indifferent stars.

Before she used her key on the front door—a key her brother had no idea she owned—she wiped some frost from a side window and peeked into the bedroom. The drapes were drawn, but she always made sure there was a crack through which she could view the show. By this time on any given evening, Bud usually had someone in bed. Sometimes she saw them doing it. Sometimes they were asleep. Tonight, however, while the room had obviously been used—the bedspread was half on the bed, half on the floor—no one was around. She could see that the lights were off in the living room. That usually meant Bud had left. Maybe he was taking his date home.

After checking the garage and discovering that her brother's car was indeed gone, she used her key and went in. Bud didn't allow her inside the cottage, but that's what made sneaking around all the more fun. It was like a secret expedition, or an archaeological dig. She loved to collect the evidence, the clues to her brother's life, at least the part to which he denied her access.

B.B. was incredibly curious about sex. She'd never slept with a man, and frankly didn't really think she'd care to, but she was still intrigued by all the romantic machinations. The food and the wine. The choice of music. And fire. Always a fire. If not in the fireplace, then candles burning here and there throughout the room. It fascinated her to think that Bud had so much energy for all these details. Over the years she'd determined that sex was terribly important to her brother. Since none of his wives or his girlfriends lasted very long, the women must be interchangeable. It didn't seem that way in the old movie classics she liked to watch on TV, but B.B. understood that movies and real life weren't always the same.

Switching on a lamp, she surveyed the front room. Everything was topsy-turvy. The coffee table was overturned, a champagne bottle, several glasses, and a tray of food scattered on the floor in front of it. Near the front drapes, a crock containing a philodendron had fallen off a credenza and smashed to pieces on the rug. Pillows were tossed here and there. A standing lamp had been knocked on the floor.

"Buddy's not going to like this," she muttered, edging her way through the mess into the bedroom. Perhaps there'd been a robbery. It had never happened before, but there was a first time for everything. Her eyes opened wide at the sight of red stains on the rug and the wall. "Oh . . . God, no," she whispered. "Not . . . not again!"

It was blood, red, dark, and ominous.

Her mind raced. She tried to think, to calm herself, to make sense of it. What was going on? She was confused. She mashed the palms of her hands hard against her temples, remembering all too clearly. After a couple of seconds she swung her head around and looked again at the stains. They were still there.

"Bud . . . you can tell me. I'm your sister. If there's anyone you can trust in this world, it's me." She hesitated, then plunged ahead. "Was it Sally? Did you have to kill her again?"

She was almost too frightened to move. Last time, B.B. had gone along in the car when he'd taken the body and dumped it in that snowy field. Had Sally come back? No, that wasn't possible. But maybe . . . maybe this was *then*.

She struggled for a context. Sometimes she lost track, got mixed up. As she tried to get her bearings her eyes were drawn to a dagger on the floor next to the bed. She leaned down and picked it up. It was sticky! She dropped it like a hot coal.

Bending over to look at it again, she realized it was familiar. "Isn't that one of my cigarette lighters?" she whispered, this time with more than a little indignation. "He took it! He just came in and took it from my collection without even asking me."

Carrying it to the kitchen, she washed the blood off. She held it under the water for a long time, dousing it with soap and scrubbing it with a scouring pad. She knew it wouldn't do the lighter part of it any good, but she couldn't have that sticky goo wrecking the dagger's beautiful hilt. When she was finally convinced it was squeaky clean, she wiped it with a paper towel and pressed it into the pocket of her cape. "If you think you can get away with this, Buddy, you've got another think coming." Her first act when she returned to the main house would be to put it back where it belonged. "You're going to get an earful when you get back," she muttered. "I have *my* rules, too."

Her indignation smoldered as she once again stepped through the mess in the living room. "It would serve you right if I just left everything the way it was." After several seconds of angry reflection, she decided that getting back at her brother at this particular moment didn't make sense.

"Well, I'm not the maid," she grumbled, her hands rising to her hips, "but I'll do a little picking up. Manderbachs don't like disorder."

28

Shortly before two A.M., Bud pulled his Mercedes into his driveway, eased the car up to the garage doors, and then turned off the motor. He sat for a moment breathing in the peaceful night air.

It was finally over. For the first time in weeks he could allow himself to relax. He'd pounded the final nail in Justin Bloom's coffin a few hours ago—or Wish Greveen's coffin. Bud was convinced now that they were one and the same person. Bloom had threatened him tonight, threatened everything he held dear. And yet in the end all he'd accomplished was to prove one simple point: Self-preservation was the strongest of all human motivations. It came as no particular shock to Bud, and yet the ruthless way he took care of business seemed to come from some part of himself he didn't recognize or remotely understand. Bud didn't consider himself a violent man, simply a man pushed to the wall. Perhaps, in the end, that was the most dangerous kind of man to be.

As he sat enjoying the beauty of the winter night, his attention was drawn to the alley. Through the bare trees in his neighbor's backyard he noticed flashing lights. For a second he thought it was a snowplow. The alley was in terrible shape from several recent snows. He'd called the city to complain about it just last week. But as the vehicle came closer Bud could see that it was a squad car. "Damn," he said under his breath. "Now what?"

He stayed in his car and waited. The cruiser slowed to a crawl next to the cottage, but didn't stop. He heaved a sigh of relief as he saw the red taillights pull onto the side street and disappear into the darkness. The police were probably just out checking the neighborhoods. Christmas eve was a notoriously bad night for family fights, even on Summit Avenue. Remembering his sister, Bud glanced up at the main house and was surprised to see a light on in her bedroom. Frustration rose in his chest. What if she'd been waiting up for him? God, how was he going to explain where he'd been?

"I wish she'd get a life," he muttered, getting out of the front seat. He started for the house. Halfway up the walk, the same flashing lights assaulted him once again. This time they came from his own driveway. The police had pulled in behind his Mercedes.

A burly officer got out of the passenger door. "Just getting home?" he asked pleasantly.

Bud turned to face the man, feeling his heart begin to race. "As a matter of fact, I am."

"I guess that means you live here."

"Why yes, I do. Is there a problem?"

The officer stepped around a mound of snow and approached. "I'm Officer Maki. We got a call at our precinct about half an hour ago. A woman reported hearing shouts and screams coming from your gatehouse shortly before midnight. Her husband didn't want her to report it, so she waited until he fell asleep and then called us. You know anything about that?"

Bud shook his head. "Not a thing."

"Have you spent any time out there tonight?"

"Yes. But I left around eleven."

"Were you alone?"

"When I left, yes. Earlier, I had some . . . friends over for a small party."

"Did it get loud, sir?"

"Of course not."

"Then, you got any idea what this woman was talking about?"

He shook his head. "Maybe she meant some other house."

"No, she was specific. Even gave us the address. Seven-fifty-one Summit Avenue." Officer Maki looked toward the cottage. "You mind if we look around?"

Bud saw no reason to object. "Sure, go ahead. Do you need me?" He noticed his sister waving at him from the kitchen window.

"Yes, sir, that would probably be a good idea."

B.B. seemed so insistent that Bud hesitated. "Would you excuse me for a minute? I need to speak with my sister first."

"We'll meet you down by the gatehouse." Maki motioned for the officer inside the car to accompany him.

Bud climbed up the back steps. B.B. was waiting for him at the door, looking typically horrific. Before bed every night, she wound her hair around pink foam curlers and then covered her head with a tight black hair net. The net always left ugly indentations in her skin when she took it off the next day. And her bathrobe was huge, plaid, and bulky, and never quite covered her abundant cleavage. The last thing she took off every night was her makeup. Tonight, it looked thicker than usual, like she'd just applied a fresh coat.

"Come in," she said breathlessly, grabbing him by the sleeve and yanking him into the back hall. She smelled heavily of perfume. White Diamonds, if he wasn't mistaken.

"What is it?" he demanded. She was holding on to his wrist so tightly that his fingers were beginning to throb.

"Is Sally . . . you know—" She raised a heavy, dark eyebrow. "All taken care of?"

"Sally? What are you talking about?"

She gave him a knowing look. "Everything's under control. Don't worry."

"B.B., you're not making any sense."

"What do the police want?"

"Some woman called and said she heard screams coming from the cook's cottage."

B.B.'s face puckered. "That's not good."

"It's ridiculous is what it is. Why are you still up?"

"I was waiting for you."

"Oh, B.B., what have I told you a thousand times. Go to bed." He gave her a hard look, then relented when he saw the hurt on her puffy face. She was *so* frustrating sometimes, but also terribly fragile. He couldn't help but love her. Who else cared enough about him to stay up and wait until he returned home? "It's freezing cold out here in the back hall. Go make us each a Scotch and soda and I'll be in in a minute."

Her frown turned to a smile. She gave him a conspiratorial wink, and then lumbered off into the kitchen, closing the interior door behind her.

Bud flipped his coat collar up around his neck and walked out to the cottage. The officers were shining their flashlights around the base of the building, looking in bushes, examining the windows. "Find anything?" he asked, shoving his hands into his coat pockets.

Officer Maki shook his head. "Everything looks okay.

Say—" He sniffed the air surrounding Bud. "Have you been handling gasoline tonight?"

"Oh . . . well, when I was driving around, I saw that the gas tank in my car was low. I'm always worried about gasline freeze in this cold. So, since I keep a gas can in my trunk in the winter, I dumped it into my tank. I probably got some on my clothes." He was explaining too much, but he didn't know how else to get out of it.

"Probably," agreed the officer. He looked Bud up and down. "That was lucky."

"What?"

"You having that gas in your trunk."

"Oh. Yeah."

"Hey, Mike, over here," called the other officer. He was crouching next to the front door.

Maki hurried over. "What have you got?"

"It looks like blood. Just a couple of drops. But we better check it out."

"Blood?" repeated Bud.

"Sir," said Maki, "we need to get into your house. The easiest way would be for you to unlock the door."

Bud glanced toward the main house, where his sister was watching from the kitchen window. What had she meant by everything's under control?

"Sir?"

"Um?"

"The door?"

"Oh, right." He felt for his keys. "I don't know what you expect to find."

Neither of the officers responded.

Once inside, Bud turned on a light. The scene that met his eyes shocked him into silence. Although the living room was reasonably neat, most of the furniture had been moved. Everything was askew. Knickknacks were jumbled together in clumps on the tabletops, or lined up in odd little rows on the bookshelves. In the middle of the coffee table sat a philodendron, its roots bare of soil, drooping over the edge of a glass pitcher. As the officers began their search, Bud's eyes were drawn to a broken pot on the floor near the front windows. Potting soil had been kicked under one of the drapes, but some of it was still embedded in the rug. "What the hell?" he said under his breath.

"Sir, would you come in here?" called one of the officers. He was standing just inside the French doors.

Bud hurried into the bedroom.

Maki had pulled back the bedspread, revealing a stained pillow. "We found blood on the carpet and the wall, so we took a look around. Can you explain this?"

Bud stared at the marks. None of them was large, but they were all clearly visible. As he bent over to touch one, Officer Maki said, "Don't do that, sir."

Bud retracted his hand. "I have no idea how this got here."

"There was no blood in the bedroom when you left earlier this evening?"

"Of course not."

"Where did you go, sir?"

"What?"

"You said you left around eleven and didn't get home until a few minutes ago. Where did you go?"

"Well, I—" He looked from face to face. "I went for a drive. I . . . you see—" He took a deep breath. "It's been a rough week for me at work. I own Manderbach's department store—I'm sure you've heard of it. Anyway, after my . . . friends left around eleven, I needed to clear my head." He knew his explanation sounded suspicious, but what could he do? He couldn't tell them the truth.

"On Christmas eve?"

Now he was getting angry. "What difference does it make what night it was?"

"About your friends. Did you part . . . on friendly terms?"

"Certainly." Bud was beginning to sweat. He hoped they couldn't read his nervousness.

Maki glanced at the other officer. "We better get a detective out here—and a crime-scene unit."

Bud's head was spinning. What was going on?

The first officer left the cottage. Through the open drapes Bud could see him trot back out to the squad car. But wait. The drapes hadn't been open when he'd left the cottage earlier in the evening. Who'd opened them?

"If you'll just have a seat in the living room," said Officer Maki, "someone will arrive in a few minutes to question you further."

"But I've done nothing wrong!"

"I understand that. But something happened here. Please, sir, just sit down."

Feeling angry and dazed, Bud sank down onto the living-room couch. He needed a drink. A stiff one. And some answers. A few minutes ago he'd been on top of the world, positive that his problems were over. Now, it seemed, Christmas eve had blessed him once again—with a new disaster.

May 15, 1959

My dearest Justin:

I'm sorry it's taken me so long to write. After my last letter to you, your stepfather became gravely ill. He was rushed to the emergency room on April 24 with chest pains. The doctors kept him in the hospital until they were sure he was all right and then sent him home. Two nights later he had a heart attack while I was away from the house. When I got home, I found him on the floor in the den. He was unconscious, but still alive. I called an ambulance and he was rushed to the hospital. Thank God he survived the attack, but the doctors tell me the chances are slim that he'll survive another.

My life has been nothing but constant running for the past few weeks. I've split my time between the station—I've taken over Cedric's duties—and the hospital. Alfred has been a big help, but he can't provide me with more hours in the day. Every minute I'm away from the hospital I worry about Cedric. His spirits are sometimes good, sometimes very bad. Yesterday he said that if Eisenhower can survive a heart attack, so can he, but then today he was very down. I know his medication makes him feel awful, but when he just stares out the window and doesn't talk, I don't know what to do. He has almost constant chest pain now. The doctors have tried everything, at least it feels like they have, but nothing seems to help. We're flying a specialist in tomorrow from Johns Hopkins. It's my hope that he will have more answers.

I don't know what I'd do if I lost Cedric. I can't even think about it without crying, and yet I'm no good to him if I can't be strong and keep a positive outlook. I know it hurt you, Justin, when I remarried, but Cedric is a good, loving man who has tried hard to be a father to you. He's been my rock for so many years now, I just can't envision life without him. Losing two men from my life in such a short time would be too much to take. That's why, deep down, I know he'll be all right. I don't believe the Good Lord gives us more than we can handle in this life, and I simply wouldn't survive if I lost Cedric as well as you. Pray for your stepfather, Justin. He needs all our prayers.

As you can imagine, I don't feel much like writing today. I'm tired and I know I'm not always thinking as clearly as I should. But since Cedric is sleeping, it seemed like a good time. Actually, there are two other matters I need to discuss with you.

First, several days ago I received a letter. There was no return address on the envelope, but the postmark said it was from Butte, Montana. When I opened it, I discovered the letter was to you from your friend Jonnie Apfenford.

All she said was that she was okay. She left Minnesota when it became clear to her that her health would suffer if she stuck around. She said she wished she could talk to you—she had a hard time believing what she'd read in the newspapers, but she had to be careful. She didn't know who to trust anymore. Her instincts told her to get lost and stay lost and that's just what she was going to do. She wished you good luck, but said you'd never hear from her again. I was glad to know she was all right, especially after what we found out about Sally Nash recently. I knew you'd be glad, too.

This next bit of information is going to upset you. Believe me when I tell you that it scared the daylights out of me. If you recall, I explained to you in a previous letter that I took all your personal papers from your apartment and stored them downstairs in that old wooden box just outside the rec room. Well, last Friday night I didn't get home from the hospital until quite late. When I put the key in the back door, I noticed that the lock was damaged. I knew immediately that someone had broken into the house.

I can't explain what I did next, Justin. Again, maybe I wasn't thinking clearly because of Cedric. Whatever the case, I walked right into the kitchen and turned on the light. Immediately, I heard noises coming from upstairs. Whoever had broken the lock was still inside the house. Well, I was frightened, of course, but I was also angry. You know me and my temper. Instead of running across the street to a neighbor's house to call the police—which is what I should have done—I turned the light back off and crept to the edge of the stairs. I thought of all your stepfather's beautiful jewelry. The idea that someone was stealing it made my blood boil.

I stood in the dark for a couple more seconds and tried to formulate a plan. I knew I couldn't physically overpower the person, but I also knew where Cedric kept a gun, so I crept to the study. Unlike the kitchen and the living room, this room had been ransacked. Cedric's books and papers were scattered all over the floor. I rushed to the desk and opened the bottom drawer, but the gun was gone.

"Looking for this?" asked a voice. Even though all the lights were off in the house, when I looked up, I could see a dark form holding a gun on me. He was big and had on a mask. It was a silk stocking, or some such thing, pulled over his head. It made him look smooth and formless.

I asked him what he wanted. He said that he'd already found what he wanted. He told me if I made a sound or caused him any trouble, he'd shoot me—just like that. He tied my hands behind my back with what felt like another silk stocking, sat me down in the desk chair, and then tied my feet. Before he left the room he told me I wasn't to report the break-in to the police. Nothing of any value had been stolen. If I did report it, I'd pay dearly for my interference. Then he said it was too bad I had to have a son like you. A murderer and a coward. He pitied me.

I sat in the dark until I heard the back door slam. The stocking around my hands was tied tightly, but after struggling with it for a few minutes I got it off. The first thing I did was to check all the doors and windows. Everything was secure. Then I got a hammer and a bunch of nails and nailed the back door shut. Cedric always said that if someone really wanted to get into your house, they'd find a way, but I had to know the house was locked up tight, at least as tight as I could make it.

I spent the next few minutes assessing the damage. What the burglar had told me was accurate. While he'd obviously looked through every part of the house, all he'd taken were your personal papers. I suspected as much after what he said.

The rest of the evening was a blur. I packed a bag and spent the night in a hotel. As I was driving away from the house I couldn't help but think about all your warnings. Believe me when I tell you that if I didn't take those warnings seriously before, I do now. I still haven't been back to the house to sleep. I go get the mail, make sure the plants are watered, and then I return to the hotel. I couldn't tell

*Cedric the truth, so I lied and said that the hotel was
closer to the hospital, which it is. I explained that I didn't
like driving home alone every night. He understood and
even agreed that the hotel was a good idea.*

*Don't worry about me, Justin, because I'm fine. But I
am apprehensive. What's going to happen to you—and to
us? With Cedric so sick, and the house no longer my safe
haven, I feel rootless, and very, very alone. I wish everything could go back to the way it was. I don't mean to
hurry you, son, but I desperately need for you to finish
your story. I understand why you've taken your time. You
were sick, and then you needed to examine your feelings,
to make sense of what happened. But please understand
my need for clarity. Especially now.*

I miss you, and send you all my love.

Mom

29

Christmas morning arrived gray and cold. Heda Bloom
stood before her living-room window and gazed at downtown St. Paul, searching the streets below for signs of life. A
thick fog obscured the skyline, making everything look ill-
defined, vague, much like her own mood. The town was
unusually quiet today, nearly empty of traffic. Watching
from her remote penthouse suite, she felt cut off from the
world, cut off also by her own physical limitations and her
growing sense of impotence.

Several hours earlier Heda had awakened from a fitful
night's sleep feeling deeply unsettled. The plan she'd come

all the way from Florida to carry out had somehow gotten away from her. Matters were no longer simple and straightforward. It had taken some time to work out, but she'd finally come to the conclusion that she was no longer the only one pulling the strings. While her attention was focused on the radio drama, someone else had entered the game.

She recalled the advice her father had once given to her older brother. When you're in the ring with another prizefighter, he said, don't ever look at the guy's hands. If you do, you're finished. Instead, watch your opponent's shoulders. They tell you where the punch is coming from. That gives you time to react, to duck out of the way and counter with your own move.

She'd never forgotten those words. Even as a kid she'd known they had a larger meaning. Right now she couldn't just watch those unseen hands and wait to be knocked down. She had to figure out who they belonged to, find the bigger picture. But that was easier said than done. Nothing was ever as clear-cut as two guys beating each other bloody in front of a roaring crowd. And yet, in a way, wasn't that a perfect metaphor for what was happening?

"Morning," muttered Dorothy, shuffling wearily into the living room. After taking a pack of cigarettes and a lighter from her purse, she joined Heda at the window.

Heda glanced over and saw that Dorothy was already dressed. "You got home earlier than I thought you would last night. Did you and Bud have a lovers' quarrel?"

Dorothy gave her a pained smile. "Hardly."

"What happened, then? I had the impression that you planned to be there for quite some time."

"He got a visitor."

"Ah."

"Don't you want to know who the visitor was?"

Not as much as Dorothy obviously wanted to tell her. "Who?"

She flicked the lighter to the tip of her cigarette. "Wish Greveen."

"Why on earth would he go see Bud Manderbach?"

"Because Bud wanted to see *him*."

Heda was confused. "What did they talk about?"

"I don't know," said Dorothy, tapping some ash into an ashtray. "Bud asked me to leave before they got down to business. I'll call Wish a little later and find out."

Heda watched a pigeon land on the building directly across from them. Since she owed Dorothy an apology, she might as well get on with it. "Listen, I'm sorry I got so upset with you last night. I'm sure you have your reasons for seeing that awful man. I just don't like being kept in the dark."

"I doubt I'll be seeing him again."

Heda's first reaction was to say "good," but instead she said, "How come?"

"I think he's pretty much finished with me. You know Bud Manderbach. Love 'em and leave 'em. Have you ordered breakfast yet?" She turned her back to the window and leaned against the ledge. Taking another drag, she said, "I'm famished."

Heda jumped at the sound of a knock on the door.

"Is our regular bodyguard on duty this morning?" asked Dorothy, stubbing out her cigarette.

"Yes," said Heda. "Nobody will get past him without being thoroughly checked out." Even so, she could feel herself tense as Dorothy opened the door.

"Excuse me," said an attractive woman. She was dressed in tight black jeans and a tan cashmere sweater. "I'd like to speak with Heda Bloom, please."

"May I ask your name?" said Dorothy.

"Why, sure. I'm Cathy Quinn. Mitzi Quinn's daughter."

Heda couldn't help but smile at the Southern drawl. The woman looked a bit like Mitzi, but could easily have passed for a fashion model. "Please," she said, moving away from the window. She used her canes to get her over to a chair. "Come in. This is a wonderful surprise. I'm delighted to meet you."

"That means you must be Heda," said Cathy, ignoring Dorothy as she passed in front of her.

Heda noticed now that the woman wasn't smiling. "Would you like to join us for breakfast? We were just going to call room service. By the way, this is my assistant, Dorothy Veneger."

Cathy gave her a stiff nod. "I can't stay. I have to leave for the airport in less than an hour."

"Really?" said Dorothy. She remained by the door, her hand on the knob. "If I'm not mistaken, I thought Mitzi said you were staying the entire week."

"No," said Cathy. "There's been a change in plans."

"I hope it's nothing serious," said Heda, pushing a pillow behind her back. She had a hard time getting comfortable in these club chairs.

"That depends on how you define 'serious.' " Cathy walked a few paces closer, examining Heda as if she were part of a science experiment. "I had to come and look at you."

"Pardon me?"

"I needed to see my grandmother with my own two eyes. I figured this would be my only chance."

"Your . . . grandmother?" Heda stared at the woman, dumbfounded.

"Mitzi Quinn is my mother. Justin Bloom was my father."

"What?" said Dorothy. She pushed away from the door and walked around in front of the woman, clutching her long strand of pearls in both hands.

"Sure. Justin Bloom convinced my mother to sleep with him before they were married—or even engaged. From what I understand, he never intended to marry her, so I guess this comes under the heading of a quick roll in the hay."

Heda blinked back her surprise, noticing that Dorothy's face betrayed a similar look of shock. As her heart began to pound, she looked at Cathy and said, "This . . . is true?"

"Of course it's true. My mother never lied to me about how I was conceived. She told me the whole story." She paused, then pursed her lips. "I suppose you think I'm here because I want something. Well, you're right. I do."

"And what would that be?" asked Dorothy.

Cathy's hands rose to her hips. "Look, Mrs. Bloom, my mother is scared to death. I've never seen her like this before. I advised her to tear up that contract and come home with me to Houston, but she says she has to stay. I finally got her to open up about some of her fears last night, but only after she'd drunk half a bottle of brandy. It seems one of the actors in the cast was murdered. And nobody knows who did it. Why didn't you stop the production, Mrs. Bloom? Weren't you scared it could happen to someone else?"

"Well, I—"

"And another thing. She's got this weird idea that Justin Bloom is still alive. That he's here, in Minnesota, and that he's going to do something terrible."

"Alive," repeated Dorothy, her expression utterly serious. "I want to understand this, Cathy. I really do. I've heard the same rumor more than once and I'd like to know how it got started. Has your mother seen him?"

"No."

"Talked to him?"

She shook her head.

"Then why does she think he's alive?"

"It's just a feeling she's got. You don't know Mama. When she gets one of her feelings, you can't shake her out of it."

"Even if he were alive," said Heda, picking up the conversation, "my son would never do anything terrible."

"Are you kidding me? He murdered a woman. And he slept with my mother and then tossed her aside as if she meant nothing to him. The man was pond scum."

"How can you say that about your father?" said Heda, struggling to her feet. Inside, she was beginning to quake.

"He wasn't my father. Jim Quinn is my father. Fathering is what someone *does*, not who someone *is*. I would think you've lived long enough to know that."

Heda felt as if a door had just clanged shut, trapping her somewhere cold, empty, and foreign. How could she have a granddaughter and not even know about it? This had to be someone else's life. It couldn't be hers.

She finally recovered enough to go on. "I'm deeply sorry my son hurt you and your mother so badly. I had no idea he had a child. Believe me when I tell you, he didn't either. You're right. Justin behaved abominably toward your mother. If I could go back and change things, I would. In my heart, I know if he were standing here right now, he'd tell you the same thing. But we both know that's not possible. Justin is dead, Cathy. If your mother thinks otherwise, she's wrong. Furthermore, the Justin I knew would never have harmed anyone, not intentionally. He was a good man caught in a terrible situation. If it's any consolation to you, before he died, he paid dearly for his mistakes." She paused. Wiping a tear from her eye, she said, "What is it you want from me, Cathy? Whatever it is, it's yours."

Cathy's anger seemed to dissipate somewhat as she pushed her hands into her back pockets. "I didn't come here to beat you up. Or maybe I did, I don't know. But what I really need is a promise. I want you to give me your word that my mother will be safe. Nothing will happen to her while she's here. And at the end of your six-week run, I want you to let her go home. No arguments. No wheedling. If you plan to extend the series another six weeks, find another actress."

Very softly, Dorothy replied, "Nothing will happen to your mother, Cathy. You have my word—and Heda's."

Cathy looked from face to face, her eyes finally settling on Heda. "I can't say it was a pleasure meeting you, but it's something I've wanted most of my life. Remember, I'll hold you to that promise." She stared at Heda for several more seconds and then turned and left.

In her wake, the silence in the room nearly crushed the life out of Heda Bloom. She staggered toward the couch and sat down.

"God, I'm so sorry," said Dorothy, helping her get comfortable.

There was another knock at the door.

Removing her glasses, Heda squeezed the bridge of her nose. "I can't talk to anyone right now. I'm going to my room to lie down. Whoever it is, get rid of them. When you're done, come in. I want to talk to you."

"Of course," said Dorothy.

Giving herself a few moments to compose herself, Dorothy stood in front of the door and closed her eyes. She didn't feel like talking to anyone either. Whoever it was, she intended to make it short. When she finally drew back the door, she found a tall, middle-aged man standing outside.

"I'm looking for Dorothy Veneger." He flashed her a badge.

Glancing at it, she asked, "Is this about Valentine Zolotow?"

"Are you Dorothy Veneger?"

"Yes."

"I'm Detective Stine, St. Paul police. Can I come in? I'd like to ask you a few questions."

She backed up a step. "What's this about?"

"Bud Manderbach."

"Bud? What about him?"

"There were some . . . problems at his house last night. I understand you were there."

She nodded.

"I'd like to talk to you about it."

It took her a few seconds to change gears. "All right," she said, pulling absently on one of her gold earrings. "We can sit in the living room. Would you like some coffee?"

"No thanks." He unzipped his coat and found a chair. He was a good-looking man. Dark hair, large dark eyes. Retrieving a notepad and a pen from the pocket of his suit, he waited until Dorothy had taken a seat across from him and then asked, "How long have you known Mr. Manderbach?"

She folded one leg over the other. "I met him at the Maxfield's bar last Sunday night. We were both alone, so we struck up a conversation."

"How would you characterize your relationship with him?"

She gave him a quizzical look. "We're . . . friends, Detective Stine."

"Romantic friends?"

The edges of her mouth curled into a smile. "I suppose you could say that."

"What were you doing at his house last night?"

"Bud invited me over for a glass of wine."

"Were the two of you alone?"

"For the first half hour, yes. Around ten, a man named Greveen, a scriptwriter I employ at WTWN, stopped by."

"Why?"

She shrugged. "Bud wanted to meet him. He was curious about the writing life, I think, and about the program Wish writes for."

The detective jotted down some notes on his notepad. "What specifically did the two men talk about?"

"Well, actually, Wish had only been there for a few minutes when Bud asked me to leave."

"Really? Why?"

"He wanted to talk to Wish alone."

"Were you upset by that?"

"I wasn't happy. But I did as he asked. I left."

The detective leaned back in his chair. "Were the two men on friendly terms when you left?"

Again, she shrugged. "Yes. I think so."

"Did either of them seem upset about anything?"

The detective was looking at her with nothing more than polite attention, and yet she could feel him studying her, weighing each answer. "Well, Wish insisted that he'd never met Bud before, but I wasn't so sure."

"Why was that?"

"At one point, Bud commented on a ring that Wish was wearing, as if he'd seen it before." She stopped and thought a little before going on. "What's all this about, Detective Stine? What happened last night?"

"Have you talked to Mr. Greveen this morning?"

"No. I was going to call him in a few minutes to wish him a Merry Christmas."

"I understand he's from Palm Beach."

"That's right."

"And he has a reputation for being somewhat of a recluse."

She nodded. "All true."

"Have you worked with him long?"

"Not really. I hired him to write the *Dallas Lane* scripts just last month. I have his résumé here, if you'd care to see it."

"I would. But first, tell me, did Mr. Greveen create the story all by himself?"

"No, Heda Bloom wrote a story-line synopsis, and he shaped it into a six-episode series—or I should say, he was in the process of doing that. Our fourth episode airs tomorrow night."

"He hasn't finished writing it?"

"No. That's why he came to town. He likes to be near the action, but not a part of it. He works in his suite downstairs."

"You didn't find that somewhat difficult? I mean, what if you didn't like the script?"

She shrugged. "It's never been a problem. I think he's amazingly talented. Have you caught any of the shows?"

"I don't know anyone who doesn't listen to your show, Ms. Veneger. It's created quite a stir."

Dorothy smiled, then realized it wasn't meant as a compliment. "You're referring to the similarity between our radio show and that old murder case."

"Is there any truth to the rumor that *Dallas Lane, Private Eye* is really Heda Bloom's attempt to set the record straight about her son?"

Dorothy looked away. "I didn't think so, at least at the beginning. But now, yes. I'm convinced that's exactly what it is. May I add that I think it was quite a brilliant stroke? I've often been in awe of her, never more than now."

"The parallels seem rather obvious to me, too. I'm just curious. How long have you known Heda Bloom?"

"Let's see. Six years, I think. I was hired shortly after my husband died."

"And in that time, has she ever discussed her son Justin with you?"

"Not until very recently."

The detective made a few more notes. "Seems to me I've heard Bud Manderbach's name being put forward as one of the men who might've been involved in the Kay Collins murder."

"Yes," agreed Dorothy, "I've heard that, too."

"But you don't believe it?"

She chose her words carefully. "I don't think Bud Manderbach is a saint, Detective Stine, but at the same time it's hard for me to picture him murdering someone in cold blood."

"Then again, Ms. Veneger, you never know about people." He turned to a clean page in his notebook. "Have you ever been in Mr. Manderbach's car?"

This new line of questioning threw her. "Sure. Several times."

"How about the trunk. Did he ever open that while you were with him?"

"Yes."

"Can you tell me what was in it?"

She closed her eyes and tried to picture the interior. "Nothing, really. He would put his briefcase inside because he was afraid that if he left it in the car, someone might steal it. But that's about it."

"You're sure? You didn't see a gas can? A large one? Red and yellow, I believe."

She shook her head. "No, nothing like that."

"Tell me, when you were at the cottage last night, did you notice if Mr. Manderbach cut himself?"

"No."

"What about you?"

"Look, Detective Stine, I don't want to seem uncooperative, but I don't think I'm going to answer any more of your questions until I know what this is all about."

He finished writing a few more lines, then clicked his pen closed. "All right. Fair enough. We had a report of a fight at Mr. Manderbach's gatehouse last night. When our officers arrived at the scene, they found fresh blood outside the house near the front door, and also in the bedroom. We won't have any details on that blood for a few days, but we suspect that someone may have been hurt. Possibly Mr. Greveen."

Dorothy sat up straight in her chair. "I'll call him right away."

"That won't be necessary, Ms. Veneger. I've already checked his room. He's not there."

"But . . . he has to be. He goes out at night sometimes, but hardly ever during the day."

"The woman who owns the hotel let me into the room a few minutes ago. His bed hadn't been slept in. Actually, Ms. Greenway gave me an interesting lead. She mentioned that when Mr. Greveen checked into the hotel, he complained that he wasn't feeling well. She suggested he go see her personal physician. His office is just up the street. Later, he apparently told her he'd scheduled a full physical for sometime this past week. What that means, Ms. Veneger, is that since Mr. Greveen seems to be missing, we may still be able to get our hands on a sample of his blood. My question to you is, did you know he'd seen this doctor?"

Thinking she heard movement, Dorothy slowly shifted her eyes from the detective to Heda's bedroom door. The last thing she wanted was for Heda to join the conversation. "Yes, I knew he'd seen a doctor. When he arrived here from Florida, he thought he had the flu. As I said, I don't know him all that well, but I think he was a bit of a hypochondriac." She folded her arms tightly over her chest. "I better get you his résumé."

"I'd also be interested in any recent photos."

"All I have is a standard head shot," she said, hurrying into her bedroom. She returned a moment later and handed the folder to the detective. "Is there any other way I can help you?" She remained standing, hoping he'd get the point and leave.

Rising from his chair, the detective flipped through the contents. "I'd like to take this with me, if you don't mind."

"Of course." She waited while he studied the photo, then accompanied him to the door.

"If I have any further questions, I'll be in touch. Oh, and one last thing. If Mr. Greveen should contact you, please inform me right away." He handed Dorothy his card.

She glanced at it. "Do you think he's still alive?"

Leaning against the door frame, he said, "This is only my opinion, you understand, but if I were you, I'd start looking for a new writer. I think it's highly unlikely you'll ever see Wish Greveen again."

30

"We got Hamms and Schmidt on tap," said the bartender, placing his beefy hands on the counter. "Blatz, Miller Lite, Summit, and Augsburger Dark in bottles. What'll it be?"

It was Saturday night and Bram was seated at a dark, crummy bar in south Minneapolis, staring at a row of bottles behind the counter. "Make it a cup of coffee."

"Coffee? You come to a dive like this on Christmas night just to have a cup of coffee? That makes sense, Mac. You must *really* be sick of your relatives."

"And don't forget the cream."

The bartender was partially right. Bram had spent most of the day with his family, opening presents, wolfing down a huge turkey dinner, and then falling asleep on the couch during the standard, insipid holiday specials.

"One cup of coffee," said the bartender, dumping it down on the counter. The cup rattled precariously in the saucer. "You want me to start you a tab? You might want to move on to a glass of milk later."

Bram raised an eyebrow. "Good idea." Glancing around the room, he realized this really *was* Pit City. The bar stank of stale smoke and sour beer, not exactly two of his favorite fragrances.

Grimacing at the foul taste of the coffee, he noticed now that the walls were covered with cheap paneling, the floor with equally cheap linoleum. The one sop to interior decoration was a series of motorcycle posters hung at odd angles over a section reserved for tables. In the back, three teenagers huddled around a Foosball game. The only other person in the room was a guy sitting at the other end of the bar eating a hamburger. "Not much business tonight."

"We've only been open an hour. It'll pick up."

"You get a lot of bikers in here?"

The bartender stuck a toothpick in his mouth. "Sorry. I left the survey results at home."

A wise guy. "Many women come in here?"

"With or without tattoos?"

Bram supposed it was a pertinent question. "I didn't know you could get that personal on a survey."

"You can't. You only get information like that from hands-on experience." He flashed Bram a lecherous smile, the toothpick clenched firmly between his teeth.

Setting the coffee cup down, Bram pushed it away. "Have you seen any women tonight? With or without tattoos." It was already a few minutes after nine. The granddaughter had said nine *sharp*.

"How come you're so interested in our clientele?"

"FBI. I'm on a case."

"Oh, right. And I'm Eliot Ness."

"I'm not joking."

He picked his teeth, eyeing Bram curiously. "Let's see your badge."

"I lost it in a bag of potato chips."

"That's what I figured." He removed the toothpick and flipped it into the garbage. "I also figure you're waiting for someone and you got stood up."

Forty-five minutes and three cups of sludge later, Bram had to admit the guy might be right. "What do I owe you?" he asked, pulling some change out of his pocket.

"Three bucks."

"For a lousy cup of coffee?"

"Too bad you lost your badge. You could arrest me." He leaned his arms on the bar while Bram retrieved his wallet. "Look, pal, how many other places are open on Christmas night? I gotta cover my overhead. Pay my staff."

"You're the only one here."

"So?"

Bram tossed three dollars on the counter and left. There was no use arguing—or tipping.

After walking half a block to his car, he spent the next few minutes scraping snow and ice off the windshield. It was turning into a nasty night. The wind had picked up and the snow was coming down hard. Once inside the car, Bram started the engine and then sat for a moment, allowing it to warm up. While the windows defrosted he had a few minutes to think.

The granddaughter's no-show seemed ominous, especially after what Sophie had learned earlier in the day. Apparently, Wish Greveen had been missing since last night. He'd had a late-night meeting with Bud Manderbach and hadn't returned to the hotel. The police couldn't say for sure that Greveen was dead, or that Bud Manderbach had murdered him, but that appeared to be the working theory.

Sophie had a theory of her own. She suggested that Bud Manderbach's intent was to sabotage the show. Bram hadn't talked to Dorothy yet, but without a completed script for next week's program, *Dallas Lane, Private Eye* would have to be put on hiatus. The worst-case scenario was that a temporary cancellation might dampen the public's interest in the series, and thus could very well quell the growing interest in the old murder case. Bram didn't want to see that happen. Justice had been delayed far too long.

On tomorrow night's radio broadcast, the public would learn that Justin Bloom had managed to get his hands on photos of the car used in the hit-and-run, and that he'd used his girlfriend to get these pictures, putting her life in great peril in the process. If Arn O'Dell really had lied about what he saw that night, if Justin Bloom hadn't murdered Kay Collins, then everything fit. The radio broadcast wasn't just another empty theory—the gospel according to Heda Bloom. It was the truth.

For weeks, residents of the Twin Cities had been speculating on how it might be possible, almost forty years after the fact, to go back and prove a man's innocence or guilt. What they were looking for, of course, was clear, undeniable proof. Bram felt certain he was the only one—other than O'Dell's granddaughter—who knew of her grandfather's letter. What that meant was, Bram had discovered the smoking gun. And yet, once again tonight, he'd been thwarted in his attempt to get his hands on it.

"Damn," he said, smacking the steering wheel with his fist. With the end of the radio show in sight, time was, as they say in the old serials, of the essence.

Remembering the call he'd made to Al Lundquist the previous night, Bram picked up his car phone and punched in the policeman's home number.

After a few rings a gruff voice answered, "Yah?"

"What a distinctly Minnesotan way to answer the phone."

"Baldric?"

"C'est moi."

"Cut the crap. You're interrupting the game."

"Oh, dear. I wouldn't want you to miss any broken bones. I'll be brief. Did you find out the name of Arn O'Dell's granddaughter?" He could hear some papers being rattled on the other end.

"Yeah, I got it. But can't this wait until tomorrow? It's fourth down and one."

Bram was elated. "No, Al, it can't. Remember, I told you this was important."

He grunted his disgust. "All right, asshole, but I gotta find my reading glasses. God knows where they are."

Bram waited nearly a minute before his friend returned to the line.

"Just in case you're interested, I just missed the touchdown."

"There's a special place in heaven for men like you."

"Okay"—he sighed—"here's the deal. According to O'Dell's old partner, the granddaughter's name is Molly Stanglund. She lives in Minneapolis—right on the border with Richfield. Want the address?"

"Yes, Al. I want the address."

"Sixty-one-thirty-one First Avenue."

Bram grabbed a pen from his pocket and wrote it on the

edge of an old take-out menu. "You can go back to your game now."

"You're a real mensch, Baldric."

"I know."

"I better not read about you and that Stanglund woman in the paper tomorrow morning."

"You won't. I'm completely domesticated. Monogamous to the core."

"That's not what I'm talking about."

"Bye, Al."

Half an hour later Bram turned off Nicollet and drove one short block to First. He'd already made the decision to approach the house cautiously.

The homes along this part of First were one story and small. A few cars were parked here and there, but generally, the neighborhood was quiet. Many of the houses were dark.

Halfway down the block, Bram switched off his headlights. As the car rolled to the end of the street, the sight that met his eyes almost took his breath away. He slammed on the brakes and skidded a good ten feet. "My God," he said, pulling the car over to the curb. As he got out all he could do was stare.

Icicles covered the house like an intricate, infinitely creepy spiderweb. Not only had the roof caved in, but all the glass was missing. Along the front of the house, the evergreen shrubs had been smashed, covered with debris and ice, and now snow. Dark, ugly stains on the exterior siding— what was left of it—revealed the extent of the fire damage. Even the air still stank of smoke. The interior was eerily silent now. In an effort to warn off curious neighbors, the police had run yellow tape all around the perimeter.

"She went up last night," said a voice from behind him.

Bram turned and found an old man standing a few feet away. He was leaning on a snow shovel. "You live around here?"

"Two doors down. Yup, it happened around midnight. The fire got a good start before anyone discovered it. The fire department got here in record time, but there wasn't much they could do."

Bram looked back at the house. "Did you know the woman who lived there?"

"Molly? Sure. Everybody knew Molly. She rented, but she was a good neighbor. Always shoveled her walk. Never made a fuss. Quite the gardener, too. She must've lived there ten years."

"Is she all right?" asked Bram, bracing himself for the worst.

"You a friend?"

He nodded.

"A close friend?"

"More on the order of an acquaintance."

"Well," the man said, adjusting his cap, "I never much liked passing on bad news, but yeah, she died in the fire. Terrible shame, too. I saw her last night around seven. She was just coming home."

Bram closed his eyes and looked away. After a couple of moments he said, "Did you speak with her?"

"Me? No, just waved from the drive. I figure she was probably asleep when it happened." He gazed up at the house with a kind of amazed reverence. "You shoulda seen that fire. It was damn incredible. Flames shooting out of every window. Smoke so thick it hurt your eyes halfway down the block. The funny thing was, her car was parked on the street the whole time the firemen were trying to put out the blaze, but"—he scratched the back of his neck—"it's gone now. I can't imagine where it went."

Bram walked a few paces closer. "Do you know how the fire got started?"

"Well, the firemen weren't sure. The best guess is, it was bad wiring on her Christmas-tree lights. It seemed like the fire got started in the living room, right around where the tree was. But you know, I walked the dog to the end of the block last night around eleven-thirty. The lights weren't on then. I woulda noticed. I don't know how the hell they coulda caused a fire if they weren't even plugged in."

It was a reasonable deduction, thought Bram. And it deserved an explanation. He couldn't help but wonder if the fire had been set on purpose, especially since Molly had revealed to him just last night that the house was being watched. "Did you see a white van around here before the fire started?"

The man thought for a moment, then shook his head. "Nope. Sorry. And I imagine all we'll see in the papers is an obituary notice. When you get to be my age, you read that section regularly."

Bram nodded. He couldn't think of much else to say. "Thanks for your time."

"Sure thing. Sorry it couldn't have been better news."

As the old guy turned his back and began to push his heavy shovel down the sidewalk, Bram returned to his car, feeling an overwhelming sense of sadness and defeat. Molly was dead. And since the letter or the knowledge of where the letter had been hidden had no doubt perished with her in the fire, his search was at an end. His hopes for the evening had been so high. Tonight he would find the answers he'd been looking for. Names. Motives. Even the proof of Bloom's innocence— the ultimate smoking gun pointing to the real murderer. But instead, all he'd found was . . . His eyes returned to the house.
Smoke.

Dear Mother:

I've waited several days, but still no letter from you. I
can't help but think that something's wrong. Overseas
mail is so frustratingly slow. Sometimes I worry that your
letters have been lost, but I know I'm just nervous and
impatient. I decided to go ahead with my story tonight.
When this reaches you, I hope everything's all right.

Each day, as soon as I wake, I begin to analyze and
reanalyze what happened last Christmas. It struck me this
morning that I must think I can change history if I just
reach some new conclusion. I suppose understanding
should equal acceptance—but, in my case, I'll never
accept what happened. Never.

The day after I took those pictures of Bud Manderbach's car, I dropped the film by the photo lab at the
paper and asked that the roll be given priority status.
Since the technician was a good friend of mine, I knew I
could trust his discretion. I didn't give him any details,
and he knew enough not to ask. This was "my" story,
Mom, and it was going to make my career. I'd be damned
if anyone else was going to break it.

The developed negatives and a contact sheet were
dropped on my desk shortly before noon. I'd been concerned that I might have mishandled the camera, but my
fears were quickly put to rest. The pictures were perfect.
The damage to the right front fender was clearly visible,
so was the license plate—and the front page of the

morning paper I'd placed next to it. I had to date the photos somehow, and that seemed not only appropriate, but appealed to my sense of irony. One way or another, my newspaper was going to get Bud Manderbach.

I called Kay right away to give her the good news, but nobody was home at her apartment. I assumed she was at work. Thinking I'd take her to lunch to celebrate, I hopped in my car and drove to Minneapolis. As expected, I found her behind the cosmetics counter, chatting with a customer. She smiled and waved, but had to complete the sale before we could talk. Once I got her alone, I asked when she could take a lunch break. Fifteen minutes later we dashed across the street to a small café.

The first thing she did was to apologize for not calling me the night before. I knew right then that everything was okay between us. While we looked at menus I asked her how she got back to her apartment. Remember, Manderbach thought she lived in my building. I figured she probably called a cab from his house. Instead of returning to my place, she just went home. It was probably too late for her to phone—not that I wasn't walking the floors hoping to hear from her. But, as it turned out, that's not what happened at all, Mom. Not by a long shot.

We ordered, and over a bowl of chowder, Kay gave me the details. After she and Bud left the garage and went to his cottage, Bud poured her a brandy to help her warm up. Her first concern, of course, was to make sure I had plenty of time to make my getaway. So, even though he'd frightened her, she played along. They talked for a while, mainly I think about his wife's reaction to his demand for a divorce. He said it was going to be a nasty fight, but he'd get what he wanted, sooner or later. Actually, he thought it might be a simple equation. The more money he promised, the quicker he'd get some action. She could, of course, contest—tie him up in court for years. But he doubted she'd turn down his offer. His freedom was going to cost him a bundle, but it was a small price to pay to be with the woman he loved.

Well, as you can imagine, I nearly vomited in my soup when I heard that load of crap. I was convinced now that he'd go to any extreme to get what he wanted. I had no doubt in my mind that the whole story was false. He'd never talked to his wife that morning, unless it was to order her to pick up his suits at the cleaners. I voiced my opinion to Kay, and she agreed—at least, I thought she did.

Around nine, Kay told Manderbach that she had to get home. He offered to drive her. When she hesitated, he pounced. Why had she lied to him about where she lived? This, as you might imagine, caught her completely off guard. She couldn't come clean and tell the truth—it was far too incriminating. After hemming and hawing for a few minutes, she finally admitted her lie and asked him how he'd found out.

He explained that he'd known she'd been lying about her real address for weeks, but since he was intrigued by the situation, and more than a little attracted to her, he played along. "You live with Sally Nash, don't you?" It was more a statement than a question. She admitted she did. Again, she asked how he knew.

"I'm your employer," he replied. "All I had to do was check your records."

I never thought of that, Mom. I was sure I'd covered all my bases, but here was something I'd missed. The fact that Manderbach had easy access to the store's employment files never entered my mind. Initially, Kay had been pretty mysterious about where she lived. I'm sure that sent him straight to the personnel office. All along, he'd been playing with her. Cat and mouse.

Kay had to think fast. She couldn't tell him about me because she knew it would get me in big trouble. So she said, "I had you drop me off at a friend's house so that I could keep my real address private. You're right. I do live with Sally. We've been friends for years. She told me all about you."

"You know nothing about me," he said. He got up and began to pace. At this point Kay said he started to get

really angry. He demanded to know what she was hiding. She said she didn't know what he was talking about. That's when he grabbed her purse and dumped the contents on the couch. Kay tried to stay calm. She asked him what he was looking for.

"A camera," he said, tossing the purse aside. Next he checked her coat.

"I don't have a camera," she said. Thank God she didn't have to lie about that.

He grabbed her by the arms. "Where is it?" he demanded. "I know what you were doing in that garage. Don't lie to me. This has been a setup from the very beginning!"

Well, she was terrified. He seemed to know everything. And he was hovering over her. Threatening her. Hurting her. "All right," she said finally. "Sally did tell me . . . about the hit-and-run."

"I knew it," he said. He sank down on the couch and put his head in his hands. Then he offered this explanation. "Look, you don't understand. In trying to do Sally a favor, you've put yourself in the middle of a terrible mess. I'm sorry, but there's nothing I can do about it now. Will you give her a message from me?"

Kay couldn't imagine what he wanted to tell Sally, but she said she would.

"I know I'm a rat. I broke a promise, but I had good reason. Tell Sally I'm going to get the front end fixed soon. I couldn't do it before. Too many people were looking for a car with just that kind of damage."

Kay nodded. At that point I think she was confused. "But why should I tell Sally that?"

"Isn't that what she sent you here to find out? That I'd taken care of the car?"

Kay said sure. That's right. But she was still confused.

Manderbach went on. "Tell her I'm sorry. I should never have let her drive that night. She didn't even have a license. And she'd been drinking. We'd both been drinking."

When I heard that, my heart stopped. Do you see now

why I told you he was slippery, Mom? He was more than slippery. He was evil!

Kay said he cried. He begged her forgiveness. It was all his fault. A life had been snuffed out, and although he wasn't driving the car, he was responsible. He accepted that. But if the police found out, he wasn't the one who'd go to jail. Sally would. Was it fair to let his bad judgment ruin an innocent young woman's life? Sally was terrified. Devastated. He'd tried everything he could to make it up to her. He'd even bought her a new car, given her some money so she could quit her job. She needed time to pull herself together. But in the end, he knew nothing would bring Olga Landauer back. They both knew it. And that knowledge had ended their affair.

Well, Kay was stunned. Confused. And worst of all, I think she believed him. It all sounded so plausible, I could see why she'd been taken in. Bud had been so distraught that she stayed with him most of the night. He finally fell asleep around three, and that's when she left him a note and then called a cab to take her home.

Sitting across from her at lunch, I could tell she was still reeling from the evening. I felt sorry for her. She always tried so hard to be fair. Very gently, I began to point out the disparities in his story. First, I reminded her of the conversation I'd had with Sally. Sally said her ex-boyfriend had "hurt" someone with something "large." Now, granted she was drunk at the time, and her words weren't terribly specific, but in context it was clear enough to me what she was saying. At the time I reminded Kay that she'd agreed.

Second, and even more importantly, I said that it made no sense for Bud to buy Sally a car to make her "feel better" if she'd just killed someone with one. That is, unless he was a really sick man, which Kay insisted he wasn't.

And finally I said that I was incredibly frustrated by Kay's inability to see how Manderbach was making the most of the situation by using it to insinuate himself further into her affections. He'd been the one to run Olga Landauer down. He'd left the scene of the accident, and was now blaming someone else for the crime. Didn't that give her some indication of the man's character?

Kay listened to me, said she understood my concerns, but had to think about it further before she could discuss it. She added that she was having dinner with Bud later that evening. I asked her why. I mean, we'd gotten what we'd come for. Why not just dump him, give him a call and tell him she'd thought it over and wasn't interested in dating him any longer. Kay said she'd already agreed to the date and didn't want to go back on her word. And also, whether I believed it or not, she was positive Bud had asked his wife for a divorce. Finally, she said she'd been in relationships before, and she certainly wasn't going to be so cruel as to end one with a phone call. I had to be patient. When it came to feelings, she knew what was best.

Since there wasn't much I could say, I pulled the contact sheet out of my pocket and showed it to her. There they were, all the pictures I'd taken the night before. She looked at them—with less enthusiasm than I'd expected—then asked what my next move would be. I said I planned to take the contact sheet and the negatives back to my apartment for safekeeping, and then I was going to drive over and talk to Sally. With what I now knew, I hoped to be able to force her hand—get her to see that it was only a matter of time before the truth came out. I didn't know all the legal ramifications, but I figured she was probably an accessory to the crime because she hadn't gone to the police right away. Yet in my mind, she was also an innocent bystander who'd been manipulated by a powerful—and thoroughly rotten—man for his own selfish purposes. I explained to Kay that I had a friend in the DA's office who might be able to help Sally, that is, if she came clean and admitted the truth. The bottom line was, the photos were good evidence, but we needed more. We needed Sally.

Kay took it all in without offering her usual suggestions. I found that odd, but assumed she was tired after her ordeal of the night before. She finished her soup, kissed me on the cheek, and then said she had to get back

*to work. Christmas was only four days away. The store
was a madhouse.*

*That reminded me of the present I wanted to buy her. It
was a diamond ring, Mom. As I said before, I already had
it picked out. After paying the bill, I walked over to
Jacob's and bought it. I was on top of the world. In just a
few days Kay and I would be officially engaged. And if the
weather cooperated, I knew just where I wanted to ask her
for her hand in marriage.*

*After stopping off at my apartment and calling to make
sure Sally was home, I drove to her apartment. Thankfully, Jonnie wasn't around, so we could talk undisturbed.
I briefly laid out what I'd learned and said I had photos of
the car used in the hit-and-run. She sat poker-faced
through it all—never said a word. I pleaded with her to
help me put Manderbach behind bars. I'll never forget
what she did, Mom. She got up, walked to the door, and
said, "I think you should leave."*

*I couldn't believe my ears. After all the work I'd put
into this story, after everything Kay had done, Sally still
wouldn't budge. I thrashed around in my mind for something to say—and I hit on an idea. "Kay's involved with
Bud Manderbach," I said.*

*Her eyes threw off a spark. "That's ridiculous. Besides,
you used that line to bait me once before. It didn't work
then and it won't work now."*

"How do you think I got the pictures of his car?"

*That gave her a moment's pause. "I don't believe you.
He'd never date someone like Kay. She's not his type.
She's much too . . . wholesome."*

*I laughed out loud because it was so true, and yet Sally
hadn't meant it as a compliment. "Well, that doesn't
change the facts. And you know what else? Bud said you
were driving the car that night. You killed Olga Landauer."*

Now her eyes flashed daggers at me. "That's a lie!"

*"Of course it is, Sally. But unless you tell the police
what you know—and fast—he may get there first. And
believe me, when a rich man tells his story, even if it's a*

lie, people listen." I didn't believe for a minute that Bud's money would make any difference—justice doesn't work that way in this country—but I knew it might hit a nerve. Sally was a poor young woman who wanted to be rich—because being rich meant you were someone. People listened to "someone," not "nobodies" like her. It played right into her fears.

I didn't get up, but waited, hoping I'd found the key that would unlock a flood of incriminating information about Bud Manderbach, but instead, Sally remained adamant. With a coldness I found chilling, she said, "Get out."

I pleaded with her to reconsider.

"Listen, Mr. Clark Kent, mild-mannered reporter for a great metropolitan newspaper, I don't ever want to see you again. Do I make myself clear?"

There wasn't much else I could say. I grabbed my hat and left.

I drove around for the next couple of hours. I must have smoked an entire pack of cigarettes while I tried to make sense of what had happened. Without Sally's eyewitness testimony, the case against Bud Manderbach was hardly a sure bet, but I didn't know what else to do.

I returned to the apartment around seven. I thought I'd make myself a sandwich and watch some TV. I figured Kay would call when she got home from her date with Manderbach. Except for the night before, we'd always talked after her dates.

When I went into the kitchen, I found a note propped against the sugar bowl. The only other person who had a key to my apartment was Kay, so I knew it had to be from her. I couldn't imagine why—or when—she'd stopped by. She'd never done it before—not unless she called first. I still have the note, Mom. I had it in my wallet on Christmas eve. I'll copy it word for word so you can read what she said.

Justin:

I don't know how to begin. You won't like what I'm about to say, so I might as well just say it. For the past few weeks

*I've tried to resist what was happening to me, but last night,
I finally had to face the truth. I haven't said anything to you
before because, deep down, I guess I'm a coward.*

*You know I love you deeply, Justin, but I've also grown
to care about another man. You know who I mean. While
you know about Bud, Bud doesn't know about you.
Tonight, I plan to tell him. I hate dishonesty, Justin. It's
impossible to love two men, so I have to make a choice. I
promise, I won't make you wait long. Today is Tuesday.
Be patient with me, darling, and realize this is the most
painful decision of my life.*

*After I talk to Bud tonight, I intend to go away. I should
be home by Thursday morning. I'll call you when I
get back. I guess Thursday evening is Christmas eve.
Funny, but a month ago I had a very different idea of what
this Christmas would bring.*

*What I tell you next may make it seem like I've already
made a choice, but let me assure you I haven't. Justin, forgive me, but I took the negatives and the photo sheet from
your bedroom drawer. I don't intend to give them back.
By the time you read this, Bud will already have moved his
father's car out of the city. For now, please trust that I'm
doing what's right.*

*I don't like having this kind of power over two men I pro-
fess to love. The fact is, I may make a decision only to find
that the man I choose no longer wants me. I guess that's a
risk I have to take. Please don't hate me, Justin. And please
try to understand that the last few weeks have been agony.
I can't go on like this. None of us can. I may be handling
this badly, but I see no other way.*

Until Thursday,
Kay

*I felt like I'd been hit by a train. At first I was dazed. I
walked around the apartment in a fog. How could this
have happened? I'd been so careful to make sure Kay
understood the kind of man Bud Manderbach really was.
Then I got out the bourbon. I started drinking. The more I*

drank, the angrier I got. She was a traitor. She'd betrayed me when I needed her most. She'd single-handedly ruined my career and at the same time allowed a guilty man to go free. You think you have a temper, Mom, well, you should see mine when I get started.

I threw plates at the wall. I broke the glass candlestick holder she bought me. I kicked furniture over. And then I went in the bedroom, took her picture off my nightstand, and threw it in the trash. I was sure Kay was just trying to soften the blow. By stealing those negatives, she'd sent me a clear message, one I'd be a fool to ignore. She was just like the rest of the women Manderbach dated, except she was more subtle. A classier act. In the end she saw that great big house of his and she sold out.

That's when the doorbell rang. I remember weaving through the mess to answer it. I was sure it would be Kay coming to apologize, to beg my forgiveness. Manderbach had confused her with his double-talk, but she'd come through for me in the end. She hadn't destroyed the negatives. How could she? She was wearing my ring. We belonged together. Nothing would separate us now.

I was as high as a kite. That doesn't excuse what happened next, but it does explain my mood. When I drew back the door, I found Mitzi standing outside. I don't know why, but I invited her in, even offered her a drink. Maybe it was because she looked so pretty in her new red dress. I hadn't seen her for over a month. She explained that she'd come to drop off my Christmas present. She couldn't return it because she'd had it monogrammed. I invited her to sit down. I'm sure she thought the place was a mess. All the broken glass. The tables upended. But she acted like there was nothing wrong.

We sat and talked. I think I cried. I know I kept drinking. It's all such a blur. I must have told her about Kay—that I hated her. That she'd betrayed me. I think I said we were finished. Mitzi stayed much too long. I know she was hoping for a reconciliation. I gave her cause to think that it was possible—though if I hadn't been drunk and feeling so sorry for *myself, I wouldn't have acted so foolishly. I just kept thinking about what Kay said. That she was in love with two men. Well, if she could love two men, why couldn't I love two women? Except I didn't. I was in love with Kay—only Kay. It was an awful night, Mom. Things got way out of hand. I'd like to forget it—I'm sure Mitzi would, too. I hope she has.*

The next morning, I had a terrible hangover, but I thought if I could just get through the day, by tomorrow, I'd know Kay's decision. Then I'd deal with it—whatever it was. In the cold light of day, it seemed inconceivable to me that Kay would pick Bud Manderbach over what we had together. I had to hold that thought. I had to believe in the woman I loved. And so I made some coffee, took a shower, and spent the rest of the day at work.

I'll finish the story tomorrow, Mom. The truth is, even though the memories are painful, I've been holding on to this retelling knowing that as long as I kept Kay alive in my letters, she would remain alive in my heart. Sometimes my worst fear is that I'll forget her, that time will dull and diminish my love, when nothing else on earth could.

Until tomorrow,
Justin

31

the day after New Year's

"This is Bram Baldric, and we have a very special guest with us today—Minnesota's own Raymond Lawless, criminal defense attorney extraordinaire." Bram adjusted his microphone, then smiled at the handsome, silver-haired man sitting opposite him. "Ray, we'll go back to our callers in a minute. But first, does it surprise you that the Kay Collins murder case, as well as the current investigation into the disappearance and possible death of Wish Greveen, have both blown up as huge stories—both locally and nationally?"

"Surprise me?" Ray gave a sarcastic chuckle. "It shouldn't come as a surprise to anyone. This is just the kind of story the national tabloids love. It's got everything—murder, mystery, betrayal, love, revenge, even, it would appear, an old love triangle." He paused for a second to collect his thoughts. "It seems to me that in the wake of the O. J. Simpson trial, people in this country are hungry for new—real-life—legal drama. What's happening in Minnesota simply provides the media with more grist for the mill. Back in the Fifties, Kay Collins's murder wasn't reported outside the state. Today, however, due to our insatiable desire to entertain ourselves with other people's tragedies, this case will no doubt be made into a national *cause célèbre*. I'll even make a prediction. In the next few months Bud Manderbach will become the focus of a media feeding frenzy. Whether he's guilty or innocent, he'll be tried and sentenced in the court of public opinion."

"You make it all sound pretty ominous."

"It is. I've always felt that if you ruin a man's reputation, you can destroy his life."

"Do you think there's enough evidence against Mr. Manderbach to bring him to trial?"

Ray sat forward, folding his hands in front of him. "That's tricky. At this point I'd have to say it looks doubtful. Hennepin County simply isn't going to waste its time and money on a trial if it doesn't have at least a fifty-fifty chance of winning."

"That's the cutoff point? Fifty percent?"

"Generally, yes. As I was preparing last night for my appearance on your show, it occurred to me that in one highly ironic sense, this current case parallels the Collins murder. Justin Bloom was never brought to trial for the death of his girlfriend, and yet in everyone's mind, he was responsible. It's common knowledge—but is it the truth?

Mr. Bloom wasn't able to put his case before a jury of his peers, so the only side of the story we've ever heard is what was written in the newspapers—and that was essentially the testimony of one man. A police officer named Arn O'Dell."

Bram desperately wanted to comment, but knew it was pointless.

"And yet," continued Ray, "everyone knows there are two sides to every story. Sometimes more. When it comes to Bud Manderbach and his current difficulties, it may turn out to be the same kind of situation. His reputation could very easily be damaged beyond repair, even though he may never be convicted—or even tried—for a crime."

"That *is* ironic," said Bram. The phone banks were jammed with calls. Lights were flashing on his console, but he resisted the urge to go to his listeners, and instead asked one more question. "You said a second ago that there wasn't enough evidence against Bud Manderbach to bring him to trial. I assume you mean that since Mr. Greveen's body hasn't been found, nobody can say for sure that he's dead, and therefore, no one can be tried for his murder."

Ray made a steeple of his fingers, then shifted his gaze to the people inside the glass control room. He seemed amused by their rapt attention. "In law, as you might expect, it's not quite that straightforward. If you want to convict a man of homicide in Minnesota, by statute you have to prove two things. First, you have to show beyond a reasonable doubt that the person allegedly murdered is indeed dead. You're right, normally a body is found, so it's not a problem. But if the body can't be located—and understand that this is rare— you may still be able to bring your case if you can prove through circumstantial and presumptive evidence that an individual is truly dead."

"Is that difficult?"

"Very difficult."

"What's the second point you have to prove?"

"Well, very simply, you have to prove that the person you have alleged to be the murderer did the crime. And let me add that each of these needs to be proved independently. That's an important point, especially in a case like this. In other words, you can't just say that Pete wanted Jack dead. Since Jack is missing, he therefore must be dead, and Pete must have murdered him. You can't use one to prove the other."

"What about the blood evidence?"

"You mean the blood found at Bud Manderbach's house? Yes, that does indicate a fight, at the very least. We'll have to wait for DNA results, but we already know that preliminary tests strongly suggest the blood belonged to Wish Greveen. And yet, as of this moment, there's still not enough evidence to prove that Mr. Greveen is dead. That's why the police are looking so hard for the body."

Bram loosened his tie. "Tell me, counselor, if Bud Manderbach wanted to retain you as his lawyer, would you take the job?"

Raymond's eyes creased with humor. "Of course I'd take it. I'd be a fool not to. But according to my sources, Mr. Manderbach has already approached two other attorneys—each of national prominence. I'm sure he'll be well represented. I would add, however, that the job I'd really like is no longer available."

"And that would be—"

"I'd like to defend Justin Bloom."

Bram laughed. "You're right. That would be difficult since the man's been dead for many years."

"I hear some people think he's still alive."

"Some people think Elvis is still alive, Ray."

"You have a point. I just wish that Justin Bloom had been brought to trial. I think he'd be a free man today if he hadn't left the country. By the way, speaking of the Collins murder, I was sorry to hear that the *Dallas Lane, Private Eye* series had been canceled."

"We're on hiatus, Ray. We're not dead yet."

"My wife and I listened with great interest. Any chance it will be back on the air soon? I'd like to hear the end of the story."

Bram sighed. "Management types are currently looking

for another writer, although I've also heard a rumor that Mr. Manderbach is threatening a lawsuit if we go ahead with the final two episodes." Glancing at the time, he continued, "We've got room for a couple of calls before we go to the news. Vern from Brooklyn Center, you're on."

"Bram?"

"Yes, Vern. Do you have a question for Raymond Lawless?"

"No, but I got one for you. Did I hear you say that Elvis was dead? It's a lie, you know. There's a pamphlet put out by one of the state militias—I forget which one—telling how they hid him in a poultry barn for years. He was real sick from all the drugs he was force-fed in Las Vegas. The government wants us to think he's dead because he was such a strong leader for those of us who still consider ourselves proud, white Americans. I would've followed him anywhere, Bram, even to the gates of hell."

"Have a nice trip, Vern. Bye."

An hour later Bram shuffled into his office, exhausted from an afternoon of nonstop talking. Some days the program took more out of him. Since Sophie was seated behind the desk, he dropped into a chair on the other side. Raking a hand through his hair, he said, "It must be the moon."

"Excuse me?" She looked up from a stack of papers.

"Did you listen to the program?"

"Some of it."

"Didn't you think there were an awful lot of weird calls today?"

She shrugged, then smiled. "You look pretty sexy when you muss your hair up like that."

"Maybe I should muss your hair up."

"Nope. Can't."

"Why not?"

"We have theatre tickets tonight."

"Theatre? When did we get those?"

"Ten minutes ago."

It now struck him that Sophie hadn't been waiting for him

like this in months. She'd been so busy, she never came to the station anymore. "To what do I owe this unexpected visit?"

"My afternoon meeting was canceled. Too many people are out with the flu, so we rescheduled for next week. Since I had some free time on my hands, I thought I'd drop by."

"You mean, it wasn't my intense animal magnetism that drew you?"

"Well, that, too, of course."

"Of course." He crossed his legs. If he were a truly kind man, he'd be happy with his good fortune and let the subject drop. "Are you telling me you didn't have any other hotel business that required your immediate attention? Sophie, this is dangerous! If you're not at the Maxfield every minute, the walls might collapse."

"Very funny. No, I thought we should have some fun tonight. It's a great play. I guarantee you'll love it."

"Right." He sighed, leaning his head back and closing his eyes.

"You don't sound thrilled."

"I am, but I'm beat."

"Christopher Plummer will pep you up."

"A relaxing dinner preceded by a couple of martinis would pep me up more."

The phone interrupted them.

"Since it's your office," said Sophie, pressing line one, "I assume it's for you." She handed him the receiver.

"This should only take a minute," he whispered. "Baldric here."

"I haven't got much time." It was Al Lundquist. "I got a fascinating little news flash for you, pal. Thought I'd pass on."

"I'm all ears. Well, almost all ears." He could feel his stomach growl.

"It's about the house that burned down last week—the one Molly Stanglund rented. It seems forensics finally got around to looking at her charred remains."

"And?"

"Stanglund didn't die in the fire. Some guy did. So far, he's a John Doe."

Bram was stunned. "Then . . . Molly is alive?"

"That would be my guess."

He put his hand over the mouthpiece and explained to Sophie what had happened. "Listen, Al, do the police know the house was rented by Arn O'Dell's granddaughter?"

"They do now. I talked to the officer in charge of the case, gave him all the particulars. Looks like we may have another homicide on our hands. Nobody down here would be a bit surprised if the body turned out to belong to Wish Greveen."

"Greveen?" Bram whistled. "That *would* be something. Will you keep me posted?"

"If I'm in the mood."

"Thanks, pal. I owe you."

After hanging up, Bram sat for a few moments in silence. He could tell Sophie was every bit as shocked as he was. And yet she seemed preoccupied by the papers in front of her. "What are you looking at?"

"It's a file on the Collins murder. I found it on your desk."

"Oh, that's the one Al gave me a while back."

"Well, look at this." She tossed him a five-by-seven glossy.

It was a picture of Justin Bloom. "I'd say this was a press photo. Sure, someone's written the name of the paper and 1958 on the back. Man, look at those clothes. Straight out of *Dragnet.*"

"Handsome guy, wasn't he?"

"I suppose."

"Now notice the ring on his left hand."

Bram glanced at it again. "So?"

"I've seen it before. Several times. The first time was when Wish Greveen checked into the hotel. He was wearing it."

Bram folded his arms over his chest. "Sophie, there have to be lots of rings like that."

"A square-cut tiger eye? Maybe. But look closer. There are two diamond baguettes on either side, where the band attaches to the setting, and the gold spreads out around it like a cat's-paw." She handed him a magnifying glass.

Holding it over the picture, he said, "Yeah, I see it."

"So think about it, honey. Justin Bloom is wearing that ring. It's rare, probably one of a kind. The year was 1958—the same year he took off for points unknown. I think it's fair to assume he was wearing it when he left. Next, forty years later Wish Greveen shows up at the Maxfield wearing what looks like the exact same ring. He keeps a low profile. Few people see him. Then he disappears. Bud Manderbach, who may be implicated in the old murder, also appears to be implicated in the disappearance of Greveen. But who really disappeared, Bram? Who *was* Wish Greveen?"

"You're saying—"

"It's simple deduction. Wish Greveen and Justin Bloom are one and the same person."

No matter how hard he tried to resist the notion, the logic was inescapable. "If it's true, do you realize what this means?"

"Justin Bloom didn't die in Europe. And for the last four weeks he was here in town, staying at the Maxfield."

Bram shook his head, thinking it through. "Do you think Bud Manderbach knew Greveen was Bloom?"

She shrugged. "I don't know. But if he did, it sure explains a lot."

His mind raced. If Molly was still alive, maybe there was an outside chance she'd try to contact him. He knew it was a long shot. If she was smart, she'd probably moved to the other side of the moon by now—and given no forwarding address.

"Bram?"

"Um?"

"Can I tell you something else?" Sophie got up and walked around the front of the desk, sitting down on the edge.

He was almost afraid to ask what it was. "Sure. What?"

"Well, I started doodling with names when I was listening to your program earlier."

"It's nice to know our topic kept you riveted to your seat."

"I only doodled during the commercials, darling."

"Good of you to clarify that, *dear*. Go on."

"Well, you know how much I like puzzles. As I was playing around I discovered—" She handed him a scratch pad. "Do you realize that the name Greveen is an anagram for the word 'revenge'?"

He stared at the words. After a few seconds he looked up. His unblinking eyes held hers.

"I think Wish Greveen, otherwise known as Justin Bloom, has been behind everything. The radio show was his revenge against Bud Manderbach."

"But, Sophie, to make such an elaborate plan work, he would've needed his mother's cooperation."

"I'm sure he had it."

He got up and sat down next to her on the desk. "Look, sweetheart, I may be wrong, but I really think Heda Bloom believes her son is dead."

"She's acting. She has to be. He's a wanted man, Bram. If the police thought he was in town, he'd be arrested. That's why she never met with Greveen once while he was here. She used Dorothy as her go-between."

"And kept Dorothy in the dark about the truth behind the radio show?"

"Maybe. Maybe not. Who knows?"

He shook his head. "But Sophie, I've talked to Heda several times since Greveen's disappearance. She seemed perfectly normal—even happy. I'd even go so far as to say she's relieved that the show has been put on hold. If Greveen truly was her son, wouldn't his disappearance and possible death cause her—at the very least—some anxiety? Or more realistically, she'd be devastated."

Sophie's enthusiasm for the conversation was starting to flag. "If you're right, we're still missing something."

Bram put his arm around her and kissed her cheek. Then he nibbled her ear. He was about to move on to her lips when she whispered, "You men. You're only interested in one thing."

"You're right. And it's not Christopher Plummer."

She leaned her head against his shoulder. "Are we done with this discussion?"

"Of course not. But I need sustenance."

"From the looks of your desk drawers, most of your sustenance comes from cookies."

With his hand, he traced the line of her jaw. "I was thinking about a nice prime-rib dinner. Wine. Candlelight. Soft music."

"You really don't want to go to the theatre tonight, do you?"

"Would it be terrible if we offered the tickets to Rudy and John?"

"I'm sure they'd be thrilled."

"What about you?"

She entwined her fingers with his. "Let's order in."

32

one week later

Bud burst into the kitchen. He slammed the door behind him, making sure it was locked and bolted, and then leaned against it and took a deep breath. "It's a madhouse out there," he shouted, looking around for his sister. "B.B.! Where the hell are you?"

For days now B.B. had been standing in the north turret, tiptoeing from window to window, peeking at the sightseers as they drove their cars slowly past the house. It seemed that everyone in the Twin Cities wanted to get a firsthand look at the scene of the crime.

"I'm here, Buddy," she called from somewhere inside the mansion's vast interior.

Bud set his briefcase down, tossed his coat over a kitchen chair, and went to find her. It had been a terrible morning.

There was no way he could get any work done at the office, especially when magazine editors, newspaper reporters, representatives of the TV tabloids, and journalists from all over the country kept calling, tying up the phone and fax lines. They all wanted the same thing: an exclusive one-on-one interview. His lawyers had been right to suggest he stay home, avoid the press and the public as much as possible. But that was easier said than done, particularly when the press and the public were camping out in his front yard. Even the cold and the snow hadn't stopped them. Mad dogs and Minnesotans, he thought to himself sourly. The English might go out into the noonday sun, but they'd never willingly venture into this god-awful wilderness.

Bud had barely made it in the back door alive. He couldn't take much more of this media abuse, and yet he'd be damned if he'd let a pack of braying hyenas chase him inside his house and make him afraid to come out. So far, neither he nor his lawyers had been able to stem the tide of public interest. His personal life had been turned upside down and inside out for the general amusement, and what was even worse, not only was there no end in sight, but the ball seemed to be picking up speed. Even his ex-wives had gotten into the fray. Driving home from the store, he'd discovered one of them being interviewed on a local talk show. While she discussed the intimate details of their stormy marriage, people at home were probably munching their morning toast. It was obscene!

Bud finally found his sister in the sunroom. With some difficulty, B.B. tore her attention away from the window and smiled at him. Then she seemed to remember something, and the smile dimmed. "You're going to be angry with me, Buddy."

"I hardly think that's likely. You're the only one in this town who's on my side." He eased down onto a chair. Raising an eyebrow, he said, "Why am I going to be angry?"

She pressed her lips together to smooth out her red lipstick. She still had on her bathrobe and slippers. "I took the phone off the hook," she said in a dejected whisper. "I couldn't stand the constant ringing. The answering machine is full and . . . this is where you're going to be mad, Buddy. I forgot what you told me about putting in a new tape."

He waved it away. "I don't give a damn about the phone calls."

Her smile returned. "I'm glad."

"I don't suppose you listened to any of them?"

"A few. A couple were personal. Some woman. I've forgotten her name."

"It was probably Giselle Tannanger." Giselle had hit the roof when he canceled their Christmas trip to New York. Since he was so busy on other fronts at the time, the fact that she'd broken off their affair in retaliation had barely registered. Now he missed her, but doubted she'd called to resume their relationship. She probably wanted to gloat.

B.B. stole one last peek out the window and then joined her brother, taking a seat on an antique fainting couch, her favorite place to nap in the afternoons. "How was work?" she said, sipping from her mug.

"What work? It's hopeless, B.B. I think I'm going to stay home until this all blows over."

"When will that be?"

"Oh, probably sometime in the next century." He grunted. "It's ridiculous, you know. I never laid a hand on that man."

B.B. lowered her eyes. "Bud?"

"Hmm?"

"You trust me, don't you?"

"What a silly question." He tipped his head back and gazed up at an oil portrait of his father. The artist had perfectly captured the little man's nastiness.

She waited, fingering the button on her nightie, then continued, "Buddy . . . you don't need to lie to me anymore. The night Wish Greveen died, I found the dagger lighter in your bedroom at the cottage. It had blood all over it, but I cleaned it off. Lucky I did, or the police would have found it. I put it back with the rest of my lighters. At first I thought you'd killed Sally all over again, but I was just mixed up." She gave him a coy smile, one that quickly turned into a pout.

"At first I was . . . upset that you took it without asking. You shouldn't do that, Buddy. It's wrong. But I forgive you. You know me. I can never stay mad at you very long."

Bud sat upright in his chair. In a voice he barely recognized as his own, he said, "The dagger lighter had blood on it?"

"That's right. Buddy, what's wrong? You seem . . . surprised."

Damn right he was surprised. His eyes hardened. "What the hell is going on here?"

B.B. glanced around the room, taking his words literally. "I don't know. The cook hasn't arrived yet. I agree, that's kind of odd. Maybe she missed her bus."

Realizing she'd misunderstood, he said, "I fired her. I caught her in my study last night, riffling through my personal papers. I'm sure she was going to sell them to a tabloid."

"But, Bud? How will we eat?" She seemed truly alarmed.

"Don't change the subject." Fixing her with a penetrating stare, he said, "You think finding that dagger means I killed Wish Greveen?"

"Didn't you?"

"No!"

Slowly, her heavy eyebrows lowered. "Then how *did* he die?"

"I don't know, but it wasn't by my hand." He got up and crossed to the front windows, turning his back on his sister. Returning to that night for the millionth time in his mind, he said, "We talked privately for about twenty minutes. I asked him who he really was. Once Dorothy was gone, he freely admitted he was Justin Bloom."

"He did?" said B.B., scrunching up her face in thought. "But . . . I don't understand."

"I demanded to know what he was up to with that radio show, but he wouldn't give me a straight answer about anything. He just kept telling me to wait and see. I'm not a patient man, B.B. I had no patience with him that night. Sure we argued, but I didn't murder him! Not that I didn't think about it. It would have been easy, but not there. Not on my own property. I'd have to be an idiot!"

"You're not an idiot, Buddy. Dad was wrong about that."

He turned around. "He left about ten-thirty. I had something I needed to do, so I took off a few minutes later. The last time I saw him, he was alive. How can I be expected to know what happened after I left? Maybe he had other enemies—but it wasn't me. I never touched a hair on his head!"

"What a confusing story," said B.B., examining the writing on her coffee mug.

Bud watched her a moment, then remembered the call he needed to make to his lawyer. "Which phone did you take off the hook?"

"The one in the kitchen. Buddy, what will we do about lunch?"

"I'll make us an omelette."

"I hate omelettes!"she shouted, pouting into her mug.

"Then I'll make us a sandwich."

"What kind?"

"B.B., we'll talk about this later."

"But I'm hungry now. We have to hire a new cook."

"I will. I'll call the service this afternoon. In the meantime go play with your sugar-bowl collection."

Her face brightened. "All right."

Since he wasn't about to carry on a business conversation in the kitchen, he hung up the phone and then walked briskly down the hall to his study. Somewhere between the two, the phone began to ring. Before he sat down, Bud grabbed the receiver and said, "Whatever this is about, I'm not interested."

"Bud . . . is that you?"

He struggled to recall the voice. "Dorothy?" He hadn't talked to her in weeks.

"I'm glad I finally got through. I only have a second, but I had to call."

He tapped a pen impatiently against the desktop. "Right. You're just like all the rest. You called to gloat."

"No, that's not it at all. Actually . . . I *was* upset when you threw me out on Christmas eve, but I'm not naive. I knew you only had lunch with me those two days so you could get close to Wish Greveen. It's not very flattering to a woman, Bud. We have egos, too. I suppose I shouldn't tell you this, but I liked your company, so I went along with it."

"Dorothy, you misjudge me. That's not true at all." Though, of course, it was. "I found you very attractive. And I would have called, but as you might imagine, I've been a bit preoccupied with my own problems."

"Bud, listen to me. I've discovered something important. It's information you need to know right away, but I don't want to tell you over the phone. We have to meet."

"What sort of information?"

In a voice barely above a whisper, she said, "It's about Wish Greveen."

"You can't just leave me hanging, Dorothy. Give me *some* clue."

More silence. Then: "He's not dead."

Very slowly, Bud sat down. "How do you know?"

"People are coming in and out of here all the time. I can't talk. Will you meet me?"

"Where?"

"There's a Lutheran church on Lafayette, just south of downtown St. Paul. It stays open until eleven every night, but nobody is ever around—well, nobody except the minister, and he usually stays in his office. I've been there a couple of times. It's quiet—and private. Nobody will see us."

"But why a church? Why not meet in a restaurant?"

"It's too public."

He saw her point. His house was off-limits for the same reason. And so was the Maxfield. "What's the name of the church?"

"St Mark's, I think. No, St. Luke's. That's it. Will you meet me there tonight at ten?"

He wrote it down. "Ten o'clock. I'll be there."

"And Bud—make sure you're not followed. I don't mean

to frighten you, but I'm scared. Really scared. Something's not right here and I refuse to be part of it any longer."

"Part of what?"

The line clicked.

B.B. appeared in the doorway, licking a spoon she'd just dipped into a carton of chocolate chip ice cream. "Buddy? I was wondering. Could you make those sandwiches now? I'm kind of in the mood for grilled cheese."

May 21, 1959

Dear Mother:

For months now, this is the moment I've dreaded. As I sit down to write I know that tonight I will finish my story. You will finally know what I know. Unless I'm caught and brought back to stand trial, the only one—other than myself—who will ever hear the truth is you. Not even Bud Manderbach himself fully understands what was at stake, or what was lost. I realize that the newspapers have already convicted me of murder, and perhaps that's as it should be. But in the end, I want you to be the judge. After you read the last page of my story, you tell me who's guilty and who's innocent.

On Thursday morning, Kay called from a phone booth at the bus station. She'd just come back from her trip out of town. I was already at work, but she knew my private number. She said that as she'd promised, she'd made her decision and now wanted to talk. It's difficult for me to explain my mood that morning, Mom. I'd had some time to think myself. I knew without a doubt that I wanted Kay—wanted to marry her. The sound of her voice gave me such hope. I was more certain than ever that she loved me—it was obvious not only by everything she said, but in the way she said it. She was so loving, so gentle, and yet frustratingly noncommittal about her decision. Still, I was an optimist. I felt certain she'd seen the error of her ways. Her future would be nothing but misery if she got mixed up with a man like Manderbach. I had to trust her good sense. And I did, Mom, really I did—because in my mind, no choice existed. Kay had simply left to get her head straight, and to figure out the best way to let Manderbach down easily.

When I asked her if she still had the photos and the negatives, she said yes. They were hidden away in a safe place. She'd had second thoughts about destroying them. I didn't press her on the subject, but I'm sure she got the point. I desperately wanted them back. The best of all possible worlds would be for her to not only agree to marry me but, as she fell into my arms, to offer them to me as a token of her love. Together, we'd take the evidence to the police and finally blow the whistle on Bud Manderbach and his drunken "accident."

As we continued to talk I pulled the engagement ring out of my pocket and admired its beauty. I could just picture the moment. For weeks I'd fantasized about asking for her hand in marriage on Christmas eve. Since that was tonight, it seemed perfect—like fate had decreed that our love was meant to be. She asked me where we should meet. I suggested "our" spot down by Minnehaha Creek. It was private—no one would bother us. And even though it was winter, the weather had been mild. Since that's where I'd first said I loved her, where I'd given her my tiger-eye ring as a token of that love, it seemed only right.

Kay agreed. She said she'd meet me there at four o'clock. I asked her if she'd talked to Bud Manderbach yet and she said no, she hadn't. She was planning to call him next. I wasn't sure how to read that, and yet the more I thought about it, the more I felt certain she'd called me first because she needed my reassurance. She had to know I still loved her. That love would give her the courage she needed to tell Manderbach what he could do with his lies. So, before she rang off, I told her she was the only woman for me. There would never be another. She said, "Until tonight, Justin."

I spent the rest of the morning on assignment. Around noon, I drove past Kay's building just to see if she was around. I wasn't trying to meet with her before the appointed time, I merely wanted to look at her—to be close. I pulled up next to the curb and watched her window for a few minutes, but when I couldn't see anyone, I gave up. I wasn't particularly disappointed since I knew we'd get together later. As I was about to leave I saw Jonnie Apfenford come out the front door. Now, you have to understand, Jonnie was never a very happy-go-lucky kind of girl, but that morning she looked positively dour. Before she stepped down onto the sidewalk, she spent a few moments surveying the street. I wondered what she was looking for. Well, of course, she spotted me right away. I waved and smiled, and then waited as she made straight for the car. Without being invited, she climbed into the front seat and said, "Drive."

"What?" I said, confused not only by the brevity of the comment, but by the intent. "Drive where?"

"Anywhere," she said. "Just go."

I didn't ask for explanations. We ended up at the Boulevard restaurant on Lyndale. I was hungry and wanted some lunch, so over egg-salad sandwiches and iced teas, she explained that Sally hadn't come home since Tuesday night. Jonnie was beside herself with worry.

I asked her if this was unusual. I mean, maybe Sally did that sort of thing all the time. Jonnie said no, Sally always came home—it might be two or three o'clock in the morning, but she would never be gone overnight without letting one of her roommates know her whereabouts. It was a house rule.

Well, as you can expect, after nearly a two-day absence,

Jonnie was terribly upset. At the same time I sensed there was something important she wasn't telling me. I wasn't in the mood to beat around the bush, so I asked her point-blank what it was. She answered my question with a question of her own. When had I last seen Sally? I replied that I'd come by the apartment to talk to her on Tuesday afternoon.

"What about?" she asked.

"It's a long story," I replied. I didn't want to get into it.

"Did it have something to do with Bud Manderbach?"

Well, I was floored. This was the first time Jonnie had ever let on that she knew anything about the whole Manderbach mess. And then the light dawned. I'd wondered for weeks if Jonnie might not be the person who'd sent me that note at the paper, the one who'd started the ball rolling. So I said, "It was you, wasn't it? You tipped me off about Sally knowing the truth behind the Landauer hit-and-run."

At this point she didn't even try to deny it, Mom. Sure, she said, she'd known all along. Sally had confided some of the details to her the night it happened, but then never said another word about it. Jonnie was torn. She didn't have any proof, merely the alcohol-soaked confession of one of her closest friends, and yet she felt that Bud Manderbach was guilty of a serious crime. Justice had to be done. She didn't want to get mixed up in it herself, so she looked around and concluded that since I'd been the reporter covering the story for the St. Paul paper, I'd be the perfect person to follow up the lead. Yet now that Sally had disappeared, Jonnie was frightened. Deeply frightened.

The fact was, Jonnie had arrived home about an hour after I'd left the apartment the previous Tuesday. She found Sally pacing the floor, furious. Sally had already called Bud Manderbach's house several times, but was finally told he wasn't expected home until evening. Jonnie said Sally was like a caged tiger. She couldn't relax. As Sally raged, Jonnie sat on the couch and listened. Little by little, the truth came out.

Sally explained that Manderbach was blaming her for

the Landauer hit-and-run, and that he'd passed this false story on to Kay. But the truth was, it had been Bud's fault—all his fault. He was drunk that night and driving like a maniac. Sally had begged him to slow down, but he just laughed. Said he loved speed. All men loved speed. Not only had Bud sideswiped Olga Landauer, knocking her down on the curb, but as Sally watched in horror he stopped the car and threw it in reverse. He knew he'd hit someone—possibly injured them—and wanted to help, but he was out of control, too drunk to watch where he was going. As Olga screamed in terror Bud backed the car up over her. That's what had finally killed her. Sally said it was hideous. Unimaginable. And then, as Bud tried to get away, he slammed into a car parked on the street. That's how he'd done the damage to the front end. Sally said all she could see as they sped away was the woman's little dog barking and yelping, yanking at the leash in the dead woman's hand.

This, as you may already realize, was new information. The police must have made a decision to withhold it from the press and the public. Only the murderer—or someone who happened to be in the car that night—could have known these details.

As we continued to talk I asked Jonnie if Sally had ever reached Bud Manderbach that evening. She said yes. She had. She'd called the mansion to make sure he was home, then left shortly before seven to go meet with him. That was the last time Jonnie had seen or heard from Sally, and she couldn't help but fear the worst. She was positive Bud Manderbach had done something to shut her up— possibly even threatening her with physical harm unless she promised to continue her silence. But Jonnie also feared that any threat Bud made had fallen on deaf ears. Before Sally left the apartment, she told Jonnie she'd made a decision. No matter what happened to her, no matter what her punishment turned out to be, she had to tell the police the truth. She wasn't going to let some slippery bastard like Manderbach wipe the floor up with her.

He'd betrayed her, and now it was payback time. But first, she intended to give him a piece of her mind.

I can only guess what happened next. I assume that Sally found Manderbach at home, and that she told him what she planned to do. Maybe he begged her forgiveness, or tried to use his charm to get her to see reason—or even tried bribing her with more money—but in the end we both know what happened. Bud Manderbach murdered Sally Nash, and then drove her body out of the city and dumped it in a frozen cornfield.

At the time I knew only that Sally was missing. Even though I hated Manderbach, I couldn't bring myself to believe he'd kill to cover his tracks. On the way to the university, where I dropped Jonnie off, I explained everything that Kay and I had learned. Jonnie knew Kay had gone out of town for two nights, but didn't know why. Now she understood.

I explained that I was meeting Kay at four, and as soon as we were done, the two of us would come back to the apartment so she could see Kay's engagement ring. Maybe by then Sally would have called or returned. I thought there was an outside possibility that she might have been detained at one of the local police precincts. Maybe she hadn't thought to call Jonnie and let her know what was happening.

That afternoon was such a crazy few hours in my life, Mom. As I think about it now I realize I was sitting at the center of a cyclone, but all I knew was that I would see my girl in a few hours. Everything was going to be all right. Sure, I was worried about Sally, and yet, for no particular reason, I'd find myself smiling. As a reporter, I was frustrated and angered by what Kay had done to sabotage my investigation, but as a man, I couldn't wait to see her, to take her in my arms and tell her how much I loved her. I spent the rest of the day running down leads for a story I was working on, but I couldn't concentrate. I was too nervous. One minute I was excited, the next terrified. At one point I did try calling around to see if I could locate Sally, but with no luck.

A few minutes before four, I walked down the hill

toward the creek. The diamond ring was in my pocket, and the promise of a beautiful, storybook future was in my heart. It was beginning to get dark, though there was enough light to see that Kay was already waiting for me. She was leaning against a tree, gazing silently at the opposite bank. The evening was quiet, the breeze almost soft. I stood for a few seconds and watched her, knowing that I wanted to capture this moment and remember it the rest of my life. She was so young, so lovely, and trying so hard to find her way, to do what was right. Once again, I felt we were kindred spirits, fated to be together.

As I walked up to her she heard the crunch of my shoes in the snow and turned. She smiled at me, Mom, but there were tears in her eyes. In that instant I knew what she'd decided. My stomach tightened. I couldn't believe she'd chosen Manderbach.

I just stood there staring at her. "Why?" I said after a couple of seconds.

She looked down. "You're strong, Justin. With or without me, you'll have a happy, successful life."

I protested, telling her she had it all wrong. Without her I'd be miserable, lonely, empty.

She held up her hand for me to stop. "Please, if you don't let me explain, you'll never understand. And if I can't make you understand, you'll hate me. I couldn't take that, Justin—knowing you hated me." She wiped a hand over her eyes and began again. "Bud is weak. He picks bad women. He's always going to pick bad women, Justin, and that's why, until the day he dies, he'll be unhappy. With me, he has a chance. I won't disappoint him. I don't care at all about his money, I care only about him. I'll help him, don't you see? Underneath, he's not what he appears. He's good and decent. And he's kind, and very gentle."

"But . . . what about Olga Landauer? He killed her in cold blood! That's not the act of a good man."

"It wasn't like that, Justin. It wasn't intentionally brutal. But you're right, he was driving that night. After a lot of soul-searching, he finally told me the truth. And that's what

broke down the final barrier between us. I know what he did was wrong, but I also understand the pain he was in. And I know he can change. I have the ability to give him back his life, to grant him a second chance. Not to do so would be wrong."

"Kay, that's crazy! Society has rules. We can't just let people get away with murder because they're in pain."

"It wasn't a cold-blooded murder, Justin. You and I both know that. It was an accident. A mistake. Oh, I understand why you're so interested in bringing Bud to justice. You're a journalist. You can't help yourself. Journalists are storytellers who need good guys and bad guys to people their stories. You deal in facts, in black and white. But real life isn't that simple. I won't let you sacrifice Bud's future on the altar of some story, Justin. He deserves better than that."

I didn't agree with her, but thought that if I argued the point, it would only alienate her further. What I asked next was self-serving, but I had to know the truth. "So . . . have you destroyed the negatives?"

Her expression grew wistful. "Bud asked me the same thing. No, they're right here." She held up her purse. "I intend to meet with him when we're done. After I present him with both the photos and the negatives, he'll understand that I mean what I say—that I can be trusted."

"But, Kay . . . I love you. You love me. You can't just walk away from what we have." I was desperate. I didn't know what to say, so I grabbed her, pulled her against me. I could smell her perfume, feel the softness of her hair.

She gave in at first. I knew she'd made a decision and wanted to stick with it, but I could also sense the conflict raging inside her. As she said, nothing was simple. After a few seconds she stiffened and pulled away. "Justin, don't make this harder than it already is." She took off my ring and handed it to me. "I can't keep this. Not now. Please, put it back on."

I protested. I wouldn't. It was hers. I'd given it to her.

"Please, Justin. I have to know it's back where it belongs. I know how much the ring means to you."

I knew by the look of determination on her face that it was useless to argue, so I did what she asked. I took off both gloves and put them in my pocket, then slipped the tiger eye back on my finger. We stood and looked at each other for several seconds. I suppose we were absorbing the finality of the moment. All I know is that neither of us knew what to say, or more specifically, how to say goodbye.

My eyes clouded with tears. I wanted to scream, to protest, to make her see my agony, but instead I took my defeat like a man.

As I was about to kiss her one last time, I saw a man slide down the opposite bank. Even in the fading twilight, I could tell he was a stranger. He had on a dark overcoat, and he was young. Early twenties. Kay turned and watched, too, as he hurried over the bridge toward us.

"Hi there," he called. "I'm looking for Kay Collins."

Kay seemed puzzled. "I'm Kay," she said.

From then on, Mom, everything happened so fast, I barely had time to think. All I could do was react. As a journalist, I know the words I'd use to describe the moment, the scene, the action, but this was different. I was inside the story—and the story was inside me.

"Are you Justin Bloom?" he asked.

"Who wants to know?" I wasn't about to give him my name. I didn't like his looks. He seemed on edge. Jumpy.

The man glanced over his shoulder, inspected the quiet woods, then turned back and smiled. "Yeah, you're Justin." Looking at Kay, he said, "I got something for you, miss. It's a message from a friend." Without warning, he drew a gun from his pocket and shot her point-blank in the head.

My mouth dropped open. For a second or two the world stopped. When it started again, I'd switched to automatic. I lunged at him and wrestled him to the ground. Somehow I managed to kick the gun away. Once he was down, I hit him hard. I pushed him back against the tree and beat the living crap out of him. All the while, Kay was lying on the ground just a few feet from us. She wasn't moving. I realized later that the bullet must have killed her instantly.

After I was sure the guy was out cold, I crawled to her side and cradled her in my arms. Words are my stock-in-trade, but nothing can describe what I felt, Mom. Nothing. It was the most horrible moment of my life. Her blood was all over me, all over the ground, the snow, the ice, and worse—I could see now that part of her head was gone. There was no doubt in my mind that she was dead.

After a while I heard the guy groaning, so I got up, located the gun, and held it on him. God, I wanted to kill him. I wanted him to feel just exactly what Kay had felt. I probably would have shot him right then and there if it hadn't been for a cop. I hadn't heard him walk up, but there he was, standing behind me, big as life in his official blue uniform. He ordered me to drop the gun.

I said, No! He didn't understand. I didn't shoot the woman. I loved her. This other guy had done it. Again, the officer demanded I put the weapon down, and finally, after he drew his own gun and pointed it at me, I dropped it in the snow at my feet. At that point he motioned for the real murderer to stand up. "You okay?" he asked.

I stopped breathing. "You know this man?"

"Shut up," said the cop. "Did you get the negatives?"

The thug answered, "Give me a break, Dad. I've been kind of busy."

"I'm not your father! Don't use that teenage slang on me. Get up and do it now."

He scrambled to his feet and retrieved the purse from under a bush. Just as Kay had said, the negatives and photos were inside.

"Here," said the cop. He pulled an envelope out of his pocket and exchanged it for the purse.

The guy counted the money and then said, "Anything else my family can ever do for you, you know where to find us."

As he disappeared into the darkness the officer, still holding the gun on me, walked a few paces closer.

I stood very still, clenched my fists, and waited for him to shoot, but for some reason, he didn't. Instead, in a very calm voice, he started talking. "Your prints are all over the murder weapon, son. Listen carefully to what I'm about to tell you. I'm going to swear you killed her. What that means is, you got two choices. You can either stay and take your chances with the law, or you can run." He lifted another envelope from his breast pocket. "If you decide to run, there's fifty thousand dollars in here, a plane ticket out of the country, and a fake passport."

I was confused. Nothing made any sense. "But . . . I don't understand. Aren't you going to . . . shoot me, too?"

"That's not part of the plan."

"What plan? Whose plan?" I was breathing so hard, I almost hyperventilated. I felt light-headed, disoriented. At that moment all I knew for sure was that I wanted to strangle the cop with my bare hands, but his gun was pointed straight at my chest. Plan or no plan, if I made a move on him, he'd shoot. I'd learned enough about men in the army to know this guy meant business.

"You can't win, kid. Manderbach set it up that way."

When I heard the name, it was like this crystal formed inside my mind. In an instant I knew it all. "It's Manderbach. He's behind this!" I looked down at Kay's lifeless body, and I understood. Tears came to my eyes. How could he do it? For God's sake, he'd won! Didn't he realize? And then it hit me. He didn't know! He must have figured that Kay had made her decision, and that she'd chosen me.

"You haven't got a prayer if you stay in town. There's a mountain of evidence stacked against you. Just look at you. You've got her blood all over your clothes."

"But why kill her and not me, too?"

"I don't know. I don't need to know." He held the envelope out to me. "If I were you, I'd take the money and disappear."

Even though I knew his solution made sense, something

prevented me from taking it. Maybe it was Kay. I couldn't just leave her there on the ground.

"One more thing," said the cop. He saw my hesitation, so he upped the ante—made his final threat. "If you don't leave the country, what happened here tonight could also happen to your mother. Be a good boy. Leave quietly and keep your mouth shut. That way, everything will be just fine."

Just fine, I thought. How could anything ever be "just fine" again? And yet, by threatening you, Mom, it was as if he waved smelling salts under my nose. Immediately, I was alert, on guard. "He wouldn't do that!" *was all I could choke out.*

"You and I both know he would. He's a smart man— smarter than both of us. Take the money, son. You can't do anything to help your girlfriend now. I'll make sure she's taken care of. I won't leave her here. If you stay, sure as I'm looking at you, you'll go to prison for her murder. You might even get the death penalty. Save yourself. It's all you've got left."

I knelt down next to Kay and took her hand. It was so cold. I kissed it, held it for a moment against my cheek. How could I leave? And yet, how could I stay? The cop was right—there was nothing more I could do except dig myself in deeper. Nobody would believe what really happened. Manderbach's plan was brutal and yet amazingly subtle. With one shot, he'd destroyed two people, saved himself, and no one would ever be the wiser.

As I got up, the cop said to me, "Police officers don't lie, son. Nobody's going to believe your story, not when they hear mine. God forgive me, but I'm part of this now, and I won't let you take me down with you."

I hesitated, but only for a moment. Stuffing the money inside my coat, I took off up the hill and never looked back. As I got to my car I saw Manderbach's Chrysler parked across the street. He must have been waiting to see the outcome. I couldn't help myself, Mom. I rushed over and banged on the hood. "You killed her!" *I exploded. I kicked the door, slammed my hands against the wind- shield, even picked up a rock and tried to smash the win-*

dows—*anything to get my hands on him. When he saw I wasn't going to give up, he started the motor.*

"You both got what you deserved," *he shouted, wiping a hand across his mouth, then over his eyes.* "You're licked, Bloom. Get the hell out of here and never come back!" *With that, he gunned the motor and roared off down the street.*

You know the rest. I went home, put on some clean clothes, and packed one small bag. I knew I didn't have much time. The flight left at six. I wrote you a quick note, dropped it in a mailbox, and then drove to the airport. I was numb, Mom. I didn't feel anything for a very long time. When I finally did, I was long gone.

And so the cop told his story, and Justin Bloom was convicted by every citizen in the good state of Minnesota. The sad truth is, that many people can't be wrong.

So, I guess we're left with the question we started with. Did Justin Bloom murder Kay Collins? I have to say, at this moment, I think he did. His rashness, his single-minded need to further his career, and his inability to grasp the obvious all consigned the woman he loved to death. Is Bud Manderbach also responsible? Without a doubt. But who bears the ultimate guilt? A selfish, self-centered bastard with no sense of right and wrong, or a decent young man, a journalist, who should have known better? As I said at the beginning, Mom, I rest my case with you.

33

Dorothy hid behind a pillar near the front of the church as Bud Manderbach entered through the vestibule. She watched in silence as he proceeded cautiously into the sanctuary, his agitation apparent from the nervous, furtive way his eyes jumped around the room. When she was certain he was alone, she moved out from the shadows and hurried down the aisle toward him. Holding a finger to her lips, she pushed him into one of the pews.

"Shhh," she said. She waited, listening to the stillness. "Are you sure you weren't followed?"

"Positive." He matched her whisper.

She sat for a moment, her eyes drifting through the empty interior. Thick white tapers in tall wrought-iron candle holders burned all around them. The flames danced and flickered, making the darkness seem alive with shadows.

"I can't wait any longer," said Bud. "Tell me what you know!"

She nodded, moving closer. "Just like I said to you on the phone, Wish Greveen isn't dead. I saw him."

He looked around suspiciously. "Are you sure no one can eavesdrop on our conversation?"

"There's no one in the church but us. Even the minister is gone tonight."

"How did you manage that?"

"It's a long story. Do you want to hear about the minister, or Greveen?"

"Greveen, of course. Where did you see him? And when?"

"Last night. I was walking back to the hotel after dinner. It was dark, but I was sure it was him."

"Were you alone?"

"Yes, thank God. He was on the other side of the street. Look, Bud, everyone thinks you murdered him. It's not fair. I couldn't just let him get away."

"Good girl," he said eagerly. "Then what?"

"Well, he entered the lobby of a hotel. The Ardmore, I think. By the time I got inside, he was standing at the reception desk talking to a clerk. They only spoke for a few seconds. The clerk handed him a piece of paper, he read it, and then he got on an elevator. Once the doors were closed and I knew he was on his way upstairs, I walked up to the clerk, made some lame excuse about thinking I knew the man with the wavy white hair, and asked what his name was. She very curtly replied that the hotel didn't give out that sort of information. After I slipped her a fifty, she had a sudden change of heart. His name was Tony Clifton. I asked how long he'd been a guest. She said a couple of weeks. His room number was 357."

"We've got him!" Bud cackled, rubbing his hands together gleefully.

"You think so?"

"I know so."

"But . . . which is his real name?" asked Dorothy.

"Neither. " Again, Bud lowered his voice. "That man is none other than Justin Bloom."

She stared at him blankly. "But . . . he's dead."

"I wish he were."

Dorothy took off her gloves, laid them in her lap, and then rested an elbow on the pew. "You can't just let him get away."

"I have to think this through very carefully. Very carefully indeed. But you did the right thing when you called. I'll never forget your . . . say—" His eyes dropped to the ring on her left hand. "Where did you get that?"

"What? The ring? My mother gave it to me."

"Your mother?" His eyes rose to hers. "What the hell are you trying to pull?"

Dorothy's voice dropped an octave. "What do you think, Bud? Take a wild guess."

A door slammed. Bud twisted around and looked back toward the vestibule just in time to see Wish Greveen walk slowly into the sanctuary. In his right hand, he held a gun.

"Greveen!" said Bud, jumping to his feet.

"Sit down!" ordered Dorothy in her new, deeper register. "We're going to have a little talk, you and me."

Bud was dumbstruck. His mouth dropped open.

"Oh, and for future reference, that man back there is a longtime friend. He helped me funnel letters to my mother when I couldn't use the U.S. mail. I spent a good part of my life abroad, you know."

Bud was so stunned, his expression didn't change for almost a minute. Finally, shutting his mouth, he sat back down. This time, he made sure there was plenty of space between them. "I don't believe . . . this."

"That I'm Justin Bloom? Better get used to it."

"But . . . I thought—"

"That my friend was Justin?" Dorothy shrugged. "Must be a case of mistaken identity."

Bud swallowed hard. "What are you going to do?"

"Well, first I think I'll remove these earrings. I never could get used to them. Women lead very uncomfortable lives, Bud. Did you know that? Most men don't."

Bud sat transfixed as he watched them come off. "This is impossible." His eyes returned to the ring. After a few seconds a look of revulsion passed over his face. "But I . . . we . . . kissed."

"Yeah, but then you know what they say. You gotta kiss a lot of frogs before you find a prince. By the way, you were definitely one of the frogs. You can't kiss for shit."

Bud seemed dazed. "Are you . . . gay?"

"Me? No. Are you?"

"No!" He removed a handkerchief from his pocket and mopped the sweat forming on his forehead. "God . . . that's disgusting. How could you . . . we—"

"Come on, Bud. It was only twice. And it's the Nineties. What's a kiss or two between pals. Besides, self-preservation causes a man to do a lot of strange things—as I'm sure you'd agree. Actually, I've been impersonating a woman for so long now, it almost feels natural. Let's see." He tapped his chin in thought. "It first started in 1962 when my mother came to Rome for a visit. We hadn't seen each other since I left the States. I knew she'd be watched carefully, either by government authorities or by one of your hirelings. Every man she met would be scrutinized. So, thinking it was my only chance to meet with her openly, to squire her around the city I'd come to love, I became a woman. Amazingly enough, it worked. After a while I became the old friend she always stayed with. I learned my craft well, don't you agree? Did you ever see the movie *Tootsie*?"

"What? No. Of course not. What's that got to do with anything?"

"You should rent it sometime. You might learn a few modern attitudes. For instance, don't call women girls. You're liable to get hit with an ashtray. I had to resist the urge several times myself." He opened his purse and tossed his earrings inside. "But . . . to get back to my story. When I returned to the States in 1987, I lived for a while in Connecticut. It didn't suit me. I wanted to be closer to my mother. After all, thanks to you, she was the only family I had left, and human attachment is still occasionally important to me. So, once again, I donned my disguise. Dorothy is as far removed from Justin Bloom as I could get. In a way, I found it oddly relaxing. From the moment I became my mother's assistant, I insisted she think of me as Dorothy, that she *call* me Dorothy, and that together, we never drop the act, not even in private. That was crucial. My life depended on how successfully we both could maintain the lie."

"This is repellent. Disgusting. I suppose now you're going to pull off the wig and show me what you really look like."

Justin yanked at his hair. "Sorry. It doesn't come off. I think I make a rather attractive older woman, don't you? I believe you called me lovely, so I assume you agree—unless you were lying." His expression turned wistful. "Actually, I've always liked the name Dorothy, ever since I saw *The Wizard of Oz* when I was a kid. Think about it for a second, Bud. It's the story of a young woman whose life is turned upside down when she finds herself lost in a faraway land. Oh, she eventually makes new friends, but it's not the same as home."

Bud glared.

Justin shut his eyes. Clicking his heels together, he repeated the words, "There's no place like home. There's no place like home." Opening them, he grinned. "I guess it works, because . . . here I am."

From the confused look on Bud's face, Justin could tell he didn't know whether to react angrily or cautiously. Caution eventually got the better of him. "Get to the point."

His grin evaporated. "All right, but first, let's go back to the movie. Dorothy finally wakes up and discovers that her sojourn in Oz was all a Technicolor dream. In my case, it was more of a noir nightmare—one I'll never wake up from."

"Why do you keep making all these movie references? You're not making any sense!"

"Oh, didn't I tell you? I owned a movie house in Rome for many years. I had to make a living somehow. And, actually, it suited me—or what was left of me. I developed quite a fondness for foreign films, although I still like the Hollywood classics the best. But come on now, Bud, you're getting me off the subject. You of all people should see the irony in choosing the name Dorothy. If I recall correctly, you like irony."

"I don't know what you're talking about." Again, he mopped his forehead.

"I've had a lot of time to think. I assume you have, too. I used to be a very earnest young man, always in a hurry, but I'm far more patient now. Age has taught me a great deal. I've learned to take my time and get it right. I laugh a lot more, too."

"Spare me your insights on aging."

Justin glanced at his ring, twisting it on his finger. "You're right, I'm circling the point. But you have to understand, I've rehearsed this conversation in my mind millions of times. This is the denouement, Bud. The final scene. We can't just rush through it." Giving him a long, measuring look, he continued, "I'm going to ask you a question, and I want an honest answer."

Bud's eyes shot around the room. "You're taping this, right?"

"Taping it? Why would I do that?"

"I'm not stupid. I see what you're doing. You get me to

say something incriminating, and then you hand the tape over to the police."

Justin laughed. "I don't trust the legal system in this country, Bud. Do you? If I taped your confession, I'd have no guarantee that justice would be done. *I'm* the one who's in charge of your fate now. Not the police. Not the courts. Not God or the devil. Just *me*."

He spoke the last word with such force that it echoed through the empty sanctuary.

"Now," he continued, returning to his more reasoned tones, "here's the question. The night you had Kay killed, why didn't you kill me, too? You could have. You probably wanted to. What stopped your hired thug from turning the gun on me?" Seeing a look of intransigence on Bud's face, he added, "The fact is, you won't leave this church alive unless you give me an answer."

"You *are* going to kill me!"

"Answer me!" Justin lunged at him, grabbed him by the lapels, and slammed him back against the pew. "That question has eaten away at me for years. Why did you let me go? *I should be dead, too!*"

Bud turned his head away, holding up his arms to ward off a blow. "You were no good to me dead. I needed you alive— but discredited. What better way than to make it look like you'd killed your girlfriend after a lovers' quarrel."

"How did you get the gun?"

"I paid Zolotow to steal it from your father's office. You obligingly covered it with your fingerprints. You even left your bloody clothes at your apartment for the police to find. But the worst thing you did was to get on that plane. It was the act of a guilty man. I never thought you'd take the bait, but you did! You took it and you ran like the coward you are." He ducked his head, expecting a blow.

"And *why* did you need to discredit me?"

"You know why."

"Tell me!"

Bud lowered his arms, but only slightly. "I couldn't be sure you hadn't made copies of the photos—that other people didn't know the truth about the hit-and-run. Since you were the man leading the attack, if I destroyed your reputation, I also destroyed your credibility. Then, if somewhere along the line, the photos surfaced, I would simply say that Kay and I had been dating, and that she planned to dump you and marry me. You were jealous. You took out your anger by trumping up some wild story about my involvement in the Landauer hit-and-run. By smearing my name, you hoped Kay would change her mind. When you saw she wasn't buying it, you killed her in a jealous rage. Don't you get it? Once people thought you'd murdered Kay and then skipped the country, they'd dismiss the hit-and-run charge as a vendetta, as a jilted lover's sick revenge."

Justin let him go, but he couldn't just sit back down—not now. They were finally getting somewhere. Stepping into the aisle, he said, "But there's more, isn't there? You had another reason for wanting me alive."

"I don't know what you mean."

He nodded to the man in the back.

Bud whirled around at the sound of a metallic tick. His eyes opened wide when he realized it was a hammer cocking.

"Figure it out, Bud. You've got ten seconds to come up with an answer."

Again, he wiped his face. "Well, sure. I saw the irony. It even appealed to me. You planned to send me to jail, to take away my freedom, so I took away yours. There are many different kinds of prisons. I wanted you to be alive so you could reflect on yours—on what you'd lost."

"It was your loss, too."

He shook his head. "No, Kay meant nothing to me. For a short time I thought I loved her. She was . . . unique. But I saw through the act eventually. She betrayed my love, just like every other woman has. I could read the writing on the wall. I wasn't pure enough for her. Not worthy enough. But Justin was. Justin Bloom, the great journalist, the mighty righter of wrongs. She met with you that night so she could give you the photos. She had them in her purse. What more proof did I need? The idea that the two of you would marry and live happily ever after, while I rotted in jail—it was impossible! Repulsive! Unthinkable!"

"So you had her killed."

"Yes!" He held Justin's eyes. "It was her punishment. She hurt me like no other woman has. I still hate her!"

Justin had been waiting almost forty years to tell Manderbach the truth. This was the moment. He allowed himself a small smile. "Except, you got part of it wrong."

Bud pressed his lips together angrily. "Yeah, like what?"

"The part where Kay and I get married and ride off into the sunset. Before you had her killed, she gave me her decision. She'd picked you. She wanted to save you from yourself. She had the negatives and the photos in her purse because she intended to make you a present of them—to prove her love. She was going to meet you next, after she gave me back my ring. This ring!" He held up his hand. "You could have had it all, you son-of-a-bitch! Kay . . . your freedom . . . even a chance at happiness. And *that's* the message I came here tonight to give you. You killed the only woman who ever loved you! What do you think of your brilliant plan now?"

"You're lying!" Bud shouted. "You have to be! She wanted you, not me."

"Did she tell you that?"

"No, not in so many words, but—" The light dawned in his eyes. "Oh, God," he said, doubling over in pain. With both hands he grabbed onto the pew in front of him and started to rock. "No," he repeated, over and over again. "You're wrong. You're making this up."

Justin watched his agony. It was strange, but he'd lived for so many years with enormity and hyperbole that he found the man's pain curiously small. "You know, Bud, not that this will interest you, but I don't believe in hope anymore."

Sitting down in one of the pews across the aisle, he picked up a hymnal and raised it to his lips. "I did believe in it, up until a few seconds ago. I'd hoped that my revenge would be sweet, something to sustain me when, years from tonight, I wondered if my actions were truly worth it. But I know now that it's not enough. Nothing will ever bring back what I lost. I think I've lived too long and seen too much. We're just two . . . pathetic old men, Bud. Two has-beens. You get one chance in this life, and we both blew it. And yet . . . I can't stop what I've started. I wouldn't, even if I could."

Running a shaky hand over his face, Bud looked up. "What do you mean?"

"I suppose you do deserve an explanation, although I'm not sure why." He touched the lipstick on his mouth, wishing he could wash it off. "After I came back to the States, I employed a series of private detectives in an effort to dig up something—anything—to put you behind bars. I thought for sure there was proof somewhere tying you to Olga Landauer's death, or Kay's, or Sally's. Did so many people have to die? Did they?"

Bud closed his eyes.

"You'll be happy to know you're safe. There's no way on earth I could touch you—unless I murdered you myself, which—at the time—seemed like more trouble than it was worth. It took a while, but I came up with another plan. When an AM radio station hit the market in the Twin Cities, I convinced my mother to buy it. Together, we would put on a revival of *Dallas Lane, Private Eye*, except the story would be true. It would be our story, yours and mine—and Kay's. I'd invite the old cast to be a part of the production. Why? Because I needed to know who you'd bribed to steal that gun from my stepfather's drawer. You gave me my answer a few minutes ago, although I already suspected it was Valentine. The bottom line is, if I couldn't convict you in the courts, I'd convict you in the court of public opinion—just like you'd done to me. It's ironic, isn't it, how we constantly find ever new ways of being ironic together?"

Bud shot him a nasty look.

"You know the rest. My plan was working, but I knew from the beginning it wouldn't be enough to bring you down. The problem was, my mother would never have agreed to a murder—even a fake one, so I had to take matters into my own hands. My friend back there is part of the medical profession, Bud. It was a simple matter for him to draw some of his blood. We waited until you were gone, and then entered the cottage. Thank God I still have my talent for picking locks. It only took a few minutes to set it up. And look what happened? Presto change-o, Bud Manderbach is now the talk of the town, suspected by millions of inquiring minds in the wrongful death of one Wish Greveen. If the police decide they have enough against you to try you for the man's 'disappearance,' then great. I hope you rot in jail. If they don't arrest you, your life has already been damaged—and it's my fondest hope that you won't soon recover. Remember, Bud, from now on, when people see you on the street, or watch you walk into a restaurant, they're going to point and whisper, snicker and sneer. There goes Bud Manderbach. He murdered Wish Greveen, maybe even Kay Collins, and just look at him. Slimy bastard. He's still a free man. Somebody should put a bullet in his back."

"This is absurd!"

"Ah, I see you've completely recovered from your momentary bout with human emotion. Take my advice, you'd best keep emotion to a minimum for the next few months. I'll bet, even as we speak, some reporter is rifling through your medicine chest while upstairs, your sister blithely catalogues her collection of teapots."

"Leave my sister out of this!"

"Gladly." Justin got up and nodded to the man in the back. "Bring me the gun and then go get the car and bring it around front."

"Why do you want the gun?" said Bud, gripping the back of the pew. His eyes dropped to the barrel as Justin pointed it at his chest. "What . . . what are you doing?"

"What does it look like?"

"But . . . you said you weren't going to shoot."

"Did I? Surely not in so many words. One last question, Bud. I should warn you. A great deal depends on your answer." He paused, walking a few paces closer. "Are you sorry?"

Bud stared at the barrel. "Sure."

He cocked the trigger. "Tell me the truth!"

Again, Bud closed his eyes. It took him almost a full minute to respond. When he did, he looked Justin square in the eye. "No. I'm not sorry. A man has to put his own interests first. That's the law of the jungle."

As they stared at each other across the abyss of years, Justin felt his finger tense over the trigger. Bud Manderbach had been a bastard to the end. He was incapable of remorse. Why should he go on living?

"Don't shoot . . . please! I . . . I'm a rich man. I can give you anything you want."

If only that were true, thought Justin.

When the horn finally honked, he released the hammer and lowered the gun to his side.

Bud wiped a hand over his brow. "What's to prevent me from telling the police the whole story—that you set everything up?"

"Well," said Justin, scratching the bottom of his chin with the gun barrel, "if you can figure out a way to do it without incriminating yourself, go for it."

"You'll be arrested!"

"Will I? First you'd have to convince the right people that the story is true, and second they'd have to find me. If I've learned anything in my life, it's how to disappear. I'm a phantom, a figment of your guilty imagination. Justin Bloom died in Europe, everyone knows that." He leaned down close to Bud's face and whispered, "But you and I know the truth. I died on Christmas eve, 1958—the night my hope, and my youth, perished."

34

Bram pulled the covers up over his head. "If it's for me, I'm in a meeting."

"It's almost one-thirty in the morning," grumbled Sophie, switching on the light next to the bed. She rubbed the sleep out of her eyes. "How could you be in a meeting?"

"All right, I'm out to lunch—or at the dentist's." He rolled over and buried his head under a pillow.

"You're out to lunch, all right." She picked up the receiver. "Yes?" After listening for several seconds, she said, "No, this is *not* Bram Baldric. This is his wife."

Snickers emanated from under the pillow. "No more cigars for you."

She banged him on the arm. "Yes, he's here. And he's in rare form. Just a minute." She dropped the receiver next to his hand. "From now on, tell your girlfriends to call during the day." She eased back under the covers.

With his head still under the pillow, he held the receiver to his ear. "This is Bram Baldric. I can't be here to answer the phone right now, but if you'd like to leave a message—"

"Mr. Baldric? Is that you?"

The voice was familiar, but he couldn't place it. "All right, speak."

"I'm sorry to wake you, but I don't have much time. This is Arn O'Dell's granddaughter."

"Molly!" he said, sitting up in bed. "How are you? *Where* are you?"

Silence. "You know my real name?"

"Look, I know you told me not to try and find you, but I was desperate. I had a friend of mine do some checking."

"It's nice to learn my life is such an open book—not that it surprises me."

Bram could hear an angry edge in her voice. "When you didn't show up at the bar, I drove over to your house."

"Then you saw why I couldn't make it."

"Yeah. I thought you'd died in the fire, Molly."

"Well, I'm unlucky, but not as unlucky as the fella who did."

"Do you know who he was?"

"Sure. It was the man who'd been watching my house— the one in the white van."

"But . . . I don't understand."

"Me neither, but I can tell you this much. I was across the street that night when I saw him approach my place on foot. A neighbor gave me the key to her house so I could feed her cat while she was away for the holidays. I watched him from her bedroom window. He was just walking around, looking in windows. I think he was trying to figure out if I was home or not. A couple minutes later an older man appeared from around the side of the house carrying something heavy. I couldn't make out what it was, but this time, I knew him."

"Who was it?"

"Bud Manderbach. My grandfather told me to memorize his face—and stay away from him. Anyway, real quick like, the first guy gets inside. I figure he kicked in a basement window because two nights before, he'd been in the back-yard examining one up real close. He lets Manderbach in through the side door. It didn't take long before I saw a flick-ering light in the living room. I knew right away they'd set a fire. I wanted to scream bloody murder—tell them to leave my goddamned house alone, but that would've been real smart, right? So instead, I called 911—disguised my voice. After I hung up, I ran back to the window. I must have sat there a good five minutes before Manderbach finally came out. The other guy never did. I figure Mr. Manderbach was just covering his tracks. He doesn't like loose ends, and that's what the guy in the white van probably was. Do you see now why I'm so frightened?"

"I do, Molly. Believe me, I do. I'm so sorry about what happened. You must be devastated, and I can't help but feel partially responsible."

"You are, Mr. Baldric. You turned my life into a toxic landfill when you announced the existence of my grand-father's letter on your talk show."

Bram didn't know what to say. Nothing would be enough.

"Look, let's cut to the chase."

"Sure. Where are you? Where've you been?"

"Driving. Thinking. The day after the house burned, I took off for Oregon. I didn't plan to come back—ever. But when I got out there, I changed my mind."

"Why?" He could tell she was smoking.

"Well, see, when I left Minnesota, I was scared to death. I was in way over my head, and I knew it. If I didn't get lost—and fast—I wasn't going to live very long. But I just kept thinking about that house. I've rented it for years, ever since I got divorced. I loved that place, Mr. Baldric. It meant the world to me. The more I thought about it, the madder I got. I spent about a week in Oregon, staying with friends, and I finally made a decision."

"To come home."

"Yeah. I got back this afternoon. I'm leaving again at first light."

"But . . . where are you going?"

"Away. That's all I'll say. And this time, I'm going to stay there."

"But . . . I'd hoped we could get together and talk."

"That's why I called. I want to meet."

Hearing this, he was immensely relieved. "Great. Just tell me when."

"Right now. As soon as you can get here. I'm staying at the Starlight Motel on Route 7, just west of Elk River. Do you need directions?"

"No, I can find it." Bram motioned for Sophie to pass him a pad and pencil. "What's the room number?"

"Seven." She took an audible drag from her cigarette.

"All right." He wrote it down. "It depends on the roads, but I think I should be there in less than an hour. Do you still have your grandfather's letter?"

"What?" She exhaled, then continued. "Nah. It got burned in the fire. We'll talk more when you get here."

"But, Molly, if you don't have the letter—"

"We're wasting time, Mr. Baldric. Remember, you owe me."

He heard the line click.

"Did she hang up?" asked Sophie, leaning over to get a better look at his notes.

"She did." He handed her the phone. "This is *so* frustrating. I've been trying for weeks to get my hands on that letter, and now it's gone. It got burned in the fire. "

"Sheesh." She flopped back against her pillow. "What incredibly rotten luck."

"The problem is, I don't know why I'm so hot and bothered. We're not even sure if the damn thing would have vindicated Justin Bloom. Not that it matters anymore." Slipping his hand over hers, he said, "Want to take a drive?"

"You mean, if I'm a good girl, I can come along this time?"

"Sarcasm doesn't become you, dear."

"Since when?"

The snow came down furiously as they sped along I-94 heading for the Elk River exit. Common wisdom in Minnesota said that if the temperatures dropped below zero, the weather would be clear and cold. Tonight, however, the common wisdom was wrong, much to Bram's growing concern. The temperatures were in the single digits below zero, while the windchill factor was somewhere in the vicinity of forty-four below.

"What an altogether splendid night," he muttered, squinting to see the road ahead.

Sophie turned the defroster fan up to high. "At least there isn't much traffic."

"It doesn't matter. I told her an hour. It's going to be at least two before we get there—possibly more."

"Well, she can see the roads are bad, honey. She'll make allowances."

Bram shook his head. "I have absolutely no confidence that I'm ever going to meet that woman face-to-face. And now, since the letter's gone, I'm not sure there's any point in risking our lives in this blizzard."

"It's not a blizzard, sweetheart, it's just your average garden-variety snowy night."

"There's something wrong with that description, Sophie."

She shrugged. "Besides, Molly must think there's a point, or she wouldn't have insisted you come."

"Yeah, maybe." The snow was starting to form drifts, which spread across the pavement like snakes, making it difficult to see where the road ended and the ditch began. "I think we should move to Florida and sell Earth shoes on the beach."

"You say that every January, Bram. I'm not even sure they make Earth shoes anymore. Maybe you should update your dream. You don't want to appear out of date."

He gave her a sideways glance. "How much farther to the turnoff?"

She switched on the map light and took a look. "We're very close. Probably another mile or two."

Half an hour later they pulled into the drive at the Starlight Motel, nearly an hour late. The sign outside said NO VACANCY. Bram assumed that most Minnesotans had the sense not to travel on a night like this. He wished he were one of them.

The parking space in front of number 7 was empty. A bad sign, he thought as he pulled into it. From the lack of snow on the ground, it looked as if someone *had* been parked there—until very recently.

"Let me check the room out first," said Bram, leaving the engine running so that Sophie wouldn't freeze to death while she waited. He slid out of the front seat and walked quickly up to the door. Bending close, he knocked and then called, "Molly? It's Bram." He waited several seconds. When no one answered, he knocked again. "Molly? I'm sorry I'm late, but the roads were a mess." He looked over his shoulder and gave Sophie a shrug. After almost a full minute he tried the handle. The door was open.

Feeling his body tense and his heart beat faster, he kicked it back. Inside, the light was on, but the room was empty. "Molly?" he called again. As his eyes searched the interior he heard a car door slam. An instant later Sophie was by his side.

"Isn't she here?" she asked, squeezing into the room in front of him.

"It appears not. I don't see a suitcase either, or any clothes."

"But the bed's been slept in," she said, moving over to examine the nightstand. "Maybe we should check the bathroom."

Bram recalled the last time he'd inspected a bathroom. Rushing to the door, he pushed it open. "Jeez," he said, bending over and resting his hands on his thighs. "That didn't do wonders for my blood pressure. She's not here."

"What are you doing!" demanded a deep voice.

Bram and Sophie turned to find a tall, heavyset man standing in the doorway, a suspicious look on his face. Since he had on a black Hell's Angels T-shirt and faded black jeans, Bram assumed he was a guest.

"Answer me," he ordered. He reached behind him and whipped a gun out of his belt.

Sophie backed up until she bumped into Bram. "We're . . . ah, looking for Molly Stanglund," she said, trying but failing to sound resolute.

"Who's *we*?" asked the man holding the gun.

"I'm Bram Baldric. And this is my wife, Sophie."

"Uh-huh. Let's see some proof."

Bram wasn't quite sure why it was necessary, but decided that under the circumstances, cooperation was in order. He carefully lifted his wallet from the back pocket of his jeans and handed it over.

Keeping the gun pointed at them, the man dropped his eyes to it briefly, then looked back up. "All right. I guess you're who you say you are. Come with me."

"Why?" asked Bram. This was getting weirder by the minute.

"I'm the manager. I got something for you."

Bram and Sophie exchanged glances, then silently fell in behind the man as he led the way down a long, badly drifted sidewalk.

Once inside the office, he said, "I been expecting you." He ducked down under an old Formica counter and then popped up on the other side. "Molly and I were good buddies, that's why she picked this motel to flop for the night. We bike together—we both own a hog. You know what that is?"

Bram smiled pleasantly. "Someone who eats too much?"

The manager gave Bram a thorough once-over. "It's a Harley. You ever done any biking, Mr. Baldric?"

"I prefer water sports."

His lips curled into a smile. "I catch your program every now and then, but I figured you for a much younger guy."

"Younger than what?"

"Where's Molly?" asked Sophie, putting an end to the banter. She rested her elbows on the stained Formica.

"Well, now," said the manager. He pulled up a stool and sat down. "She waited until close to three, but just didn't feel comfortable sticking around any longer, so she took off."

"Will she be back?" asked Bram.

"Nope." He removed an envelope from the top drawer and pushed it across the counter. "But she left you this."

Bram picked it up. There was something invitingly heavy inside, but he didn't want to open it until they got back to the car. "Thanks," he said, holding the door open for his wife.

"Don't mention it, Mr. Baldric. See you on the radio."

"Open it!" demanded Sophie, rubbing her gloved hands together to keep them warm.

Bram started the engine. The first order of business was to get the heater going. Once that was accomplished, he flipped on the dome light. Taking off one glove, he ripped back the flap. Inside was a letter and a key. He held the key up to the light, examining both sides, then handed it to Sophie. "It has a number on it."

"I'm not blind. Hold the letter up so I can read it, too."

Dear Mr. Baldric,

I'm not a very good writer, but I thought I'd put something down on paper because I can't wait around here any longer. Like I told you on the phone, the letter from my grandfather got burned. I thought I had it hidden so well no one would ever find it, not even if they broke into my house, which I thought was not only possible, but likely. I never figured on a fire.

I'll tell you briefly what it said. My grandfather took a bribe from a man named Manderbach. Manderbach wanted him to lie about what took place on Christmas eve 1958. See, Justin Bloom didn't murder his girlfriend, some guy who was hired by Manderbach did. The reason my grandfather lied was because my grandmother was very ill. She'd had three operations, but needed a fourth. My grandfather had basically mortgaged everything they had to pay for the first three operations. He didn't have anything else left, so he took the money Manderbach offered him. The sad thing is, my grandmother died during that last surgery. My grandfather was an honest cop, up until then. He had strong reasons for what he did, and I don't hold it against him. He resigned from the force about a year later. He fished a lot after that, but his health pretty much went downhill.

The two of us were always close. I moved to Oregon in my early twenties, and that's where he sent me the letter telling me the truth. He said he couldn't tell anyone else in the family, the disgrace would kill them, but he had to tell someone, so he picked me. He was dying when he wrote the letter. He asked me to come home because he had something to give me.

I took a leave of absence from my job and came home to Minnesota. On his deathbed, he handed me a packet. I had no idea what was in it. He said, burn that letter I sent you. Don't ever let anyone see it. And later, he said, if Manderbach ever tried to bother me, or anyone else in the family, I should give the packet to the police—but only if absolutely necessary. He told me to keep the packet somewhere safe and not to open it. He died three days later.

I took the packet with me when I went back to Oregon. That's what I went to get when I left here two weeks ago. Right now it's in one of those lockers at the bus station. The one in Minneapolis. The number is on the key. I finally opened the package. It's some photos of an old car. One side of the front end is pretty messed up. And there are some negatives, too. My grandfather made copies to give to Manderbach, but kept the originals. But what's really important is there's a full confession signed by my grandfather. He even had it witnessed by some friend of his, so I think it's legal. But I don't know if it's something you could use in a court of law. I thought you might know. I listened to part of your program this afternoon, and I heard that Lawless guy talk about the old murder case. Maybe you should give the packet to him. He sounded pretty smart on the subject.

That's about it. I never would have gone to Oregon to get the packet if my house hadn't burned down. It's funny how things work out sometimes.

Have a nice life, Mr. Baldric.

Very truly yours,
Molly Stanglund

Bram looked up, feeling such a rush he could barely contain himself. "My God, we've got it!" He hit the steering wheel with his fists and whooped with delight. "This is the proof no one thought existed!"

"Talk about the key to Pandora's box," said Sophie, holding it under the map light.

Bram hugged her, then threw the car into reverse and backed out of the parking spot.

"What's our next move?" she asked, strapping on her seat belt. They slid onto an icy street, nearly hitting a parked car as the Explorer made an unscheduled one-hundred-and-eighty-degree turn.

"Next stop, the Greyhound bus depot."

"In this blizzard?"

"We're Minnesotans. We're tough. We're resourceful."

"And we got rocks for brains."

"Yes!" He looked both ways, then fishtailed onto the highway. Skidding between two immense snowdrifts, they sped off into the snowy night.

Sophie's Christmas
Cookie Cookbook

Ethel's Favorite Fruitcake Cookies

3	cups mixed candied fruit
1½	cups raisins
1½	cups currants
1	cup chopped mixed nuts (pecans, walnuts, almonds)
2½	cups flour
½	tsp. baking powder
½	tsp. salt
1	tsp. each ground cinnamon, allspice, and cloves
½	cup (1 stick) butter
3	eggs, separated
1½	cups brown sugar
1½	tsps. vinegar
½	cup evaporated milk
½	cup brandy

Mix fruit and nuts with one cup of the flour. Set aside. Add soda, salt, and spices to the rest of the flour. Cream the butter and sugar, then add the yolks and mix. Add vinegar to the milk and combine with the creamed mixture. Add remaining flour, stirring well. Add brandy and floured fruit mix. Beat egg whites until stiff. Fold into mixture. Drop by spoonfuls onto greased cookie sheet. Bake in a 325-degree oven for 10 to 15 minutes, or until slightly browned.

Norwegian Sandbakkelse

For these cookies you will need sandbakkel forms, available in most kitchen/cooking stores.

³/₄	cup white granulated sugar
1	cup butter
1	egg
15	blanched almonds, ground in food processor
1	tsp. almond extract
2¹/₂	cups flour

Cream sugar and butter. Add egg, almonds, and extract. Add flour and press into sandbakkel forms. Bake in oven, 350 degrees, until golden brown—about 10 minutes.

Merry Winter Cookies

³/₄	cup shortening
1	cup white granulated sugar
1	egg, beaten
¹/₄	cup molasses
2	cups sifted flour
2¹/₂	tsps. soda
1	tsp. cinnamon
1	tsp. ginger
	confectioner's sugar

Cream the shortening and sugar. Add egg and molasses. Combine the flour, soda, and spices. Stir flour mixture into creamed mixture. Chill. Form the dough into balls the size of a walnut and roll in powdered sugar. Place 2 inches apart on a greased cookie sheet. Bake at 375 degrees for 10 minutes, or until done.

Ella Anderson's Best Sugar Cookies

1	cup powdered sugar
1	cup white granulated sugar
1	cup butter
1	cup oil

2	eggs
4	cups plus 4 heaping T. of flour
1	tsp. baking soda
1	tsp. salt
1	tsp. cream of tartar

Cream the sugar, butter, and oil together. Beat in eggs. Mix dry ingredients together and add to creamed mixture. Drop by heaping teaspoons onto greased cookie sheet. Press down slightly with the flat part of a glass dipped in sugar. Decorate with colored sugars, nuts, cherries—any Christmas decorations you like.

Bake for 10 minutes at 350 degrees, or until slightly golden.

Mincemeat Cookies

1	cup butter
1 1/2	cups sugar
3	eggs
1	9-oz. package prepared mincemeat
3 1/4	cups flour
1	tsp. baking soda
1/2	tsp. salt

Cream shortening and sugar. Add eggs and beat well. Combine dry ingredients and add to creamed mixture. Crumble mincemeat and stir into mix. Bake 10–12 minutes at 350 degrees on a greased cookie sheet.

Russian Tea Cakes

1	cup soft butter
1/2	cup powdered sugar
1	tsp. vanilla
2 1/4	cups flour

¼   tsp. salt
1   cup ground walnuts
      powdered sugar

Cream butter and sugar. Add vanilla. Grind walnuts in a
food processor. Add flour and salt to the creamed mixture,
then ground nuts. Chill in refrigerator for one hour. Roll into
walnut-size balls. Bake on an ungreased cookie sheet at 350
degrees 10–12 minutes, or until slightly browned.

When slightly cool, roll in powdered sugar. When completely cool, roll in powdered sugar again. Before serving,
roll in powdered sugar one last time.

Norwegian Sugar Cookies

1   cup butter
2   cups brown sugar
2   eggs
2   cups flour
1   tsp. salt
1   tsp. baking soda dissolved in a little water (1 T. or so)
¾   cup coconut
1   cup raisins
2   cups rolled oatmeal (grind this in a food processor)

Cream butter and sugar. Add the eggs and beat well. Mix the
dry ingredients together. Add to creamed mixture. Add
raisins, oats, and coconut. Drop by teaspoonfuls onto
ungreased cookie sheet. Bake 10–12 minutes at 350 degrees.

Finnish Cookie Sticks
(Suomalaiset Puikot)

1	cup soft butter
1/2	cup sugar
1	egg
1	tsp. almond extract
1/4	tsp. salt
3	cups flour

Coating: 1 beaten egg, sugar (can use colored Christmas sugars), 1/2 cup chopped almonds

Cream butter and sugar. Add eggs and extract and mix well. Stir in dry ingredients, blending well. Work the dough with the hands until smooth. Shape into long rolls, about 1/2 inch thick. Cut into 2-inch lengths and roll in beaten egg, then in sugar, and then in the chopped almonds. Place on a lightly greased baking sheet. Bake 350 degrees until just barely golden.

Chocolate Meringue Kringles

These cookies are much lower in fat than those containing butter and whole eggs.

12	oz. chocolate (chocolate chips work fine)
5	egg whites
1	cup granulated sugar
1/2	tsp. vanilla
1	cup chopped macadamia nuts (or walnuts, or pecans)

Melt the chocolate in the top of a double boiler. Set aside to cool to room temperature. Allow egg whites to come to room temperature and then beat until they form soft peaks. Very slowly, add the sugar—a tablespoon at a time. Beat well after each addition. Beat the mixture until thick and glossy. Fold the chocolate into the egg whites with a rubber spatula. Add vanilla and nuts. Drop immediately on a cookie sheet lined with parchment paper. These cookies will spread, so allow two inches between cookies. Bake at 350 degrees for 10 to 12 minutes. (The centers will still be slightly moist.) After removing them from the oven, let them sit a minute or two to firm before removing them to a rack to cool.